D1646917

GATHERING CLOUDS

GATHERING CLOUDS

BOOK ONE OF THE NETHERGATE TRILOGY

DEREK H SKINNER

The Book Guild Ltd

First published in Great Britain in 2018 by
The Book Guild Ltd
9 Priory Business Park
Wistow Road, Kibworth
Leicestershire, LE8 0RX
Freephone: 0800 999 2982
www.bookguild.co.uk
Email: info@bookguild.co.uk
Twitter: @bookguild

Copyright © 2018 Derek H Skinner

The right of Derek H Skinner to be identified as the author of this
work has been asserted by him in accordance with the
Copyright, Design and Patents Act 1988.

All rights reserved. No part of this publication may be
reproduced, transmitted, or stored in a retrieval system, in any form or by any means,
without permission in writing from the publisher, nor be otherwise circulated in
any form of binding or cover other than that in which it is published and without
a similar condition being imposed on the subsequent purchaser.

This work is entirely fictitious and bears no resemblance to any persons living or dead.

Typeset in Aldine401 BT

Printed and bound in Great Britain by CPI Group (UK) Ltd, Croydon, CR0 4YY

ISBN 978 1912575 206

British Library Cataloguing in Publication Data.
A catalogue record for this book is available from the British Library.

*To Jacqueline, my wife, as an apology for all the things I have neglected
to do during the Nethergate Trilogy's long gestation.*

BAINTE DEN STOC

WITHDRAWN FROM DÚN LAOGHAIRE-RATHDOWN
COUNTY LIBRARY STOCK

1

The People Of Nethergate

Silas Killcaid, Deputy Overseer to the vast Nethergate tobacco estate, was soaked and in a foul temper. His boots leaked, and his feet felt like leaden lumps of ice. He had swapped his saddle for a horse-drawn buggy to give himself some cover from the incessant deluge from the glowering Kentucky skies. Even so he had been forced to spend most his day outside his wagon to ensure the slaves turned in a proper day's work. The other Overseers were simply 'trusted' slaves and were as likely to cut corners as were their charges. It was only the crack and snip of the 'Rattler', his beloved whip, that had kept the planting programme going.

The slaves of Nethergate were mute in their misery. No-one had the heart to sing, when so often just a dull melody might sometimes lift the spirits. Even the uncomplaining mules that brought the fresh seedlings on sledges, sagged in their traces, their head and ears drooping in the downpour.

Now however the light had faded and even Silas Killcaid had to acknowledge that little more could be achieved. He had blown three long blasts on his whistle to signify the end of work. Before the last blast was swallowed in the splatter of rain on the sodden ground, there was a flurry of movement and purpose the like of which had been lacking the entire working day. The mules lifted their heads, lines of slaves miraculously formed in the gathering gloom and the other overseers, imbued with sudden vocal enthusiasm, began mustering and chivvying their sullen charges back to the slave lines.

With one impulsive gesture Killcaid whipped the rain from the thick, black mat of his beard, glistening like jet in the gathering gloom. Under the shadow of his dripping hat the hook of his nose and the gimlet glare in his eyes somehow caught what light there was and threw it back in defiance. Although still in his early twenties, his face bore the chiselled features that told of a harsh upbringing and a determination to meet whatever life had to offer and to force it to his will. No-one had reached their quota for that day and all would have to labour at twice the rate on the morrow. He would surely see to that.

Once Silas Killcaid had checked over what work had been completed, he clambered up into the buggy and twitched the reins. The horse, as eager as he to find shelter, set off at a cracking pace, its wheels throwing up a fine arc of spray. Neither horse nor Killcaid spotted the lone child toiling slowly behind the last slave gang as it vanished into the murk.

Ruth was barely five years old. This was her first year in the fields. Today she felt proud, for it was the first time she had been working on her own without her mother to guide her. Her mother was soon to be delivered of another child and had been allowed to work back in the cabins. Ruth was quick and eager to please, but it had been back-breaking work for one so young and without her 'Mammy', who always made things a little easier for her. All the same she longed to tell her mother of her day and what she had done on her own. Her thin, sodden smock wrapped her body in a chill embrace. Her bare feet were clogged with mud spreading between her toes and further hampering her progress. With her head bent into the driving rain, she could not match the eager pace of the other slaves, their minds set on the shelter of their wood cabins and the evening meal.

Ruth had been born into servitude. Since the abolition of the African trade, most slaves now were home bred. Some, like Ruth, were not pure Negro, but owed their origins to often random liaisons, or sometimes to the drunken lusts of their white masters.

Killcaid felt a sharp jolt and the buggy rocked. The horse skittered sideways as a shape was thrown briefly into the air. He thought it might have been a dog or a small deer. He calmed the horse and looked behind him but could see nothing. The thought of the supper that surely awaited him back in his house and the sensuous black arms of his new housekeeper beckoned him on.

After a hundred yards, he stopped the wagon and swore. "Darn it! Darn it to Hell!" It hadn't been a dog and a deer would have avoided the horse. He knew it must have been a child. There had been a number working that day. Cursing afresh, he turned the horse about and retraced his route, his concern not so much for the victim, as for the possible loss of an asset to the estate. Mr Styles, the plantation owner, would not be pleased and Killcaid had his eye on the job of Morrison the Head Overseer. He was rarely to be seen in the fields these days and it was only his long service to two generations of the Masters of Nethergate that kept him employed. Silas Killcaid could not afford to make a mistake.

He found her eventually, lying just off the track, her leg bent awkwardly under her inert body. She lay very still. "Damn the girl!" he muttered to himself. Why could she not have got out of his way?

At first, he thought she was dead, but a low moan escaped from the huddled shape. Hastily he gathered her up and laid her small form on the seat beside him. Even in her present condition, he was struck by the child's perfectly formed features and high cheek bones that in time would blossom into a woman of exceptional beauty. Killcaid had an eye for beauty. Without thinking why, he reached out a hand and wiped a mud smear from her cheek. Then turning the buggy once more, he made for Nethergate House where he knew he would find Morella. Morella would know what to do.

Nethergate House loomed vast in the gathering gloom, its white, wood walls, and red tiles shiny with the rain. It owed its name, 'Nethergate', to a small village from whence the first American Styles had come, the younger son of the then Squire Styles of Nethergate in the County of Suffolk, England. In America, the family had prospered so well that Adrian Styles, grandson of the first American Styles, had embarked upon the ambitious construction of the bigger, portico mansion of Nethergate Hall, to replace the lesser grandeur of Nethergate House. Nethergate Hall was to be a true reflection of Adrian Styles' status in the New World.

Shouting for Morella, Killcaid carried his limp burden into the slave quarters at the back of Nethergate House. Morella shimmied in, her great, bustling bulk moving with surprising grace and assurance for all her size. Morella, a house servant to the Styles for as long as anyone could remember, was a practical woman with herbal, medical and mystical skills that were famed for miles about. She had tended her master's two sons and successfully tackled all the accidents and ailments that befell them as they had progressed from infancy to maturity. She had treated their parents too and when necessary the slaves as well. Thus, she had earned her privileged place in the quarters at the back of the big house.

She at once took charge of the casualty. She nodded after a brief examination and Killcaid left, confident she would not fail him, and that Mr Styles would not suffer the financial loss of one more of the farm's stock.

Ruth was undoubtedly an attractive child, her features and form not yet harshened with toil. Her countenance and gentle colouring were a touching tribute to the sometimes-stunning results of the often brutal co-junction of the races. The child was barely conscious as Morella cleansed her body, dressed her wounds and then reset and splinted her fractured leg. As she worked she hummed, high pitched, in a language known only to herself.

When she was well on with her healing task she was joined by Mary Styles, wife to Adrian Styles, Nethergate's Master. Morella's mistress had been drawn by the commotion in the back yard.

Mary's features were etched with concern when she saw what Morella was doing. She had a gentle face, not by any means beautiful in the classic mould, but a face of which a man would never tire, and which would grow old with grace. She still looked young, but with just a touch of the thickening and stiffness of middle age.

Morella was not surprised at her arrival, for Mary was a caring and kindly mistress. Coming from a Northern family she was a stranger to slavery and still found it difficult to come to terms with the concept of owning another human being. She treated her house slaves as a Christian lady should, in much the same manner as she had always treated her servants at home in New York. But there was no doubting the difference between servant and slave, for these people had distinct, childlike expectations from their owners, born of a total dependence. It distressed her that they had no prospects, no ambitions other than to ease their lot in life, no hopes other than that they would find themselves with a kindly Master when old age sapped their usefulness and their purpose in being kept alive. That thought, when it had first come to her had shocked her, but now she was a part of it. Try as she might though, she could not quite reconcile her Christian beliefs with the ownership of another human soul.

It had all seemed so simple when she had first met Adrian on one of his periodic visits North to negotiate the export of the tobacco crop. He was handsome and assured, every bit the Southern gentleman. She loved the way he spoke and his old-world courtesy. Their friendship had quickly blossomed into romance. Her family approved. Her father, Henry Bragg, was a manufacturer of farming machinery and saw possible openings in Southern estates as slave labour became more expensive to maintain. Soon it was accepted that the two families would be united and Mary had moved South into Nethergate House as Mrs Mary Styles. She had rapidly grown to love the old house and secretly dreaded the imminent move into the artificial grandeur of Nethergate Hall, now nearly complete.

Ruth opened her eyes and stared back up at the faces above her, one black one white. She had the wide-eyed, unblinking gaze of a trapped animal, passive and resigned to whatever they might do to her. Mary had dutifully born two sons, but she had always longed for a daughter. She felt a stirring in her heart at this child's youth and vulnerability. But Morella saw something else in those innocent staring eyes. She reeled back with a startled cry.

"O Mistress Mary, O Mistress," she gasped, clasping her head, the whites of her eyes rolling back in her black face.

"Whatever's the matter Morella?" asked Mary.

"I sees the most dreadful things Mistress," and she shook her greying head. Then in tones of deep foreboding she added, "This chile, she goin' to give you great heartache. I see it all. I sees it wid mine own eyes!"

"What utter nonsense you talk sometimes Morella!" chided Mary, "She is just a little girl. She's hurt and frightened and we must do our Christian duty by her." All the same, she felt

6

a sudden chill, for in the past Morella's sudden revelations had often proved prescient. Morella's great frame shuddered briefly and then she returned to her duties as if nothing had been said. She had given her warning. Now she dismissed her own fearful forebodings as quickly as they had come into her mind, in the strange way that things so often did. Besides, her own heart too had warmed to the bewitching charm of this small and fearful child.

2

Ruth Finds A New Home

Ruth's earliest memory of Nethergate was of a dim, wood cabin made with split timbers, with a beaten-earth floor and just a door and a single window to let in the light. The roof was wooden too but covered with reed thatch from the nearby swamps down at the creek. There was the friendly smell of the wood fire, spiced with the aroma of whatever was cooking and always the warm, intimate smell of closely packed human bodies and flies, flies, flies.

Outside there would be the sound of her mother singing to the thumping rhythm as she pounded maize into flour. When all the slaves returned from the fields, the outside world would burst into sudden animation with the commotion, chatter and laughter of a hundred voices rejoicing at the end of another day of toil.

Later, her horizons widened to the rows of slave huts, stretching as far as the eye could see under the wide Kentucky sky. There had been a succession of 'fathers', until one seemed to become a permanent fixture. But the identity of her real father she never discovered, and her mother would never say for the shame of it. She guessed by her complexion that he had been a white man and she often in small ways was made to feel the stigma of it, even at her young age.

Ruth had never even seen the big house in which her owner lived. As soon as she was old enough to walk there was work to be done. At first there were simple tasks, helping about the cabin, then further afield with her mother harvesting what was to be gathered in the woodlands down by the bayou, too marshy to be suitable for tobacco-growing. Later when her mother was working again, she learnt to forage on her own. At five she was put to work in the tobacco fields. It had been a source of pride, a rite of passage. For her, childhood was over.

Because of her accident, Ruth now found herself in a very strange world indeed. She had never slept in a proper bed with sheets before, or in a room that had windows that let in so much light, or in a building that was not thick with the familiar acrid reek of wood smoke. For a moment, the solidity of the walls and structure made her fearful, as if they might fall in and crush her and the air was almost too pure to breathe.

Morella came bustling in with some food. Ruth sat up, now hungry despite the soreness of her body and still her amazement grew at the bright luxury of her surroundings. Her hands investigated the bedding and she wondered at how it could feel so warm where she lay yet so cool to her exploring touch. Then she lifted the proffered bowl to her lips. She smiled at the smiling face of Morella and Morella's heart melted.

Mary came in to see her too and stayed a while talking. At first, Ruth had been too shy to say much, for she had never spoken to a white lady before and could not stop staring. But she soon warmed to Mary's tender and motherly nature.

As she recovered she was given small tasks to do about the house, hobbling along on crutches, swinging her splinted leg after her. Gradually she ceased to be in awe of her surroundings and her natural sunny and willing disposition asserted itself. Wherever she was, somehow there was always laughter and smiles. As she abandoned crutches and splints she was given more to do. The question of her returning to the fields somehow never arose. By a process more of absorption than any conscious decision, she was adopted into the household staff, though still a frequent visitor to her mother and the slave cabins.

She became a great favourite with her Mistress. Mary's personal maid Daisy, who had served the previous Mistresses of Nethergate House, was getting on in years and was slowing down with rheumatism. It seemed the natural thing that Ruth should be her understudy. When they all moved into the grandeur of Nethergate Hall, Daisy had found the servants' stairs difficult to manage and Ruth assumed even more of her duties. When finally, she suffered a fall, Ruth took over entirely. Daisy eased into a gentle retirement, doing such small tasks about the house as her failing health allowed.

As the years passed, the bond between Ruth and her mistress grew ever stronger. Ruth was naturally intelligent and quick to respond to her Mistress's needs. Mary for her part began to treat Ruth more as a friend and confidant than a slave. Though it was against the law, she arranged for all her household slaves to be introduced to the mysteries of the written word. It was a skill very few slaves enjoyed. But Ruth, she personally taught to read and write. She also encouraged in her a real talent for drawing. Ruth was her apology, her appeasement, to the unease she still felt about owning slaves, although technically they belonged to the estate and not to her personally. Ruth, for her part, became devoted to her mistress. She soon lost much of the patois of the slaves and in every way adopted the manners and mores of those she served. As she matured she became a very great beauty indeed. It wasn't long before she became conscious of the way Mark, Mary's oldest boy, watched her.

Although barely in her teens, she was aware of her growing

womanhood and the effect she had on men generally. She was doubly flattered by Mark's attentions and intrigued by the way her femininity appealed to both black and white men alike. At times, she would experiment and coyly play up to what instinctively she knew men expected of her, unaware in her innocence that she was playing with fire.

Mark was a handsome, aristocratic-looking man, dark haired with blue, inscrutable eyes and warm, sensual lips. He was a man used to getting his own way. His mother, though, had no illusions about her elder son and had seen the way he looked at Ruth. One day when Ruth was brushing Mary's hair and the early morning sun was streaming in through the windows she said suddenly, "Have a care Ruth where my oldest boy is concerned. I've seen the way he watches you."

"Yes Missus," she had replied, wondering whether this was a warning or a rebuke. After that she tried to ignore the eyes of this disturbing young man.

Then one evening she received a message to go to her mistress immediately in the billiard room. It was an unusual request, for normally the billiard room was the haunt of the menfolk. There must however be a reason and she hastened to obey. When she arrived, she found the room empty. Puzzled, she turned to go. Only then did she see Mark standing behind the door. Slowly and deliberately he pushed the door to and leant against it. She heard the key click in the lock as he turned it behind his back. Ruth turned cold. He had been drinking. A thin dribble ran down the corner of his mouth.

"This 'as been a long-time cumin' Ruth," he slurred.

She stood, frozen with fear.

"Come 'ere. Come to Mark, you knows you wants to," he said in a wheedling voice. His face was slack from the drink and his lips moist with his own drool. How could she have thought him handsome?

She remained, rooted to the spot. Suddenly his features flushed with anger.

"Come 'ere nigger when I tells 'e!" he exploded.

Trembling she took one or two hesitant steps towards him.

"Closer," he demanded thickly. She obeyed until she was an arm's length from him.

"Now, unbutton your chemise fo' me." She did not move.

"Do as you're bid. Damn you!" His voice crackled with menace.

She fumbled at the buttons of her dress, but her fingers trembled too much to do her bidding. He took one step towards her and ripped her chemise apart so that the buttons rattled to the floor like beads from a broken necklace. She tried to cover herself with her hands, but with one violent gesture he tore the dress from her shoulders so that her hands were briefly pinioned to her side. She stood facing him her shoulders bare, her breasts heaving with her panic-stricken breathing and the violent beating of her heart.

For a moment, he stood before her, drinking in her nakedness.

"God! You're beautiful for a nigger," he croaked hoarsely, almost to himself. Then his hands reached out towards the firm pink roundness of her breasts and he touched her.

For Ruth, it was like a dagger of fire; the outrage, the sense of violation, the degradation of her situation. Without thinking she freed her hand and it flew to his face with a violent crack. Then she gasped at the awful thing she had done. She had raised her hand to her white master. She had struck him. She was a criminal.

Mark's face bore a look of utter astonishment as slowly his hand reached to his smarting cheek where she had hit him. Then fire kindled in his eyes until they blazed with fury. With a low guttural rumble from deep within his chest, he lashed out at her. Blow after blow struck her and she fell, her head spinning. Then he was upon her his weight crushing her to the floor, one hand about her throat. Barely conscious, she struggled for breath. She was only dimly aware of his frantic fury as he ripped and tore at her clothing. His strength and passion overwhelmed her dazed resistance until she knew she lay defenceless and open to him.

For a moment, his weight left her. Hope soared as she gasped and gagged for air. Then she glimpsed him kneeling over her fumbling for the swollen enormity of his desire. Then he was upon her once more, one hand still about her throat. The sharpness of the pain drove through her. Her whole body was shaken like a rag doll with the frenzied violence of his passion. Then at last, again and again and again he shuddered, and she felt the molten heat of his lust subsiding within her. His body went limp. Slowly she felt his weight lift from her. It was all over. Then almost as an afterthought, his hand left her throat, but by then, mercifully, she had lost consciousness.

It was Morella, with her instinct for any creature in distress, who came to find her. Morella who spirited her away to the slave quarters where she could be cared for, Morella who made excuses to her mistress and advised her to keep away for fear of some imagined contagion.

As for Ruth, though she had been born and bred a slave she had always felt that at the very core of her being, in her thoughts, in the inner recesses of her mind, there was a tiny part of herself that was free and hers alone. Now, that freedom had been violated. Her body was no longer her own. Only when her bruises had sunk into the dusky bronze of her complexion did she return to her duties. Mary took one look at her and knew what had happened, for Mary knew her son.

13

3

Ambitions

When Mary told Adrian about what she suspected Mark had done to Ruth, his reaction had surprised her, for he did not greet the news with shock or outrage. It was almost as if Mark had been guilty of a breach of good manners, nothing more. He had promised to talk to him about it when the occasion might arise.

Mary had lost her temper at this. "Adrian! How can you take this with such a lack of concern?" she had stormed. "Mark has brutally raped the poor girl. Taken her by force!"

In his turn Adrian seemed surprised by the reaction of his wife. "As I said my dear, I will mention it to him and let him know how you feel about it." Then he had added, as if in justification for Mark's conduct, "She is a very pretty girl."

Mary felt a sharp retort coming to her lips at this seemingly casual response to her outrage, but she was wise enough to let the matter lie, for she realised that there was a fundamental difference between her views and her husband's on such matters, both as a woman and as someone who had not been born and bred with slavery. Instead she vowed that she would do all she could to make it up to Ruth in some way. In any event she doubted that any rebuke from Adrian would have much influence on her wayward son. Mark's relationship with his father was even worse than that with his mother. She had long felt her influence waning as her son grew older and ever more errant. It grieved her that he seemed incapable of showing love to either of his parents and she worried and wondered where she had gone wrong and where it would all end.

Mark had never been easy in his father's company. His father, he reckoned, had old fashioned ideas about the dutiful relationship between father and son which had never featured in his reckoning. They were too similar in temperament. Both could only see things from their own point of view. Both were proudly nailed to their own opinions. Mary had done her best over the years to sooth bruised egos, but as Mark grew older and still more headstrong, her blandishments failed to achieve even the barest outward signs of civility between the two.

Their difference lay rooted in the view they held of the source of all their wealth and prosperity. Mark's father was justly proud of Nethergate and of what he and his forebears had achieved over the years. He intended to make sure that there should be no let-up under his watch. It was his ambition that the Styles name should surge down through the pantheon of American history riding on the wealth generated by the Nethergate Estate. To this end he made sure that he understood every facet of the tobacco operation himself. Above all though, he studied the marketing, for he knew that this would give him the edge over his competitors. In negotiating the price and when to bring his leaf onto the market he had an uncanny instinct that was the envy of his fellow planters. There was little to choose between growers when it came to farming techniques, but in reading the market for the coming year and in producing the type of tobacco leaf that the market most desired lay the true path to success and the accumulation of wealth. In that talent, Adrian had no equal. He was determined that Mark should continue in a like vein once the time came for him to hand the reins over to the next generation.

Although Adrian had little love for Silas Killcaid, now his Head Overseer, he was not blind to this man's talents, infinitely superior to those of his predecessor and so essential to the estate's prosperity. Nor did he doubt his loyalty. Silas Killcaid had a wholehearted commitment to Nethergate and to its Master. He may have been rough and unchristian, but he was his right-hand man in working the land and managing the slaves. His chief quality, as far as the latter were concerned, was the fear he engendered amongst the workforce. His temper and harshness of character were a byword. No slave dared to defy him or to shirk under his watchful eye. He had also built up a network of informants so that nothing went on within the slave community without his knowledge. It wasn't necessarily the number of slaves that a plantation might own that dictated a plantation's prosperity, more it was the work that could be got from each individual. No-one shirked under Killcaid's gimlet eyes.

Out in the fields Killcaid would spend the long hours of the slaves' day practising with his 'Rattler'. The hiss and crack of the rawhide whip kept heads down. None dared look up from their toil for fear of tasting the Rattler's bite. It was said he could remove a man's ear from ten paces and that you would never even detect the movement of his wrist. It was well known too that he would allot the easier tasks or reduce the work quota for young female slaves in exchange for other favours to ease the monotony of his day. The rest of the slave community welcomed such interludes, for only then did the Rattler fall silent. Adrian was aware of all this and his Puritanical side was repelled, but no man is perfect and there had been no complaints.

Killcaid's select band of lesser overseers vied with each other in their diligence and loyalty to Killcaid himself. Every aspiring slave sought to curry favour so that he too might be chosen as a whip-hand and thus exchange hard labour for the laying on of the lash, albeit upon the backs of his brothers. Thus did Silas Killcaid control his workforce and in so doing enhance his value to his employer. His attitude to slaves, though, was typical of most of his peers on other estates. He excelled only perhaps in his wanton cruelty and complete lack of compassion.

Adrian, like Killcaid, thoroughly understood his slave workforce. He'd grown up with slaves. Slaves were warm, simple-hearted folk, like small children. As a young boy, as a toddler even, they had been a constant presence, there to do his will, to answer his every need. The ubiquitous chorus of, "Yes Masser Adrian. Right away Masser Adrian," forever ringing in his ears, as with a childlike anxiety to please, grown men had scuttled away to do his bidding. Field slaves, when he had met them, had been equally unctuous to please.

With household slaves, his relationship had of course been much warmer. He had suckled from a black breast, sought comfort from black arms and been lulled to sleep by black harmonies. As he grew older his favourite place in the house was the kitchen where he was ever assured of a loving welcome and some tasty treat. Countless times he had ridden piggyback on the broad shoulders of the houseboys, squealing with delight as they bucked, reared and galloped about the lawns of Nethergate House. He loved the warm, acrid smell of their sweat, so different from the white man's body odour. He had felt their frames shake with laughter or vibrate with their sometimes-deep bass singing voices. He had listened to their tales and visited the worlds of their imagination and been comforted when upset or angry. He would have trusted them with his very soul. Yet as he grew older he had heard stories of slaves turning against their masters and could not believe it of any of their slaves, always so docile and willing. Then came the shock of the Nat Turner rebellion of 1831 which caused every slave owner to look with a different eye upon their work hands.

The rebellion did not change the slave owner's basic view of the slave, but it made them look with a wary eye for any lack of willingness or sign of rebellion and led to harsh and savage punishment meted out to some as a lesson for others.

Like the rest of his Southern country-folk, Adrian did not believe that the slaves had the same feeling or understanding as white folk. They did not love or comprehend as whites did. They were born to harshness, particularly those who worked in the fields. It was their lot in life. They would not work without the lash. If their working conditions were eased, they would simply work less and expect more. Slaves over the years had acquired a skill for avoiding work and effort with a cunning the equal of no other creature on earth. They were capable of wilfully misunderstanding even the most meticulous of instructions where an advantage was to be gained. Without the lick of the lash, there would be no more profitability and the whole Southern way of life would be imperilled.

If Adrian chose to allow Silas his head on the management of the slave stock, he was not totally blind to their other needs. He ensured that they were well fed, watered and housed much as the Nethergate groom exercised his care for the quality of his livestock. Latterly, urged on by Mary, he had gone further than his own good sense allowed by additionally improving the conditions in which they lived in the slave lines. At her prompting, he even employed a slave to trap the game which abounded in the bayou, to ensure a plentiful supply of good fresh meat. This was the task of Old Mo, an ex-trapper's slave who, unlike his erstwhile master, had survived after being scalped by Indians out West. Whenever possible he permitted the slaves their Sundays as a day of rest and worship. He had built for them a place of prayer and had hired a freed slave as their preacher. Killcaid had only reluctantly tolerated such indulgencies with a tight-lipped refusal to comment.

Adrian had safely left the day-to-day running of the estate

to Silas. His chief anxiety now however was centred on Mark. Mark had showed no sign of developing his father's feel for the estate and for Nethergate's future. He had intended to allow Mark gradually to take over the administration of the estate under his guidance until he was satisfied that he had learnt the ropes. Then he meant to pursue his ultimate ambition on forging a political future for the family in the Kentucky State legislature. After that, he allowed himself to dream of even higher attainments.

Thus far though, Mark had shown no inclination to take a more active part in the running of Nethergate. To Mark it seemed, the Nethergate Estate was simply there to be milked for his own indulgence, to his father's simmering rage and frustration.

4

The Confrontation

Thus far Adrian Styles had tolerated much of Mark's excesses
with the thought that he might yet be prepared to learn and
follow in his father's footsteps, but Mark showed nothing but a
casual disinterest in the subject so dear to his father's heart. He
was not proving a willing pupil, nor did he show the respect due
to his parent and mentor, usually such a feature of the Southern
culture. This particularly raised his father's ire, accustomed
as he was to the regard and deference due to his position in
the community. It undermined his status. A man could hardly
demand the esteem of others if he could not control his own
son. Yet it was precisely for this reason that Mark defied his
father's wishes, for in so doing it enhanced his own status
among those whom he wished to impress. This was another
source of conflict between father and son. Its roots lay deep
back in the past.

Many of the neighbouring estates had been founded by the
second sons of English aristocratic families. Their immediate
progeny had honed their skills in developing these vast new
enterprises. With success came good living. Gradually their
issue had become more self-indulgent, basking in the luxuries

and mores of a slave owning society and ever more flaunting the cachet of their aristocratic connections. Mark's roots though were not in the ranks of the aristocracy. He sprang from yeoman stock. Few in the New World would give the matter any further thought, but it mattered to Mark. He was all too aware of the distinction. Now however, the strength of Nethergate made him every bit the equal of those with a finer pedigree and he meant to gain acceptance into their inner circle by his own dash and daring.

Mark's new friends were a hard and fast living lot. Mark vied with the best of them in daring and outrageous conduct. Nethergate could well afford his excesses. Adrian had at first indulged his wild behaviour, hoping that it was but the temporary expression of a youthful exuberance. But far from stopping, Mark's extravagances gained momentum. His father's firm Protestant instincts began to assert themselves. He could not see the necessity for such displays of wantonness. Not without a certain grim satisfaction, he curtailed the release of further funds necessary to bankroll Mark's new tastes. This infuriated Mark and became an ever-growing source of conflict between them.

Mark, not to be outdone, now took to gambling to make up the shortfall. Such was his success that it was rumoured that he seemed to have Lady Luck standing not so much at his elbow, but somehow concealed somewhere up his sleeve, such was the near-miraculous way in which the right cards seemed to spring into his hands at the very moment it was wanted. He was too skilled to be caught out, but the rumours abounded. This caused further friction between father and son, for Adrian placed great value upon probity and the family honour. A showdown was inevitable if Adrian was ever to hold up his head among his peers.

It came after Mark took part in a week-long carousal of excesses and debauchery centred on a neighbouring estate, notorious for such goings on. The party spilled over into the local town greatly to the outrage of its citizenry. During one escapade, Mark had been identified as the one who rode down and killed an unfortunate slave who had been too slow to get out of his way. Mark had refused to pay compensation to the owner, who farmed one of the lesser plantations. The aggrieved party had accordingly asked Adrian to make good the loss of his much-valued hand and Adrian had felt obliged so to do.

On his return, Mark was summoned to his father's study, a deliberate strategy on the part of his father to remind him of past humiliations, for the study at Nethergate was the traditional seat of governance. He was not offered a seat, so with casual unconcern he took possession of the most commodious armchair and cocking one leg over the arm, sunk into its depths. As was the intention, it was too much for his father.

"Damn you for an insolent puppy!" he exploded, "You've cost me near a thousand dollars in compensation for the nigger you rode down. And by God I'll see it comes out of your allowance. See if I don't. You're draggin' the family name through the mire," continued Adrian, warming to his theme, "gallivantin' about with those idle good-for-nothings with more money than sense. You're no damned use to man nor beast."

Mark gazed up at his father with a languid lack of concern and raised one quizzical eyebrow. "Is that all Father?" he asked insolently, for he knew just how to goad his father.

Adrian lurched to his feet sending his chair crashing over behind him. Barely able to contain himself he leant forward over his desk glowering at his son and seething with rage. Such was his fury that he found it hard to speak, but at last he found the words. "This time you've gone too far. I'll have no more of it. I'll thank you to show a proper interest of the running of this estate and the opinion of our neighbours, or by God I'll make sure that your brother has the running of it and the ownership too."

Adrian had not meant to say this, but his anger ran on ahead of him. Now it was said and there could be no backing down.

Mark considered this. He was stung by the prospect of losing money for the dead nigger for which he felt more irritation than guilt. But he would soon replace that at the card tables. To be disinherited though was another matter and he had to acknowledge it was the one weakness in his position. But he doubted his father would have the resolve to do it, once his choler had cooled. There had been many previous threats, but none so specific. He realised too that for his father, it would be a public signal of weakness to his fellow planters to show he was unable to control his older son to the extent of giving the reins to the runt of the litter. Few had much regard for Anthony's ability to run such an enterprise as Nethergate. Everyone knew that his brother Anthony wasn't half the man he was. But his own dander was rising as it always did on such occasions.

"You know full well Sir," he replied evenly, in a deliberately provocative drawl, "that Killcaid will run rings round my brother. He'll end up syphoning off the estate profits and Anthony won't have an inkling of what's happening. I am the only one that can keep Killcaid in his place and you know it." This was true and his father in secret acknowledged it.

Nevertheless, such was his anger that Adrian this time was determined to teach his wayward son a lesson. "You worthless young braggart!" he roared, "I shall call for Forbes this very day and have Anthony put in your place. See if I don't."

Further high words then erupted between them until Mark stormed out, satisfied that when his temper cooled, his father would never carry out his threat.

That satisfaction was shaken the next day however, when Brian Forbes, the family solicitor, called to see his father. His father made sure that Mark should see them together so that the message to him would not be lost. To emphasise the point the pair were accompanied by Anthony, Mark's younger brother, as always looking awkward and uncomfortable in his father's presence. Anthony, to his brother's contempt, had taken training as a solicitor and now worked for a living as a junior partner in the offices of Forbes and Sons, Family Solicitors. Anthony, as a junior member of the firm, had never been involved directly in family or estate business. That had always been left to Forbes Senior. The presence of Anthony was to show his wayward son who now was the heir apparent. The message was clear to Mark. His father, this time, meant business.

In the dark recesses of his mind Mark began to ponder ways of stopping him.

5

A Family Tragedy

Initially Ruth thought it must have been the shock her body had received over her encounter with Mark that had caused her periods to cease. As time passed though, she could no longer hide the truth from herself. She had to acknowledge with increasing outrage, that she was now pregnant with Mark's child.

Only Morella knew. At first Ruth hated the incubus growing within her. It was as if Mark had not only raped her but was now cultivating his poison within her and possessing her with his evil nature, over and again, with every moment of every day. In the quiet of the night she would try to relax her stomach muscles and then pummel her belly with her fists as tears of humiliation flowed down her cheeks. It was a constant reminder of what Mark had stolen from her. At last, unable to stand the hatred she felt for her own body and what it was nurturing, she appealed to Morella.

"Please Morella," she begged, "you must get rid of this thing that is within me. I hates it so. I can never love the child it will become."

Morella enfolded her to her ample bosom. Her aroma filled

Ruth's senses with comfort. "Hush chile," she murmured, stroking and caressing her hair, "Hush chile. Yoh' must wait a little while yet. Maybe you won' alus feel this way. Then maybe we'll see, eh?"

"Never," cried Ruth.

But Morella had been right. Gradually Ruth's feeling for what grew inside her began to change. It was not its fault that it had started life in the way it had, but the child was hers now and hers alone. Only it wasn't hers. It was the Master's and eventually, in the fullness of time, it would become Mark's, to do with as he wished. But even with that realisation, she recognised that she now thought of it as a child, her child and not as if it were a malignant growth. Mark would not know, would not care even if he guessed that it was his seed she carried. She would turn evil into good, hatred into love. It was a new life in God's image, that's what the preacher said. Now she could place her hands wide over her belly as if in this way, she could encompass and cradle the tiny thing that grew within her. When she was alone she would talk to it and quietly sing to it by way of apology for her previous feelings and to reassure it in case it might have sensed that she had ever wished it harm.

Ruth managed to conceal her condition from her Mistress, fearful of what she might do. She was certain that Mary would expect her to leave the comforts of Nethergate Hall. Above all she feared leaving the service of Mary herself. With the prospect of parting she had to acknowledge how much she owed to Mary's kindness and too how much she cared for her mistress.

Such matters however were driven from all their minds by news of far greater concern. Adrian Styles the Master of Nethergate was seriously ill. He had travelled to New York to negotiate the sale of next year's tobacco harvest. There he had met some Northern contagion and was laid low. Mary left in haste to be by his side. A month later, she returned pale, drawn and dressed in black.

Mark to his intense gratification was now the new master of Nethergate, whatever his father's plans might have been. He had though received a visit from Forbes and with it a shock as to the further provisions of his father's will.

As the new Master, Mark's first act was to suggest to his mother that she might like to move back into Nethergate House, the old house, built by the first master of Nethergate. For Mark, it was an act of revenge against his father for certain changes to his will that had been revealed by Forbes after his father's untimely death. It was a message to his mother too, should there be any doubt as to who was now Master of Nethergate. Mary, though, had no stomach at such a time for a fight and indeed no objections to the move, for in truth she was fonder of the old house, her first marital home, than the impersonality and grandeur of Nethergate Hall. It held happy memories for her of the years of her marriage to Adrian. She felt closer to him there than at Nethergate Hall. Naturally, Ruth and Morella moved with her. Ruth was greatly relieved for now there was less of a chance of her meeting up again with Mark before her child was born.

Mary still had not realised Ruth's condition and Ruth dreaded the moment when she would have to confess how things stood, particularly whilst her mistress was mourning the loss of her husband. Although she still managed to conceal the swelling of her belly, it was the sickness that gave her away in front of her mistress. Appalled by the weakness of her own body, she fully expected to be punished. But Mary was full of concern.

"You poor, poor child," she said when Ruth had recovered. Then after a long pause, she almost whispered, "Was it Master Mark?"

Ruth could only nod in assent. For what seemed like an age

to Ruth, Mary simply looked at her. To Mary, it was simply the worst manifestation in a very personal way of all her fears about the casual manner such matters were viewed in the South. Even her beloved Adrian had been immune to such goings on. Then with sudden resolution she came to a decision. She became in a moment very business-like.

"You know my son will not care two figs for what he has done," she said, "but nevertheless, the fact remains that you are now carrying my grandson."

At this awful truth, Ruth burst into tears. She had never thought of her child in this way. "O Missus, O Missus, I is so sorry."

"Hush child. I know it was no fault of yours. But what's to do now? That's the question." But she had already come to her decision. "No grandchild of mine," she announced, "is going to be born a slave." It was an option that had not occurred to Ruth, for every child born to a slave was automatically a slave too, no matter who the father might be. That was the law, as logical and as irrefutable as the Christian nature of the State itself. Ruth's heart gave a sudden lurch of joy, more so at the totally unexpected nature of the consequence of that awful event in the billiard room.

"You mean Missus…" She hardly dared voice the thought.

"Yes Ruth. We'll make a free woman of you."

"O Missus, O Missus," was all she could say, her heart was so full.

"It's no more than you deserve my child, after what you've been through. I shall see to it this very day."

The tears sprang to Ruth's eyes, she was so full of joy at the sudden and unexpected turn of events. She tried to speak, but all she could do was incoherently to sob out her gratitude. Then an awful thought occurred to her.

"But what about you Mistress? Will I still be able to be your maid?"

Mary in her turn was overwhelmed by Ruth's reaction and now at her concern for her, midst her own sudden delight. She felt her arms moving out towards Ruth and the two women fell into an embrace, both now with tears in their eyes. Mary drew great comfort from the sincerity of Ruth's reaction. It was the first time since Adrian's death that she had felt comforted by the affection of another human being. It brought to her mind with a sudden rush how dear to her Ruth was, and how much more than just a maid she had become.

"Of course you may remain here if that is your wish my dear, but as a free woman in my service."

At that moment Ruth felt the first movement of the child within her. She gasped with the surprise of it and her hands flew to her belly. It was as if her unborn child was rejoicing within her. Mary realised at once what had happened and smiled gently.

"You must go now Ruth my dear. I have things to do, not the least of which will be to see Mr Forbes to get the necessary papers drawn up."

Ruth left then. She seemed to be walking on air. A free woman! It seemed too incredible even to think of. And she could still serve her mistress. When she was a free woman Mark could never touch her again. She would be his equal at least in the eyes of the law.

All that day she went about her duties with her heart singing with joy, going over and over in her mind all the things she would do as a free woman and how the world suddenly would be a different place. When, earlier than usual, she received a summons to her mistress's room she rushed along, seeming to be skating on air. As soon as she opened the door however, she knew that something was wrong.

"O Ruth, I am so sorry," burst out Mary as soon as she saw her.

"What is it Missus?"

"It's Master Mark. He won't hear of it."

"But I's your woman Missus."

"Yes, Ruth dear, you are indeed mine, but with Adrian gone, Mark is now the legal owner of all the hands on the estate. He refuses to grant you your freedom. He says we need all the younger women since the African trade was stopped." She was clearly as distressed at the news as Ruth. "He treats people like cattle. Since he has become Master of Nethergate, I confess I no longer know him as the son I once had. He has grown so hard and wilful."

Waves of bitterness and anger by turns swept through her. So, Master Mark had won after all! How could she ever have even dreamt of freedom, of being his equal and free from him?

Whilst she was still trying to come to terms with this devastating news there was a knock at the door and Morella entered. For Mary, it had been a terrible dilemma, for what she contemplated now was no more than the murder of her own grandchild.

"Ruth, I know how you must feel, but I have in all conscience to offer you this way out. Though I cannot say I could ever approve of such a course. But I would never blame you for taking it." For a time, she seemed to be wrestling with her conscience, then in a low voice she said, "Morella can make sure you do not have this baby."

"O Mistress," wailed Morella, deeply distressed, "Did'na I just see this happ'nin, all dem years ago?"

Ruth knew just what it had cost her mistress to call for Morella and how it went against all her Christian principles.

"No Missus," she said. "This chile is my chile. Tis not its fault the manner of its being."

Mary seemed to be struggling with emotions too deep for words. Her eyes brimmed with tears when at last she spoke, "Bless you Ruth my dear. Truly if anyone ever deserved to be free it is you. Someday I promise you, I will see that you and the child you carry, my own grandchild, will truly get their freedom."

"O Missus, I knows you will and God bless you for it."

6

Back To The Plantation

What plans his father had set in motion shortly before his death, Mark discovered when Mr Forbes had visited the house when Adrian's death had been confirmed, but this time as Mark's not Adrian's solicitor.

"Before he departed for New York," Mr Forbes began, with a lawyer's urbane neutrality, "your father instructed me, in the event of his death, to draw up papers explaining that due to…" and here he coughed discreetly, "what he described as your wayward behaviour, the whole estate should be left in trust to his wife, Mrs Mary Styles. It would be up to her to decide when and who should take over the management of the estate and the entire inheritance, when she deemed the time to be right."

"What!" exploded Mark, "Curse him to hell. Do you mean to say my damned father has disinherited me?"

"Not at all Sir. It was his intention that your mother should be the person to decide the moment for either you or your brother to take over the running of the estate. In the meantime, he seemed to think that the management of the estate could be safely left in your mother's hands. Unusual, I must confess, but he seemed to think that she would be more than equal to the task."

Only then, when it was too late, did Mark realise that he had finally pushed his father too far. He had never thought for a moment he would dare to take such drastic action. He ground his teeth in impotent fury at his father's revenge from beyond the grave. He had noted with a grim satisfaction, the change in attitude of so many who had previously condemned him, now that it was assumed he was the new Master of Nethergate. All that would change, but chiefly he raged against the scorn that he would endure from his erstwhile companions in debauchery.

"My Mother!" he exploded, "What does my Mother know about running a place like this? Killcaid will run rings round her. Does she know of this?" he asked.

"But of course, Sir. She has already been to see me with a letter dictated by your father in New York and signed a few days before he died. It conformed with the wishes he had already voiced to me as to his intentions. He was going to finalise the arrangements with me after his return. At the time, of course there was no particular urgency. What I have is a draft of what I believed him to have in mind."

Mark finally gave way to the anger and frustration of his new situation and railed and cursed against both his parents in the coarsest of terms. Such was his passion that he at first failed to register that Forbes had continued speaking.

"I have had to advise your mother that what I hold is simply what I believe to have been your father's intention, which he would have confirmed or otherwise on his return. Your father was too ill to write and dictated his final will to your mother who wrote it down for him. He signed it, but there were no witnesses. I have had to advise your mother that since it was she who had written down your father's wishes and since she was the beneficiary it is unlikely that the deposition would be accepted by any court. In addition, the signature is so unlike your father's normal hand as to give rise to reasonable doubt as to its authenticity. It was shortly after this that your father lapsed into his final coma, before he died."

Slowly what Mr Forbes was saying had begun to register.

"You – you mean I could still be the new Master of Nethergate after all?"

"The draft I hold is no more than just that – a draft – and the document in your mother's own hand would not be acceptable by any court without there being witnesses. I have had to advise your mother, that in my view your father's original will still stands legally as his final testament. In answer to your question, yes, I believe you to be the new Master of Nethergate."

"Haaah!" Mark let out a great roar of triumph and relief. He was Master of Nethergate after all, despite his father's wishes. All the same he was consumed with anger that his father had dared to take this step. He still considered that in the end he would not have implemented it, but it had nevertheless given him a nasty shock.

On his father's death, Mark had observed all the niceties of mourning expected of him, but when Forbes had revealed his father's intentions, he felt he no longer had any reason to mourn. Within a week of the funeral, to the mortification of his mother, he was out carousing with his friends. The very idea of a decent period of mourning was forgotten. The running of the estate was left entirely in the hands of Silas Killcaid, who now indulged his appetites without restraint.

It is doubtful if Mark even thought of what had happened between Ruth and him, other than to be enraged at the memory of her insolence in daring to strike him. Ruth hid from going anywhere where she might be seen by the new Master. But one day she was at the back of the old house when he rode by and saw her over the hedge. She was then too far gone to be able to hide her condition. Shortly after, she heard Master Mark talking to his mother in the garden. His voice was raised in anger.

"I tell you Ma'am. I'll have no nigger girl farrowing in any of my houses. She goes back to the compound to spawn with her own kind." At these words, a chill crept over her.

She heard the low voice of her mistress remonstrating with her son and then his voice again exploding in anger. "Rest assured Ma'am, if you defy me I will sell her this very day and send her down the river whatsoever condition she's in! Either that or she'll marry the child's father. Do we know who that is?"

Mary's reply was too low for her to catch. But the guffaw of ridicule that followed her reply bore ample evidence as to his attitude to the news.

And so it was that Ruth found herself once again back among the cabins from whence she had come so long ago and working once more in the tobacco fields. It was hard work having grown accustomed to the luxury and less physical routine of a lady's maid and harder still whilst carrying her child. Her natural refinement born of the life she had lived and indeed the difference in her way of speaking marked her apart from the rest. But she had never looked down upon her fellow slaves from her position of privilege and had many acts of kindness to her credit. Nevertheless, there were still some who resented her presence among them and mistrusted her, believing her to be an instrument of their owner and a willing, if discarded, plaything of the white man. Their own growing uncertainties too, bred from the enhanced power of Killcaid and the maverick management of Mark, had broken up the unity of the slaves and set family against family. There were rumours that Mark again planned a tranche of selling to pay off further debts. However tyrannical the regime under which a slave lived might be, the thought of the slave market and an uncertain future, was always worse.

Her own mother attended to Ruth's needs as much as she could, to repay the many kindnesses she had received from her daughter. Morella too was a frequent visitor and brought food and gifts from her Mistress.

When Ruth's son was born, Mary herself came to visit her and held the child.

"What are you going to call him?" she asked.

"May I call him Matthew?" Ruth asked. The significance was not lost on Mary, for Matthew was the middle name of Adrian, her husband, whose untimely death she still bitterly mourned.

"Of course you can my dear," she replied, wondering as often before at the faithfulness and devotion of this little slave girl. "I shall be honoured, and I have no doubt that my husband would too. God rest his soul and God bless you too, Ruth."

She came many more times whenever she was able, to see and play with Matthew, particularly when Mark was away from the estate.

7

A Fatal Reckoning

As the years passed Mark grew ever more wilful and profligate in his habits and so the plantation business began to suffer. The drying sheds were left unrepaired. The crops were no longer entirely weed-free and allowed to grow wild and the quality of the leaves harvested fell. Sales were dictated by the constant need for cash. Mark, hungry as ever for immediate gain, felt no need to read the market and plan as his father had done. The sale of slave stock increased so that all the hands felt insecure. He split families who had been together for generations and sold off their children mostly to go down south to the rice fields where labour was scarce, but prices high. In the rice fields swamp disease was rife and few lived to an old age. To compensate for the lack of hands, Killcaid drove the remaining slaves ever harder. The slaves groaned under the burden. Gone now even was the Sunday day of rest.

Every day was a day of unmitigated toil. The slave lines became a sombre and silent place, where many huts were empty, where many more mourned the loss or absence of loved ones and where the men and women were too bone weary even to rejoice and sing at the end of a working day.

Tempers were short and families bickered and squabbled amongst themselves. There was muttering too and unrest in the cabins at night and dark talk of desperate measures. Ruth did her best to shield Matthew from the worsening conditions and tried to occupy his mind by teaching him to read and write with materials eagerly supplied by Mary.

Matters came to a head when the slave dealers once again visited the farm to look over the stock prior to yet another tranche of selling. The dreaded traders came with Mark and Killcaid to survey the stock out working in the tobacco fields. Mark and the dealers dismounted. Killcaid, ever with his whip flicking and cracking, strode among the slaves as they lay resting at midday. There was a mood of almost mutinous unease. Ruth was there too with her young son, his pale bronzed skin contrasting to those about him and always drawing the eyes of the slave traders.

Matthew was now a young boy, just ten years of age, full of merriment and mischief and as playful as a kitten despite the conditions in which he lived. He was a great favourite with the rest of the slaves despite his different appearance, for he brought laughter to their lives. He had a talent for mimicry and would clown about lampooning those who wielded the lash, but in such a way that even they were drawn to his humour and indulged his antics. When the hated Killcaid was not around, it was the aping of Killcaid himself, which brought out the greatest hilarity. But there was also a steely core to his nature that spoke of hidden depths and resolve. Even the older boys treated him with an acceptance not enjoyed by his peers by age, for he would stand up to any of them with an impetuous courage and resolve that was simply best avoided. He was a willing worker in the field, pleased to display skills that were way ahead of his years, but if he was wronged he nursed a sense of indignation that bordered on the reckless. It was this knowledge that kept his mother ever vigilant at his side and still working in the fields. Without regard for Mary's often stated wish that she should resume her place as her lady's maid, she always refused for fear of what her son would do without her restraining hand. Mary was saddened at this refusal and blamed herself, believing that it was caused by the bitterness of Ruth's disappointment over the offer of her freedom that Mark had so swiftly vetoed.

Mark did not quite know in his own mind what his attitude was to Matthew. He knew, without ever acknowledging it, that he must have sired the child for he could see much of himself mirrored in the child's appearance. He could not help being a little curious. He had watched the boy. His antics had amused him at first. He could even see some of his own rebellious traits of character emerging. But his presence was always a reminder of being struck by a slave and his own loss of control. He would like to have got rid of Ruth too, for she still defied him in her own way. On the rare occasions when they met she treated him with a contempt and disdain in her eyes that fell just short of insolence. She had paid the price, but he knew that despite the resentment she engendered in him, his mother would never sanction her sale. In some matters now he had to defer to his mother's wishes for she had persuaded her father in New York to invest heavily in the estate. He wasn't certain whether she knew that he had fathered Ruth's child and the thought made him uneasy and further threw the weight of advantage on his mother's side.

Mary Styles' support was assuming an ever-greater significance, for he feared that because of his financial problems he might have need to seek yet further financial backing from his grandfather in the North. He knew his mother had a special regard for Ruth and that he must tread carefully as far as she was concerned, but that did not stop him playing on Ruth's fears of what might happen to them both.

When one of the slave traders paused where Matthew stood,

Mark came quickly to his side. The trader was a rough-looking man, though clearly a man of means. He wore quality clothes, but they were stained and dirty. He had not been near a barber for some few days for his face was black with stubble. His hands were dirty and his nails ringed in filth.

He reached out to Matthew and held his jaw pinching it hard so that Matthew opened his mouth. The trader peered in examining the state of his young teeth. Then bringing his own rough face close to the smooth complexion of the child, barked out, "Breathe out nigger boy." Too startled to do otherwise Matthew obliged and the trader sniffed at his breath. "Hmm," he grunted, "Sweet as new-mown hay." Then he ran his hands over the boy's body squeezing and probing intimately. Ruth's heart was in her mouth, for there was the growing stiffness of rebellion about her child's stance that Ruth knew only too well.

The trader leant over and spoke quietly in Mark's ear. Both men gave a snort of crude laughter. Mark's cruel eyes caught the look of panic in Ruth's face and a slow contemptuous smile played about his lips.

"Yes," he said to the trader, his eyes not leaving Ruth's face, "that one can go too, but I warn you there's a good price upon him for what you want him for." Then he added, "He's a beautiful boy, that's for sure. Some as 'ed pay a fortune for a lad like that. Eh?" and he nodded to the trader with a lascivious leer and the air was filled with their coarse and knowing guffaws.

Ruth turned cold with fear and revulsion. All the pride and scorn that had sustained her were swept aside. With a cry of desperation, she fell to the ground and grasped at Mark's knees.

"O Massa'! O Massa' please I beg you." He looked down at her with cold contempt and kicked her away. At the same time, he nodded at one of the black overseers standing nearby, who brought down his whip in a stinging crack across her bare shoulders which blazed red at the impact. But she hardly felt the bite of the lash, so desperate was her distress.

"Please Massa'. Don't take away my child. Don't take away my boy, I beg you. Let me go with him. Please."

He turned. "What?" he said, "And lose good breeding stock. It's high time you had a husband. When we're rid of your child we shall give you Shemper Jacob as your man. What d'you think on that? Eh!" Jacob was a sickly hand who no-one would buy so disfigured was he from the smallpox. No woman would lie with him either and he was caught satisfying his frustrations by his own hand so often that he had acquired the nickname of Shemper. With a savage laugh at this final insult, Mark turned on his heel and the group moved away to where other slaves were sheltering in the midday heat.

Ruth felt nothing. Whether he really meant what he said, she did not know. She was drained of feeling. It was as if she had already ceased to exist. Mark's horse was standing nearby. It was a fine animal with a temper as fiery as that of its owner. Ruth released her hold on Matthew and asked the man standing next to her to continue holding him and to keep him looking away. Matthew, quelled by his mother's anxiety, struggled to follow her with his eyes, but the man held him firmly despite his struggles.

Ruth moved towards Mark's horse. Stooping to the ground she picked up a sharp stone. She made no attempt to hide what she was doing. Watched by the others she moved slowly and deliberately to Mark's horse and wedged the stone under the horse's saddle. The stallion snorted and moved restlessly, but eventually settled as Ruth soothed him. Then Ruth returned to her boy and held him so tight that he struggled to be free. No-one said a word. Everyone had seen what she had done. By their silence, they too had assumed responsibility for what might now ensue. All eyes were now fixed on the stallion waiting for the drama to be played out.

Their business complete, the three white men returned to their horses. Mark sensed the silence from the watchers and paused, seeking to decipher the rows of inscrutable faces. He interpreted their hostility to the break-up of yet more families and to the yet further efforts that would be demanded of the remainder with the erosion of their number.

"What's the matter with you all? Frightened of a little hard work? You had it too good under my father, that not so Mr Killcaid?" he added turning to the overseer.

"Surely is Master Mark," agreed Killcaid, "Have to chivvy them up a bit more. Me and the Rattler, eh!" He gave a short laugh and cracked his whip above the heads of the sullen, black watchers. Normally they would have shrunk back from the snap of the lash. This time though they stood their ground in silent solidarity. Mark stared back at them, unable to understand the meaning behind this change in their normal submissiveness.

One by one the white men swung up into their saddles. Mark threw a final glance at the silently watching slaves and then followed suit.

Straight away, his mount reared up. With an oath, Mark brought down his whip savagely across the horse's rump, striking again and again, trying to beat it into submission. This only caused the animal to become yet more crazed. It bucked and reared at the discomfort under his saddle and then set off at a ferocious, circular gallop, bucking and kicking, doing everything in its power to be rid of his rider and the pain he brought with him.

No man could have stayed on its back so wild was its movement. With a final bound Mark was thrown, spinning high into the air to come crashing heavily and awkwardly to the ground. He did not move.

The slaves stood in shocked stillness, staring at where their Master had fallen. Some went over to the agitated horse and secured it. Ruth released Matthew from her frantic embrace and gazed in horror at where Mark lay. A sudden spasm ran through his body ending in a shuddering gasp. She was incapable of any feeling at the sight of his crumpled form lying broken on the ground.

There was a small movement in the crowd of black men standing by Mark's horse. A sharp stone was being passed from hand to hand in silent accord until it ended up in the hand of Ruth. She held it warm in her hands for a moment and then let it fall to the ground at her feet. Then she looked about for her son.

Matthew was standing over the fallen body. He stared without understanding into the unblinking eyes that were so strikingly like his own. He stared into the eyes of the father he had never known, stared without comprehension as the life force slowly ebbed away.

8

A New Master For Nethergate

Anthony Styles, Mark's younger brother, truly mourned the passing of Mark. Not it must be admitted due to any brotherly affection, for there was none, but solely for the fear he now felt at the prospect of becoming the new Master of Nethergate. He had never expected such a role in life. This had been Mark's destiny, not his. Mark was the one to carry forward the family name. Mark had been tall, with imperial good looks. He was so evidently the master of his world. People may not have liked him, they may have feared him even, but they knew him for what he was and the power he held and accepted him accordingly.

Anthony had no such natural authority and was painfully aware of his own inadequacies. True, he was tall like his brother, but he was stooped as if apologising for the presumption of his own stature. His face in repose was a perpetual apology. No-one had ever expected much of him, least of all his parents. What small triumphs had come his way had been to the apparent amazement of his father and to the perhaps too obvious delight of his mother.

Mark, by contrast, had never basked in even such watery

parental approval, for so much more had been expected of him and in any event, he did not need it. He had from an early age stiffened at his mother's embraces and spurned the love she offered as an unworthy weakness. His father's approval he scorned.

Anthony, for his part, had craved the love and approval of both his parents. His mother was always there ready to satisfy this need, but his father was harder to please. When sometimes he received some grudging acknowledgement from that quarter, his delight was so obvious as to be embarrassing. Such praises though, when they came, were not lost on Mark and he tormented his brother mercilessly with the bile of his jealousy. His lips would curl in a sarcastic sneer and he would remark, "Ain't we jus' the purest little copper-bottomed boy then?" and Anthony would cringe, his shoulders would rise defensively and he would feel his bladder loosening. Privately, Mark coined the nickname 'Copper' for his brother and Anthony hated the word whenever it was uttered.

On leaving school, Anthony had trained as a lawyer and had joined Bill Forbes and Sons, Attorneys at Law. Forbes Senior was the family solicitor. They were a small firm of country lawyers in premises in the nearby township of New Haven. His father had bought him a partnership in the firm. For Anthony, it was the answer to his prayers, for he longed for just such a mundane life as this, encircled in the arms of the law, where things were either right or wrong or if challenged forcefully enough could be either half right or half wrong. Few decisions had to be taken and when they were, the Law was always there to hide behind.

Most of the plantation owners had their business with Forbes. His presence in the firm had brought with it a ripple of modest acclaim for Anthony, for people respected the Styles name. Thus, without any effort on his part, he was given the respect and deference due to one whose connections were much valued.

As the years passed, to his own surprise, he proved to be no passenger in the firm. In a quiet, unassuming way he was quite competent as a lawyer and soon gained a reputation for care and discretion. He knew he was not going to set the legal world alight, the thought would have terrified him, but the business was enough for him to make a comfortable living and to keep his wife Amelia and George, his son, in the manner to which they had grown accustomed. For the first time in his life he felt appreciated for his own worth. In short, he was happy and content and asked for nothing more than that his life should continue in this modest mould.

Now all this had been shattered by his brother's untimely death. In life and in death his brother had brought him nothing but misery.

Whilst Anthony bitterly resented the death of his brother, Amelia, his wife, could barely conceal her delight. She had sharp features and thin disapproving lips and wore a perpetual expression of one who has just encountered a rather unpleasant smell. Whereas Anthony grieved for the loss of the easy comfort and familiarity of his old, humbler way of life, Amelia hungered now for the prospect of an altogether grander style of living. She had great ambitions too for George. Now they could afford it, he would be enrolled in one of the great schools in the North where she imagined he would be trained to be a true gentleman of the South.

"Anthony dear," she announced, barely a week after Mark's accident, "we must of course wait a suitable period to acknowledge poor Mark's untimely departure." She was now too refined to use such an ugly word as, 'death'. "And then we must hold a grand opening occasion to show them all how we mean to carry on at Nethergate Hall. George must be there too."

Anthony, mute in his own secret misery, merely nodded.

There was something different, he noted, about his wife since Mark's death. Her voice had taken on an altogether more strident tone. It seemed to have gone up half an octave. She seemed to speak in pronouncements. She, who had once humbly basked in the reflected grandeur of being closely related to one of the most respected names in the State, now unbelievably was seated upon that very throne herself. She was, he feared, determined to make the most of it.

At his lowest ebb, Anthony had even toyed with the idea of selling Nethergate, but he had too much innate respect for the founding spirit of his forebears to let that thought take hold. In any event, he knew that Amelia would never have forgiven him. For Anthony, each new day was like waking on the dawn of his own execution. How he yearned for the simple certainties of his old way of life and the satisfaction of knowing when a job was well done and that he had done it.

As to the running of the great Nethergate Estate, he had little idea how this should be accomplished. It was not his role and he had been too much in awe of his father to have dared to show an interest as to how his father accomplished so mammoth a task. He quickly discovered though, that he need have had no worries on that score for Silas Killcaid was all too ready to shoulder the burden. As a child, he had always been terrified of the black-bearded, ferret-eyed figure of his father's Head Overseer. He remembered when he was very young, hiding behind his father's legs when Killcaid approached. That fear had remained as he grew older. Now it came crowding back whenever he had dealings with him, however hard he tried to remind himself of their changed relationship.

For every tentative inquiry Anthony raised, Killcaid had a positive and assertive answer. Answers moreover that were couched with such covert condescension as barely to conceal Killcaid's disappointment that the New Master had not been cast in the same mould as his predecessors.

"Leave things to me Mr Styles. Your father and brother al'us did. Been doin' the job near all my life as you well knows. Managing niggers is like second nature to the likes o' me," and he caressed his bull-hide whip as if it were a field marshal's baton. Any doubts Anthony may have had about his methods, he suppressed. He would let him handle things he told himself, until he had the measure of the undertaking himself. Then he thought he might assume a more positive direction as to how things should be run. It was the sensible thing to do after all and Anthony Styles was nothing if not a sensible man.

Only in the matter of the marketing was Killcaid a little less than confident, glossing over the conduct of such matters with an airy wave of the hand. The Masters of Nethergate had always taken care of this aspect of the affairs of the estate and Anthony knew it. Anthony however in this respect held a secret weapon.

The memory of when he had first stepped into his father's study as the new Master of Nethergate was forever with him. He felt like an interloper as he sat in his father's chair. One of the maids had come in abruptly not realising that anyone was there, and he had leapt to his feet with a guilty start as if he had been caught out. It even smelt of his father, for Mark, when he had been Master, had rarely used the room. Perhaps it reminded Mark too much of past humiliations. Somehow, though he was the same build as his father, he felt dwarfed by it all, like a toddler scuffling about in a grown-up's shoes. Everything was on too grand a scale.

It seemed wrong to look through his father's things, like voyeurism. There were mementos of his childhood and Mark's. Then in a bound leather folder he came across miniature portraits of Mark and himself. Under each were two lockets of fine child's hair each neatly labelled in his father's meticulous hand. The leather was much worn as though it had been opened many times. He felt a sudden surge of grief and longing for his father. For a moment tears sprang to his eyes, tears that he had never shed when he had been told of his father's death, for he was always too much in awe of his father to have felt any feelings of love. Now here was evidence that his father had loved them both in his own way and in quiet moments had treasured and pondered over these reminders of their childhood.

He had also discovered, in his father's desk, detailed instructions concerning the marketing of the tobacco crop addressed to Mark in his father's own neat hand and labelled, 'Instructions for the Selling'. He must have written it after one of his many disputes with Mark to ensure that at least he might have a bench mark to follow.

Such was the contempt his brother had felt for his father, that the letter had remained unopened. From it Anthony could follow much of his father's thinking and methods in the selling of the farm produce. With his lawyer training, he was readily able to understand the document and for the first time felt a thin wash of confidence in his ability to master at least some aspects of his new role.

With an air of condescension which mirrored Killcaid's own, he felt bold enough to be able tentatively to place a patronising hand upon Killcaid's shoulder and to assure him, "You may safely leave matters of the sale of our harvest to me Silas. I am aware of my father's dealings with Mr Slater, and the role he plays in the negotiation of prices. I have my own ideas too about when we might place the bulk of our produce on the market to meet the shipping and other business considerations."

He had the satisfaction of witnessing on Silas Killcaid's face an expression of bemused amazement. For the first time, he thought he detected a wary look of respect creep into his eye.

"Yes Mr Styles. You certainly seem to have such matters

under your belt." Then he added, "It is your lawyer training I suppose," which somehow implied that such a calling was an unworthy excuse for this apparent understanding. Certainly, Killcaid implied, it was far less worthy a talent in the great scheme of things, than the actual farming of tobacco and the managing of slaves.

The most severe shock for Anthony, though, was now to learn how desperate the finances of the plantation really were, after the profligate years under the direction of his elder brother. The manpower had been reduced to such a degree that they barely had enough hands to take in the harvest for that year, let alone prepare for the next. The drying sheds were sadly in need of refurbishment and the estate generally was much run down.

Harder still though was the task of explaining this to Amelia who was looking forward to a time of unlimited spending and socialising. His pleas fell on deaf ears and were dismissed with withering contempt. "Are you trying to tell me my dear," she proclaimed, "that the near largest estate and plantations in the entire State of Kentucky cannot afford a few dollars of modest expenditure to announce our accession?"

"Amelia dearest, things are in a parlous state. Mark squandered the assets here as if there were no tomorrow. We owe money, more than I can possibly say. We need to take things steady, to retrench, to harbour our assets and only then gradually to rebuild the profitability of the estate."

"Don't be so silly," she retorted. "You're talking like a lawyer again. We live in a different world now. You must remember your new position. You'll be telling me next that we cannot afford George's schooling." She was right there. He had delayed the enrolment of George but decided on the spur of the moment to select a better time to tell his wife. She, for her part, was not going to allow his excuses and lack of social ambition to stand in her way. It seemed she had forgotten that unlike her, he had been born into this world.

With no-one in whom he could confide, Anthony became increasingly dependent upon Killcaid who was not slow to take advantage of the situation. Anthony could never shake off his feeling of inferiority. He fell to picking up on comments made by Killcaid and then to repeating them back as if they were his own deliberations.

"Well done Mr Styles," Killcaid would say. "You're learnin' quick." Then Anthony would bask in the approval of his subordinate, in much the same way as he had longed for the approval of his father.

Mary Styles had watched with compassion her youngest son's early struggles to fit into his new clothes. She had been naturally distressed at the sudden death of Mark, but he had been hard to love, even as a small child. He had always struggled out of any embrace and stiffened at the first sign of affection. She had learnt to accept him as he was, but she had grown almost to fear the man he became when he was Master of Nethergate. But no mother can ever totally defy the bonds that bind her to her children.

Now she feared for her youngest son so unfitted for his new role. Any advice she tendered, though, was pushed aside and she soon realised how much such 'interference' was resented by Amelia, the new Mistress of Nethergate Hall. She was also quickly aware of the all embracing influence Killcaid began to exert over the new Master.

In one matter though, she was quietly elated. Upon Mark's death, she had quickly seized the opportunity of uncertainty to recall Ruth to her personal service and Matthew with her. Now at last she had her grandson and his mother under her own roof in Nethergate House, much to the chagrin of Killcaid, who still insisted he needed every hand he could get for field work.

Her next step was to fulfil the promise she had made to Ruth, but in this she needed the agreement of Nethergate's new Master. There was however another problem and that was what to do with Ursula, the new lady's maid she had taken on to replace Ruth.

9

Introducing Ursula

Ursula's arrival in Nethergate House had been for Mary one of the few victories she had won against Killcaid and indirectly against the wishes of Mark during the time he was Master of Nethergate. When Ruth had left Nethergate House because of Mark's threats to sell her, Mary had been forced to call back Daisy out of retirement to her duties as lady's maid, but it was not a satisfactory arrangement. Daisy was now much too old. Whenever she raised the matter of redeploying Ruth back into her personal service after Matthew was born, Mark always refused. He was not going to let Ruth return to the relative ease of his mother's household. When finally she had worn him down by promising to ask her father in New York for another tranche of money to support the estate, it had been Ruth herself who had declined to come, due to her fear of what might happen to Matthew if left alone as a field hand. Matthew had acquired the particular enmity of Killcaid, partly due to his ability to mimic and lampoon the overseer to the delight of the other slaves and partly due to a stubborn refusal to be cowed. He was the lonely slave who would meet Killcaid's stare and not look down.

For as long as there was hope of Ruth returning, Mary held back from finding a full-time replacement for her – that was until Ursula arrived on the scene.

Ursula had come into Mary's service in a quite unusual way, mainly because of Killcaid's duplicity and his appetite for a pretty face. Killcaid, and his cronies from other estates, often visited the slave market in New Haven at the quarterly slave markets. In the past, it had been to purchase new hands or to exchange those who were beginning to fade, but now, frequently fuelled with rum, it was simply to enjoy the spectacle. The slave market sale was a pageant that ran the gamut of human emotions. Like public hangings, it attracted large groups of spectators wishing to witness human emotion in the raw.

Gone perhaps were the more bizarre exhibitions of behaviour when the slaves were gaunt and fresh-shipped from the African continent and some of the women were even bare breasted. They would jabber like monkeys with their incomprehensible heathen gibberish and react like wild animals too, to the touch of the goad or stick. When shackled and manacled, they were herded onto the sales platform, most would cling together for mutual comfort. Others would stare out dumb with misery, white eyed and resigned to whatever fate awaited them. Nowadays though, with the abolition of the African trade, slave sales were altogether more civilised affairs. It was seldom necessary even to manacle the slaves.

A large sale would bring in fellow overseers from the adjoining estates and sometimes the owners themselves, though mostly these came from the smaller concerns. All those there reckoned themselves to be good judges of slave flesh and the sort of work that could be gotten from them.

There was something too about slaves en masse that brought an indefinable frisson of excitement to Killcaid and his ilk. It had something to do with the raw manifestation of power; of the immutable rightness and order of a world where black was so markedly subservient to white. It was about fear in a way too, from the huge predominance of black faces wherever one looked. Above all it was a statement that God and rightness still ruled on earth as assuredly they did in heaven too.

Slave markets would bring in traders and stalls from miles about, jugglers and singers, musicians and performers, all adding to the scrum and hubbub of humanity. The markets too had an odour that was unique. There was of course the usual smell of the slave, the urine-sweetness of their sweat, so different from the aroma of the white man and there was too the indefinable whiff of anxiety and fear. It was a heady mix.

The crowd about the raised sale platform would delight in the patter of the auctioneer. They would also shout at those up for sale. Occasionally some poor, benighted slave would join in the pantomime and ape and mime to the audience to gain a laugh, as if it might perhaps better his lot. It never did. The auctioneer would play to the crowd too and over embellish some wretch with a grandiose description of talent. That was guaranteed to get the crowd going.

"This here fine Negro. Strong as an ox," and a stooped, aged figure would shuffle forward on the selling platform and the crowd would burst out laughing.

Then the serious stuff, "Good worker. Bain't never had no cause to be beat. Willing and friendly. Got many years fine labour ahead o' him yet. Worked most of his life for Mr Fellows. Never been no trouble. Now what am I bid? What am I bid? Who'll give me nine hundred dollars?"

"I know that nigger! Frail as a daisy an' sick as a parrot. Sixty-year-old if he's a day," someone might yell.

"Always knew you couldn't count," the auctioneer might retort, "Particular when it comes to buying a drink." There would be general laughter and the sales and good-natured repartee would continue as black souls changed hands.

On this particular day though, Killcaid's eye had been

caught by the group of slaves awaiting sale rather than those already on the platform. They were huddled together under the shade of the oak in the usual place on the slave market square. All of them were squatting, clustered together in family groups, or sometimes just alone with their anxiety. All wore their best clothes and their best looks. Most wore their Sunday clothes to look their best, with faces to match. Those without such attire were clothed in white shirts belonging to the slave traders, thus to display their wares to greatest advantage. Some had little bundles of their possessions where they had managed to collect anything, but the majority had nothing. All were eager to please in the hopes of attracting a good master, the whites of their eyes portraying their apprehension.

All of them were to be cut adrift from a familiar world to be cast into uncertainty. However harsh that old world might have been, however cruel their owners, somehow it was always better than the world of the unknown. Most of all they dreaded the big dealers who were interested in numbers only. For then they would be shipped down south for work on the sugar or rice plantations where conditions were notorious, but prices were higher, and a handsome trading profit was to be made by the traders. Those thus traded were condemned to a future without hope.

What had caught Killcaid's eye on this occasion was a mother and her child. They were embracing each other, huddled together for comfort. It was the child though who held his attention. She was a girl who, regardless of the uncertainty of the circumstances in which she now found herself, was still looking about her with the bright intelligent eyes of a lively kitten. Where most eyes were downcast, hers were surveying the scene with interest, despite the uncertainty and the clear anxiety of her mother.

Killcaid felt a tightening at the pit of his stomach. He knew what he liked. Perhaps not quite as young as this one, but he could wait. His eyes travelled to the mother. She looked sturdy enough, then he spotted a small movement of her hands. He watched her carefully and how the child seemed to be more than usually solicitous to her mother's needs. When their turn came, and they moved together to stand up on the raised selling platform, his suspicions were confirmed. The mother seemed to stumble as together they mounted the steps. No-one would have noticed unless they were watching closely. No-one who wasn't so well versed in how the devious mind of a nigger worked would have understood the signs he was seeing. Now he was sure.

"A fine mulatto girl and her dam," the auctioneer began, entering his sales pitch. "Fine domestics. Well trained for duties in the home. Part of the estate of the late Ebenezer Sparrow, maker of his justly famed meat pies. T'was his particular wish that the pair be sold together. I'll take bids for the two o' them, then each separate if there be no takers for the brace. Now what am I bid? Who'll start at fifteen hundred dollars?" Several heads nodded. The bidding was brisk and soon reached eighteen fifty. Then Killcaid intervened.

"The dam's half blind!" he yelled. A hush fell over the crowd. Killcaid was watching the girl. At his announcement, her hand flew to her mouth and he knew he was right.

"What d'you mean?" shouted the auctioneer with some indignation. This was taking banter too far. Killcaid tossed a dime onto the platform.

"Tell her to pick it up and she can keep it."

All eyes were on the mulatto woman. Her daughter whispered to her. She turned and strode confidently across the platform towards where the coin had fallen. She passed where the coin sparkled in the sun. Then stooped as if to pick it up and with a sudden cry of alarm, pitched out over the edge of the dais. She picked herself up. Then clearly disorientated tried to find again the steps onto the stand. No-one moved to help her.

A gasp ran around the onlookers. It was clear that she was as near blind as made no difference.

The child ran to her mother, visibly concerned. With her daughter's help the pair once more clambered onto the sales podium. The auctioneer coughed. "We'll er…" he hesitated. "Well now don't that jes' take the cake? Reckon we better start the bidding over again," he announced. "Who'll give me a thousand for the pair."

There was no response.

"Eight hundred. Come on now. The little one'll be worth double that alone in a year or two."

Still no bids. Then with a sigh the auctioneer announced, "For a separate sale then."

At this announcement, a thin keening cry came from the mulatto woman's lips. It seemed to go on and on for an impossible length of time. Then with a gagging, gasping intake of breath she burst into an impassioned plea to the auctioneer and the gathered crowd of onlookers. "Please Massa', Oh please, please don' take ma daughter 'way fro me. She all I have. She my eyes. I can work as good as any. She all I have. She all I have," and she broke down into long sobs of distress.

The crowd savoured the drama of the moment. Some were quite moved by her anguish and a murmur of sympathy briefly rippled through the onlookers. But it didn't last.

"It's all put on," muttered one unsympathetic voice.

"They don' feel same as what we do," mumbled another and the crowd began to take a more pragmatic view, almost as if ashamed of being taken in by such a human display of emotion.

Then a thin small voice cut through the throng.

"Please don' take my Mamma 'way from me," then almost inaudibly, "Please," and the small girl clung protectively to her mother.

Once again, the crowd fell silent.

"Seven Hundred Dollars for 'em both!"

Mother and daughter shot looks of the deepest gratitude in the direction of the voice.

"Sold!" barked the auctioneer hastily unless there should be any second thoughts, "Sold to Mr Killcaid and the Nethergate Estate." Their moment in the limelight had gone and they were mustered away to join the growing crowd of slaves who had found new masters.

Both mother and daughter were housed in the slave pound overnight whilst bills of sale were drawn up and signed and to allow for the celebrations by buyer and seller alike that always followed market day.

In the early hours of the morning the pound was astir as the slave convoy moving south began to assemble for an early start to catch the river boat. Two men with lanterns came to where the mulatto woman was asleep with her child in her arms.

They shook her roughly. "You're coming with us."

Both struggled into wakefulness. Confused they rose to their feet. "Not you little'en. It's just your Mam," said one of the men.

"You're making a mistake," cried the woman, a note of hysteria creeping into her voice. "We both 'bin sol' to Nethergate."

"Only the little'en. You been sold on – goin' down south wi'us."

In the end, it took four of them to take away the woman. Not before she had been whipped and bludgeoned into a state of near insensibility and her daughter had been shackled, for she fought as fiercely as her mother.

In irons and still sobbing was how Ursula arrived at Nethergate, for given the chance she would have thrown herself under any horse or carriage that they passed on the journey. Killcaid had done a deal with the dealers going South. He had paid the handlers two hundred dollars to take the blind woman off his hands. He still reckoned he had made a profit on the sale.

Once the girl had been broken in a little, he looked forward to other delights.

But Killcaid was destined to be disappointed. Mary, when the child arrived, had been talking to Mark and was a witness to her condition. She was appalled at such a young child being held in chains and above all at the child's utter distress. Indignantly she had asked why the child was being treated in this way.

"She got the temper of a cornered rat, that little one. It's for her own safety," Killcaid had replied.

"But she's so young. What on earth do you want her for?"

"She'll work in the fields, like the rest," Killcaid had replied. He resented Mary's interference and looked to Mark to support him.

Then an idea had occurred to Mary. She turned straight to Mark

"Look at her Mark," she had argued, "She's much too young to give much in the fields. It'll coarsen her and she'll lose in value. I need a lady's maid now Ruth's gone. Let me train her up and she'll fetch a far better price when you come to sell her."

Mark considered what his mother had said. It had made sense and would finally stop her from trying to get Ruth back. He nodded his agreement.

Killcaid protested. "She's young yet, but she'll train up good. We need her on the fields, particular with harvest coming. Every hand counts."

Mark never took kindly to his orders being questioned and his eyes hardened. Killcaid was much too wary of Mark's temper to have dared to take the matter further and grudgingly had mumbled his acceptance with a poor grace.

Thus, Ursula came to Nethergate House, distressed, tearful and resentful. Mary was appalled when she later heard what Killcaid had done to her mother.

She was determined to change Ursula's tears to laughter and to bring some happiness back into her life.

10

First Meeting

When Mary learnt the full story of Ursula's earlier life and the perfidious way in which she had been treated, her sympathy knew no bounds. Ebenezer Sparrow, Ursula's previous owner, was a kindly master. He had kept on Ursula's mother when she began to show signs of going blind. Many would have sold her, before her condition became too marked and her value dropped, but in truth she managed her duties about the kitchens much as she always had. She knew where everything was kept, and Ursula was for ever at her side to be her eyes. Besides, he loved her apple pies. The old man was fond of them both. Ursula with her warm sunny smile, her young laughter and her concern for her mother and for him too, made him smile and feel comfortable as he got older. He had always promised them that they would have their freedom when he died, together with a small gift of money to help them on their way. The old man's sudden death from a stroke had devastated them both, but they could not help but feel a tremor of excitement at the prospect of freedom. They began excitedly to plan their new future.

Mr Sparrow's daughter Alice, a stranger to them both, had

arrived a short time after his death, full of a concern and regret at his passing confessing a devotion to her father she had never shown in his lifetime. She knew of her father's intention to grant them both their freedom but asked them if they would stay on until the house and its contents were sold. She managed to keep her sadness at bay by keeping busy in carrying out a very thorough inventory of the house and its contents before her sister arrived.

Dorothy, the sister, arrived the next day. Immediately there was discord such as the old house had not known for decades, whilst their father lay cold and still in the upstairs bedroom. Dorothy insisted that she inspect the inventory made out by her sister and promptly made out one of her own.

Dorothy then asked to go and pay her last respects to the corpse of her father and Ursula and her mother escorted her upstairs to where he lay in his darkened bedroom. They withdrew to the door to allow her time to be alone with her father. In doing so they nearly collided with Alice who was watching her sister through the half open door. Suddenly she let out a banshee howl. "Oh no you don't!" she screamed, rushing into the room, "I know your game. He promised those rings to my husband."

Saddened that their old Master should be the silent witness to so much discord, the two slaves quietly withdrew, leaving his two grieving daughters fighting over his dead hand with such vigour that his old bones seemed once more to become jostled into animation.

That evening though, a strange harmony seemed to have overcome the sorrowing pair, who took to conversing in whispers and stopping their conversations altogether when either of the two slaves were in the room. The next day the family lawyer arrived to be present at the opening of the cast-iron safe that Ebenezer kept in his study. The sisters had been unable to find their father's key to the safe and had to await the arrival of the lawyers. But when the lawyers tried to open the safe they were unable to move the handle. It was Ursula's mother who had to show them the trick of it, for she had to carry out a like service for old Ebenezer as he became frailer. She was excited too, for Ebenezer had often showed her the documents he had prepared for her freedom and that of her daughter, before her sight began to fail. She knew their precise location in the safe and tried to grasp them to show them to the lawyer as the door swung open. But he was too quick and pushed her out the way to grasp all the documents in the safe. He started to thumb through them, but now she could not see the envelope her master had so often shown her.

"The papers for the freedom of Ursula and me are there. It was Mr Sparrow's promise that we be free when he died. That not so?" she asked appealing to Alice who initially had seemed to be aware of her father's wishes. But Alice slowly shook her head.

"First I heard on it," she murmured, but without much conviction.

The lawyer glanced meaningfully at the two sisters and then made a pretence of again thumbing through the documents and shook his head.

"But he showed it me. He showed it me. He say this here's you and Ursula's freedom when I pass on."

"Nuttin' here," said the lawyer, splaying out the documents for the slave to see, but of course she could neither see nor could she read. "That not so?" he asked the two sisters. They both nodded their heads without bothering to look. Thus, Ursula and her mother were cheated of their freedom and the chain of events began that had led to their tragic separation.

The uncertainty of her future and her anxiety for the welfare of her mother had at first overshadowed Ursula's start at Nethergate House. But Mary's motherly instincts, never far below the surface, came to the fore. Assisted by Morella, between them they did their very best to comfort the child. A child's grief at the loss of her mother is perhaps the hardest of all crosses to bear. There are no words or deeds that can heal such a devastation. Bit by bit though, Mary and Morella began patiently to win Ursula's trust

For Mary's part, she had always keenly felt the loss of Ruth in her household and the presence of Ursula partly filled a void in her life. To offer some hope to the grieving child, she promised Ursula to try and find out where her mother had gone and to see what she could do to bring her back, but Mary had little real hope. She spoke to Anthony who at that time was anxious to prove his ability as a lawyer and he brought to bear all influence he could muster.

Of Ursula's mother, there was no trace. The sale to Nethergate was recorded and that was the last paper record. Killcaid's sale had been by word of mouth. It was not unusual. He had authority to answer for the estate in such matters and had simply exchanged Ursula's mother under a perfectly legal verbal contract. When questioned he just shrugged his shoulders. She would have been no use on Nethergate, whereas he had got her daughter for a good price. He couldn't remember the name of the trader. By now she would be in the deep South. She could be anywhere. Like so many others before her, she had simply vanished.

As the months passed however, Ursula's natural resilience began to reassert itself under the guidance of Mary and Morella. Ursula was still a bit shy of Mary, but she warmed to the great bulk of Morella's presence, her chuckling throaty laugh and her endless good humour. She began to smile and sometimes to laugh too.

As with all her house slaves Mary was anxious that they should all learn how to read and write. Strangely this proved to be more beneficial than anything else. The mysteries of the written word, to Ursula the magical domain of the white man alone, were slowly unravelled for her. In her own mind, she was determined that she would never be cheated as she was convinced her mother had been cheated, in part because she could not read. It proved to be an addictive new challenge and Ursula applied herself with diligence and determination. She was a bright child with a natural curiosity and intelligence and learnt quickly. She delighted too in the pleasure her new knowledge seemed to give her mistress.

She was adept too at learning her new duties as lady's maid and Mary became more and more delighted at the consequences of her fortuitous intervention. Gradually Ursula relaxed in the presence of Mary and began to respond to her natural warmth of character. She took great pride in arranging Mary's hair when Mary explained how she liked it and in laying out the clothes she was to wear. She was particularly excited when there was entertaining to be done and Mary's hair was done in a special way and grand clothing had to be set out and her mistress laced in. She learnt too about the various potions and unguents that white ladies applied and their various uses. Soon she was almost as good as Ruth had been, but of course she lacked Ruth's maturity and Mary could never quite confide in her in the way that came to her so naturally with Ruth, sharing as they did the secret of Matthew's conception.

Bit by bit Ursula's true character was restored. She had a natural zest for living and revelled in the unexpected turn her life had taken, though as always in moments of quiet her thoughts would turn with sadness to her mother. Her delight in all the new things was infectious and she was always bubbling over with laughter. She would skip and clap her hands in unrestrained delight at each new discovery. Though at times, not appropriate behaviour for a slave, Mary tolerated it for the inner warmth it gave her that she could bring so much delight into a life seemingly so blighted.

"Oh, Lordy Miss! Ain't that jus' princey?" she would exclaim with delight and her face would light up with a beaming grin. Then she would chuckle with a merriment that brought happiness to everyone near her. Mary had no idea where she had picked up that expression, but it always made her smile. In the evenings, Mary would get Ursula to read to her which she did with ever increasing confidence. She even allowed her to read to her some of her more mundane correspondence. She was a very apt pupil.

Despite her natural sorrow at the unexpected death of Mark, she had been quick to grasp the opportunity to get both Ruth and her grandson Matthew back under her own roof before Anthony began to take over the reins of the estate. She had expected Killcaid to resist when she had made the necessary arrangements, but he had raised little objection, but then he remarked, "You'll not be needing Ursula then?" and she knew the way his mind was turning.

"She's yet to complete her training," she responded, but she knew it would only be a matter of time before she would have to surrender her.

Ursula by then had grown into a very pleasing and presentable member of any household and would fetch a good price. But she knew that was not what Killcaid had in mind.

"The new Master of Nethergate must decide that one," she had replied evasively when Killcaid pressed her further, but clearly Killcaid was looking to getting Ursula back under his control. When she learnt that Amelia, the new Mistress of Nethergate, had no personal maid, the solution seemed heaven-sent.

She explained the situation to Ursula. "Would you like to move to the big house?" she had asked. At the news Ursula's face had fallen, but then the thought of serving at Nethergate Hall, where so much more seemed to be happening, began to appeal to her sense of adventure. In truth, things had been difficult when Ruth had returned to Mary's household, for Mary had two maids and they were forever tripping over each other in their efforts to serve their mistress. It was clear too that Ruth had her mistress's ear in a way that she could not rival.

All the slaves from Nethergate Hall adopted an assumption of superiority over the others employed in lesser establishments about the estate. In a way, it was a promotion. Besides, there was a boot boy who worked there whom she had met when he was sent on an errand to the Hall.

"Will I be able to come and see you and Morella?" she had asked.

"Of course you will," Mary had assured her, "It will be a good deal more lively at the Hall than here, but I shall miss you and you must come and see us as often as you can."

"I will Ma'am. I surely will."

That afternoon she was taken up with Mary to meet Amelia. It was an awkward meeting. Amelia had always been respectful to Mary as the past Lady of Nethergate and her mother-in-law, but now she felt that she had a new status to live up to.

When Mary proffered Ursula as her future lady's maid she looked her up and down with apparent distaste. What she saw was a girl bright looking, neat and clean, eyes downcast with respect. She could find nothing to criticise. Such was her nature, though, that she could not but think that somehow in accepting this offer she would be giving in to her mother-in-law's wishes and perhaps admitting an infiltrator into the midst of her own household.

"She's very young for such a position," she pronounced at last. "I had thought of going to Martins," she added, naming a well-known purveyor of specialist slaves in New Haven, 'for a properly trained lady's maid." The sting in the tail was not lost on Mary and she inwardly stiffened. She had never much cared for Anthony's choice of a spouse.

"I have had *some* experience with personal servants," she replied in measured tones, knowing that Amelia had not and biting back a sharper retort that had sprung to her lips. The two women faced each other with unspoken hostility. Amelia was very conscious of the fact that Mary had been the first mistress of Nethergate Hall and she could not get it out of her mind that she was being judged by the older woman.

Just then the door burst open and Amelia's son rushed in. "Grandmamma!" he cried with delight and ran to embrace his grandmother. "I was told you were here. Now we have moved in you must come and see us every day."

"I don't know about that dear," replied Mary, eyeing her daughter-in-law. "But you may come to see me as often as you like."

George's glance, for the first time, fell upon Ursula. "Who's this?" he asked. Mary explained that she did not need two lady's maids, now that Ruth had returned and added that his mother would probably be seeking a maid from Martins. George looked at Ursula and liked what he saw. "Oh, come on Mamma. You were only saying this morning how much you needed help upstairs. Please say 'yes', then I can show Grandmamma my new rooms."

Amelia had not wished for such open hostility between herself and Mary but felt she had made her point as to whose voice now carried most weight. She was glad now to have an excuse to relent. "Oh, very well Dear."

"Ah sure won't let you down Missus. Ah'sl work real hard and I's real well trained under Mrs Styles, here," said the object of all their deliberations. There was a silence and all eyes turned on Ursula. No-one had expected her to have an opinion and no-one knew quite what to say.

It was Mary who spoke first. "I expect Mrs Styles will want

you to go down to the slave quarters where they will show you where you are to sleep. That is unless Mrs Styles wants you to sleep in the annex to the master bedroom."

Amelia reacted immediately to the latter thought. "No. You must go down with the others to the quarters," she said.

"Thank you, Missus," said Ursula demurely and gave a little bob.

"Come Grandmamma," said George, "come and see my rooms."

As they left George glanced behind him. At that moment, Ursula glanced up as she too was about to leave. For a moment, their eyes met, and Ursula forgot about her boot boy.

11

The New Mistress Of Nethergate Hall

Not everyone owned slaves in the South. Anthony had inherited some of his mother's attitudes to slavery and had always employed servants in his modest household in New Haven, rather than slaves. Thus, Amelia had never owned slaves before she came to Nethergate Hall and was unsure quite how to treat them. She had always secretly envied the assured way others seemed to deal with slave ownership and sought in her own mind to emulate their casual poise. To have become the Mistress of Nethergate was a 'dream come true', but the reality was not quite as she had imagined. There were problems to deal with, directions to give, decisions to be made and she was never quite sure whom she could trust and who was trying to pull the wool over her eyes.

Samuel ran the household. He was a mature negro with a crisp, grizzled cap of curly hair, a deep voice, a natural dignity about him that declared that there was nothing in life that could ruffle his equanimity. He had seen four Masters of Nethergate come and go and kept his counsel and judgement on them all.

Samuel seemed to be a rock upon which she could build her

trust, but somehow in the vast knowledge he seemed to have in the running of the house their roles were subtly reversed. She began to feel subordinate to his calm logic, doing things at his behest, agreeing always with the devastating force of his experience. She longed just for once to prove him wrong and to take control herself.

Things were now very different in the house from when Mark had been there. The house slaves had learnt to fear Mark and his uncertain mood swings. But despite the rigid rule that Samuel enforced, the house slaves were quick to exploit the uncertainty they sensed in their new owners. In a thousand different ways, they tried to make their life just that bit easier.

"Massa' Mark al'us did it this way," or even, "When Massa' Adrian was here we al'us did it that way." Anthony, she felt, was no help. Despite his own memories of his childhood at Nethergate House, he was inclined never to challenge such utterances. Amelia though was made of sterner stuff and began to sense the way things were going. A resolution began to form and harden within her. She was not going to become the fiddle upon which her slaves played tunes of their own choosing.

Though there was nothing Amelia could point to, nothing she could define, she was aware that bit by bit she was losing the battle for mastery of her own household. For her it was war, not just a gentle game to be pursued with a wry sense of humour where every little advantage was a pyrrhic victory to be savoured and shared, as it was for the slaves. They had nothing to lose and a lifetime to perfect and hone their skills. For her it was a grim contest where every skirmish had to be won and the enemy defeated at every turn. Nothing could pass without criticism, no contact made without a rebuke or a sour look. Above all she yearned to bring Samuel down from his lofty throne, to humiliate him and to bring him to heel.

Her chance came when an old house-slave called secretly at the slave's quarters in the dead of night. He had been sold by Mark when he needed more money to settle a debt. Now he had escaped from the even greater tyranny of his new master and was trying to reach Canada where he would be free. When he arrived at Nethergate Hall he was sick and at the end of his tether. There was no way he could continue in his present condition. Samuel had sheltered him in the slave's quarters until he was well enough to be on his way.

But in any community under stress there is always someone who will act for their own advantage. One of the women slaves, seeking advantage, had told Amelia what Samuel had done. This was her chance. She called for Samuel.

He stood before her with his usual calm dignity.

"What's this I hear Samuel, 'bout you sheltering an escaped slave, a fugitive, here in my house?" she intoned with outraged indignation.

He seemed to have expected her question and registered no surprise.

"It is true Missus. I don't deny it," he said. Imperceptibly his chin rose as if bracing himself to face down the storm that was about to break about him. "I is truly sorry," he added.

"Sorry!" she exploded. "Sorry! Is that all you can say? Harbouring a criminal from justice under my roof and you're sorry!"

"He was sick Missus. He used to work for Master Mark and Master Adrian before him. I could not turn him away."

She couldn't believe what she was hearing. "You could not turn a felon away from my house. What right have you to say who lives under my roof? Whose authority rules in this household, yours or mine?" There at last was the nub of the matter.

Samuel stood before her his head held high. She was not reaching him and her anger mounted. This was the chance she had been waiting for and she felt it slipping away from her. Samuel said nothing. Then with great dignity in deep, measured, sepulchral tones he said, "For everyone that asketh, receiveth; and he that seeketh, findeth and to him that knocks it shall be opened."

This was what came of allowing slaves to have their own places of worship and their own pastors. They didn't understand what they were hearing. She was beside herself with rage.

"Don't you dare quote the Bible at me," she raged. "I know just how to deal with those who choose to ignore the law. You will ask Mr Styles to come to the house right away. Now you may go."

"Yes Missus. As you wish." With his dignity unruffled, he bowed and left.

He won't feel that way for long, she reflected as she waited for her husband to come. In New Haven, there were public whipping posts. Here offenders, usually from those employing only a small numbers of slaves, could be brought to be suitably punished. It was the public nature of such an event which appealed to Amelia in her vendetta with Samuel. She intended that he should be taken there and publiclt scourged. She could have given the task to Killcaid, but this way, she reasoned, everyone would know of her resolution and Samuel would be properly humiliated.

When Anthony arrived, he was appalled at her proposal. He had known Samuel all his life. The man was like an uncle to him and had cared for him throughout his childhood. He had ridden on his back and played hide and seek with him. He was like one of the family. Besides he was known and respected among the neighbourhood, most of whom had known him all their lives. He was like an institution. For once he dared to defy his wife.

"Amelia my dear, surely there is a less public way in which we can deal with this matter…" But he got no further.

Amelia now had her temper truly roused. "If you do not see to this Anthony," she fumed, "then I will report the matter to the Militia. Harbouring an escaped slave is a criminal offence and I will not be a party to it in my house. He will get a good deal more than a public flogging then."

What she said was true and Anthony knew she would carry out her threat. Two days later Samuel was taken to New Haven. A quietness fell over all the slaves working at Nethergate Hall as Samuel was led to the tumbrels that did the rounds of the settlements and took the slaves to New Haven for punishment. His tumbrel was crowded with mostly younger slaves. At first there was some joking and banter from the other miscreants at Samuel's age and fall from grace, as he was led to the cart and shackled to the side. But Samuel's silent dignity suppressed all mockery as they lurched and rocked away.

The return journey was a complete contrast. Only Samuel was standing like a sentinel rock with the same rigid composure he had displayed on his departure. The rest were bloodied and cowed in the depths of the cart, nursing their misery. There was no need for shackles now. The cart stopped and Samuel stiffly alighted. The back of his shirt was stained and crisp with blood showing the pattern of his wounds. Morella was there, and she hastened to him and bore him off to administer her balm.

Amelia was informed of his return. Now she reflected, she had created the sort of respect she craved. To her surprise, he was on duty at the dinner table as usual orchestrating the occasion with his usual calm efficiency. Only a little stiffness in his posture and a certain pastiness of complexion hinted at his ordeal. He responded to all of them, including Amelia herself, with the same respectful deference he always displayed. It was as if nothing had happened.

Amelia began to wonder if she had won after all. But a change had taken place that was to have far reaching effects on the future for them all. On the surface, Samuel remained as ever the urbane and dignified servant, but now from being a passive supporter of all who sought their freedom he had resolved to play an altogether more active part.

It was into this situation that Ursula arrived as the new lady's maid to Amelia Styles, Mistress of Nethergate Hall.

12

Uneasy Lies The Head

Ursula had few things to bring with her from Nethergate House. Her most treasured possession was a tiny brooch her mother had given her which she always kept in a secret place about her, where she could feel it whenever she felt the need. There were some bright stones she had picked up which had a special significance for her alone, a ring that Mary had given her which she never dared to wear, some personal items and two dresses for Sunday church and special occasions.

She gazed about the small room where she had slept at Nethergate House with the other female slaves and thought of her mother as she always did when something significant was happening in her life. She was sad to leave Morella, Mary, and Nethergate House and the friends she had made there, but excited at the prospect of being a part of the infinitely more prestigious Nethergate Hall, despite some of the stories she had heard about her new mistress. She would serve her with all the devotion she had shown to Mary. That way she would earn her trust, and nothing would go wrong.

She said goodbye to Mary and then sought out Morella who enfolded her in her ample bosom. "Now you take good care o' yourself." Then she added, "and you take great care of your new mistress," but it sounded to Ursula's ears more like a warning than advice and she drew back to look into Morella's face. But it seemed as if Morella herself had not understood why she had said it in that way.

She wrapped up all her possessions in a canvas bag Morella had given her and set off for her new life at Nethergate Hall. She liked the clothes she was given to wear in her new job and admired her reflection in the pond by the kitchen pump.

Samuel himself greeted her and arranged for her to be directed to the room where the female slaves slept. She was shown to the truckle bed which was to be hers. She stowed her bag under the bed and prepared to go to serve her new mistress.

As she was about to leave she found Samuel waiting for her. He called her over. For a moment, he was silent, scrutinising her. Then seeming to make up his mind, he said, "Ursula, have a great care how you serve your new Mistress. She's not like the old Mistress of Nethergate whom we all loved."

He would say no more. She had heard of what had happened to Samuel, but she renewed her determination to give her new mistress no reason to complain of how she served her. She could not imagine why her new mistress had decided to treat Samuel in the way she had, but the slaves often wondered at the decisions taken by their white owners. Sometimes they seemed to make no sense at all. She noticed that he still winced if he moved suddenly and wondered at what it must have been like to have one's pain and anguish witnessed by so many onlookers.

The rest of the household staff seemed strangely reluctant to talk to her as if in some way, she was tainted, or that they did not fully trust her. There was none of the easy banter and laughter she had known at Nethergate House, but then she did not know them as she had known those working for Mrs Styles the elder.

It was early evening when she made her way upstairs

and knocked nervously on Amelia's door. A voice, rather too loud bade her come in. Amelia was not used to having slaves in the more private rooms of her home and reacted with her usual assertiveness. Under all the bluster, Ursula thought she detected a certain wariness.

To her surprise, Ursula found that she knew far more about her new duties than did her new mistress who evidently was not quite sure what a lady's maid actually did. In a way, this gave her an advantage, but she was much too cautious to let this show. She laid out the clothes that Amelia indicated as she had done for Mary and Amelia seemed pleased. She offered to brush her hair as she had always done for Mary.

"That what you did for Mrs Styles?" asked Amelia.

"Sure is Ma'am," replied Ursula and began gently to brush her new mistress's hair. At her first touch Amelia stiffened imperceptibly, as one might react to an insect crawling upon one's skin. Despite her gentle brushing, she never once relaxed to enjoy the rhythmic, sweeping motion, as Mary always did. She set Amelia's hair at her direction and Amelia seemed pleased enough with the result, but only then when personal contact had ceased, did she seem at ease.

She found the various components for make-up and made them up at Amelia's direction, but Amelia applied them herself. She then asked when Amelia would like the bed prepared and when she would like help with undressing for the night.

"No!" Amelia had snapped back. Then as if surprised at her own reaction, she had added more softly, "No, thank you Ursula, that will be all."

Ursula had left then. She was puzzled by the reaction and the tension she had felt whenever she touched her, but when all her duties were done, she was pleased by how her first day had gone. She retired to her own bed with a heart buoyed up with hope for the morrow and the days yet to come, convinced that the stories she had heard about Amelia were greatly exaggerated. Amelia, she felt, was just very reserved.

The next morning, she roused Amelia. Whilst she was helping her to dress, there was a gentle knock at the door and Anthony entered.

"Good morning Massa'," she said bobbing respectfully. He seemed surprised to see her and nodded in her direction. Thereafter it was as if she did not exist. But Ursula was used to this. White folk often spoke amongst themselves as if their slaves were simply pieces of furniture, sometimes uttering personal asides for their ears only, when but a few inches away would be the impassive face of a slave. From the manner Anthony spoke to his wife, it was quite clear as to who was the more dominant of the two. It was also apparent as to how uneasy both were in their new roles.

Ursula was quick to pick up the undercurrents of tension within the household. She determined to try to remain aloof from all factions. Amelia however had other plans. It was part of the reason that she had allowed herself to be persuaded to accept Ursula. She saw in Ursula a potential weapon to be used to defeat the foe as a spy within the ranks of the enemy.

In those moments of intimacy when Ursula was alone with her and working at her directions she began to quiz her about how things were in the slave quarters. At first Ursula replied with honesty, for she thought Amelia was genuinely interested in what a slave's life was like, but then she detected a different resonance to her questions. She began to realise what Amelia was trying to do. She noted too that her probing always somehow turned to Samuel and his loyalty.

Gradually she became more cautious and circumspect in her replies, pleading the ignorance of one newly joined. Amelia for her part did not fail to notice the change and began to treat Ursula with growing hostility. If she was not going to be with her, then she was yet another of those against her like the rest and needed to be treated accordingly and brought into line. Over the weeks, to Ursula's distress, she became increasingly critical of her work.

"You stupid girl!" she would say, "What on earth made you think of putting that necklace with that dress? You should have learnt by now that I would never choose those two together." Ursula would know that the last time she had worn it she had selected that necklace to go with it, for she kept a written record of all such parings, using the writing skills she had acquired under Mary's careful tutelage.

The first time she had mildly disagreed thinking Mrs Styles had forgotten. "I really do recall Missus you wearing that dress with that necklace. You say the two greens complement each other."

Amelia's face had flushed red. She spun round and slapped Ursula's face so hard as to bring tears to her eyes. "How dare you contradict me!" she screamed, her face twisted with rage. Ursula's hand flew to her cheek, shocked by the sudden violence. She could feel the ridges made by the blow. Old Ebenezer had never struck her, or her mother, and Mary would never have thought of such a thing. She had heard of others treating their slaves in such a way, but this was the first time it had happened to her. She was stung more by the humiliation than by the smart of the blow.

"I – I is so sorry Missus. I did not mean to be rude," she stammered.

"You can lay out the blue dress," continued Amelia, her voice suddenly calm, as if nothing had happened, "then you may continue with my hair. I want it to be perfect for this evening." How could she be so enraged one moment and then act as if nothing had happened the next? It was almost as if she was two different people.

Ursula was at a loss to understand these sudden mood changes, or as to why her mistress reacted so violently. When she went downstairs though the rest of the household were quick to notice the livid marks and ridges upon her cheek and for the first time reacted with sympathy. Now that they felt she was one of them they opened with an out pouring of tales of the tyranny under which they all lived. For the first time, she realised why conversations had sometimes ceased as she walked into a room. For the first time, too, she felt the tug of the brotherhood of those who share in bondage.

Still though, Ursula tried to remain loyal to her mistress as best she could and hoped that the sudden outburst was but an isolated incident. However, the next day an event took place that was to have a profound influence on her future. She had been putting the final touches to Amelia's hair, when she suddenly announced, "Ursula, I have been thinking. Do you have any other name other than Ursula?"

"No Miss jus' Ursula and Styles now of course." It was a strange question for her mistress must surely know that all slaves assumed the surname of those for whom they worked, like in a marriage.

"I have an aunt called Ursula. You must change your name. It is not fitting that you should share the same name as my aunt."

A pit suddenly seemed to open in Ursula's world. "You mean change my name from Ursula?"

"Of course I do, you stupid child," snapped Amelia. She had no idea of the terror which was now gripping Ursula's mind.

Her name was who she was. If her name was changed her mother would never be able to find her. Her mother had given her that name. It was her name given before God. It was the only thing she had that was truly her own. It was as if her mistress were taking away her soul, for surely God would not know her by any other name than the one given before Him.

"But… but Missus, it is my name," she protested. "It's what my mammy chose for me. I cannot change my name."

"Nonsense child! Of course you can, if I say so. I shall call you Angela – Little Angel. There, is that not a good enough name for you?"

Ursula was appalled. She didn't really understand why this shocked her so. But it was as if her whole identity was being snatched from her. If she wasn't Ursula, who was she? It was as if she was denying her own mother, denying God himself. She would become a lost soul, abandoned and crying in the wilderness. The thought appalled her.

"No Missus. No. You can't do that. I is Ursula. Ursula is my name." It was the worst thing she could have done. With a cry of rage Amelia leapt to her feet scattering brushes and combs.

"You will answer to whatever name I choose to give you. Damn you for your impertinence!" she muttered through clenched teeth. Once again, unprepared for the blow, Ursula felt the stinging impact of her mistress's hand on her cheek. With a strangled cry of distress, she turned and ran from the room.

"Come back here this instant!" cried Amelia, her voice rising in indignation at this sudden show of independence. "Angela! Come here!" But by that time Ursula had left the room. It was the first time she had ever disobeyed an order. But in her present distress she was heedless of the consequences.

Sobbing with misery she rushed down the corridor, determined that somehow, she would keep her name. Rounding a corner, she cannoned into the arms of George.

13

Breaking Free

Ruth had settled back to her duties at Nethergate House as if she had never been away. She loved her Mistress for her gentleness and compassion. In her turn Mary loved Ruth as the daughter she had never had. But now Mary's affection was coloured by the guilty knowledge of what her son had done to Ruth. But Ruth's feelings for her mistress were subtly altered too by the guilt she bore for, however unintentionally, being the cause of Mark's death. She doubted that even Mary could find it in her Christian soul to forgive such a sin as that.

On his arrival at Nethergate House, Matthew was at first overawed by the grandeur of his new home. Ruth had her room adjacent to those of her mistress and Matthew was allotted a small room further down the corridor. As Mrs Styles' personal slaves, they lived apart from the slaves' quarters. He was taken about the airy-huge and echoing rooms of Nethergate House by his grandmother, who longed to acknowledge their relationship, but never quite dared. So many of his gestures and mannerisms tugged poignantly at her heartstrings as reminiscent of Mark; Mark as a small boy, before he became so self-willed. Where she wondered had she and Adrian gone so wrong. But with Matthew perhaps there would be another chance, if only she could find a way. He held a very special place in her heart and she could not help but treat him as a very favoured member of her household.

Nominally, for convention's sake and to appease Killcaid, Matthew was employed as houseboy to carry out general duties about Nethergate House as specified by his mistress. At first, he was treated with some suspicion by the other slaves for the clear favouritism shown to him by Mary. But their affection for both Mary and Ruth and Matthew's own sunny disposition soon dissipated these reservations. Such was Matthew's insatiable curiosity and energy though, that he seemed at first to be everywhere at once, sometime carpenter, sometime shoe-smith, plumber, stable-hand and gardener. Because of the nebulous nature of his own duties as houseboy, he could be helpmate to all who served the house. Anything that lightened a slave's lot was to be welcomed and Matthew became ever more popular for the delight he seemed to derive from sharing in the work of others. His vigour knew no bounds and with the passing of time he became ever more integrated into the smooth running of the household and thus unwittingly even further beyond the grasp of Killcaid. And too he had another priceless asset. By his mimicry and his sense of humour he could make people laugh, and laughter was a God-given anodyne to ease the slaves unenviable lot. They all loved to laugh.

Leisure time did not feature much in a slave's daily round, except perhaps on Sundays if the needs of the tobacco fields allowed. But it did feature in Matthew's. His mother had taught him how to read and write and now, in Mary's household where all her staff were encouraged in these skills, Matthew received particular attention. Mary gave him free run of the extensive library that Adrian, and his family, had built up and directed and encouraged his reading. Matthew found it a fascinating place as his vocabulary and knowledge increased. It gave him a glimpse of a life beyond the narrow horizons of slavery and the confines of the Nethergate Estate, to a strange new world that seemed to exist beyond its borders, populated by strange people and unimaginable things that formed weird shapes in his mind.

He also roamed the estate at will lending a hand when he saw the need but avoiding as much as he could the watchful eyes of Killcaid and his overseers. Often, he would simply gaze from a distance at the rows of bent backs humped in toil, tending the tobacco crops, with the overseers the only ones standing erect. It was a world that had been his own, a world he had been born into. Sometimes they would sing sad, rhythmic songs, rich with harmonies and the sound would float across the fields and fill him with strange longings.

As he grew older though, he found himself spending more of his time away from the house, in the swamp about the bayou. He loved it for its wildness and for its brooding secrets. In the middle of the swamps he discovered areas of dry, fertile land where wild life abounded. They had remained hidden because the only way to reach them was through the swamps themselves and no-one was interested in doing that.

Matthew painstakingly made his own secret routes through the swamp lands utilising islands of firmer vegetation and fallen trees to create his own private pathways taking his clues from where the animals went. He indulged himself in the notion that this was his land. Sometimes he would strut about with his chest thrown out as if he owned it, an impossibility for a slave. Even then a vague idea was beginning to take shape in his mind which became more defined when he discovered that after all he was not the only one who roamed about these secret places.

He had been stealthily following the delicately pointed trail left by deer when something different caught his eye. He stopped and examined the trees about him. One of them was bent over under tension. Cautiously he approached it and saw that it had been tethered to the ground and held down by ropes. Following the lines of the ropes he saw that it was a trap that would hoist an unfortunate creature off the ground and suspend it helpless in the air. He was struck by the cunning of it and was stepping closer to examine its working when a voice rung out, "Jes' you leave that alone boy or 'twill be the worst for thee."

He spun round to be confronted by the unmistakeable figure of Old Mo. Old Mohair, known by all as Old Mo, had been the slave of a trapper and a backwoodsman, who had been killed by the Indians. Both he and Old Mo had been scalped, by Mohawk Indians, but Old Mo had survived. The slave children used to chant, "Old No-hair, Old No-hair," until reprimanded by their parents or chased off by Old Mo himself. Somehow, 'No-hair' and 'Mohawk' had come combined until he was simply known by all as, Old Mo. He had been purchased by Killcaid because of his skill as a trapper and procurer of wild meat.

Killcaid had done the buying and was too drunk at the time to fully examine his purchase. When he saw the suppurating sore that was Old Mo's head, he thrashed him for keeping his hat on his head and for not letting on.

However, Old Mo turned out to be another of Morella's success stories. She had ensured that the infection that had prevented a complete healing was kept at bay. Now, although his head was scarred and pitted the flesh had grown across it and the wound had healed as much as such a wound could. He still always wore a hat for the sun was painful to him. He had however proved a great success at trapping and providing meat for the slaves and for the overseers too. He had in fact turned out to be one of the more inspired of Killcaid's purchases.

Now confronted by Old Mo who looked none too pleased, Matthew could not contain his admiration. "That's the darndest, cleverest thing I ever did see. Did you do it?"

It was the best thing Matthew could have said. Before long Old Mo was in full spate telling the avid young listener all about his traps and how he set them out. To have a listener and particularly someone who clearly admired his skills was a totally new experience for Old Mo and a very pleasant one at that. When he had finished, Matthew burst out, "You must show me how you do it all Old Mo, for I've jes' got to learn."

Old Mo was a wily old fox. He had lived wild with his previous owner and had a taste for solitude, but he knew that he was getting old and that sooner or later he would be unable to provide as much for the pot as once he did. He knew that once his usefulness declined Killcaid would get rid of him and that as an old slave, nothing but a downhill spiral awaited him into a squalor, such that death would come as a welcome friend.

Old Mo however had no intention of following that route. He had laid plans whereby he would remain the master of his own destiny. The only question was when to take the decisive step from which there could be no turning back. Now with his unexpected meeting with Matthew, he saw the possibility of delaying that decision just a little bit longer. It would give him more time to perfect his plans. It all depended on how useful this other pair of hands would be. He soon found in Matthew a very able apprentice indeed. Thus began a partnership that proved greatly beneficial to them both.

Matthew, for his part, was fascinated by Old Mo and by his tales of life outside of Nethergate. He told of his experiences among the Indians too, the people who had left such a scar upon him. He was extraordinarily generous in his judgement considering the wound that he bore. "They's goodly folk once you gets to know 'em. Do you know that there is not a word in their language for lying or deceit? They have their own rules. It's only when us breaks dem rules they acts ornery. Trouble is not all de white folks know what dem rules is. Dem Indians they jus' lumps us all together. Dat's how I come to lose my ol' grey locks, only in dem days they wasn't as grey as my beard is now. Lucky thing dey don't want that hey!" he added with a throaty chuckle, stroking his stubbly grey chin.

In quiet moments, when they were together, heads bent and hands busy in the intricate business of preparing nets or traps, his mind would wander back to memories of his youth and childhood. He told Matthew of earlier days in a distant land beyond the seas; the wild life in Africa, the great open plains, the night time grunting of the lions, the wild, manic laughter of the hyena and the great majesty of the elephants with their deep base rumbling that carried for miles and of other game in profusion. He told too of the tribal meetings, the rhythm of dancing to the beat of drums and the raids against other tribes. It was all a misty, mystical past, somehow not of this world at all, but within it Matthew felt the yearning every slave feels for a different place, a country where men can move where the fancy takes them, where they can do and say what they wish and where no man belongs body and soul to another. It made no difference that there never had been such a place, for in the slave's mind it was a reality or maybe for some just an imagining of where every slave would go when a merciful God chose to take him.

Old Mo knew who Matthew was, though he had little to do with the other slaves, for he kept himself to himself. He preferred it that way. Little by little he began to take Matthew into his confidence about his own plans, but not to the extent of sharing his ultimate secret. He schooled him in his skills; how to lay traps, how to hunt with a spear and how to catch fish with net, line and harpoon. He was impressed with how Matthew moved about the swamps and how well he knew the parts that, so far, he had explored. Matthew was quick to learn, so much so that the meat for the cabins and the overseers began to experience something of a glut.

Old Mo also showed him what fruits and wild vegetables

were good to eat. Together they would gather them to enhance the meals of the slaves and of Killcaid and his other overseers. In the big house, the slaves had long ago acquired the art of feeding themselves well from what was purchased for their white masters, but these additional gifts were especially welcome among the cabins.

With Matthew's help, Old Mo's reputation began to achieve something of a renaissance. Both agreed to keep quiet about Matthew's role in the new prosperity. When there was too much meat for Old Mo to carry back to the cabins he instructed Matthew to take it to the kennels where the Racoon Hounds were kept.

"Best give dem dogs a treat," he would say whenever their booty was too plentiful. "That way there's baint nothin' left for any to see." So, on his journeys home Matthew would often stop by the pack of Racoon Hounds when the huntsman was away and feed them the spare carcasses. He liked the dogs and enjoyed the hungry appeal in their eyes and their clamour when they sensed his approach. Sometimes he would move in among them and enjoy their closeness, their wet friendly noses and the urgent pressure of their bodies. Often, he would get them to sit before he threw in the meat as he had seen the huntsman do. It satisfied a hunger within the heart of every slave, the need to command and to be obeyed.

But in the closed life of a plantation secrets could not remain hidden for long, such deception as Old Mo and he had spun could not be expected to last forever.

14

A Taste Of Freedom

Back in Nethergate House, Mary Styles was content for a while with the small victory of prizing Ruth and Matthew away from labour in the fields and the harsh law of Killcaid. Selfishly, she indulged in the joy of having Ruth close to her and above all in watching over Matthew as he matured. So many of his mannerisms and expressions brought Mark to mind and did much to assuage the anguish she felt at his sudden death.

She had planned to wait until the plantation became profitable once more before trying again to fulfil the promise of freedom she had made to Ruth all those years ago. But that prosperity was slow in coming for the estate was now burdened by the lavish entertainments and indulgences of Amelia Styles. She decided eventually that the recompense for the evil done to Ruth by Mark could wait no longer. In addition, things were getting difficult with their Northern shippers in the wholesale tobacco market. There was much anti-slavery propaganda about. The tobacco industry was closely linked to slavery in people's minds in the North. Some warehouses had been attacked and burnt out. None of their produce was affected, but the insurance and transport costs had risen with the perceived additional risks. All this had cut into the estate's profitability.

Nevertheless, now that some five years had passed since Anthony took over as Master, Mary judged that the time was ripe to ask once more for the freedom of Ruth and that of her own grandson. She had noted with alarm how Anthony seemed increasingly to depend upon Killcaid for almost every decision and judged that the sooner she broached the subject the better, lest Anthony fall completely under the influence of his overseer.

When she had chosen her moment, Anthony's response had been all she had feared.

"Dearest Mamma, things are not as they were when dear Father was alive. Mark left the estate with so many debts. Our family in the North have, I know, been more than generous with the loans they have given, but I must soon repay them, or the estate will become theirs by default."

"But Anthony we still hold well over a hundred slaves," she had argued, "surely the release of just two from bondage would not make any real difference?"

"You must understand Mamma; how different things are now. With the anti-slavery movement gathering momentum in the North, any weakness on our part could lead to unrest and unreal expectations among the field hands here. The nigger has got to be kept in his place. Any softening now could lead to trouble later." Mary could hear Killcaid speaking and again she regretted his influence over her son. "Apart from that," he continued adopting a tone of masculine condescension, "we still have a long way to go to full recovery, now that all this new uncertainty has caused costs to soar and profits to plummet."

Why did men have to assume that women had no understanding of economic matters thought Mary? Adrian, for all she had loved him, had been just the same. "I would have to replace them from field hands," he resumed, "and Killcaid would never allow it."

91

She was about to burst out with, 'who is Master, you or Killcaid?', but knew this would only anger him. At the mention of Killcaid's name she knew she had probably lost at least this round. Nevertheless, she pressed on.

"Well at least see what he says," she had ended lamely. Anthony promised he would.

Mary too was toying with another notion. It was a long time since she had visited her family in the north or spent any time there. She had for some time been considering the idea of a prolonged visit before the rumblings of war between North and South became a reality and travel became restricted. She wanted too to school Ruth for her new role as a free woman when that occasion should arise. Accordingly, she broache the subject with her, at their moment of greatest relaxation, when Ruth was brushing her hair.

"What would you think to a trip to New York Ruth?"

Ruth was immediately enthusiastic for any change to the routine and rhythm of Nethergate was welcome.

"Ah would take dat very well Ma'am. You knows that."

"Good," said Mary, "for I want this to be an extra special visit for you."

"Why so Ma'am?" came Ruth's intrigued reply.

"Years ago Ruth, I promised you your freedom for the great wrong that was done to you. At the time, it was not in my gift to give, but I have not forgotten that promise and I will keep it come what may. When we go to the North I want my father to know about Matthew. I want him to see you and to get to know you as a person, before I tell him that you are the mother of his great grandson by blood, so that he does not prejudge the situation. I want him to think of Matthew as his great grandson as I think of him as now as one of my grandsons."

Ruth was moved at this sudden frank revelation as to how her mistress really felt about Matthew. Despite the depths of her emotion at this revelation all she could think to say was simply, "I thank you Ma'am. Truly I thank you." But she meant it from the bottom of her heart. She longed to confess the part she had played in the death of Mary's son and she craved with all her being to be forgiven, but she knew the two events could be mutually destructive.

True to his word Anthony broached the matter of Ruth's freedom when next he and Killcaid met. Anthony had come out to see the hands at work, planting next year's crop, always a time of optimism and hope for the future.

"You must do what you think best Mr Styles," replied Killcaid after Anthony had broached the subject, "but you know better 'an I how things stands. Nethergate House is expensive enough to run – let alone the Hall," he added, getting in a sly dig at the ever more lavish costs incurred by Amelia. "If you do as your mother wishes we'd have to buy in new hands and you knows what that 'ud cost."

"It might encourage the others to work harder," tentatively suggested Anthony, but even to his own ears, his argument lacked any real conviction.

"I doubt it Sir," replied Killcaid dismissively, "Besides..." he started and then stopped.

"Besides what?" asked Anthony.

"I very much doubt it would stop there."

"Why so?"

"Do you think for a moment that she would want the freedom of the dam without its whelp?" he asked.

It was a thought that had not occurred to Anthony, but he saw immediately that what he said was true. Killcaid gathered himself and Anthony suspected he was in line for another of Killcaid's diatribes on his favourite theme. He wasn't to be disappointed.

Killcaid paused before answering as if pondering a new and weighty matter that he had long been considering. "Slaves is such ornery critters, but don't 'e be fooled by their docile manner," he began. "Now is no time to get soft with the nigger. Quite the opposite. We must remind him of his place. Where would they be if they's had to fend for 'emselves? Eh? They'd all starve in a month." Then he added ominously, "Remember Harper's Ferry."

This last remark, as Killcaid well knew, was bound to resonate with his boss. Harper's Ferry was still fresh in everyone's minds. An abortive rising of armed slaves, led by John Brown, a white man, ending in his execution. It had sent a shudder of dread down through the Southern States. It had been all over in less than forty-eight hours. But the truth was as nothing compared to the crazed and unsubstantiated rumours, that spread like wildfire after the event. White families had been murdered in their beds by those setting off to join the renegades, babies had been brained, whole families murdered in their sleep and their homes burnt about them.

Every mother drew her child a little bit closer and every father eyed even the most trustworthy servant with a new suspicion after that event. They were singing a song about it in the northern states with a catchy tune, 'John Brown's Body Lies A 'mouldering in his Grave'. The slaves everywhere were innocently whistling and humming the tune too, like a subtle flag of defiance.

Killcaid well knew how mention of Harper's Ferry would play on his employer's fears. Not so much on Anthony himself, who from his earliest days had always had slaves about him, but on his wife's unreasoned imaginings for she both hated and feared the black faces that now surrounded her in her home. Killcaid though had another axe to grind. He had often watched Ruth when she was working in the fields when Mark was Master of Nethergate and let his imagination wonder. However, he knew there was something about her and Master Mark and he had kept his hands off her, for Mark was a man he would never have dared to cross.

Her son Matthew with his quaint little ways and his mastery of mimicry was a different matter entirely. He knew how Matthew aped the other overseers and himself. He had once come across a crowd of slaves roaring with laughter as they crowded about their diminutive entertainer. A crack of his whip had broken them up, but he could see the laughter and mockery lingering in their eyes. They all fell back, and he was left confronting the child who met his stare with insolent insouciance. He had known then that this was a slave to be watched.

Killcaid was a man with a long memory. He never forgot an insult or let a slight slip by unavenged no matter how long it might take. And Matthew had in his mind amassed a considerable score of both. His whole success as overseer depended upon the fear he engendered in the hearts of his charges and his intimate knowledge of each one of them. Matthew though from the earliest days was the only slave who could meet his eye and refused to look down. He read in those eyes, strangely blue for a nigger, a look of quizzical amusement as if he could see through all Killcaid's posturing and was enjoying the joke. He longed to see those eyes widen with fear and to dominate Matthew as he did the others. Matthew had got under his skin and even troubled his sleep.

He had watched how Matthew had been affected by his new life in Nethergate House and could do nothing but grind his teeth in impotent fury that a slave should be given such freedoms and should adopt such an air of superiority. Matthew too had lately taken to riding about the estate to exercise the horses that were still held in the stables at Nethergate House, the building of the new stables at Nethergate Hall having ceased when Master Adrian had died.

There had been one occasion that lingered particularly in Killcaid's mind, when he had stopped Matthew. He had been on foot, but Matthew had been mounted. Matthew had leant casually forward, one elbow resting on his knee and looked down on him from his mount's superior height with a look of amusement dancing in his eyes at the juxtaposing their relative positions. In his hand was a riding whip which he tapped gently into the palm of his other hand in a parody of the way that Killcaid so often toyed with the Rattler. The meaning was not lost on Killcaid, but for a moment it was as if Mark Styles was looking down on him and he looked away unable to meet his eye. Then his anger had erupted at that moment of weakness. He ordered Matthew to dismount. In response Matthew had deliberately dug his heel into the horse's other flank and had pretended the animal was proving too lively to control. With a rueful grin and a cheery wave, he had ridden prancing off leaving Killcaid to nurse his fury. But after that encounter, there was no doubt in Killcaid's mind as to whose blood coursed through Matthew's veins.

After that encounter Killcaid had become more incensed than ever at the slave's arrogant swagger and superior ways, for he knew that Matthew had detected that sudden moment of weakness. It irked him to see the boy apparently running free. He had even heard that the old Mrs Styles encouraged her household slaves to learn to read and write and he suspected Matthew could do both, a skill he had barely mastered himself. It was in his view asking for trouble and giving slaves expectations way above their station. Matthew should have been working in the fields and earning his keep as he had done when Mark was Master of Nethergate.

A sly look crept into Killcaid's eye now that Anthony was asking him if Ruth should be granted her freedom and probably with her child as well. He saw an opportunity to even old scores. "You know far better than I, Mr Styles, the dangers of setting up expectations among the niggers," he ventured. "All this talk in the North about the gainful employ of slaves for wages trickles down. It unsettles 'em. We all depends upon the proper working of the system we has here. Without proper work, they'd soon be running wild, stealing and robbing and Lord knows what besides. Then where'd we all be? Our women 'ed never sleep secure in their beds. Do it for one, set one of 'em free and soon they'd all be jammerin' for't and runnin' riot."

For a moment, the vision of Amelia wide-eyed and fearful, cringing before a rampaging crowd of crazed slaves sprang to Anthony's mind. Despite the difficulties his wife's extravagances had created for him he was still devoted to her and the thought of her being harmed appalled him. There were so many slaves, so many black faces in every community, particularly on the plantations. Only occasionally, though, had there been any trouble. He well remembered when he was a boy, his father talking in hushed tones of Nat Turner's rebellion of 1831 with its religious overtones and the indiscriminate slaughter of white folks that had ensued. Now there was Harper's Ferry. Anthony could do nothing but nod in mute agreement.

Killcaid paused to let these ideas take hold, then ruefully shaking his head he continued, "But there's far too many at Nethergate House. There's hands there that should by rights be field hands. God knows we have need of them. Take that boy of Ruth's, he's a big lad now. I see the boy riding about the estate as if he owned the place. Damned if I don't. Blessed if I know what he does at your mother's place. High time he had a proper job o' work, a 'fore he gets ideas above 'is station, if you ask me Master Anthony."

Anthony was all too aware of the truth in Killcaid's last assertion. He had seen Matthew riding about the estate and wondered vaguely what his mother used him for. What Killcaid said made sense. All the same he could not afford to press his mother too hard, for her father had indeed been more than generous with loans to the estate. Then another thought occurred to him.

"Listen," he said, "I know my mother plans a visit to her kinsfolk in the North quite soon. She'll take Ruth with her. Perhaps then would be a better time to make changes. Now that war with the north seems possible, she is likely to be away for some time."

Killcaid could barely hide his triumph. It was as if Anthony was voicing his own thoughts. Revenge would be even sweeter for the savouring of it. Once the old Mrs Styles was away there would be nothing to stop him redeploying Matthew in the fields again. It would take less than a month when the time came he reckoned, to break the arrogant little scab. That would put an end to his condescending and lordly ways. Killcaid knew that he would sleep now with much more comforting dreams.

15

All In A Name

George Styles was a solitary child, not by nature, but now by circumstances. At Nethergate there was no-one his mother, Amelia, judged fit to be his companion and there were no children of his age on the nearby properties. Things had been different in their old home in New Haven where he had a wide circle of friends of his own age. There, he had had plenty to call on or visit, but his mother now regarded them as 'unsuitable'. As a consequence, he led a lonely life, though he had to admit, it had its compensations. It wasn't all bad by any means.

His father, as the new Master of Nethergate, had little time to spare for him. Mostly now he seemed to carry the cares of the world on his shoulders. He had lost the resilience and confidence he had possessed when he worked as a lawyer. As for his mother, she it seemed to him was only interested in displaying him to their guests when she had company, for which occasions he had to get dressed in his best clothes. It was a procedure he detested. He much preferred the freedom of old clothes. His promised schooling at the best of boarding schools in the North had somehow not materialised and so far, he had had to make do with a series of tutors.

The Pastor called most weekdays to teach him his Latin or to read Virgil's Aeneid and then to set him sums. There was also a weekly visit from Mrs Broadstairs who taught him Music Theory, the piano and the flute, both of which he enjoyed. This coming Fall though, he would be going north away from Nethergate to a school in New England, where at seventeen his education would be finished before going to college, or so he had been promised. He longed for that time to come. But now he was aware of other longings too, ever since Ursula had cannoned into him so unexpectedly in the corridor upstairs.

She had been crying and deeply distressed, but all he could think of was the warmth of her body so close to his and the firm feel of her hard, young breasts against his chest. Such was her misery that she had clung to him for a moment needing nothing more than the comfort of another human being, without thinking who that might be. When she had realised to whom she was clinging she had broken free with a cry of apology. But it seemed to him that there had been but the briefest instant when she had remained in his arms just a second longer than she really needed to. It was that thought that now lingered uppermost in his mind and so unsettled him. He had gone over the incident a thousand times since and their conversation when they had separated.

"Why Ursula, whatever is the matter?" he had asked.

"Oh, Master George! Forgive me. I is so sorry."

"What is it?"

She had shaken her head at that, but he insisted until grudgingly she declared, "It's my name Master George," she had sobbed, "My Mistress, your mother, she want to give me another name. But Ursula's ma name. It the only thing I have that is really my own. It's me. It's who I am. My Mam she never find me now wi' a different name."

"If that's all it is," he said, "why I'll go see Mamma right away."

"Oh No!" she had cried appalled at the idea. "She'll think I have been going behind her back." With that she had fled down the corridor. He had watched her go, his emotions in a turmoil, but determined to do all he could to help her.

His mother had been strangely hostile when he had mentioned his encounter to her and how distressed Ursula had seemed.

"That little hussy been talking out of turn?" she had exploded. "I'll teach her to come crying to you. She's mine to call her what I want to. Angela she is and Angela she'll stay. She should be grateful I have chosen a nice name for her." Her anger began to feed upon itself. "The arrogance of the little slattern! She ran out of this room as if she owned the place. She deliberately disobeys me. I've a good mind to have her whipped same as I did for Samuel."

George was appalled at the unexpected way his attempt to help Ursula had turned out.

"No Mamma really," he had protested. "She could not have known I was just coming around the corner. Had we not collided she would never have spoken to me. It was *me* that asked *her*."

"Collided, did you? I'll bet the little schemer had it all planned. Just because she's a pretty face, she thought she could run rings round you."

When his mother was in this sort of mood there was no arguing with her. She had never been like this at New Haven. She had got worse of late, ever since Samuel had been flogged. But she hadn't finished yet, "Mark my words George, you'll have the running of this place someday. You've got to show them who's boss. If you're weak now it will return to haunt you a thousand times later."

"Yes Mamma," he had replied and hastily made his exit. Even so his thoughts lingered on Ursula. He felt guilt about feeling this way about a slave, but then he argued she didn't really look like a normal nigger. Her skin was creamy brown, and her features were more like those of a European. She was more Arab perhaps, or even Mediterranean than Negro he argued as if that made a difference.

Though he missed his old friends, George tried to make the most of his new circumstances and to enjoy all he now had to divert him. But it was hard to make the most of it when there was no-one to share it with. He enjoyed being his own entertainer. He spent much of his time playing his flute, reading or going for long walks with his gun and with Trixie, his dog, for company. He wasn't bored exactly, but he did hanker after someone his own age to talk to.

Instead of company he would weave wild adventures to himself in which he played the hero or led a band of prospector adventurers breaking new grounds to the west, fighting the Indian tribes or solving great mysteries. But now increasingly it seemed that Ursula crept into his mind and featured more and more in his reveries.

He took to visiting his mother, more than he had done before, so that he could watch Ursula, now always addressed as Angela, as she worked. Occasionally she would look in his direction when his mother's attention was elsewhere, and it seemed to him, she smiled. He longed to catch her on her own, but his mother was as vigilant as a hawk and no doubt suspected his sudden change of habit.

He could understand now how his mother's harshness with Ursula distressed the girl and how she seemed to shrink whenever she was addressed by her new name. At times, she deliberately failed to respond, and his mother would stride over and slap her sharply for her lack of attention. But chiefly it was the cruelty of his mother's language and the harshness of her tongue that distressed him and made him wonder why his mother had changed so much. Ursula never looked in his direction when such moments occurred. He sensed that partly she did not wish him to be a witness to her humiliation, but at the same time she welcomed his unspoken support for her in her misery. Frequently he would try to distract his mother by asking her a question or changing the subject, but it never seemed to work.

Sometimes his mother would attempt to draw him into her criticism of Ursula's work and slowness of understanding. Ursula knew that his presence spurred his mother on to ever greater cruelty. She longed for him to go so that his mother's ire would cool, but at the same time she wanted him to stay.

For his part, George craved to be able to see Ursula just to talk. Sometimes when his mother was away or visiting, he would wander down to the slaves' quarters, hoping to see her. But somehow Samuel would always be there to ask with his gentle dignity whom he sought and George would find himself stammering in confusion. Samuel watched over the younger servant girls like a father perhaps having seen how owners and their sons treated these young women. Then, quite unexpectedly, his perseverance was greeted with success.

16

The Gauntlet Thrown Down

On the morning of April 12th 1861, beneath overcast skies, the Confederate guns of Charleston opened fire on the Union Forces besieged in Fort Sumner. The gauntlet had been thrown down, the challenge accepted and the war between north and south had begun.

The news reached Nethergate Hall as Anthony and Amelia were sitting down to breakfast. They rarely breakfasted together, but on this occasion, they were both due to embark on a long-planned trip to Belmont where Anthony was planning to arrange the shipping of some of this year's crop down the Mississippi. It was the coachman who had brought the news hot from the telegraph at the railhead.

"Kentucky's sure to remain neutral," remarked Anthony to Amelia, "At least that's a blessing. This year's harvest should not be much affected, though no doubt insurance costs will soar."

"No doubt," murmured Amelia, not much interested. "It was bound to come sooner or later. I was thinking, we can hardly now send George to finish his schooling in New England. His current tutors seem to be doing a pretty good job in any case. If we are to be spared the expense of a college education, perhaps now we might consider the new curtaining in the ballroom?"

Thus was the future education of George determined and balanced against more pressing needs. He was in any event fast approaching an age where further schooling might be considered unnecessary. George's father had little say in the matter, as indeed he did in most domestic concerns.

George, however, had a natural curiosity and never found his studies arduous or irksome and enjoyed the opportunity to discuss and dispute with his tutors. He missed the companionship of those of his own age that he had enjoyed before coming to Nethergate and had been eager to widen his educational horizons. He wanted to learn as much as he could about the running of the estate too, but his father rarely felt inclined to discuss estate business with him. It was a subject in which he felt ill at ease and would rather not think about unless he had to.

George's studies were an enjoyable diversion from the tensions at home and he would often wander down to the river that meandered through the grounds of Nethergate House where the library created by an earlier Styles had remained intact on Adrian's move to Nethergate Hall. In the solitude of the grounds he would seek a favoured place under the shelter of the trees to settle down to study undisturbed. On this occasion too, after his parents had departed on their trip to Belmont, he was enjoying the feeling of freedom which their absence invariably gave. His wanderings had led him towards Nethergate House. He thought he might visit his grandmother when he got tired of his studies, an altogether pleasant prospect for the afternoon.

He was comfortably seated in the bole of a favourite tree when his eye was caught by movement from the direction of his grandmother's house. A female figure had come from the house and was making her way towards the river. It was Ursula.

As she approached he saw her more clearly. Her hair was loose and flowing. He had not realised it was so long, concealed as it always was under a mob cap. Her mistress away, she was now wearing a dress of bright blue gingham that set off the honey dew of her complexion. He thought he had never seen so entrancing a sight in all his life.

Overcome by a sudden shyness he hastily sunk down under the cover of the tree where he sat, lest she should think he was spying on her. When he looked up again she was gone. Then he spotted her. She too was seated in the shade of a tree, the dappled sunlight filtering through the roof of leaves made her dress dance like a live thing. She had a book open on her knee with her finger hunting each word.

Suddenly, as though she could feel the intensity of his gaze, she looked up and their eyes met. With a startled cry, she jumped to her feet.

"Oh, Master George," she cried, "I's so sorry. I thought I was on my own," then realising that she held a book in her hands and that he might think she had taken it, she stammered, "Mrs Styles, the old Mrs Styles that is, she give me this to read, truly she did."

George, who was almost as confused as Ursula herself, hastened to reassure her, "Of course she did," he answered, "I know how she likes to teach all her household to read and write, or those as can take to it."

For a moment, both stood under the cool of the trees, looking at each other, neither knowing what to say. Both were acutely aware of the other and the difference in their status. Both too were aware of the emotions that coursed through their own minds at this chance meeting.

"What are you reading Ursula?" he asked at last, breaking the tension. At the sound of her name she flashed him a sudden smile, for all now had been told to address her by her new name.

She told him. "It was a book I started to read when I was at Nethergate House. There were bits I never could understand."

"Perhaps I might help," he suggested diffidently.

"Oh, would you?" and the two sat down side by side as if it were the most natural thing in the world, the book shared between them beside the gently flowing river under the intimate shelter of the canopy above.

It was not long before their hands touched as she chased the words across the page; his hands large and strong hers small and delicate. The touch lingered longer than it should and turned into a gentle caress. Their eyes strayed from the page. She looked up and he stared down, trying to read her face. Such longing passed between them, that neither dared put into words. Then bending towards her he gently brushed her brow with his lips. He felt a tremor pass through her as she gazed up at him and then finally their lips met in a long lingering kiss that dispelled all their doubts.

At last she broke away.

"O Massa' George!" she gasped, "What must you think of me? I's not that sort o' girl," as if what had passed between them was all her doing. With a sudden cry, she jumped to her feet and turned towards him as if to say something then abruptly turned and ran from him.

Confused at her sudden departure, George sat for a moment where he was aware only of the wild beating of his heart and the riot of emotions that were coursing through his young body. Then suddenly he realised he was still holding the book that they had been reading.

"Ursula!" he cried, "Ursula – your book."

The fleeing figure hesitated. Then she halted and turned back towards him. He caught up with her. Once more master and slave faced each other, but things were different now. Both were acutely aware of the sudden flaring of passion that had passed between them. Neither knew where it might lead or what it might mean for them both.

George broke the silence between them. "Here," he said, proffering the book they had been reading, "look I kept the place for you."

Gently she took the book from him and their eyes met again.

"Thank you," she said, and both knew that it was not just for returning the book, but more for what had passed between them.

"Ursula," he stammered, "Ursula, I – I do care for you."

"O Massa' George," she murmured, "and I for you."

With that she turned and fled. Both fearful now of the riot of their own emotions, both acutely conscious that things would never be the same again.

17

A Meeting Of A Different Kind

George had long taken to roaming the estate with his hunting rifle and his retriever, Trixie. He rarely went down to the creek, for the ground there was wild, treacherous and boggy and his father had in any event forbidden him to wander there for it was a place where sometimes escaped slaves would camp out in safety in the bayou. But now, since his meeting with Ursula, it seemed the only place to go where he could be certain to be alone with the turbulent riot of his thoughts. It was too somehow a rite of passage as if by coming here he was breaking free from the wearing authority of his parents.

Ursula and he had only managed fleeting meetings since his parents' return, but their eyes had spoken more than words could convey. Slowly though, the lands about the bayou had begun to exert their magic on him. There was the hint of danger wherever he trod, the wildness and untamed nature of the woodlands and swamps and the milling confusion of wildlife that abounded there matched his new mood of defiance and independence. The riot of nature's sounds too fascinated him. The way all fell silent at his approach as if a covert conductor had raised a secret baton and the orchestra was poised at the ready. Then when he stood still, the sounds slowly swelled once more to full volume as if he were a part of that vast chaotic orchestra of life.

He had recently joined the Confederate Militia, mainly to support his father who, because of his position at Nethergate, was an honorary Captain of the local guard. They did little but drill, musket handling practice and basic cavalry movements taken from old British army cavalry manuals. He was anxious to excel in this new military environment. He knew he was viewed with condescension by those whose whole life had been on the plantations and was anxious to prove them wrong. The lands about the bayou were secluded enough for him to practise his drills unseen and to exercise his aiming and firing skills too.

Perhaps it was because of these distractions that he failed at first to detect the tell-tale signs that he was not alone.

At first it was only the vaguest feeling of unease. After a time, he became certain that he was being watched. Then he noticed that Trixie seemed to be sniffing the air, but not in the excited way as when he detected game, but somehow with an air of wariness. He had a growing certainty now that he was not the sole wanderer in this wilderness. He became more and more curious. Somehow, he did not think it might be an escaped slave, for none had been reported and there were too many eager to enjoy the bounty from their capture. The mystery began to intrigue him.

On each visit now, he became more certain. Sometimes Trixie would stare intently into the undergrowth and utter a low growl. Once he caught sight of movement. A bush had been agitated when there was no wind. He had crept up close with his gun at the ready, but there was nothing there. Just some flattened undergrowth. It could have been where a deer had been lying up during the heat of the day.

Then he had seen him; a fleeting glimpse of a young man about his own age running across an area of swamp. The figure was dressed as a slave. What was extraordinary though was that he appeared to be dancing above the swamp itself, leaving no trace other than widening ripples on its watery surface. For the moment that he was visible, George held his breath, for surely, he must succumb to the grip of the morass and be sucked into its embrace. But the figure moved seemingly flying over the mire, buoyed up by invisible hands. Then as quickly as it had appeared the apparition vanished, swallowed into the swampland green as if digested by the vegetation itself.

For a moment, he wondered if it had not been a figment of his imagination, a trick of the sunlight streaming through the swamp's canopy. His thoughts turned to tales of the Will of the Wisp and he felt a cold prickle of fear run up his spine. But it had been too vivid, too real for that. He attempted to follow where the figure had gone, but soon he was up to his knees in cloying, sucking mud and then had the greatest difficulty in extricating both himself and Trixie, who had loyally followed him, part way into danger.

He would have liked to ask his father if people still lived in the bayou swamplands. Perhaps they were the survivors of the original Indian tribes who had once inhabited these lands before the white man came. He wondered whether they had developed some secret method of traversing the wetlands in much the same way as the native Indians used snow shoes to traverse the icy landscapes in the north. To do so, though, would reveal where he had been. Anyway, his father was far too busy in estate affairs to spend time with him.

"O Massa' George, where hab you been?" remonstrated Manuel for the umpteenth time at George's muddied clothes.

"Never you mind Manuel. Just you keep that mouth o' your'n buttoned tight," George would reply with a wink.

"Sure will Baas," was Manuel's inevitable response.

Manuel was his personal boy. Amelia had discovered that most young men of George's age had their personal boys much as the ancient sons of Rome had had their whipping boys. Manuel, as far as anyone knew or cared, was in his early thirties. She had carefully chosen him for this role in the sure knowledge that he would be her eyes and ears about what her son was up to. Manuel had learnt over time that it paid to appear slightly stupid and ever anxious to please his white masters. No-one ever considered him capable of holding a notion of his own, let alone of doing anything other than what he was bid. He was seemingly ideal for Amelia's purposes and was clearly terrified of her and her waspish ways. She had also discovered that his fear of her was as nothing to that of his terror of Killcaid. As a youth, he had been a field slave and the particular target for Killcaid's malicious humour. The mere mention of the name 'Killcaid' would reduce him to stuttering incoherence. Amelia knew just how to play upon this weakness and was more than content with her choice.

But Manuel was not all that he seemed. He had after time formed a liking for Master George, for his warm and friendly manner, for little acts of kindness and consideration, but above all for the trust he put in him. Despite his fear of Amelia, he had developed a loyalty towards George and a determination to protect him as much as he could from his mother's prying eye.

Accordingly, he would nod his head obediently at George's request for secrecy and take away his muddied clothes and boots, anxious for his own sake to hide the evidence and avoid the dire consequence of not revealing his young master's secrets should Amelia question him.

Then the day arrived when George met his Will of the Wisp and that event raised more questions than it answered.

George had been negotiating a particularly difficult part of the swampland, made more hazardous by recent rains, when with a rush something swept past his face and thudded into the bog oak beside him. He stopped dead. Not an inch from his face was the shaft of a spear still quivering from the force of its delivery. Standing a few yards off was the young man he had seen so fleetingly. He was dressed as a slave, but he did not have the look or bearing of a slave. His skin was dark, but not with the hue of the Negro. In his hand, he held another spear, ready to throw. For a moment, the two youths stood facing each other, George with his hands tightening on his rifle and the slave with his spear poised. The sun was shining from behind the stranger's face so that George could not see his features. Then the stranger spoke.

"You listen good young Massa' George." He uttered the word 'Massa' as if it were a term of abuse. "This here's my territory and you ain't welcome here!" George was too startled to say anything. He thought of the obvious retort that this land belonged to his father, but somehow it did not seem relevant. How did he know his name? And how dared he address him with such barely concealed contempt? "Now," continued the boy, "You can give me back my spear and be warned, if you come here again then next time you will be on the end of it!"

Obediently George pulled at the spear embedded in the tree, but it would not budge. With an impatient snort of scorn, the slave strode forward and with one swift jerk removed the spear. Then in a flurry of the undergrowth, he vanished.

"Wait!" cried George, recovering at last. "Wait. Who are you?" In that moment of closeness, he felt sure he had seen him before. But all he heard by way of reply was the mocking calling of the Marsh Clapper Rails which abounded in those parts, soon to be joined by the full orchestra of the bayou, but somehow now mocking him.

For a long time, George stood still going over in his mind all he had seen and all the things he would and should have said had he had time to think. It was his bearing though that had arrested George's attention. There had been an air of aristocratic hauteur about him as he gazed contemptuously at George, knowing that he could not see him properly. It was as

113

if George was the interloper. Now that he had gone George felt angry at being spoken to in such a manner and by a slave, but at the same time he was intrigued and wanted to learn more about him.

"I'll be back, never fear," he shouted, but his only reply was the sudden, sullen silence of the birds.

Matthew heard that defiant cry from a distance. He paused in thought, reflecting on the implications of his owner's son's sudden interest in what he regarded as his territory and anxious also for Old Mo's sake that no-one might know of the help he was now giving him. Then once more he made his own secret way back over ground he knew was firm under foot to where he always met Old Mo. On balance, he thought that little good would come from George's sudden appearance. It added to the general sense of foreboding he had following his latest meeting with Killcaid.

On that occasion, he had been on horseback as usual, exercising one of the old Mrs Styles' horses. To his intense surprise, Killcaid had been affability itself at Matthew's whimsical greeting, which he knew normally so enraged the overseer and caused him such secret amusement. This time though there had been a glint of triumph in Killcaid's eye that was hard for him to read, making him instantly wary. Something he was sure was afoot. Whatever it was would not be to his benefit, of that he was certain. For if ever Killcaid looked content someone else was sure to suffer. Matthew had a feeling that that someone was going to be him.

18

A Friendship Is Forged

Back home that night George quizzed Manuel as to who this wild youth might be. At first Manuel denied all knowledge of matters so close to home. Manuel knew who George had met, for only one slave had the freedom of movement that Matthew enjoyed. Manuel's eyes shifted with unease and he could not meet his master's gaze. George guessed he was not revealing all he knew. Matthew had many friends among the rest of the slaves. Everyone knew of his silent mockery of Killcaid and enjoyed his mimicry on the occasions when the slaves had their few holidays. Old Mo had also let it be known that Matthew was a friend of his and all were anxious now to keep on the right side of that strange old trapper-slave for the benefits of fresh meat. Even the small children who used to follow the strange old man chanting out his peculiarities were now hushed and rebuked by the others.

Bit by bit George managed to winkle out from Manuel who the young slave might be. George knew Ruth, as his grandmother's personal maid, and just recalled her son, the strange, reserved young slave called Matthew who was part of her household, but who always withdrew whenever he visited.

He recalled too seeing Matthew riding about on the estate's horses.

Once the gates were open however, Manuel spilled out all he knew about Matthew, including who his father was rumoured to be, for gossip about their betters was the elixir of life to the slave community and Manuel was anxious to prove his value to his new master. He stopped short however of mentioning anything of the manner of Mark's death.

Manuel told too of Matthew's languid contempt for the fearsome overseer, plain for all to see and of the fury and frustration of Killcaid at his present inability to do anything about it. The thought that intrigued George now, though, was the startling revelation that Matthew and he probably both shared the same grandmother and that they were, if the stories were true, cousins by blood. It was a novel thought. It explained a lot about Matthew's appearance and aloofness of manner for a slave.

Once Manuel started it was hard to stop him. George learnt about the deep resentment that simmered among the slave community when Mark had been Master and how many of the slaves had been sold to pay off his debts. Families which for generations had been together were split up. Their menfolk had been shipped off to the slave market at Louisville and sold down the river to the rice estates near the mouth of the Mississippi where slaves were either worked to an early death or succumbed to swamp fever.

Now that George knew the identity of his 'Will of the Wisp' he no longer felt intimidated by the mystery. He determined that he would return the next day in defiance of Matthew's edict and confront him with what he now knew. They were after all kinsmen now. He also wanted to know how he managed to move so freely over the surface of the bayou.

Accordingly, he made his way to where they had last met and began calling his name. After a fruitless half hour, he was about to give up when with a rustle of undergrowth Matthew suddenly appeared.

"Follow me," was all he said and vanished from sight, before George could say a word. George had no alternative but to do as he requested. Matthew set up a fast pace following a trail George could hardly see and he was soon out of breath. He could glimpse Matthew just ahead of him and hastened to catch him up, anxious not to appear a laggard and to prove himself every bit as fit as his guide. If it was to be some sort of test of stamina, he was determined not to be found lacking.

It was his undoing. Suddenly without warning the ground seemed to surge up towards him. A noose tightened about his leg and he was swung off his feet and left dangling some five feet from the ground. But he was not entirely powerless for he had still managed to keep a grip on his rifle.

The shock of his predicament was soon replaced by anger.

"Let me down, damn you! I know who you are. You're Matthew, Ruth's son. Let me down or I swear it'll be the worse for you," he bellowed trying to bring his rifle to bear as he slowly gyrated on the end of the rope. It was the worst thing he could have said. Matthew's response was to place his hands on his hips and roar with laughter.

"O Massa'," he parodied in the patois of the slaves, "Ah is too foolish to unnerstan what yo' am say-in'. How you 'spec me to undo dis here contraption? I is nuttin' but a stupid nigger." Then a rashness overtook him and the simmering resentment at the difference in their two stations in life overwhelmed him. "How does it feel hey! Now you knows just how us niggers feels, all a-dangling on the end of a rope for yo' white folks to yank whenever yo' wishes."

"Let me down or I swear I'll shoot you like a dog," roared George.

"And then?" queried Matthew, speaking in normal tones and letting the question hang, "then, you will remain swinging here until you rot, with nothin' but my carcass and the crows for company."

"What do you want?" asked George, the hopelessness of his situation suddenly dawning on him.

"Want?" echoed his captor, "I warned you not to come down here and now it seems you have blundered into one of Old Mo's traps," he replied innocently.

Truly, Matthew suddenly realised, he did not know the answer to George's question. What did he want? He had deliberately led George to Old Mo's trap, but he had not really considered what would come next. He knew who George was. He suspected that he was probably as lonely as he was himself, but he had the natural suspicion all slaves have of their white masters.

"How do I know you won't blame me fo' all this and get me a whipping?" he asked of his new master now dangling on the end of his rope and entirely at his mercy.

The hopelessness of his situation was not lost on George and he had to think fast. He wasn't quite sure how much Matthew knew about the nature of his origins. He knew slaves rarely reveal the fathers of children sired by white folk, for the shame it brought from among their own kind. He wondered how true Manuel's revelations might be, but his grandmother's indulgence of Matthew seemed to bear it all out.

"I won't," he said in answer to Matthew's last question. "Why would I? You and I – well we're practically brothers."

"What d'you mean?" asked Matthew, intrigued at this sudden bizarre revelation.

"'Cos your father was my Uncle Mark. We share the same grandmother."

A stunned silence followed this revelation. Matthew had always wondered who his father might be, but as far as his mother was concerned the subject was taboo. He was only too aware of how different he was from the rest of the slaves, both in looks and in the colour of his skin. He longed to be more like the rest and to be accepted as one of them. In the end, he had found approval and acceptance by his refusal to be cowed by Killcaid and by the laughter he generated with his clowning and his mimicry. He had always suspected, though, that there was more to the special treatment he received at his mistress's hands than just the favouritism given to the child of a much-valued slave. But Mrs Styles anyway was different from other slave owners in the way she treated her charges. All the same it was hard to think of Mrs Styles, the matriarchal white lady of the Nethergate Estate, as his grandmother. He thought he had much to ask his mother.

"Why'd you think I came back here, after last time?" continued George, now sensing that this was all a revelation to Matthew. "I want us to be friends but leaving me twisting in the air like this don't make conversation easy. In fact, I can tell you it's not at all comfortable."

This last understatement made Matthew smile. He hadn't expected George to react this way and what he had just said, intrigued him. In some strange way, he felt himself warming to this young white man as if he had somehow known him for years. Then suddenly he made up his mind. If George wanted to be friends, then who was he to turn down the offer?

"OK," he said. "Hold tight."

With that Matthew unhitched the rope and let George drop to the ground. George sat, rubbing at his ankle staring long and hard at Matthew, so different from the other slaves. While he was dangling from the end of a rope their roles had truly been reversed. Then the strangeness of what he had just experienced began to dawn on him. He saw how he must have looked dangling by one leg on the end of a rope completely at the mercy of one of his father's slaves.

The ridiculousness of the situation struck him. He began to chuckle. Soon he was shaking with laughter. Then Matthew joined in, for laughter is infectious. Soon both young men were whooping and hollering, not really knowing why, but each somehow sensing the need they both had of a friend of their own age to breach the loneliness in their lives and to relieve the tension of the moment. Thus, in this strange way, a friendship between these two lonely outcasts was forged. Soon they fell to talking as if they had been old friends and equals. Matthew even explained how he moved with such apparent ease over the swamp. It was simply his knowledge of where the firm bits of the bayou lay.

Matthew accompanied George back to the estate and then as if by an unspoken agreement, they separated for it was not right that slave and master should be seen sharing such amity. But the warmth they shared in the sudden birth of their strange kinship and friendship remained as the answer to the isolation that consumed them both.

As for Matthew, he had much he wished to ask of his mother.

19

Secrets Revealed

Most days Ruth had time to herself when she had finished dressing her mistress for the evening. This was a time which she tried to devote to her son when he was free from the many things which seemed to absorb and distract him. He always returned to the house for the evening meal, for no slaves were allowed free to roam after dark, though she suspected that her son ignored this law when the mood took him. She was free then until it was time for her to go upstairs again to help her mistress undress and prepare for bed.

On the evening of Matthew's meeting with George, Ruth found Matthew waiting for her in her rooms. She could see from his face that he had something important which he wished to discuss. She suspected that it might be the question of his origins which had always been with him a preoccupation and a source of natural curiosity. She prepared to prevaricate once again as she had always done in the past.

However, she was not prepared for his open declaration of the truth.

"Is it true Mama that my real father was Master Mark?"

Faced with such an open declaration, she could not contradict him.

"Who you bin talking to?" she asked, but he noted that she did not deny it.

"That don't matter. Is it true Mammy?"

Ruth knew this moment must surely come someday. Matthew still remembered the dramatic death of the Master but had no idea of how it related to him. But now there was no escape from his probing. Above all she did not want him to think of her as someone who would willingly give herself to her white masters. She knew too that now he must be told the whole story including the manner of his father's death.

"It's not as it may seem to you Matti'. I've never been the sort of woman that gave herself to anyone, let alone a white man. It happened when I was very young, not as old as you are now. He forced himself on me. But I struck him. Imagine that? Me a slave girl striking the future Master of Nethergate. That's what made him so wild. I was beat bad. Beat so that I was barely conscious. Then he took. I had no say in the matter."

For the first time, Matthew saw his mother as a woman. She was in her early thirties and he knew that she was still very attractive to men. He'd seen the way they looked at her. Yet she had never taken a husband as most of the other slave women did.

He remembered Mark from when he had worked in the fields. He felt again the fear his mother had of the slave traders. He remembered her pleading on her knees before Master Mark. This was so unlike his mother that her fear had filled him with unease and afterwards her holding him so tight it hurt. Then someone else holding him and making him look away. He thought then that he had always known that somehow his mother had played some special part in the drama that had followed. But all such thoughts had been eclipsed by his memories first of the wild leaping horse and

122

then of looking dispassionately into the face of the dying man, staring into his eyes as the life ebbed from them. He had felt no pity, for all had hated Master Mark for his cruelty and his harshness and the heedless way he split families and sold off their menfolk. He had felt only curiosity. He wondered if he would have felt any different had he known that the man was his father. He could feel nothing for him now and doubted that he would have felt any different had he known the truth. The man was a white man and inhabited a different world to his.

"I saw him die," said Matthew. "At the time, I was only curious. I watched him. I was thinking, 'this is important', I must remember this. He fell from his horse that was kicking and jumping about 'ntil he was thrown. Never saw a horse so wild."

Ruth wrestled with the desire not to let him know what she had done, but she felt it better that he should hear it all now from her own lips. Then he could judge her.

"It was the time when the estate was going downhill, even more swiftly than now. Master Mark was selling off slaves to pay his gambling and gaming debts. He was splitting up families who had been together for years. He wanted to sell you to a slave dealer to become the plaything of some debauched white man. I couldn't let that happen so I placed a stone under his saddle, knowing that his horse would throw him. It was me that caused the horse to behave in the way it did. I didn't know he'd die though... but I hoped he would," she added with sudden vehemence. "Everyone as was there knew what I done, but no-one ever breathed a word. Now you know too. The Mistress, she don't know. It would break her heart if she were told, but it is a guilt I hold every day of my life, what I did to her son and she always so good to me."

Matthew looked long and hard at his mother. She could read nothing in his stare. He had a lot to digest. He saw his mother now, as another human being, one who had been tried and who had found her own resolution. His heart went out to her. He could understand her bitterness at her treatment by her owner and too the anguish of the guilt she bore in causing the mistress she so loved such distress. He was overcome with a sudden wave of affection for this handsome woman who had retained so much of her humanity and dignity in the face of so much adversity. Silently he reached out to grasp her hand. She held his hand to her cheek in silent gratitude. They remained like that for a long time each deep in their own thoughts, but each drinking in that special love and trust that only a mother and her child can share.

"You don't condemn me Matthew?" she asked at last, drawing away and there was a quiver in her voice.

"No Mama. 'Course I don't. I think you was very brave. But why you never get married since, like most folks do? There some mighty good men down there in the cabins. You could have had other chillen. I could have had brothers and sisters like most folk do."

Ruth didn't answer. She was wondering how much she could bare herself and her inner thoughts to her son. At last she spoke. "There is deep shame in lying with a white man. Most folk assume people do it to gain favour with the white folks. No doubt some do an' some say that's just what I did. There is shame too in having a white man's chile. I always needed to be with you when you was very young afore you learn to look after yourself. You is so different from the other slaves. They don't trust folks that's different from them. It's like you bin tainted with the white blood that flows in your veins."

"But why did you not take another man for a husband?" he repeated.

"It's hard to explain Matti'. You were my blessing from God that He give me to make up for what Master Mark take away from me. Then instead of being grateful and trusting in God, like a good Christian should, I committed the worst sin of all. I took another's life, because I couldn't trust God not to let them take you away from me. This is my punishment. This, an' the guilt I feel every day I see the Mistress. For I can never dare tell her that it was me as took away her son."

Matthew had much to consider. Then another thought occurred to him. "The Mistress? Does she know who my father was?"

"A' course she do. That why you allus get such special treatment, why we both come here when Mark died. But she could never let the other white folks know you was her gran'chile. But I sees the way she watches you. She loves you like any real grandmother should. I can tell. But she can never say so to the rest of the world and neither must you."

Matthew pondered all his mother had revealed. He knew he was different from the other slaves. It was why instinctively he had always sought their approval in laughter, in mimicry of the white men and in aping and goading Killcaid and the other overseers. It was why he had always sought to help them in their work as much as he could. But he still felt an alien. He realised now that he could never truly be one of them. He would always bear the mark of his mother's shame. Equally he could never be a part of the white man's world. He was condemned forever to inhabit a shadowy no man's land, neither beast nor fowl. For a moment, he felt crushed by the sudden weight of the truth. But then he drew in his breath and set back his shoulders. If this was to be his destiny, then he would face it head on.

Ruth watched her son and her heart went out to him.

20

Friendship Blossoms

Over the following months, George began to share in the strange life which his slave friend so evidently enjoyed whilst he was in the marshlands and out of the reach of Killcaid and his overseers. George too grew to enjoy the wildness of the bayou; its humidity, the constant murmur and hum of its insect life, the orchestra of birdsong, the mysterious sudden disturbance of unseen wildlife and the convulsive eruption of alligator fish in the swamp waters. Matthew revealed some of the secret routes in the marshlands to George. He showed him the markings which denoted where there were firm pathways beneath the watery surface which had enabled him to appear to dance over the treacherous terrain. He even shared some of the skills Old Mo had taught him. But an inbred caution led him to keep silent about the help he gave to that irascible old man. These two parts of his life he kept in separate compartments, for he was certain that Old Mo would vanish like a morning mist at the mere thought of meeting up with the son of his owner.

Together they hunted and trapped, vied with each other in feats of daring or wrestled and fought in mock battles and trials of strength. Matthew soon came to realise that he was immensely the stronger of the two but allowed George his fair share of victories. They even shared in the task of building a dug out canoe, for Matthew dared not use Old Mo's canoe lest George should realise the closeness between Old Mo and his new-found companion. It gave George the chance to show that he was just as capable of hard sustained physical labour as Matthew. Though soon his hands were blistered, he carried on regardless. Both were proud of the result. With their own boat, they explored more of the bayou and got down to the serious business of fishing. Both enjoyed the concentration required by that joint endeavour and the silent companionship it fostered.

In other moments of quiet, the two youths would squat down on one of their favourite islands of dry land amid the swamp and would talk of their different worlds. George would share his love of books and the stories he had read. He was astonished at the memory and understanding that Matthew seemed to have and his hunger for more knowledge, gleaned up to now mostly from the library in Nethergate House. Few slaves outside those at Nethergate House had been taught to read or write as Matthew had, for it was against the law. But Matthew had grasped every opportunity with both hands and had benefited greatly. But it was a random education with no clear pattern to it.

Matthew had discovered a flute in Nethergate House and had taught himself to play. George loved the flute too and had avidly drawn from the affection Mrs Broadstairs, his music teacher, also had for the instrument. He passed on to Matthew much of what he had acquired by way of technique and understanding from her and introduced him to many of the finer points of the instrument. Sometimes it seemed that even the birds stopped their clamour to listen to their playing.

Matthew for his part taught George many of the tunes

the slaves played in their rare moments of recreation and the haunting melodies they sang in the fields to divert their minds from the endless cycle of toil.

They spoke too of women as young men will. George had shared with Matthew his feelings for Ursula and had been surprised at the anger in his response.

"Then why don't you jus' take her and do what you will. After all she' your property. You can do what you like." George realised he had struck a raw nerve and in future kept off the subject. He could not know that Matthew was thinking of his own mother and what had befallen her at the hands of Master Mark.

Only when the talk turned to slavery and of the war did the two really differ. As far as the war was concerned they were of course on different sides. Both accepted this as given and largely kept off the subject. George had conversed with his grandmother over the years and assimilated some of her ideas from the anti-slavery North. But the practicality of the system for harvesting tobacco, with its need for intensive labour, was of course all too evident to George as a future plantation owner.

"Grandmamma always says that everyone is equal in the sight of God and that no man has the right to hold another in bondage," George had once remarked.

Matthew always secretly resented George's easy talk of 'Grandmamma' and the affection and familiarity it implied. Though they shared the same relationship he could not think of Mrs Styles as anything other than the grand and distant Mistress of Nethergate House, despite his awareness now of their tie by blood.

"She I know," continued George, unaware of Matthew's resentment, "finds slavery hard to live with, to own a fellow human being, body and soul.

"Nobody owns my soul, but the good Lord himself," rumbled Matthew, sullenly.

"But without slaves who would plant the Tobacco seedlings, who would weed, top and sucker them and bring in the leaves and smoke them dry, who would pack and press them? You need people to do that. They don't have no machines that can do that."

"They do up North," retorted Matthew, "the farmers there have machines that can do most anything."

"But growing corn is easy. Tobacco must be tended and cared for every step of the way. Only human hands can do that, Brother." They had fallen to addressing each other thus in the privacy of their shared life in the bayou. George used the term now anxious to take the heat out of the words he sensed Matthew was about to utter.

"You mean slave hands," retorted Matthew angrily holding out his own two hands in front of George's face and the two youths glared at each other. Then Matthew added softly, "Brother," and placed a hand on George's shoulder. Both relaxed, their differences evaporating as suddenly as they had arisen. Resentment never lasted long between them, for their friendship and the relief from their mutual isolation meant more to each of them than any passing divergences about their contrasting prospects in life.

After one such argument, George, anxious to restore peace, had made a momentous declaration.

Matthew had been making a heartfelt statement of his own feelings in the matter. "You cannot possibly understand Brother, what it feels like to know that you are *owned* by another human being like a horse or a dog – that when it comes to it, you have no voice in any of the major decisions which affect your life. You and I, we call each other 'Brother' now and so we are in the sight of God, but there will come a day when you are Master here of Nethergate. I will have to call you, 'Massa'' and do as I am bid. Yes Massa'. No Massa'. Will I be 'Brother' then?"

George looked long and hard at Matthew. The weight of his future responsibilities weighed suddenly heavy upon him. Matthew could not possibly know how much he envied him his seeming freedom to roam the estate almost as he chose, free from any real duties in his grandmother's household. But George could not know how deeply Matthew in his turn envied him in his freedom to be the master of his own destiny, free to have a say about his future and above all, freedom from the shackles of slavery. Then George came to a sudden decision.

"When I am master of Nethergate," he said, "I promise you, the first thing I shall do is to grant you your freedom. You will never have to call me Massa'. You will always be 'Brother' to me."

Matthew felt the tears spring to his eyes. In a sudden surge of gratitude, he proffered his hand and the two boys solemnly shook upon the momentous pledge like the brothers they truly were. Thus, the two young men talked, vied with each other and sported together under the cathedral-like canopy of the woodland swamp and the great Cypress trees.

But events were taking place now outside the monastic isolation of Nethergate that could do nothing but divide friendships; divide families and indeed the whole nation. For the country was now truly at war with itself and the killing had started in earnest.

21

The Distant Rumblings Of War

Matthew was unusually well informed about the political situation in Kentucky as were most of the slaves who showed any concern for the progress of the two warring sides. Since his humiliation at the hands of Amelia Styles, Samuel had abandoned his hitherto aloof silence as the chief servant and custodian of the secrets of the big house and started to play a much more positive role within the slave community. He was an avid listener and reported all the conversations he heard from the influential people who flocked to Amelia's soirees. Thus, the slave body was kept well informed about the progress of the war and the opinions of their 'betters'.

It never ceased to amaze Samuel how the white men who came to the house seemed to assume that those who waited at table, ever alert to their bidding, should be no better able to follow the thread of a conversation than the furniture besides which they stood. Samuel, protected from suspicion by his long and close service to the Styles family, had for some time been a secret link for those slaves seeking to escape bondage. This indeed had been the cause of his public humiliation at Amelia's hands. Now he was part of another underground organisation which was beginning to form. It was led by those idealists in the North who were outraged at the very idea that slavery could exist in the 'land of the free'. It was that same land which their forebears had sought to create when they too had escaped from another sort of bondage from across the water. These organisations were led by enlightened whites of the North, but now drew in, in increasing numbers, the slaves themselves who were beginning to form a web of intrigue that was becoming ever more active.

As the war progressed, Matthew and George fell to discussing the gradually evolving military situation from a curiously dispassionate standpoint. Both were aware of where each other's sympathies lay, but they managed mostly to put that aside when reviewing the war's progress. Only rarely did their tempers flare, but it was soon put aside, for there was little they could do about it and both saw no reason why it should destroy their friendship.

Matthew saw all whites as his enemies, but George pointed out that even in the South, not all whites supported the Confederate cause. There were certainly enlightened idealists who favoured the cause of the North and many others who did not own slaves or were not dependent upon their labour and saw no reason to upset their lives for the cause of the nigger and his freedom. There was also the whole sub-culture of the poor whites who feared that the emergence of free blacks would usurp their place at the poor end of the economy and leave them struggling to survive.

"But when it comes down to it," George maintained, "you have to admit that slave labour is the engine that drives the economy in all the great estates in the south. Most great civilisations in the past have thrived on the product of slave labour. It is a natural condition of mankind. Without the work of slaves, the whole country's economy would falter and then we'd all be in a mess. It isn't the slavery issue that fires up the

Goddamn Yankees," he added with some truth, "it's the fear that the Confederate States could form a new country and then they would lose all the wealth the South generates with the European trade in tobacco and cotton."

"But if all that wealth comes from the work of us slaves, ain't it only right that we should have a share in all that prosperity? I has read some of 'dem books in Mrs Styles' library 'bout the 'rights of man'. I is a man. Ah don' hear nuttin' 'bout my rights."

There the two would have to leave it, for there was no agreement to be found across that great divide. Unlike many families, which became irreconcilably split over such issues, both knew instinctively when to abandon their disputes for the sake of their friendship.

Curiously, in religious matters they were united, but both from quite different standpoints. Matthew was a devout follower of Aaron the preacher, a freed slave, who Adrian Styles had appointed and was still in post, though getting old now. He was a staunch Quaker and an evangelist and had forthright views on the evils of slavery. He had been kept on under sufferance under Mark, who was wise enough to realise the unrest his dismissal would rouse.

Many thought that Aaron, with Samuel, were linked with the Underground Railroad which spirited runaways through the hands of activists and sympathisers across America to the Canadian border. At least that was their aim, but few escapes were planned affairs. Mostly slaves would be driven by the cruelty, ill-treatment or injustice of the moment, to flee from their persecutors without any plan, save the desire to be free from their immediate suffering. Often it was purely a matter of luck if they happened to fall into the hands of a sympathiser, or someone in the know, who might then pass them onto the Underground Railroad. More often, driven by want and hunger, or totally lost, they would be captured or betrayed, for there was usually a generous bounty to be had for the return of a runaway.

It was a curious feature of the first part of the war that the old laws about property still applied to runaways caught in Yankee territory. They were returned to their Confederate owners and the bounty claimed despite the war being in part about the abolition of slavery. It seemed to slaves that everyone's hand was turned against them. The rewards to be had led to an industry of 'bounty hunters'. Renowned for their cunning and ruthlessness in seeking out fleeing slaves. These agents made rich pickings from the trade in captured slaves and from accepting bribes for their silence from those who sheltered them.

Aaron ministered to his flock on the Nethergate Estate and his church was always full on those increasingly rare Sundays when his congregation was free from work in the fields and always on Christmas Days when all were free to worship. His flock filled the air with their enthusiasm and praise and leapt about as lively as a field of crickets. They were supremely confident that the Good Lord had a place for them in a heaven that was free from slavery, suffering and strife and from their white masters. Matthew loved these services and the spontaneous joy they evoked.

The white folk on the estate, by contrast, were orthodox Protestants who hatted and bonneted, sombrely and soberly paraded their conviction for all to see as they dutifully trekked to church. George found in himself an answering chord to this sombre, earnest declaration of faith. Every Sunday the Styles family would ride to Bentham Springs, their nearest church, in a convoy of carriages or on horseback where, reassuringly, God in his heaven and his army of angels and archangels were all in white. There the services were sedate and sincere, and salvation was assured to the righteous in seemly and serious tones. If ever the sermons touched on the issue of slavery, the congregation was asked to recall the parable of the talents and reminded that St Paul had bidden the runaway to go back to his master. So, all was right and ordered in the best of all possible worlds.

There was one aspect of all this that Matthew could never understand and for which George was hard put to find a logical explanation and that was how the North could be engaged in conflict over the issue of slavery, yet still returned those very slaves if apprehended, as captives to their owners in the South. "It's jus' the law o' the land," George would attempt to explain. "I suppose it is part of what the North was originally trying to do before the two sides split. It's jus' the rights of property, like stealing by finding."

That always riled Matthew. "So, us slaves is jus' property, like a barrel of nuts." They usually stopped at this point in an argument for fear of their tempers fraying, for both knew that that indeed was just what most slaves were to their white owners.

"Where I'm with you Brother," George would often say to cool things down, "is in despising those as makes a living by hunting down slaves and claiming the bounty for their capture."

"And de government in the North as takes the farms and living away from any they ketch sheltering a runaway."

"It's the new laws the North brought in to try and keep the South on side, I suppose," George would say, but neither were convinced by that.

"But even so," Matthew observed each time, "there are still brave people of conscience who are prepared to help the runaway, whatever the consequences."

"Yeh," George would concede, "but they are few and far between. S' far as you're concerned, it's better you stay here where you are safe rather than risk all in trying to get to Canada."

"Unless of course I joined the Yankee Army down here in Southern territory where there's fightin' to be done. They takes us in then, whilst they still returns those as escaped further North. Now how mad is that? They takes the wives and families too of those down here as wants to join the Yankee Army, houses them and gives them an education. They calls us Contraband Troops and pays us good money. Some even bears arms and fights too." It was an exciting thought for Matthew and one he had toyed with more than once.

"Then Brother," George would say, "Ah would be forced to kill you. Best I start now." At which point very often they would fall to fooling around and wrestling in mock combat, for the very idea of doing real harm to each other was so preposterous. Such light-hearted resolution of differences was not often repeated in many Southern families where brother fought against brother and father against son, fought and often died on opposing sides.

George, with his father, was of course already nominally a member of the local Militia and committed to the Confederate cause. His father, because of the number of slaves he owned, was excused military service. George had no such exemption and was aware of his own lack of military skills which he sought to put right before his time came to join the conflict. His commitment was due to what was expected of him and in this respect the Styles family were united.

Kentucky's role in the struggle was however far from one sided. Matthew, through the ears of Samuel, was almost as well informed as was George who had sat through many of the political discussions taking place at Nethergate House. Kentucky had, after supporting one side then the other, finally declared herself neutral and sought to play a conciliatory role to bring both sides together. But it soon became apparent that opinions were too deeply divided and feelings too entrenched, for this ever to be a feasible option. Instead Kentucky became a battleground for both sides to bleed out their differences with men fighting on either side with equal passion and conviction.

Much of the state, including Nethergate itself, was under the control of the Yankees.

The struggle had special resonance for George and Matthew, for both were now old enough to join in the struggle and felt the pull and the excitement common to all young men at the prospect of adventure. For Matthew, the consequences of joining the Union cause would be dire, for he would be an escaped slave and could never again come back to Nethergate or, perhaps ever, see his mother again. There was too the promise George had given him to grant him his freedom. That would not be possible once he joined the Yankee Army. It was not a choice to be taken lightly. But if the Union side won, then slavery itself might be abolished and then he imagined himself coming back as a conquering hero covered in glory, parading in triumph through the plantation fields. As for George, his position at Nethergate guaranteed him the bars of a Second Lieutenant whenever he felt ready. But for him there was a reluctance to leave Nethergate for thoughts of Ursula and the fear of what his mother might yet do to her. His greatest anxiety was that if he went away he might come back to find that she had been sold.

22

The War Comes To Nethergate

The war between North and South had had little impact thus far upon the even tenor of life on the Nethergate Estate. There had been much talk among the slaves as to what the outcome might be for them. Some burned with the desire for a Northern victory and the freedom to move north with their families and to start life afresh in the burgeoning industries of the north. Others, particularly the more elderly who had known no other life but slavery, supported the cause of their owners. They were full of dread for an uncertain future as age sapped their usefulness. They wished for nothing more than to continue in their bondage praying that their masters would honour their obligations to them.

George had listened at his mother's gatherings to the talk about the battles so far with their appalling casualty figures on both sides. To the majority though, they were simply numbers unless they included a loved one. Few could imagine the carnage of the battlefield unless they had witnessed the slaughter first hand. Only the plantation owners and white society were passionate about following the course of the war and many of those had already joined up to the Confederate cause. Some though had taken an opposite view with family members on both sides. There was much bitterness and dissention within the Commonwealth of Kentucky.

There were plenty of stories too and pictures and paintings depicting the industrial poverty of the north, aimed mainly at the poor whites. Images in pamphlets and periodicals abounded showing the squalor in which many families lived in the industrial cities with jobs at the whim of mine and factory owners. Starvation and death was the inevitable lot of those who through injury, illness or ill luck could no longer find work. Such a stark contrast to the southern states portraying the aging nigger, his gnarled old hands resting upon his cane as he watched the world go by from his cabin door in relaxed and contented retirement. In a curious way, the niggers looked down on the poor whites as lesser creatures than themselves.

Only once had the war come close to Nethergate. There had been great excitement when a squadron of cavalry rode through on their way to Bowling Green. Even the overseers had stopped to watch the spectacle. The slaves resting on hoe and fork watched the tossing heads of the horses as they rode through. The martial clatter and creaking of the harnesses, the stern weather-ruddy faces of the soldiers, and the mud splattered horses, all told of a resolute purpose and of the certainty and utter invincibility of the Confederate cause.

At the front were two Officers with gold braid on their shoulders riding magnificent hunters whose flanks gleamed with recent grooming, despite the mire on stomach and hocks. They both wore impressive moustaches showing that these two were clearly professional men of war. At their horses' heels trotted two fine greyhounds as if ready to join in the sport that warfare offered. All knew of the superiority of the Southern cavalry over anything the North could muster. Surely nothing could withstand such military extravagance.

There was great interest too when the baggage train rumbled through the estate for there amongst the soldiers were one or two black faces, wearing Confederate uniforms, clearly part of the struggle too. A cheer went up from the fields when they came into view and they waved back with bright-toothed grins. None carried weapons though like the rest of the soldiers.

The next day when they were all at work they had stopped and looked up in wonder at the sudden roll of thunder that came out of the west under the clear Kentucky sky. Then realisation dawned that it was the angry rumble of the guns sounding as if the very hills were at war. All marvelled that such power could be produced by the hand of man. On and on it seemed to go, salvo answering salvo all gathering together into one endless discordant grumbling and booming. The slaves glanced at each other in wonder that mankind could muster such titanic forces to their bidding. When at last it abated, they could hear the angry snap and crackle of rifle and musket like dry pine needles thrown suddenly onto a fire. With it came the knowledge that even as they listened men were dying in their droves. That night the cabins were full of excited talk and speculation.

The next day the excitement grew, for on that day they had witnessed the soldiers returning from the conflict. It was clear from the soldiers' deportment that it had all fallen far short of a victory. The soldiers' heads were down and there was no response to the tentative cheer the slaves offered, which quickly died on their lips at the dispirited faces of the men. Only one officer now rode at the head of the troops and only one greyhound trod at his heels. There were few now on horseback and there was no suggestion of military formations as they streamed past in broken ranks in one long dispirited convoy. Many bore the marks of battle, torn and dirtied uniforms, bandaged limbs and the occasional blood stain. Some were wounded and bore the marks of attempted dressings, their desire to remain with their companions stronger than their longing to lie down and rest. What few horses remained fit, carried those unable to walk. Many of the horses were bloodied and some limped. Those that were no longer able to carry a mount were nursed along by their erstwhile riders. At one point one such pair fell away from the line, the horse clearly unable to go on. The soldier stood by his mount caressing its nose and speaking to it for what seemed an age. Then a sudden shot rang out and the soldier was swallowed once more in the stream of human misery leaving a black mound twitching by the roadside.

Only one or two wagons now lurched and jolted after the soldiers. The groans and cries that came from within bore witness to the nature of their cargo. Of the bulk of the baggage train which had so confidently followed the soldiers into battle a few days before, there was no sign. To the back of one of the wagons George noted one of the fine hunters he had seen a few days before, but now its head was down and it seemed barely able to walk. Beside it, limped a lone and trembling dog, ears down, tail firmly planted betwixt its legs.

George, watching the sorry spectacle, felt a sudden surge of savage loyalty to the Confederate cause, a longing to be one of their number, to play his part and to avenge those left, stiffened and dead on the field of battle. He wanted to play his part in this great adventure before it was all too late, and history had passed him by. What right had the Northern states to impose their will and their way of life upon the South? He saw in his mind the broad parkland about the Nethergate estate and Nethergate Hall set like a jewel in its midst. Then he thought of the grime and squalor of the great Northern industrial towns. He was gripped by anger at their presumption and perhaps for the first time felt a real hatred for his northern country-folk. Were it not for his preoccupation with Ursula he thought that he might have volunteered that very moment. He turned away from the spectre of defeat as it threaded its sorry way through the estate, feeling a rush of guilt at his own selfishness.

23

Sickness And Freedom

Matthew had led a charmed life as far as the usual childhood ailments were concerned. He had hardly known a day's sickness. Now as a young man he was tall and straight and ready to shrug off whatever ailments the world might throw at him. Ruth was therefore more than usually concerned when Matthew one day complained of a sore throat and loss of appetite. Within twenty-four hours the fever was upon him. He lay tossing and turning on his bed, the sheets sodden with the fever sweats, barely conscious of the visitations of his mother, Morella and Mrs Styles, their concerns etched deeply into their faces.

The family doctor was called from New Haven. He diagnosed swamp fever and prescribed his own brand of medicine, but Matthew refused to take it. Then he lapsed into a coma and was only dimly conscious of the ghostly ministering of the women floating in and out of his awareness. For over a fortnight he hovered between life and death. At last, as suddenly as it had arrived, the fever left him, and he woke one morning clear-headed, the world white, still and somehow pristine about him. He was as weak as a new born kitten.

It was another fortnight before he was strong enough to venture outside again. There was great rejoicing in the household, for Matthew was a popular figure with his fellow slaves, regardless of his special status and all were relieved to see him recovered. All too had noted the distress of their Mistress. Many too might have wondered why she should be quite so upset at the illness of a slave, albeit a much favoured one. Such was the affection that they all had for Mrs Styles that her evident relief and happiness at Matthew's recovery was a cause for double rejoicing.

When it was clear that there was no longer any danger Mary Styles announced her intention of travelling north on her long-delayed visit to her family. Ruth of course was to travel with her. The household was thrown into a bustle of activity.

For Ruth, this journey had a special significance. It was to be a journey into a totally new world, a journey that filled her with both fear and excitement. Ruth had often gone over in her mind that conversation she had had with her Mistress when she had first broached the matter of their journey to see her family in New York. She knew that for a slave to masquerade as a free woman was against the law and that if she let her Mistress down then they would both be in trouble. However, she suspected that she was likely to suffer more than her Mistress, but she was prepared to take the added risk. She knew it was in part for the benefit of Matthew, as a way for Mary to persuade her father to accept Matthew as his great grandson in the same way as she too had accepted him as her grandson by blood. She had been practising her new role of learning to address her Mistress as a lady's companion would and no longer as a lady's maid. The two of them in the secrecy of her rooms had been playing out their roles together. It became a game they enacted each evening. Mary bade her to sit down with her and encouraged her protégée to voice opinions and to join in imagined conversations and schooled her in the current views and opinions. But in truth Ruth had observed so much already that she felt reasonably secure in her new guise.

It had been a conspiracy that the two had shared like a guilty schoolgirl secret. Mary had taken a particular delight in all the subterfuge. There were papers ready allowing them both to travel in their new guise. Anthony had raised no objections to Ruth travelling with his mother and had warned her of the consequences should Ruth take advantage of finding herself in Union Territory and decide to stay there. But Mary had pointed out that with her son still on the estate, she would hardly defect. The two women had worked out their relationship and how they met and a complete family history for Ruth. There had been shopping trips to the big emporia in Clarksville when the two of them had entered the changing rooms together for fittings, but the clothes were for Ruth and not for Mary. The shop assistants were puzzled as to why this lady of mature years should seem to take such delight in clothing intended for a lady far younger and they had both enjoyed their obvious mystification. When seamstresses were necessary it was explained that Mary had a daughter with an identical shape to her maid. Their disapproval at a slave being allowed to try on some of their clothing was all too apparent. It was as if she was contaminated in some way. Until this moment it had all been a game. Now with an actual date set for their departure, the prospect was unnerving enough to cause Ruth some sleepless nights.

"When we leave Nethergate, you will leave as a slave," explained Mary, not for the first time. "At our first stop we will make the transformation. You will emerge as simply my companion. Lots of widowed ladies my age take a poorer relation or a friend of a friend with them for the companionship and everyone will assume that is who you are. No-one will ever suspect. You have many of the features of a European and skin colour lighter than many a Spaniard of my acquaintance."

Ruth felt a growing surge of excitement as the date for their departure drew nearer and an overwhelming sense of gratitude to her mistress. At the same time, she was filled with dread at the thought of masquerading as a white woman and the consequences and possible humiliation of discovery. Just the thought of living life as a free woman, even for a short time, was a heady tonic. She wondered whether she could pull it off. It was an outrageous thing to do, to break the law in this way, but her whole being revelled at the thought.

She wondered how she would feel when for a few magic weeks, she would be able to shed the shackles of slavery and be truly herself. She thought too of her return. How would she react to being a slave again after tasting the heady wine of freedom? It was a thought that she was certain had not occurred to her mistress, but she thrust it to the back of her mind, determined to make the most of the weeks of adventure that lay ahead. For Ruth, it was a Cinderella moment, for Mary it was striking out against the very idea of slavery.

There was however one other individual who anticipated the date of their departure with perhaps a greater eagerness than did the two ladies concerned. When Killcaid learnt of their plans, he had immediately reminded Anthony of his promise concerning the re-employment of Matthew back in the fields. Anthony had not demurred, but only insisted that nothing should be done until they had both departed for New York. Killcaid savoured the moment.

24

Old Mo's Secret

Whilst Ruth was contemplating the new adventure in her life, Matthew was considering the implications of another event destined to change his life too.

When Matthew was fully recovered and beginning to regain his strength, Morella came to see him to fulfil a promise she had made to Old Mo during his sickness. She had not realised how important Old Mo had become to Matthew and his message had almost slipped her mind, but for the curious piece of cloth he had given her. She drew Matthew aside and presented him with the remnant of cloth which she pulled out from under her waistband.

"This fo' you Matthew. It come from Old Mo." She handed it over to Matthew as if it were a sacred relic.

Matthew was puzzled. Why on earth should Old Mo want to send him a piece of sacking? "What is it?" he asked.

"There's things on it," advised Morella. "Old Mo wanted particular fo' you to have it afore he left. He kept pressin' me. Yo' be sure to give it to young Matthew he say. There were tears in his eyes."

Sudden alarm filled Matthew. "Afore he left? Where is Old

Mo?" he asked, already dreading what he might hear, for he had not yet felt well enough to venture down to the bayou.

"A' course you don' know," replied Morella. "Old Mo suddenly got lazy. Stopped producing all the food he been a'getting for the overseers and fo' dem niggers in the cabins too. So Killcaid he ups and tells him to keep the game coming or he will sell him." She snorted with contempt for Killcaid. "He be gone now well over a two week."

"Oh no!" An involuntary cry of grief escaped from Matthew's lips. He was overwhelmed. He felt a searing sense of loss. He had not realised how fond he had grown of the intrepid, indomitable old trapper with his fund of stories and his wisdom and knowledge of the world as he saw it. He had accepted his lot in life as a slave but had never owned the superiority of his white masters or lost his own sense of self. Within the bounds of slavery, he had shone out as a truly free spirit. Now he had gone, and Matthew would never see him again. Even Old Mo could not survive for long in the world where age alone would condemn him. He would be at the very end of the slave chain, fit for little but the most menial of tasks. He would be worked for as long as he breathed and was capable and then left to die through lack of care and medication. Not for the first time a burning sense of bitterness and resentment engulfed Matthew and for those who owned him too, body and soul.

He also felt an irrational sense of guilt. Had he been well he might have persuaded George to intervene. In any event, if he had been there to help Old Mo it would never have happened. It was all his fault. The enigmatic mystery and fascination of the bayou would never be quite the same again. Then his eye fell on the piece of sacking that Old Mo had wanted him to have. He knew that Old Mo could not write, but did it contain a message? He remembered how Old Mo had always said that he had a plan for the end of his life and how his friendship with

Matthew and Matthew's help had brought him more time to see it through.

It seemed though that time had run out for Old Mo, before his plans could be perfected. Now he had been shipped off somewhere to end his life in a spiral of misery and deprivation that in the end would break even his feisty old spirit.

He opened out the piece of sacking. On it there were designs etched in charcoal. He turned it round and round, not making any sense of it. Along one corner there ran it seemed a random wavering line. Then in a fold of the hessian he recognised what looked like the outline of a boat and suddenly it all began to make sense. There was the creek on the river where Old Mo had hidden the dug out and a fish entwined by an eel, where he had taught Matthew the ways of catching fish and eels. There was a pattern of trails which Matthew recognised. Gradually the whole puzzle fell into place. Then Matthew spotted one area that he did not recognise, a trail he did not know, marked with crosses. At the end of it there was what looked like a cabin decorated about with necklaces of beads.

Consumed with curiosity he declared himself fit enough to venture out once more on horseback and straight away made his way down to the bayou. He was buoyed up with hope too. Despite talking to those who had seen Old Mo shipped off to the slave market, such was his confidence in the spirited old man he had come so much to admire, that he half hoped he might somehow be there still.

The tobacco was nearing harvest time and he had no choice but to pass by where some of the slaves were busy hoeing between the plants and cutting the first leaves. As he passed one of the slaves recognised him and waved a cheery greeting, for all had been aware of his sickness.

"Glad to see yo' up and about Boy." Spotting the movement and hearing the cry of welcome, the others looked up and spontaneously followed suit with cries of greeting. Then as one they looked away and resumed their toil. The reason became apparent, for riding towards him was Killcaid. Matthew stood his ground.

Killcaid reigned in beside him.

"Mighty glad to see you have recovered," he said, then added with a humourless chuckle, "We all thought we was goin' to have a runaway on our hands."

Matthew nodded politely. He wasn't entirely sure what Killcaid meant.

"Well good day to you Mr Killcaid," he said. In his present weakened state, he had no wish to tangle with Killcaid and turned to go. But Killcaid laid a restraining hand upon his bridle.

"I hear you was very near a runaway to the Promised Land," he said by way of explanation for his previous remark. And he chuckled dryly at his own witticism. Then his face took on a look of stony menace. "Remember this boy, no-one escapes from Killcaid that easy, most of all you. Even if yo's dead, you'll never get away from me. I'll come after you to the very gates of hell and back."

Then it was he who turned and left leaving Matthew wondering precisely what Killcaid had meant, but never doubting for a moment the man's implacable hatred.

However, the excitement of deciphering Old Mo's map soon banished any feelings of foreboding and he hastened into the leafy shelter of the bayou. He tethered his horse where there was a bit of grazing and ventured deeper into the swampland to where Mo and he had concealed the dug out. It was still there only partially filled with rainwater which he soon spilled out, the effort, though, was a reminder of his weakened state. Paddling the canoe through the weed-thick waters, he was soon able to locate the tracks they had always used, but try as he might he could not locate the track marked with crosses. Then it dawned upon him that it might not be a track at all, but perhaps another watercourse. He soon found it, partly concealed by vegetation and hard to spot if you were not looking out for it. Soon he was poling up the channel noting the crosses carved on the trees, following it until it split. He was full of doubt as to which route to take until he spotted on the bark of one of the swamp cypress trees another small cross. After that the route was easy to follow and soon the stream ran into a small lake that must have been the source of the watercourse. At one point the vegetation had been trampled down and there was a small jetty. Matthew tied up the boat and followed the track that led up towards higher ground. Following the crosses, Matthew was led to a small clump of trees. Thrusting his way through he was met with a sight which made him gasp in astonishment.

What now lay before him was Old Mo's secret, his solution for when he grew old. The thought of how it had been so cruelly snatched away from him before it could bear fruit filled Matthew with the deepest remorse. If only he could have been there to help Old Mo with his daily quota of game, this would never have happened.

This was Old Mo's retreat, where he meant to seize his freedom at a time of his own choosing. Here in this secluded secret spot, he had bit by bit over the years constructed his retirement home. On some five acres of rising ground he had built a sturdy log cabin complete with a veranda for him to sit out and enjoy the sun. All about he had planted patches of vegetables and fruits, which now bore the signs of a month's neglect. This was the necklace that Matthew had seen on the map.

Almost as if approaching a shrine, Matthew edged forward. The door creaked open. He still half expected to find the old man waiting for him. The stale musty smell of a house too

151

long shut up met his nostrils, but otherwise the cabin bore little signs of neglect. Old Mo had thought of everything. All was spick and span. Two serviceable chairs and a table, a fireplace of stone and even a stove for cooking, goodness knows where he had got that from, but Old Mo was nothing if not resourceful. There were shelves on which plates and pans were neatly stacked. In one corner, there was a bed with animal skins for blankets. It was in every sense a ready-for-occupation retirement home. Suddenly, all about him Matthew felt the presence of Old Mo. He had the strangest feeling that if he were to turn about Old Mo would be standing there, just behind him with his battered and greasy hat still firmly planted on his scarred old crown. There would be that sparkling twinkle in his eye that belied the often-sour look of his face in repose. Matthew's eyes filled with tears as he thought how cruelly Old Mo had been robbed of this, the fruits of all his labours. Killcaid must have moved more quickly than Old Mo had anticipated, robbing him of the chance to pre-empt his departure by making his own escape to his own promised land. He felt his eyes stinging with tears at the thought of Old Mo, at the eleventh hour being robbed of this, his final bid for freedom.

Then almost as if Old Mo himself were speaking, a thought came to him in a sudden exhilarating rush. This was his chance now – made possible by the labours of that indomitable old trapper. He could take hold of his own destiny as Old Mo had tried to take hold of his. A plan was already forming in his mind. Once his mother was away he would make a break for freedom. Not even George would know. He would ride out the hunt and clamour of his escape and all the posters and rewards that Killcaid would broadcast about, simply by living in Old Mo's cabin. Then, after a month or two, when all hue and cry had subsided, he would make his break for freedom and join the Yankee Army. He would be a soldier, playing his own small part in freeing his brother slaves. The thought and his own sudden resolution were intoxicating. Yet he would not be rushed. He would need to take a careful inventory of all that was here and consider all his needs for at least three months and then at a time of his choosing, just as Old Mo had planned, seize his freedom from slavery.

25

A Victim Of The Bayou

Matthew's rapid recovery continued, now enhanced by his new resolve to decide upon his own future. Whilst the rest of the household was preoccupied with preparing for his Mistress's journey north, he had paid further visits to Old Mo's retreat. He began slowly to transport those other necessities down to the cabin in preparation for a prolonged stay. He had also set about restoring Old Mo's garden of fruit and vegetables from the month of neglect following his sale. It was not an unfamiliar task, drawing as he did from the knowledge acquired from helping the gardener at Nethergate House. He continued to meet up with George who was mightily glad to see him restored to good health and they resumed their friendship and meetings down in the bayou. George though now seemed to be increasingly concerned with seeking ways of meeting up with Ursula.

Matthew was careful to keep Old Mo's secret from George. However deep their friendship, the difference between slave and free would perhaps always lie between them until Matthew was himself a free man. That would not be until either George fulfilled his promise, or until Matthew achieved that aim himself. In any case he wanted to save his friend from the necessity of lying when the moment came for him to put his plan into action.

As the time for the departure of Mrs Styles and his mother drew near, his excitement mounted. He felt sad at the parting from his mother and longed to confide in her. She had always been such a dogged and determined figure, always there for him. Now she was going away. He knew how much she had suffered and how resolutely she had protected him from the overseers and most of all from Killcaid. She had too over the years prevented him from falling victim to the wilful impulses of his own character. He longed to tell her how much he cared for her and how deeply he respected all that she had done for him, but he knew she would immediately sense that something was afoot, and he did not want to implicate her. He decided instead that he would wait until both had finally left for New York. Then he would write her a letter explaining what he had done and why and put into words all the love, affection and respect he felt for her. He would leave it in her room for her to find on her return.

When the time finally came for them to say goodbye he held her in a tight embrace, so much so that afterwards she looked at him quizzically, as she had so often done when he was a child and she suspected him of some mischief. Unexpectedly too, Mrs Styles embraced him briefly as they were about to depart, but with an unexpected warmth.

Both women were excited at the prospect of their travels. For Mrs Styles, it was a return to where she had lived as a child. She longed to see her father again. Her mother was not well, but her father had not enlarged upon her ailments, other than to say that she had become increasingly forgetful and vague.

Ruth too was filled with excitement in anticipation of her first taste of real freedom when she would leave the life of a slave behind her. It was an exhilarating prospect. She had never really been away from Nethergate apart from the recent shopping trips with Mary. It was the first time too that she had been separated from her son. She wondered at the unusual demonstration of affection at their parting. Maybe he too felt the tug of their departure as she did. Perhaps she might have read more into it had she not been so preoccupied with her own forthcoming adventure.

Silas Killcaid had been awaiting their departure too, but with a vengeful anticipation. He had been savouring this moment ever since the Master had promised him he could have Matthew as a field hand during old Mrs Styles' absence. He wasted no time. The carriage had barely swept down the long drive, loaded with baggage, before he had reminded Anthony yet again of his promise. Anthony had merely nodded, knowing this day would surely come and hoping that he might somehow return Matthew to Nethergate House when he got news of his mother's return.

Silas Killcaid sent two of his overseers to Nethergate House to find and fetch Matthew. Killcaid relished the moment when he would wipe that studied look of arrogance off Matthew's face. He had so many scores to settle. He had never really tried to analyse his aversion to Matthew, but then self-analysis was not in Silas's nature. It was just that the boy was so condescending and somehow contemptuous of Killcaid's position and of Killcaid himself. He was convinced that with the advantage of some learning and his power of mimicry he was not only laughing at him but inducing laughter in others too. He could not bear the thought of the scorn that comes with laughter. Hitherto protected by old Mrs Styles, Matthew had been immune. Not anymore. Killcaid relished the months ahead. His tongue ran across his thin lips in anticipation.

Matthew however was not at Nethergate House. The

Overseers had been warned not to come away empty handed, so they settled down to wait for his return.

George had been due his music lesson on the day of his grandmother's departure and after waving her a fond farewell he had returned to Nethergate Hall. He had seen Matthew, but the two boys remained as strangers when others were about. He had watched Matthew riding beside the carriage down to see Mary and his mother off the estate before returning to Nethergate House.

After his music lesson, George had gone to his rooms to prepare for another visit to the bayou later that day. There he found Manuel preparing his things for his master's afternoon outing. It was then that he learnt of Killcaid's plans, for they were common knowledge among the slaves. News of the overseers' presence at Nethergate House had spread with alacrity.

Manuel in his slow lugubrious way was shaking his head.

"Don't reckon on a couple of chuck-peas fo' dat poor Matthew now Mr Killcaid got his hooks in him," he muttered.

"What d' you mean?" asked George, immediately alert.

Manuel explained the situation and what Killcaid intended to do in the absence of old Mrs Styles. As soon as he heard the news George was full of concern for his friend and straight away resolved to warn him of the danger. He ordered Manuel to bring his horse immediately. He was in a lather of anxiety lest his warning should come too late. He had to warn Matthew of the danger before he returned to Nethergate House.

He set off at a gallop following the route his grandmother had taken. But the road off the estate was clear of travellers. George knew that Matthew would not have gone too far along the road without a travel certificate, which in the haste of departure he doubted Matthew would have obtained. He therefore concluded that by now Matthew must have returned to the estate. It was possible that he had gone straight to their rendezvous down in the bayou and not returned to Nethergate House. He might still be in time to warn him.

Accordingly, he headed straight down to the bayou. He tethered his horse in the usual spot, well hidden from any likely prying eyes, and made his way down to the place where he and Matthew usually met. There was an old log there under which they would place a set number of twigs. It was a code they had agreed to indicate where in the bayou they might be. The space under the log was empty. George stared about him listening hard, but all he could hear was the whispering intimacy of the swamp life teaming about him, the wandering call of the birds high in the Cypress tree canopy above his head and the mocking chuckles of the gallinules. Everything seemed set to scorn his growing sense of crisis.

George knew that once Matthew returned to Nethergate House he would be in the hands of Killcaid. His father would do nothing to rescue his mother's favoured household slave. The thought of what life would be like without Matthew's friendship and company already filled him with a sense of loss. Precisely what the two of them could do about the situation was still vague at the back of his mind. All that was necessary for the moment was to warn Matthew in time for him to escape falling into the hands of Silas Killcaid.

With a caution born of respect George followed the various secret trails ever deeper into the swamp to places he and Matthew had visited before. In desperation now, he began to call out Matthew's name, but his cries seemed but puny bleating, swallowed up in the enormous, lonely expanse of the marsh.

Such was his anxiety to find Matthew that he allowed his concentration to lapse. In his haste, he did not take the usual care that Matthew had instilled into him when venturing into the more dangerous parts of the bayou. For a time, he had been ankle deep in water following the signs that he and Matthew had laid.

He stopped suddenly. He did not recognise the spot in which he now stood. All their way-marks were etched on prominent trees or other features. There was nothing here he recognised. Although he had been splashing through water the ground remained firm enough under his feet. Now the water was half way to his knees. Already the weed was closing over where he had been. His back-trail was vanishing as he looked. A thin icicle of fear crept over him freezing his mind with indecision. A water snake swam past him. At least it knew where it was going. Then he turned, telling himself to keep calm. With infinite care, he began to edge his way back. Step by step he retraced his route over the way he thought he had come, searching for a familiar landmark.

Suddenly the ground gave way under his feet. 'Lie flat'! It was what Matthew always said. He'd done it too when Matthew was with him one time. 'Above all keep calm', was what Matthew always repeated. He could hear him saying it now, but it was all very well when there were two of you. Now he was alone. He felt the panic rising within him and he began to struggle. Straight away his legs were gripped in the unyielding quagmire. The more he struggled the deeper he foundered. Each time he tried to pull one leg free, the other was forced yet more deeply into the bog.

His curses soon gave way to cries of panic. He had never felt so alone. Surely this was not how it was all going to end. The mire was nearly up to his waist now. Every movement simply sucked him deeper in. There was nothing under his feet to push against. His cries now became screams of terror.

Exhausted at last he stopped, aware of the thumping of his heart and the hopelessness of his situation. He had failed to warn Matthew and now Matthew would be in the clutches of Killcaid and any vain hope that he might hear his cries and come to his rescue were dashed. Old Mo had long since been sold. There was no-one to hear his cries. A strange calm seemed to wash over him. He tried now to lie back in the water as Matthew had shown him, but now the lower half of his body was too firmly embedded for it to make any difference. He thought of his parents, but mostly he thought of Ursula. Would she grieve for him? How he wished things could have been different between them. If only she had not been a slave. If ever he got out of this he vowed he would confess his love for her, shout it from the rooftops. He would not let his parents stand in his way.

"I love you!" he shouted as if that would make his vow known to all the world. But there was no-one to hear him and he fell silent. He felt the water creeping ever higher over his waist.

Slowly the swamp came alive again, no longer stilled by his terrified cries. The sounds of life going on about him suddenly took on an awesome significance. He heard them as if for the very first time. They would go on today, tomorrow for maybe a hundred years or more whereas he would be sucked into the bowels of the earth, to suffer a slow and agonising death?

Tears sprang to his eyes as he gave way to despair and to a whole world of sorrow for what might have been. But mostly it was for him and for Ursula. With his despair came a welling up of protest at the cruelty of fate which found expression in one last long bellow of dissent.

"No! No! – No!" he cried.

26

Rescue At A Cost

It is almost impossible to keep things secret in a slave compound. Rumours abound. Information and the power that it gives is the life-blood of such communities. Thus, the doings of master and mistress in which one's own future is inextricably interwoven becomes a constant source of speculation and innuendo. The activities of fellow slaves also take on an added importance as each slave seeks to better his lot sometimes even at the expense of his companions. But then that is only human nature, common to slave and freeman alike. The timely passing on of information often becomes a matter for fine judgement as to whether the recipient might someday be able to repay that kindness.

Thus it was that as Matthew returned to the estate, bound for Nethergate House and the two waiting overseers, he was waved down by Laticia. Laticia was one of the young slaves who had recently been a house-slave to Killcaid, with all that that implied. He though had grown tired of her and she had been replaced by another. She had lost her influence and was thus seeking to build bridges and to forge other alliances.

Matthew reigned in his mount and stared down curiously at where she stood.

"What is it Laticia?" he asked, still wary of her and not certain whether she still held any influence with Killcaid.

"It be just what I have heard," she started, "Maybe 'tis important, but there again maybe it baint," she added with a shrug of her pretty shoulders.

"What is?" asked Matthew, curious despite himself.

"It's just as I heard say that once the Mistress has left for the north, Killcaid means to take you back to work in the fields."

This was not the first time that Matthew had heard such talk, but now coming from someone who had been so close to Killcaid, he felt he dare not ignore the warnings. He had not expected Killcaid to act so quickly after the departure of the old Mrs Styles. He had already added enough to the items in Old Mo's cabin to ensure his survival, but he had not taken down any personal items for fear of alerting his mother. Almost everything else could be classed as luxuries.

For a moment, he hesitated at this news. He considered riding after his mother and appealing to Mrs Styles. But what would he say? He could hardly expect her to delay her departure and return on the word of a slave's rumour. He had just not anticipated that Killcaid would have dared to move so soon. But he had not reckoned on the vindictiveness of Nethergate's black-hearted overseer either.

Matthew remembered his time in the fields as a boy, the sting of the lash and the degradation of being treated like a pack animal, prodded, whipped, goaded and occasionally rewarded for good work. Chiefly he remembered the humiliation it brought with it. He had made the resolution long ago, but now was the first time he had acknowledged it even to himself. He would never go back to working in the fields again. He would never play the placid packhorse, the farmhand slave. No. Now was to be the moment in which he took the direction of his life into his own hands.

"Thanks, Laticia. I won't forget this," he said. She smiled, happy that she had found an ally in Matthew.

"What will you do?" she asked full of apparent concern.

"Head up north," he said as if coming to a sudden decision, "maybe try to reach Canada or join the Yankees," he added. With that he turned his horse and headed for the road out of the estate. He was filled with a strange elation. He had done it. He had taken the decision and acted upon it. He wasn't fully prepared, but no matter. There would be no turning back now. He had at last taken control of his own life.

As soon as he was out of sight of Laticia, he changed direction and took the track for the bayou. He had no doubt that Old Mo's retreat would never be discovered by anyone without a thorough knowledge of the bayou and all its treacherous ways. His head was already full of how he would live over the next month or so. It would be truly a 'return to nature', as he had read about in the writings of Rousseau in old Mrs Styles' library. He would live out this ideal until he judged the time was right to join the Yankee Army. Then he would fight for the freedom of all slaves. He felt as if he were truly alive for the first time in his whole life. Now his life had a sense of purpose. Such was his inner elation that he let out a great holler of pure elation that caused his horse to dance and skitter in the road.

On the edge of the swamplands he halted and released the horse. It would find its own way back. He hoped his pursuers would think he had abandoned it because a mounted slave would be more conspicuous than one on foot.

Back at Nethergate House, the overseers waited with growing anxiety and uncertainty, hoping for his return, but not daring to go back to Killcaid empty handed. Soon the news of Matthew's escape was everywhere, but no-one dared to tell Killcaid for fear of his rage, no-one that is except Laticia.

For Laticia it was a simple choice. This way she was backing both horses and maybe it might just bring her back into Killcaid's favour.

"Ah seed dat Matthew boy," she told him. "'Bout two hour ago. He stop by me an say, 'Ah hears dat Killcaid is after me. Ah's not waitin', ah's high-tailin' it right out'a here.' Said he were heading to join the Yankees and that's the truth! Then I come direct to find you Silas, I surely did." With that she put a tentative hand on Killcaid's arm.

Killcaid swore and his eyes blazed with fury. He pushed Laticia roughly aside. An escaped slave was a priority. It was one of the few excuses to divert manpower from the fields. It would be a warning for them all, of the fate that would be theirs should any of them decide to follow suit and desert their workplace. The sooner the pursuit started the better the chance of a capture, before the fugitive had the opportunity to contact those who might shelter him before nightfall.

Laticia was brusquely questioned and revealed the direction in which she had seen Matthew heading. Killcaid gathered together a posse, from the field hands who could ride, and sent for the horses. His little band were delighted at the prospect of some diversion from the tedium of tending the tobacco plants. All was jostle and excitement. Killcaid considered calling out the coonhounds, but this would take too much time, knowing that mounted Matthew would travel a considerable distance. He determined to follow Matthew's trail whilst it was still warm. He would surely follow the road at the point he had left Laticia to cover as much mileage as possible.

Soon the hue and cry was well underway, with the riders following the road and another group of the youngest and fittest going on foot. They were to take a short cut through the estate that met up with the road going north, hoping to cut Matthew off. In truth, the slaves all enjoyed such activities. Whilst hoping that one of their number might make his escape, they were not immune to the rewards that awaited the captors. Besides, it was a welcome diversion from the monotony of the fields. Whatever the outcome the pursuers intended to make as much of the diversion as they could. With whoops and hollers they set about each allotted task making as much noise and clamour as they dared, hoping thereby at least to give the fugitive as much warning as they could of their approach.

Meanwhile, far from the clamour of pursuit, Matthew was heading deeper into the shelter of the bayou. He was still buoyed up with the euphoria of at last taking hold of his own destiny and the excitement of a new future. It felt good.

The lush green shelter of the bayou enfolded him like an old friend. For the first time since his decision to run he felt safe and secure. Cautiously he made his way to where he had left Old Mo's dug out, being careful to leave no trace of his passing. When he reached it, he paused, listening carefully for any sound of pursuit.

Slowly the familiar clamour of the bayou returned to wash reassuringly about him. Then he heard it: a far-away, distant cry, a cry of distress, but not the sound of a beast in pain. He listened hard, trying to separate the new sound from the babble of noise about him. The cry came again. Unbelievably it sounded like someone shouting his name. Then the cries became less distinct. His first thought was that it might be a trap. Then the shouts became edged with panic. George! It could only be George who would seek for him in the bayou. Surely, he would not have joined the chase? Despite their friendship, George was after all a white man and would be the owner of slaves someday, his owner even. Newly a fugitive, he read treachery at every turn.

No. Not George. He dismissed the thought and dug in the paddle surging towards the commotion. The noise of his own exertions drowned out the cries. He stopped again, listening hard. It was difficult to be sure of their direction. The voice had now taken on a new note, tinged with despair and hopelessness. Then came one last, long sobbing cry of regret. "No. No. No!"

"I'm coming! I'm coming!" he shouted.

27

The Rescue

George fell silent. The water about him felt warm, heated by his own body and his frantic struggles. He was overcome by the sadness and pointlessness of his situation. How could all just end like this in slow suffocation? He imagined the moment when the waters would reach his mouth and his nose and his desperate last struggles for air and for life and he gave way to hopelessness.

Matthew had been listening hard. Hearing now no new sounds he headed in the direction of that last desperate cry. He knew now that George must be in some terrible danger. He dug deep with his paddles wishing that the dug out was a little less cumbersome.

His sense of direction did not betray him. Suddenly Matthew burst in upon the scene of George's peril. He was appalled by the sight which met his eyes.

"What the hell you bin thinking of?" was all he could say. "I warned you of the dangers of going off our routes."

"Thank God you're here. I was looking for you," sobbed his friend. "I needed to warn you about Killcaid. He's after you. You gotta help me. I'm stuck fast."

The words struck home like an arrow. How could he have doubted his friend? How could he have thought it was part of a trap? Now here he was facing a ghastly death and all because of him. Matthew quickly set about in a frenzied attempt to free his friend. George clung to him frantically almost causing the dug out to capsize in his anxiety.

"Steady George! You'll have us both in the water," shouted Matthew fighting to free himself. "Hang on to the boat. See if you can ease yourself free?" George's panic subsided. He tried to do as Matthew suggested, but he could not get sufficient purchase. Matthew tried to pull him free, but the dug out began to fill with water. As the two boys struggled Matthew explained how he had already been warned of Killcaid's intentions by Laticia and had decided to make a bid for freedom.

The two boys kept trying everything they could think of to ease George from the swamp's deadly hold, but the quagmire was not to be so easily cheated of its victim. The suction about George's body was too much for their combined strengths alone.

Both young men were nearing exhaustion. George's eyes held a mute appeal, but he could not bring himself to ask for Matthew to go for help. Both knew that if Matthew were to do so, his bid for freedom would be short-lived with dire consequences.

It was Matthew who took the decision. "I can't free you on my own, Brother," he muttered. "I must get help. It's the only way."

"Find Manuel," gasped George, "I can trust him. Tell him I said that Killcaid must never hear of this."

Matthew nodded and quickly made a lattice of branches to support George so that he would not sink deeper. "Hang on Brother. I'll be back." With these words of encouragement, he left his friend and headed back, bound now for Nethergate Hall where he hoped to find Manuel. He knew that Samuel up at the

Hall could be relied upon too. He just hoped that news of his escape would not yet have spread too widely.

But there could be no hiding the curiosity his presence aroused once he reached the Nethergate Estate. His mud bespattered appearance was advertisement enough. As Matthew approached the house he was surrounded by a small group under two overseers. They clearly were aware of his bid for freedom and were anxious to claim the reward from Killcaid for his capture. Somehow though, Matthew's decision to decide upon his own future had given him an inner authority. The peril of his friend added further force to his voice.

"Master George is trapped up to his chest in the bayou. He is sinking fast. Any man who hinders me now will be responsible for the young Master's death."

Such was the conviction of his words that the clamour instantly died. The hands which held him, fell away. They all were struck by the sudden drama of the situation and by the terrible appearance of Matthew and the vigour of his words. Immediately he began to fire off orders. Pointing at each group in turn he issued his instructions.

"Ropes and tackle! Get pulleys! As many long ladders as you can find! Go to it now!" Used to obedience the crowd began to scatter at his command. Seeing control slipping from his grasp one of the overseers tried to intervene.

"Stop!" he ordered, "You can't let him go." But his voice lacked conviction. It was more of a plea than an order.

Matthew met the overseer's eye in a brief battle of wills. The overseer looked down.

"Do as I say," said Matthew in a softer voice, but in a tone that expected obedience. The men and the two overseers scattered to his bidding.

As they reassembled he gave further meticulous instructions as to how they were to follow him into the perilous territory of the bayou. There was hardly a murmur now as grim-faced the small group set out on their hazardous journey. For many it was their first venture into the bayou, linked as it was to a fear of the dread spirits that all believed lurked there ready to claim the lives of the unwary. Matthew noticed that one of the overseers had stayed with them. The other he assumed had gone to find Killcaid. He gave him a nod of encouragement and approval. The overseer replied with a wry look of understanding, acknowledging the consequences to himself, but at the same time conceding Matthew's right of leadership.

Managing the ladders was particularly difficult and the ropes too snagged on the vegetation as Matthew led the rescue party into the bayou. Their progress was agonisingly slow for the men, lacking Matthew's confidence, were full of anxiety as they felt the movement of the vegetation beneath their feet. Matthew was getting yet more anxious as to whether George would still be there. Would the swamp claim his exhausted body before they could reach him? He longed to go on ahead but dare not leave his charges. They had to pause often to allow those carrying the ladders to catch up and rest. Despite his apprehension, Matthew experienced a strange feeling of euphoria at the way in which these men accepted his authority without question and were now risking their own lives at his behest. He felt a strange surge of pride and affection for his motley group of followers.

At last they reached the spot where Matthew had left the boat. He turned to the others and demanded absolute silence and stillness. Then gathering his breath, he shouted at the top of his voice, "George! Can you hear me?"

Everyone listened, scarcely daring to breathe. There was no sound but the sucking of the swamp at their feet as they all sought to keep their balance and fight against the greedy appetite of the quagmire.

Matthew's anxiety was written large across his face. "All

together. On my signal, shout his name and then absolute stillness."

"Master George!"

Together they roared his name. A startled hush fell over the bayou. Everything seemed to be stilled and listening. They all heard it then. A thin answering cry crept back, full of hope and full of despair at the same time. Galvanised into action the small group redoubled their efforts. Matthew took the first ladder and dragged it in the direction of George's voice using the dug out. Then bursting through the vegetation, he was there. "Thank God," gasped George, relief and hope in his voice, "I thought you'd never get here."

But their troubles had barely begun. It was never going to be an easy task to extricate George from the grip of the mud. Soon all were floundering in the morass themselves, spending almost as much energy in preventing themselves from becoming trapped as in easing George from his prison. Matthew seemed to be everywhere, directing where they should string the ropes and pulleys, encouraging those who seemed to be flagging and controlling those pulling on the ropes. Bit by bit George was slowly torn from the relentless suction of the swamp.

Then with one final heave, he was free. Every man was covered from head to foot in mud, the black hair of the negros' now all turned brown. An exhausted cry rang from every throat as George was released and dragged across to where there was firmer ground. At the moment of triumph some collapsed into the mud, others burst out with a spontaneous cheer. One of their number began to chuckle the noise coming deep from within his chest. Soon all were laughing and slapping each other on the back so that the mud flew about in showers. Matthew looked about him smiling with a profound satisfaction. He had led these men into danger and they had followed without question. Now they had been successful. His eyes turned to

171

George who was staggering to his feet, covered as were the rest in the leaf green slime. He held out his hand to Matthew and in front of them all, the two young men solemnly shook hands and embraced. Then shouting and laughing they hugged each other in an outpouring of relief. Slowly the laughter died away as the slaves witnessed this rite of passage, not fully understanding what they saw, but somehow knowing it was momentous and that they all had had a part in it.

Leaving the ladders and ropes, for now all were too exhausted to carry them, they began to make their way out of the swamp. It was then that the ordeal that George had endured began to take its toll. One moment he was staggering on with the rest, the next he had collapsed to the ground, barely conscious with fatigue and the shock of his nightmare experience.

Willing hands were soon about him and the exhausted band continued their way. George, now pale and trembling from the shock of his ordeal, was barely able to move and had to be helped by the stronger slaves. But Matthew's thoughts were moving forward to their return. He was only too aware of his own physical weakness after the epic struggle of the last few hours. Every instinct cried out now to leave his heroic band of helpers and make good his own escape. One glance at George was enough to tell him that there was now no way that he could rely on him to follow the trail out of the bayou. His head was hanging forward on his chest. He was barely conscious. Yet he knew what awaited him should he continue to guide them all back out of the bayou. He called a halt to rest. Immediately all collapsed where they stood, too exhausted to seek a more comfortable resting place.

Matthew surveyed the bedraggled group. They could surely find their way out from here. It was not too far. He alone was standing. He took one step to distance himself from the men. One of them looked up at his movement. It was the man who had started all the laughter at their success. In his eyes, he read the man's belief that under his guidance they would all find their way out to safetly. He realised suddenly that these men would do his bidding no matter what he asked of them, not because they were slaves and bred to obedience, but because they trusted him. He felt a strange stirring deep within himself, as if just for a moment he had suddenly glimpsed a secret half-recognised part of himself that one day he might fully embrace and understand. He looked again about his exhausted little army of helpers and felt a surge of affection, like a father for his children. The decision was made.

"Come," he urged, "No time to linger. We must get Massa' George back. He doesn't look too good." Wearily but obediently his exhausted band staggered to their feet and half carrying George, continued. Once they reached the edge of the bayou, George was mounted on his horse, still tethered where he had earlier left it and the little band of rescuers made good time escorting him back to Nethergate Hall.

The news of Matthew's dramatic appearance and the launching of the rescue mission had swept through the slave community as they returned from the fields. It was not long before all knew of the peril facing George and too of Matthew's sudden and dramatic re-appearance. When the small band of muddied heroes emerged from the trees lining the bayou with their burden the waiting slaves ran forward to greet them. Although evening was now quite far advanced, few had thought of returning to the slave lines, despite the usual nightly curfew.

The rescuers, Matthew among them, collapsed to the ground, whilst George was led off by fresh hands guiding his horse to Nethergate Hall. They were surrounded by the chattering group of their fellows anxious to hear the details of the drama. But suddenly all fell silent. The crowd parted from the back to reveal Killcaid on horseback, redolent with menace, hefting his bull-hide whip from hand to hand. There was a look of unbridled triumph across his face. Either side of him were two of his most burly overseers and the other overseers who had rushed off to find Killcaid when Matthew first emerged from the bayou. He now took hold of the horses as the rest dismounted.

Matthew staggered to his feet, but his body was too exhausted for him to attempt flight. The two overseers gripped him. To struggle was useless.

"Well, well, well," gloated Killcaid, "what has we here? Ah do believe as we has captured a runaway." A slow smile spread across his face, his pretence of warmth betrayed by the cruel and humourless gleam of triumph in his eyes.

Killcaid turned once more to Matthew, who despite his weariness was still trying to hold his head high in defiance. He addressed the overseers holding onto Matthew. "And we all knows what we does with runaways?"

"Why Mr Killcaid, I suppose we flogs the living daylights out o' the," one of them replied. Then a curious thing happened. From the ranks of the exhausted little band of rescuers came a low growl of protest. Every man stirred despite their exhaustion. Some staggered slowly yet deliberately to their feet.

A look of astonishment briefly flashed across Killcaid's features and his hand went automatically to his bull-hide whip. Killcaid was not slow to recognise what he now saw. There was in the movement an expression of sullen rebellion and a sense of unity of purpose he had never seen before in the slaves of Nethergate. The war he thought had given them all expectations above their lot in life. Once again it seemed to him that Matthew was at the root of it all. He would crush it now before it could give itself a name and find expression in action of any sort.

"Well now," muttered Killcaid, his bearded jaw thrust aggressively forward and his eyes sharp with menace, "Seems we have a little disagreement here. DOES WE!" He roared out the last two words. "Whoever wants to express his disagreement can join young Matthew here in the House of Correction."

There were no takers, but the mutinous mood of the little crowd remained in their surly looks and slow response.

Despite his own numbed exhaustion, Matthew felt a curious sense of pride in the men who had been inspired to make this spontaneous gesture of defiance, but his concern now was for them and what might befall them at Killcaid's hands.

"I'm sure that when the Master hears what you have all done," he said, addressing his little crowd of helpers, "he will thank you from the bottom of his heart for your bravery, as indeed do I. But let there be no foolishness now. Let the Master show his gratitude. There will be no flogging I'm sure, once the Master hears what we have done this day," for all knew that a visit to the House of Correction was almost always followed by a justly deserved flogging, particularly when there had been an attempted escape.

Killcaid was no fool. He allowed Matthew's message to sink in, then in a softer more conciliatory tone, despite his inner rage at the young slave's arrogant effrontery, he added, "I will have words with the Master myself. No doubt he'll be very grateful to those as played a part in the rescue of the young Master. He may be prepared to grant you a day, even two days off field labour for your efforts. He is a fair-minded man. What he may find harder to forgive though is a slave as runs away, jus' from the mere thought of doing a day's work in the 'baccy fields, such as you and I does every day of our lives. Eh?" he added looking fixedly at Matthew.

Thus did Killcaid defuse the situation and take upon himself the credit, if credit there was, for the Master's bounty. At the same time, he was trying to drive a wedge between Matthew and the other slaves, for all knew and envied his privileged position in Nethergate House and the indulgence he enjoyed from old Mrs Styles. Then addressing the two burly overseers holding Matthew, he growled, "To the House of Correction with him." Turning to the rescuers he added, "I'll put in a good word for Matthew here with the Master and we'll see what he says." With that he turned and made his way up to the Hall, leaving the slaves to disperse and make their way back to the cabins in the evening gloom.

Whilst at Nethergate House Matthew had been spared the sight of floggings, but he remembered them well from when he had been much smaller and worked in the fields with his mother. All field slaves were compelled to attend as a lesson to any other would-be miscreant. It was the thought of others witnessing his humiliation that he found hardest to bear, for already he had inherited much of the native pride of his father. All the same he doubted that when Mr Styles heard the true story, he would allow the flogging to take place. But at the same time, he wondered, knowing the hold that Silas Killcaid had over George's father. He watched the retreating figure of Killcaid as he made his way up to the Hall and wondered what other villainy he had planned.

"Come on," said one of the Overseers, "it's the House of Correction for you boy." With that Matthew was led away. It wasn't where he had expected to spend the night, but he was so dog tired he reckoned he could sleep anywhere.

28

The Journey To New York

Mary and Ruth's journey away from the Slave States had been uneventful as far as Mary was concerned, but for Ruth it had been the most exciting journey of her life. They had travelled from Nethergate to the railroad hotel in Nashville. Mary had booked a suite of rooms and had let the hotel know that she was expecting to be joined by a friend. Ruth had carried the baggage up through the servant's entrance from the Nethergate carriage. The baggage porter, one of the town's poor whites, had indolently watched the driver and Ruth unload their mistress's luggage and bring it in to the stairway. Tilting back on his chair, chewing a wad of tobacco he watched Ruth with a speculative eye, as she struggled with the cases.

After the second trip, his attitude got to her and she remarked, with some asperity, "Ain't you supposed to help us doin' this?"

"Don't see no reason to git off ma backside if'n thar's niggers to do it fo' me." Then he spat out a mouthful of black tobacco juice with practised precision into a bucket he kept beside his chair. "That's unless you want to make it worth ma' while," and he gave a lecherous leer. Ruth continued with her task, refusing now to even acknowledge his presence, but conscious all the while of his scrutiny.

When they were alone in Mary's room and Ruth had rested, it was time for the metamorphosis to take place.

"Are you sure you want to go ahead with this?" asked Mary, giving Ruth one last chance to withdraw, for both knew that what she proposed was against the law and by the nature of things the law would deal more harshly with Ruth than it would with her mistress.

Ruth had already made up her mind. She had grown up in Nethergate House and had been a daily witness to the manners and customs of southern ladies. When she was younger she had often tried on the clothes of her mistress when she was away. She had pretended to be a fine Southern lady herself, before the uncritical eye of the mirror. Now however it was to be for real, but still she felt no qualms about the plan, only as to whether she could carry it off.

"No Ma'am. I is ready to go on, for Matthew's sake, if for no other reason."

"And I too for Matthew's sake," re-joined Mary. Mary had been generous in supplying an impressive wardrobe of dresses and other personal items that a woman of the status of companion would be expected to wear. They had had a lot of fun purchasing the items and Ruth had made many of the dresses herself.

She used some of her mistress's make-up and changed the arrangement of her hair to a fashionably restrained style. Then both women admired their handiwork. Ruth, looking in the mirror, saw a genteel mature lady, smart yet discreet in her style of dress.

"My!" said Mary, admiring her handiwork, "But you're a handsome woman and that's for sure." Ruth smiled at the compliment, staring long and hard at the transformation in the mirror and admiring what she saw. Truly her features and her colouring would enable her to pass for a European of perhaps Spanish extraction, but it was the shock of seeing herself presented in such a different guise that chiefly held her attention. A few pieces of cloth, cosmetics and a changed hairstyle and she was seeing a new woman, no longer a slave. The set of the shoulders, the angle of the head of the woman in the mirror declared their own story. Ruth felt a surge of confidence. For the first time, she felt she could really carry out Mary's plan. Both women pronounced themselves satisfied.

Then came the first test. Ruth left the hotel unobserved by a side door. She came around to the front, feeling that everyone was looking at her and would immediately see through her subterfuge. Then she remembered the woman in the mirror and squared her shoulders and raised her head. She approached the front desk where one of the under-managers was on duty.

He sized her up and categorised her as hotel staff do. "Can I help you Madam?" he asked. His tone was deferential and respectful. There was something else too. Suddenly she realised that he found her attractive as a woman and wanted to impress. She was well used to men looking at her in this way, but now there was a difference. Before it was the look of a man who just saw her as a vehicle for the satisfaction of his carnal desires. Now she felt there was a difference, a need for him first to win her approval, perhaps for no more of a reward than just a smile. She smiled.

"I am meeting a Mrs Styles here," she said, "I believe she is expecting me."

"Indeed, yes Madam. She wanted you to be shown up to her rooms. If I may?" and he inclined his head respectfully for her to follow him. At the same time, he clicked his fingers and gestured for the bell boy to take over the desk. She knew it was all for her benefit to show how much he was in control of things. She followed him dutifully up the stairs. He stopped outside Mrs Styles' rooms and deferentially knocked. Mary came to the door after a due pause.

"Ah Ruth dear, you found me. Do come in."

"Thank you," said Ruth to her escort and he bowed and beamed with gratitude at her acknowledgement.

In those few brief moments, a totally new world had been revealed to Ruth. She had been living in it all her life without knowing that it existed. It was a world where she counted for something, where she could give pleasure to strangers by simply acknowledging their existence and the service that they gave. She fancied it would take a lot of getting used to.

The first crisis though came the next day when they were preparing to leave the hotel to catch the train at Nashville. Ruth had sent for the porter to take their bags downstairs and load them onto the carriage going to the railroad station. There was a knock at the door. When she opened it, her heart sank. The porter waiting to carry down their luggage was the same man who had refused to help her with the cases the day before. He had spent so much time staring lecherously at her that she felt he could not fail but to recognise her now.

His eyes though betrayed not a flicker of recognition. Dutifully he did her bidding in every respect, doffing his uniform cap politely at her every request and keeping his eyes lowered. Even when she tipped him when he had completed his task and he looked her in the face, she read only a submissive desire to please and earn a reward. That taught her another lesson. People only see what they expected to see.

The whole of the remaining journey to New York was a steep learning curve for Ruth, but she met every challenge with burgeoning confidence. Mary was a willing tutor and helped and advised her on the way with an increasing respect for the manner in which her protégée was mastering her new role.

When they reached New York, they both felt that she was as ready as she could ever be to face the greatest challenge of all, that of meeting Mary's family and being accepted as her mistress's companion and friend. Not only would she have to pass muster on their first meeting, but she would have to maintain the illusion over a protracted period and avoid all the countless pitfalls and snares that familiarity might spread out before her. It was a daunting prospect, but Ruth felt her spirits rising to the challenge.

29

The House Of Correction

Matthew was too weary to even try to struggle. His hands were tied behind his back and a pole inserted through his elbows. With brutal jerks Killcaid's 'trusties' half carried half dragged him away from the other slaves. This performance was in case Killcaid should chance to look back from his progress up to Nethergate Hall. Once out of sight though, the rough treatment ceased, the pole was withdrawn, his hands were freed, and he was permitted to walk at his own weary pace. The overseers were in no hurry. They had been given a special task and it was as well to spin it out for as long as possible.

Matthew tried to remain optimistic, but inwardly his heart sank, for he knew only too well the punishment that might yet await him. He remembered as a child, how Zeb, a slave who had endured a flogging by Killcaid, had allowed him to run his hands over the scars on his back. His shoulders were grooved by the bite of the lash. He remembered how his small fingers had traced the hard ridges and furrows impossibly huge to his tiny hands, yet glassy-smooth to the touch. He had lost half his tongue and always spoke as through a mouthful of pebbles.

"Did it hurt?" he had asked, his eyes wide with childish wonder at how anyone could survive such a flaying.

"Only at first," was the reply, "after a bit, you lose the feeling for each stroke. You jus' floats in a sea where there aint nothin' but pain. Thet's how I los' my tongue – bit it clean through. Didn't know what I were doin'."

At the time, he didn't see how it was possible to bite one's tongue off without knowing it. He was only too aware of the pain of a bitten tongue. It was impossible to imagine pain so intense that you wouldn't feel biting off your own tongue. The memory came back to him now and his body tightened with dread.

Meanwhile Killcaid had other plans to set in motion. George, now barely conscious, had already been taken to the big house. Manuel, full of concern for his young master, went to follow, but Killcaid held him back. Then holding him by his ear he whispered, "Now, when you gets to see the Master, be sure to tell who it were that rescued the young Master. Understand?"

Manuel looked puzzled, then hesitatingly murmured, "You mean Matthew?" At this he received a smart clip that set his head ringing.

Clearly it was the wrong answer. "It were Matthew as *lured* the young master into the swamp in the first place, isn't that what I heard you say?"

Slowly Manuel nodded his head. He was rewarded by the rare accolade of a smile from Killcaid. "And was it not myself and the other overseers that led the rescue party and pulled young Master George in the nick o' time from the prospect of a horrible death?"

Circles of white appeared in Manuel's eyes. Killcaid gave his ear a savage twist. "I understand, Boss," he said vigorously nodding his head.

"Good," drawled Killcaid, "and it is your opinion that

Matthew was deliberately trying to lead your young master into danger. Do I make myself clear?" Manuel was now bobbing his head as fast as it would go, for no-one dared defy Killcaid. With that now firmly understood, he was dismissed and rushed away in hot pursuit of his master, rubbing furiously at his tortured ear.

Allowing time for the initial fuss to die down Killcaid then reported to the Master himself. By then Manuel's version of events had spread and he was ushered in almost as if he had been a guest of the house. Now that George was safe, his father's anxiety had given way to anger at the boy's disobedience.

"Damn the lad," were his first words to Killcaid, "I have forbidden him to go down to the Creek alone. It's not that he don't have enough places to roam in."

Killcaid shook his head. "T'was not the lad's fault Sir, if you'll pardon me saying so. It seems that that rogue Matthew, Ruth's boy, were at the root of it. Lured him there in some way. It was I fear a deliberate attempt to trap the lad." Then turning to Manuel who was still lingering at his side he barked, "That not so boy?"

Manuel hesitated a fraction of a second. Then he caught the look in Killcaid's eye which set his head wagging and his tongue chattering as though his life depended on it, as indeed it did.

"Oh yes Massa'. That surely so. Surely am. Dat Matthew he left a message fo' Massa' George to meet him down by de bayou an' he would learn summat to his advantage, but I dunno what it was." He gave a convincing performance. No-one dared gainsay Killcaid.

But Killcaid was not finished yet. He turned to face Anthony, "Like you wanted Mr Styles, I sent for Matthew to set him to work in the fields where he belongs. But the lad was too grand for that. He ups and away on one of your horses. I sent a posse out to bring him back. But he got clean

184

away. Then it seemed he sneaks back; no doubt cooking up this scheme to lure young George into the swamps seeking revenge. I'm sure the lad has some special hold over the young Master. Darned if I knows what though. Had I not got there just in time…" and he left the rest hanging in the air.

Anthony swore again. This seemed to confirm all that Killcaid had said of Matthew before his mother had left for the north. After his conversation with Killcaid, he had taken special note of Matthew whenever he met him when visiting his mother. He noted the special treatment and freedom he seemed to enjoy, but he was a good-looking upright young man with a presence and dignity of bearing unusual in a slave. Matthew had always been polite and respectful. In fact, he had rather taken to the lad, though his good impression had been somewhat tempered by his own mother's obvious fondness for him, which he viewed not without a twinge of jealousy. He did not recall her being so solicitous when he and Mark were young.

It seemed though as in so many other matters about the estate, that Killcaid had been right all along. His mother had been sheltering a viper in her bosom. When she returned, he would show her just how wrong she had been to put her trust in Matthew. He had repaid that trust, by hazarding the life of her own grandson. He almost wished that his mother was still at home. Then he could show her now just how much she had been mistaken about the youth and the dire consequences of putting so much trust in a slave.

Having received the heartfelt gratitude of George's father and of Amelia, Killcaid then turned his attention with considerable satisfaction to what all along he had been inwardly savouring, the utter subjugation of Matthew. For far too long now Matthew had been a thorn in his side. A flogging was guaranteed to break the proudest will. His tongue ran along his lower lip as he anticipated the process of supressing

185

that wild spirit. With the absence of his protector, the timing was perfect.

"I have arranged for the lad to be flogged as a lesson to them all," he continued, "I assume you will be attending. Young Master George too if he's up to it, after that ornery nigger near killed him."

Anthony wavered at this. Getting Matthew to work in the fields was one thing, but to have him flogged and scarred for life was quite another. His mother would never forgive him. But Amelia, who had hitherto said nothing, saw this as a way of justifying the flogging she had ordered for Samuel which she knew had not received the approval of her husband or Mrs Styles.

"Quite right Mr Killcaid. He's a poisonous little worm. Deserves all he gets. A good flogging will be a lesson to them all." Thus it was decided.

Few would sleep easy with the prospect of such a dawn as awaited Matthew. Killcaid had in mind another refinement to bring yet further misery to those bleak small hours where the human spirit is at its lowest ebb.

He made his way in a leisurely fashion to the House of Correction, relishing the triumph yet to come. When he arrived, he found Matthew slumped to the ground, manacled to one of the pillars set into the floor. He was filthy, still covered in the mud from the swamp. Despite his discomforted posture, he was fast asleep with the sleep of the exhausted.

For a moment Killcaid stood looking down at the slumbering youth. There was something noble and graceful in his awkward posture despite the dried mud of the swamp, something of the grace of 'the dying slave', though Killcaid could not put a name to it. Killcaid was never immune to beauty in whatever form it might take. For a moment, he was struck as one might admire the nobility of stag at bay before the hounds can reach it.

The moment passed as he recalled again Matthew's condescending air of superiority that never failed to get under his skin. He remembered that once when he had looked away from Matthew's stare. He remembered his gift for mimicry and ground his teeth at the feeling of always being the butt of all his jibes, yet never able to prove it. Resentment once again welled up within him. He aimed a savage kick at the slumbering slave.

30

A Companion In

The House Of Correction

The House of Correction was a cabin where miscreants were held, manacled to posts set in the floor to await their punishment the following day. It was placed in the middle and forward of the line of cabins so that it was the first thing that most of the slaves would see when they emerged each morning. It was a reminder of the price of disobedience. It was a building like the other cabins, but Killcaid had opened it up on three sides. Thus, those inside could contemplate the whipping posts and others outside could ponder on the penalties of stepping out of line. Sometimes Killcaid would order that the miscreant be released during the small hours. This added a further refinement of uncertainty to the punishment. The victim would never know for sure but lived in hope until the last moment.

When, however, the slaves were roused in the morning and a dark figure could be observed still slumped on the ground in the House of Correction, all knew what was to follow. It produced a strangely ambivalent reaction. Of course, there was sympathy for the unfortunate sufferer, but there was also a strange sense of relief that this time someone else was the victim. There was too that voyeuristic and curiously human fascination in witnessing another soul's torment and pain. Also, it meant that the working day would be later in starting, for every flogging had to be witnessed by the rest of the slave community in the cabins. Even a flogging was a welcome diversion from the unending drudgery of labouring among the tobacco fields.

Such was the depths of his exhaustion, that the impact of Killcaid's boot and the pain of the kick only slowly roused Matthew from his slumber. At the sight of Killcaid though, he struggled to his feet, glaring his defiance like a chained bear, full of fury and boldness even in defeat.

Killcaid held all the cards and knew it. He was prepared now to allow the youth his posturing for the greater satisfaction of witnessing his inevitable humiliation. For a full minute, he stood there saying nothing, allowing his mere presence to cow the lad.

"Thought you could get away from Killcaid, did you?" He spoke at last in short, savage sentences, punctuating each statement with a savage blow from the weighted end of his beloved 'Rattler'.

"No-one gets away from Killcaid, eh boy? Eh!" and he waited till Matthew nodded his head. "Well now yous'll feel the penalty for escaping, eh? Feel the thirsty tongue of the lash a'lappin up your blood boy. Think on that. Sometin' you'll never forget, eh boy? Ah can promise you that." He chuckled mirthlessly as his hand stroked at his beard. He moistened his lips as if he could already taste the acrid tang of Matthew's blood. "Now they's all gone away at the old house, yous'll git no help from thar'. Eh boy? How that feel?" and he thrust his face inches away from Matthew's so that Matthew involuntarily shrank from the foetid stench of the slave master's foul breath.

Matthew realized the truth of Killcaid's statement, but he felt sure that once George had recovered and discovered what was going to happen to him he would put a stop to it. However strongly the Master might be under the thumb of his Chief Overseer he could never allow his son's rescuer to face such treatment. Killcaid turned to go and then paused as if a sudden thought had occurred to him.

"Oh. In case you was thinking that The Young Master might put in a word for you, then think on't again. The Master knows as it was me and some of the other overseers as came to the Young Master's aid and Manuel, bless him, has sworn the truth of that before the Angel Gabriel an' all the Heavenly Hosts." Then he added innocently. "The Master seems to think as it were you as lured young Master George into the swamp in the first place. How he got hold of that idea I cannot think, but he's sure spittin' fury at the thought of it. Such treachery after you gettin' such kind treatment from the old Mistress too."

Matthew's heart sank, but still he was determined not to give Killcaid the satisfaction of seeing it. But Killcaid was not finished and had yet one more refinement to offer. "Thought you'd like a little company. For the night is long, as they say and I thought you might like a little diversion. We has another candidate for a flogging tomorrow. Caught stealing food he was." He beckoned with his whip and another figure shambled into view, sobbing with fear. At the sight of Killcaid he burst into a torrent of incoherent pleading, begging for forgiveness and to be spared the lash. The man spoke in a barely coherent babble. Matthew immediately recognised Zeb, the slave who had bitten off his own tongue.

"It were never me Massa'. I swear it. I never stole nothing. Why would I do dat eh? I don' want no trouble. I never stole, honest to God I never. I learn good my lesson de fus time. Please Massa' no more, no more, I beg you O' Massa', please. I beg…" His voice faded into unintelligible sobbing. Killcaid simply nodded to the man holding him and he was manacled to one of the posts.

With a shock, Matthew recalled his previous meeting with Zeb and the way his childish fingers had once wandered over the smooth ridges and furrows left by his previous flogging.

Clearly the thought of another scourging was more than the poor man could bear. Killcaid's purpose was not lost on Matthew. He intended that Matthew should have Zeb's whimpering, sobbing company through the long night to further subdue his spirits before his own ordeal in the morning.

The hopelessness of his predicament was now all too apparent. There was no escaping the iron shackles that held him. Ignoring Killcaid he tried to comfort his distraught companion. Killcaid listened to Matthew's futile efforts. Then with a low chuckle of satisfaction he left, well pleased with this added enhancement to Matthew's discomfiture.

31

A Visitor In The Night

The evening of an eventful day was drawing in. The slaves were coming in from the fields and those who had been part of the posse hunting Matthew were also returning. By now the story of George's rescue was on everyone's lips, but not the story that Killcaid was telling. Despite their sympathy no-one dared come near to where Matthew was held, for Killcaid had placed two of his overseers to act as guards and no doubt to see who showed any untoward compassion for the prisoners. The most the more daring ones could manage was a cautious wave when the guards were looking the other way. For the first time in his life Matthew felt truly isolated.

Despite his limbs aching from the exertions of the day and the bruising from Killcaid's beating, his whole being yearned for sleep. His companion now made that impossible. He was rocking to and fro on his heels uttering a high pitched keening cry of misery at every breath. The slaves went about their normal tasks in preparing food, trying hard not to look in their direction, but all the time acutely aware of the two condemned men. The smell of food made Matthew realise how hungry he was.

After a time though, the slaves grew bolder. A small crowd gathered in the gloom, just far away enough for none to be recognised. Normally the slaves would go to their individual cabins to have their evening meal in family groups. This evening though many chose to gather about the House of Correction. No-one spoke out loud, no-one sang. When they did communicate, it was in low whispers, which as the crowd swelled became a low rumble, sounding increasingly menacing to the two overseers. They exchanged anxious glances intensely aware of the hostility growing about them in the darkness.

Eventually a small girl bravely approached, clumsily carrying two beakers of water spilling most in the nervousness of her mission. The overseers watched her, sensing the will of the crowd just beyond their vision. They said nothing, did nothing, only too aware of the will of those in the shadows. The young girl held the water first for Zeb who greedily sucked at the contents and then shyly to Matthew's lips. Emboldened by the success of the little girl other children came and so bit by bit the two were fed and watered. Thus, through their children, the rest of the slaves expressed their sympathy and solidarity with the convicted pair.

There had too been a curious undercurrent of excitement in the slave community that evening spread by those who had helped Matthew in the rescue. True, they had been all too willing to capture Matthew when he first emerged from the bayou just to please Killcaid, but then they had embarked upon their mission of mercy. In the end, the success of that mission had in a curious way defied the will of the overseers. It was something they as slaves had achieved on their own. Then the overseers witnessed a scene that for them at least was the expression of an immense unspoken threat. There was to be no singing that night instead the crowd about the House of Correction began to hum. That way no-one could tell from whom the sounds came. The humming gradually became a tune, one tune and then another. The first was John Brown's Body and then other songs of slavery known to them all. It was somehow proof that they could do things for themselves, despite the orders of those set above them. The overseers faced a set of steely faces, lips tight sealed, eyes expressionless and yet from their throng came the deep harmonious expression of their wrongs. The two overseers looked at each other with fear in their eyes.

With the onset of night though, the crowd gradually dispersed. The slaves entered their cabins to sleep the sleep of the exhausted before the next day's unremitting toil. Hearts were subdued at the injustices that awaited their rising in the coming day. There was a deep sense of outrage that Zeb should be made to endure yet another flogging and there was also sympathy and respect for Matthew, despite his youth and the privileges he enjoyed. But there was something else too. There was a stirring of the blood. The day had not been without its special significance.

Others though still looked forward to the later start in the fields and the usually a reduction in the day's quota that followed a flogging. Thus did Killcaid reduce the chances of a deeper underswell of resentment building up when one of their number received such a dreadful punishment. Everyone expected that Zeb at least would not be there in the morning to receive his punishment.

The noises of the night gradually closed in. It had been a long time since Matthew had slept among the slave cabins. But the presence of so many sleeping souls and the awareness of so much sympathy gave him no consolation for the dread of what the morrow would bring. He thought of Ruth, no longer as a child yearning for his mother's comforting arms, but now as a soldier's mind might stray to home and loved ones in the still of the night before a coming engagement. But the balm of sleep was denied him by the lamentations of his companion.

All his efforts so far, though, had failed to quell the dread in Zeb's mind. He mumbled and sobbed in an outpouring of terrors at revisiting that dreadful ordeal he had endured once before. Despite Matthew's determination not to allow his companion's fears to play upon his mind, he could not be immune to his woeful babbling. There were moments when he longed to shout out for silence, but with an effort he forbore, understanding the older man's horror. Even their guards found old Zeb's moans hard to endure and shouted for him to be silent. Shortly before dawn the lamentations ceased and he at last lapsed into a troubled sleep.

Matthew too began to relax, but sleep was denied him. The hours just before dawn are when the spirit is at its lowest ebb. Matthew felt his eyes begin to water. He clenched them tight shut to hide the weakness from himself. It was at that moment that he heard someone moving cautiously around the hut. A huge figure was briefly silhouetted against the gradually lightening sky. Matthew's heart leapt. It was Morella.

Matthew had known Morella all his life. She was a loving, but at the same time a rather awesome, figure to him. As a young boy, he had been frightened of her, but he soon discovered the gentle compassion at the core of her character. She was getting old and moved with the slow, ponderous grace of a galleon under full sail. But she had lost none of her skills and he knew that he would soon have need of all the healing care she could give him. Perhaps she had come to give him something that would enable him to endure the pain to come?

What she had brought him was water in a flask which she held to his lips as he eagerly drank. Then she whispered instructions in his ear. In so doing she brought him something of even greater value than a potion to relieve the pain – hope. She also had a plan to lessen his companion's ordeal.

No sooner had Morella left it seemed that the cabins began to stir. His unfortunate companion awoke with a sobbing whimper of dread. His hopes that Killcaid might at the eleventh hour grant him a reprieve died with the breaking of the dawn. The spectacle was to be staged just when there was light enough for all to witness the event and as little working time as possible was lost after the later start. The bright shafts of the morning sun were just creeping down the tree trunks in the slave compound, touching them with fire, when four overseers came to collect Matthew and his companion. They were released from the manacles that held them and their arms pinioned to their sides. Just as they did so, a small child ran in from outside with a jug of water. The slaves motioned her to go away, but with an authority beyond her years she disdainfully ignored them. She was a child of exceptional beauty with wide innocent eyes which somehow shamed the slaves from stopping her. She came first to Matthew and held a beaker to his lips, then turned to his fellow victim and rendered the same service. Only Matthew saw her empty a phial of liquid into the drink.

The old man was pathetically grateful for this small token of sympathy. But no sooner had he been released than he fell to the ground. He had lost the power of his limbs so great was his dread of what was to come. His britches too bore the stain and disgrace of his terror. He was dragged out to the whipping post. His shirt was removed. There was a gasp from the crowd as the ridges and scars from his previous flogging were revealed for all to see. A low murmur of sympathy ran through the onlookers for all had expected that he at least would have been reprieved during the night. Impassively the overseers buckled his sagging body to the flogging frame with leather straps. None would have guessed that he was there simply so that Matthew would witness his own fate yet to come. But then few would have been aware of Killcaid's obsessional desire for the utter humiliation of Mary Styles' favoured slave.

Killcaid, a craggy, bearded figure, stood, savouring the spectacle, his mouth working as though he would taste the terror of his victims. Slightly behind stood the Master. Close to him was the smaller figure of George. Surely George would speak out now and put a stop to it all. But it seemed that George was simply there to witness his humiliation and there would be no intervention.

As Zeb was being prepared Killcaid's eyes were on Matthew's face alone, watching and hoping to see the signs of the old man's terror mirrored there. He was disappointed. At last he nodded to the slave holding the nine-tailed whip who knew that any lack of enthusiasm on his part might bring him a taste of his own medicine. He threw his arms wide drawing the whip back as far as he could go. The lash sighed in the early morning air. It fell with a soft, leaden thud onto the victim's bare back. Like a marionette suddenly jerked into a grotesque parody of life, Zeb's limp form leapt into sudden animation, straining every fibre against his restraints. An impossibly high wail broke from his lips to be abruptly severed by the second fall of the lash.

Killcaid's eyes glittered. "Don't he squeal?" he muttered.

At the third stroke, the victim's back began to open up. Blow fell upon blow. Now only groans escaped his lips. At each stroke, a fine mist of blood rose from his writhing torso. Then mercifully quickly the victim's head suddenly dropped, and he ceased to respond to the flaying. Morella's potion had taken effect and the old man was unconscious. Killcaid let the lash fall a few more times then nodded, and the beating ceased. The bloodied form was dragged away by two of his friends his toes dragging a trail flecked with blood in the sand. The slaves gently laid him face down on the ground. Morella broke away from the crowd and surged forth to administer her soothing balms whilst her patient was still beyond pain.

Killcaid watched unmoved. He had no objections to Morella's ministrations, for the sooner he healed, the sooner his victim would be back to work. Instead he turned to where Matthew was standing, trembling now despite himself, at what he had just witnessed. A thin, tight little smile played about Killcaid's lips as he saw Matthew's reaction. Matthew's response though was more in anger and indignation than fear of what now awaited him.

"Your turn now boy," said Killcaid.

32

Matthew Faces A Flogging

The two slaves holding Matthew began to urge him towards the whipping post where the ground was already darkened by Zeb's blood.

Now that it was happening, the fear suddenly left him. Instead he burned with battle fever.

"I can walk there on my own," he declared, shaking himself free from his escorts. They fell back, awed by his sudden rush of determination. In the gathering light, he strode to the whipping post, a slender, youthful figure dwarfed by the bulk of the full-grown men about him. He removed his shirt and tied it about his waist. At the whipping brace, he slipped his feet into the vacated leather traces and held out his hands for his escorts to secure with the leather thongs. He held his head fearlessly erect. A scarcely audible hiss of escaping breath came from the mouths of the watching slaves and their ranks stirred as if a shiver had passed through them all. A flicker of doubt crossed Killcaid's face. There were over a hundred hostile slaves gathered before him. For the first time, he became aware of the weight of their numbers and of their hatred. Then with a snort of contempt he turned his back on them. No-one stirred. All the same he was glad that he could feel the comforting shape of his pistol in his pocket.

George, even in the morning light, still pale from his ordeal of the day before, was talking urgently to his father gesturing animatedly with his hands. Up until then he had not seen who the second victim was to be. The Master was shaking his head and was clearly getting very angry. George turned to go, but his father held him. The two faced each other, both aware of the public nature of their disagreement in the presence of the slaves. Killcaid hastened to the Master's side.

"I can't think why you wish to defend the boy," George's father was saying, "after what he tried to do to you."

"But Father it wasn't like that at all," insisted George with vigour.

Killcaid intruded and with an air of finality declared, "I don't know what hold Matthew has over the young Master Mr Styles but let us call for Manuel. He will surely tell us what happened."

Manuel was quickly fetched. "Was it I or him?" he demanded, pointing with his bearded chin to where the defiant Matthew stood, "what organised Master George's rescue?"

Manuel dare not look at his young master as he murmured to Killcaid with eyes downcast, "It were you Massa' Killcaid. Surely was you."

"You *lie!*" exploded George. He took one stride to Manuel and struck him hard in the face, something he had never done to Manuel or to any other slave. Immediately he was filled with remorse. As for Manuel, he wished his young master had struck him twice as hard. It would perhaps have helped to assuage his sense of guilt and betrayal.

Turning to his father, George said, "On my honour as your son I swear to you that it was Matthew who rescued me from the grip of the bayou." Such was his son's passionate intensity, that for a moment his father was inclined to believe him, but Killcaid immediately intervened.

Killcaid never liked to be called to justify himself and his own ire began to rise at the suspicion that these two youngsters, whom he considered no more than mere boys, might mean more to each other than he had guessed. He spoke earnestly to Anthony for a moment about how it would look if they were suddenly to postpone Matthew's punishment. Trying to escape alone warranted such a penalty. It would be a clear sign of weakness that would undermine his own position as Master of Nethergate, particularly at a time when the war with the North was causing ripples of rebellion among all slave communities.

Then suddenly an idea occurred to his fertile mind which would sever for ever any empathy the two youths might share. He whispered urgently into the Master's ear. Anthony was a ready listener if for no other reason than jealousy for the affection his own mother seemed to have for the boy. At first the Master hesitated at what Killcaid was proposing. But he was still angry with his George for his disobedience in venturing into the bayou and partly for the shock at the realisation that he might so nearly have lost him. After a moment, he nodded his assent. Killcaid turned smiling, unable to hide his satisfaction at the turn of events, for no friendship could possibly survive what he now had in mind.

Killcaid strode over to where George was standing and ushered him forward to where Matthew was secured to the whipping post. For a moment, George thought that Matthew was to be released.

"Now is your chance to prove what you is made of Sir," said Killcaid. "Your father has agreed that you need to show the men that you will be a firm master to them in your turn." With that he took the lash from the hands of the overseer who was preparing to execute the whipping and handed it to George.

George turned red with indignation. "I'll do no such thing!"

201

he exploded, suddenly realising what was expected of him. "It is an injustice and you know it!"

"Then Sir," re-joined Killcaid with silky persuasion, "I shall do it myself." His eyebrows rose in a mock sincerity, "I leave it to you to judge who will lay it on the harder," he added. Once again, he proffered the lash to George.

There was no doubt that a flogging from Killcaid would be infinitely worse than one administered by him, but every fibre of his being revolted at the idea.

George took the whip, then staring at his father he threw it on the ground. A gasp escaped from the watching crowd. His father shot him a look like thunder at this open display of defiance in front of the work hands.

"Then I do believe it will be up to me Mr Styles to administer just punishment," declared Silas Killcaid striding towards the abandoned whip.

"You do it Brother." It was Matthew whispering urgently. George hesitated a moment and then retrieved the whip before Killcaid could reach it. Ignoring him he turned back to where Matthew was held at the whipping post, desperately trying to think of a way out.

Killcaid turned his back on the two boys a cynical smile playing about his lips. No friendship could survive such an ordeal and anyway he had meant all along to finish it off himself.

"Can you ever forgive me?" hissed George to his friend, "It's either me or Killcaid."

"I won't have to," whispered Matthew between clenched teeth.

Then it seemed that everything happened at once. Morella who had visited him the previous night had rubbed on to his wrists and ankles an oil that she had assured him would, 'make them as slippery as the skin of an eel'. Whilst Killcaid had been in earnest conversation with the Master he had worked his feet free and now his hands also had slipped through the leather bindings. With a defiant yell, he leapt free of the whipping post and rushed to where Morella was still kneeling, administering to the prone figure of Zeb as she had instructed him to do the previous night. The readied crowd parted as if by magic and the fugitive vanished from sight. Then the crowd closed in once more like a trapdoor shutting.

For a moment, all were too stunned to react.

"Stop him!" yelled Killcaid leaping in pursuit, suddenly aware that his victim was about to escape. His overseers instantly rallied and began cracking their whips. The crowd of sullen watchers burst into spontaneous animation.

Order, in the blinking of an eye, changed into chaos. Everyone seemed to be running in different directions at once getting in each other's way. It was a scene of total pandemonium.

"I got him boss," went up a cry and everyone surged towards the spot stumbling and falling over each other in their haste to be in at the kill.

"He got away," came a despairing shout, to be followed by another holler from a different direction.

"I got the little varmint. Got him good." At once the crowd surged in that direction whilst Killcaid and his overseers helplessly cracked their whips to try and restore order to the scene.

"That's not him!" came another shout.

"Damn me so it aint. These nigger boys dey all look de same." There was a burst of laughter at this.

"There he goes!" came another shout and the unruly crowd surged in still another direction, whooping and hollering in delight at the utter confusion they had created.

"Damn the little devil, he slipped away agin."

"There he is," went up another shout. The slaves were finding it hard to stop their laughter. This was truly a turning of the tables. The gentle assumption of stupidity was hitherto their only weapon to frustrate and get back at their masters. Now together they were discovering another weapon. They were finding something as heady as corn liquor itself; mass disobedience under the pretence of doing their master's bidding. It mattered not that one or two felt the bite of the lash now and again, for now it was they who were baiting Killcaid and his helpers. Now they, in a strange way, held the whip.

"There he is!" and the crowd surged off once more. This way and that they rushed like terriers hunting rats in a barn, everyone shouting and now openly laughing. Killcaid was no fool and realised the danger he would face if the mood were to change.

He brought out his pistol and fired.

Everything stopped. Everyone stood still, shocked into silence. "Now you all listen and listen good!" roared Killcaid seizing the moment's stillness. "The fun is over. You is all on your way out to the fields. You can forget breakfast. Anyone today who steps out o'place they know what's waiting for them on the morrow and every other mornin' till you all falls back into line." Then turning to one of his overseers, he uttered the words that caused every slave to catch his breath. "Fetch me them damned coon hounds and horses too!"

Then, turning to Anthony who had been an impotent witness to the chaos that had so suddenly erupted about him, he asked, "I take it I has your permission Mr Styles?" Anthony had never seen slaves behave like this and had for the first time experienced a real fear of what might happen were their humour suddenly to change into open rebellion. Thoughts of Nat Turner's heartless killing of his kindly white master and the subsequent rebellion and slaughter of nearly two score white men, women, children and even babies and the more recent uprising under John Brown, filled his mind with dread. Anthony could only nod in agreement.

"But be sure to ride close to the hounds though," he

cautioned. "My mother would not wish the lad seriously harmed."

George, on the other hand, still smarting after his father's refusal to believe him, was delighted at his friend's escape and wracked his brains as to what he might yet do to help him. But he too had felt the fear at the sudden turn of events and the revelation of what might happen were the slaves to realise the power that they already possessed but failed to use. His father turned and started back to where their horses had been tethered.

"Come George. This is Killcaid's business."

Still feeling like Judas for taking the whip, George could only follow, praying that his friend might yet escape and wondering if truly he would have laid on the lash.

Killcaid's decision to use hounds had further changed the mood of the restless crowd. Everyone dreaded the thought of being hunted down like a wild beast. Every slave knew what the dogs could do to a man once they were let loose after a runaway. Unless the hunters were sharp upon the scene to whip-off the dogs, the fugitive risked being literally torn to pieces. Furthermore, the Nethergate pack was well known as a killer pack. Slowly the slaves began to lapse back into some subdued semblance of order whilst horses and hounds were gathered, and the hunting party organised.

Hilarity had given way to a mood of surly resentment. Despite the crack of whips and the harsh shouts of the overseers the men moved like sleepwalkers as if a sullen lethargy had taken hold of them all. A resemblance of calm was restored as once again they assumed their mantle of dumb obedience and shuffled off to the fields and their other work places. But something remained. For a moment, a spark had been kindled. No-one would forget that moment. For a few heady seconds, it was they who had been in command, they who had called the shots. For a moment, they had had a taste of the freedom of being the masters of their own destiny. Perhaps the thought had not yet even formed in their minds, but they all knew in their bones that the chemistry had changed, the spark was still there. It was just waiting to be fanned into flame.

Killcaid was astute enough to realise the danger that he had faced. Once the men were back at work he would resume his hunt for Matthew with a few of his trusted men. Inwardly he seethed with anger at the turn of events but contented himself with the thought of how much more Matthew would suffer now. For the first time, his fertile mind began to toy with the possibility that this might be the time to rid himself finally of the threat that Matthew posed. If he delayed the arrival of the horsemen, the hounds would do his work even more effectively than the 'Rattler'. They would teach the slaves a lesson they would never forget. It would engender a fear and dread that would cow them into obedience. He savoured the thought and smiled in grim anticipation. On horseback, they would soon overhaul the fleeing fugitive, however fast he might run. He would never escape the hounds with such a short advantage of time and with a scent so fresh. It was clear where Matthew was heading, for the bayou was the only possible refuge. It was a good five miles off. He would never reach it before the hounds were upon him.

Horses arrived for Killcaid and his party. Then the moment he had been waiting for when the mounted huntsman arrived in a sea of excited hounds, tails rigidly erect at the prospect of a hunt, the air full of their eager clamour. Their innocent and joyful anticipation such a contrast to the evil nature of their purpose. Silas Killcaid was seething with vengeful fury at the turn of events. Whatever the outcome, his authority had once again been publicly flouted by this insolent slave. The more he pondered the more certain he became that this should be a permanent solution to the canker that was Matthew. So long as he sheltered under the protection of the old Mistress he would forever be a focus for unrest and a thorn in his side.

But the blame would be on the Master's shoulders, not his, for the Master had agreed the loosing of the hounds. The more he thought, the more his resolve hardened. It was the perfect solution. The hounds would be allowed to run their course. The rest would learn their lesson from it and there would be no more of the covert defiance that underlined the morning's events.

His only regret was that in that circumstance, he would not have the satisfaction of being in at the kill. Even so his stomach tightened in anticipation. There would be no going back.

33

Mary's Father Henry Bragg

Whilst Matthew was facing his ordeal back at Nethergate, his mother was facing a challenge of a different sort in New York. She had been fearing the meeting with Mary's father. She felt she already knew him from how Mary had described him in the past. She imagined a pugnacious, formidable man, skilled in the ways of the world who would instantly see through the deception of her new status. She thought hard of Matthew ensnared for life in the hopeless mesh of slavery and steeled herself for the test to come. It would all be for him.

Mary's father, Henry Bragg, came from that energetic and forceful element of the New World that grasped each opportunity life offered and shook from it every ounce of profit that was to be had. He was one of that aggressive band of industrial entrepreneurs who had been the first to thrust their heads over the economic parapet, as America became an industrial powerhouse in its own right. Now she was a worthy competitor with that old and privileged world across the Atlantic which so often laid down the ground rules that others were forced to follow. Rules, it may be said, that overtly and without shame always worked to their advantage.

Mary had left home at eighteen and, unlike her sister, had always been dutiful to her father's wishes. Her sister, Caroline, had been just the opposite. She had inherited her father's stubborn wilfulness and defied him at every step of the way. Despite their difference in temperament, she had been very close to her sister and had often comforted her following her frequent spats with their father. Their mother always supported their father's point of view and it was always to Mary, some ten years older than her, that Caroline would come to pour out her anger and frustration and to seek comfort.

When Adrian Styles had come on the scene, the only doubts she had had about accepting his proposal were due to what would become of Caroline, left alone with her father's disapproval. She had been right too. Caroline had rejected her parents' choice of a suitable husband and had run away with a young journalist she had met at a Protestant church meeting.

Mary had resumed her role as mentor, by letter. Caroline had been disowned by her father, but she had been blissfully happy in poverty with her journalist husband. Mary had sent her money when she could. Adrian had of course supported his father-in-law's point of view. Then had come news of her tragic death in childbirth. It was only in his grief and when it was too late, that her father had become reconciled to his youngest daughter and had recognised, mirrored in her, his own restless and rebellious nature. Many months later Mary had received a parcel containing all the pathetic mementos of Caroline's short life. It had been the last act of her heart-broken husband, before he took his own life. She had never told her father of this bequest. It would only have added to his remorse.

Her death had marked the sad decline of Caroline's mother who could never come to terms with her abandonment of her own daughter. Henry in his grief had tried to contact his erstwhile son-in-law to recapture some of their life together, only to discover that he had taken his own life some four weeks after the death of Caroline. They had both been buried in a pauper's grave, but no-one could tell him where.

Henry Bragg had been proud of Mary's marriage to a southern gentleman and she had basked in his approval. She had not seen him for many years. Now in his early eighties, he was still a sprightly and vigorous man with but the merest suggestion of a paunch. He was carefully dressed and sported a white, exquisitely trimmed beard that framed a slightly florid complexion. But it was the sparkling blue of his eyes, dancing with energy and merriment, that as always arrested her attention. He was, she thought, the very epitome of a man of power and prosperity. He bore his age well.

He greeted his daughter with affection. Mary introduced Ruth as her friend and companion. Henry responded by kissing her hand. Ruth had been prepared for this greeting, but all the same it seemed a strange custom to Ruth. She fought to hide how new the experience was to her.

Henry was full of charm and chatter, most of which he seemed to direct towards Ruth. She realised with a sudden shock that he found her attractive and was in a mild way flirting with her. Ruth in her turn warmed to the gallant old gentleman who was trying so hard to mimic the old-world courtesy of the South, which he so much admired.

There was such a multitude of differences to her new status, it was like trying to catch snow-flakes in a blizzard. But people see what they want to see and interpret things how they expect them to be. She still found it strange to accept how people went out of their way to try and please her, whereas before her approval had been of no account. Nevertheless, she slowly began to relax and even to enjoy herself but was careful not for a moment to lower her guard.

Standing behind Henry Bragg, unnoticed in the entrance Hall, was an elderly lady who shuffled forward when the flurry of formal greetings was over. She came up to Mary peering with

210

the frank curiosity of a child into her face. On her own face there was, at first, not a flicker of recognition. Then she brought up a wandering hand and traced the outline of her features with her fingers as one who is blind might do. Mary stood quite still while this tactile interrogation took place. There was an awkward silence in which everyone avoided eye contact.

"Caroline?" said the old lady at last, her voice seeming to rise with sudden hope.

"No Mother, Caroline's gone away. It's Mary," said Mrs Styles, moving to embrace her mother, but her mother's arms remained limply at her sides.

"Mary?" said the old lady in a quavering, querulous tone, as if she was hearing the name for the first time.

"Your oldest daughter Mamma," explained Mary gently.

Suddenly the old lady turned towards where Ruth was standing, "And who is this?" she asked sharply looking challengingly at Ruth.

"It's Ruth Mother, my companion and friend," explained Mary, "she's come with me all the way from Nethergate."

"Nethergate? Nethergate?" queried her mother without comprehension and as if the word meant nothing to her. Then suddenly she went rigid and stared directly at Ruth. Her eyes sparkled with sudden intelligence. She pronounced, "You ain't no lady's companion. You're a nigger."

Ruth went cold. How could this mad old lady have suddenly seen through her deception? She looked to Mary, but it was Henry Bragg who recovered first.

"Come Rebecca my dearest," he said, "it is time for your rest. We've kept you going far too long, just to see Mary's homecoming." He put his arm round his wife's shoulders. Immediately the tension left her, and she relaxed trustingly, like a weary child pleased to do his bidding. Then, flashing a look of apology to Ruth and Mary, he murmured, "You mustn't take offence at the things she says. It is not her that says these things." Then with a tenderness that seemed so at odds with the rest of his nature, Henry Bragg ushered his wife from the room.

Ruth had glanced about the room after Rebecca's announcement, but only read sympathy and understanding on every face. Mary had known of her mother's deteriorating condition but had not been prepared for how far she had retreated from reality. "You mustn't care for what she says," she whispered to Ruth as the two women were shown to their rooms.

"She was dead right though, wasn't she?" muttered Ruth under her breath. Mary gave her a wry smile.

Their cases had been brought up from the station rail cart. Ruth's maid, a young white girl called Maggie, was very respectful and awed at serving a grand Southern Lady. She asked where Ruth wished her things to be unpacked. All the time Ruth was feeling as if she had suddenly come to a world where everything had been turned upside down. Her instincts were to do all the things for herself, but she knew she must at all costs keep the deception alive. She knew too that whilst one might dupe one's social peers it was infinitely more difficult to deceive a servant.

Hot water had been brought into the room and Ruth gladly allowed Maggie to clean away the smut and grime of their long journey and prepare her for her next ordeal of dining with the family. Keeping the pretence, particularly after the shock of Mrs Bragg's apparent prescience, was going to be hard work indeed. She wondered if others thought the same way as Mary's mother. Only time would tell, but it did not make things any easier for her.

34

On The Run

Matthew had not witnessed the pantomime that followed his escape into the crowd. As far as he was concerned, he had dived full tilt into the mass of slave bodies which had somehow miraculously parted in front of him and then had immediately closed behind him. Not a soul had impeded his progress. They had split like the Red Sea for the children of Israel, for Morella had prepared them well. He had a long way to go. The lands about the creek, where safety lay, were a good five miles distant. The terrain was flat where the tobacco grew. It might be possible to hide among the crop itself and slowly work his way to the bayou. But instinct told him that his best chances lay in reaching refuge as quickly as possible. His recent illness had weakened him and the ordeal of the past few days had further sapped his stamina. In his heart, he didn't reckon much to his chances, but there could be no turning back now. So far there had been no signs of pursuit. He looked over his shoulder, but all he could hear was the distant wild shouting of the slaves and could only wonder at what was happening.

Soon the plantation buildings were out of sight and the first flickering hopes of success began to take hold. He slackened his pace to gain his breath and to husband his energy, now that the first adrenalin rush of his escape was over. He had not realised how weak he was.

A sudden shot rang out. The distant clamour died immediately. He stopped to listen. The sudden silence was ominous. Something had changed. He broke into a run again. His thoughts turned to George. Would he really have laid on the lash? But then what would he have done in George's shoes? The notion of Killcaid administering the beating instead was unthinkable, not for the pain that he would have endured, but for the enjoyment that Killcaid would derive from the act. Most of all though, it would have been the humiliation as the pain of the lash broke down his resolve and he was reduced to a whimpering cowering parody of his former self. No-one could suffer the lash without crying out in the end. He shuddered at the thought of it.

It seemed he had been going for ages. All he could hear now was the labouring of his own breath and the thudding of his heart. Then suddenly he stopped. His ears had caught a distant musical note that rose and fell on the morning breeze. It was a sound to chill the heart and loosen the bowels of any fugitive slave, the clamour of the Nethergate Coonhounds. He felt his chest tighten and his breath shorten in panic. He knew well what that sound meant.

The pack at Nethergate had been introduced by Mark Styles. They were the very finest black and tan Coonhounds bred for their ability to follow a scent both on the ground and airborne. Originally the old planters had favoured the English Foxhound to hunt the racoon, the nearest native substitute they could find to the wily old English fox. But they had failed when it came to racoon hunting, for unsportingly the racoon often took refuge up trees to the utter mystification of hounds bred to the ways of the English fox. These hounds had eventually been crossed with bloodhounds and other breeds to produce the Coonhound. Now, the ingenuity of man had found a more sinister use for the breed, in hunting down a human quarry.

The pack at Nethergate had been trained to perfection. As such they were much in demand by the neighbouring plantation owners. They had a justifiable reputation. Unless the huntsmen kept them firmly in check though, they would tear and worry at their prey much as their kind tore at the racoon and in their distant past, the fox. Occasionally the hunters would arrive at the scene too late to save the wretched fugitive. There might be some financial loss, but the cost was usually considered worth it for the deterrent effect it had on others who might contemplate a similar urge for freedom.

It had taken Killcaid longer than he would have liked to restore order. By the liberal application of the whip his overseers had eventually set the slaves off, sullen without breakfast, to their allotted tasks. Spread about the estate, they could not draw courage from each other. The disorder of the morning was a thing of the past. After a hard and arduous day's labour among the tobacco plants it would soon be forgotten. Now the excited barking and clamour of the coonhounds filled the air. It would send a chilling message to every hand on Nethergate and Killcaid hoped particularly that it would carry to their quarry. Often it was enough to send the terrified runaway scrabbling for the nearest refuge where the hounds would ring him until the hunters arrived. The mounted huntsman nodded to Killcaid that all was ready and waited for the expected order to start the hunt.

Killcaid's mood had changed. His impotent fury at the conduct of the slaves had given way to one of vengeful anticipation. Slaves rarely escaped the Nethergate pack. Now Silas Killcaid was preparing to enjoy and savour the excitement of the chase. There was nothing quite like the exhilaration of hunting a human quarry. It was so much more challenging than the pursuit of the racoon. For Killcaid, slave hunting was the ultimate expression of the superiority of the white man over the Negro. The Negro was reduced to his true primitive state, meeting an animal's fate and dying with grunts and shrill screams as an animal died.

The old Mrs Styles might be enraged at the loss of a favourite slave, but whatever she might think he was only following the Master's orders and if the hunters were delayed, these accidents did sometimes occur. He still had not quite made up his mind if he dared let the hunt end that way, but he wanted to with a yearning he hardly dared to acknowledge it was so intense.

The clamour and excitement of the hounds had now reached fever pitch, but still Killcaid held them back. The bayou was the only sanctuary that Matthew could seek. He knew Matthew was weakened by his ordeal of the day before, by a sleepless night of fear and by his recent illness. He wanted Matthew to get a good start so that he would feel to the full the terror of the hunted as the hounds inevitably gained on him. He would know there could be no escape. He would cling to hope until hope turned to despair and he would finally seek refuge from the jaws of the hounds and face instead the humiliation of recapture. But he might of course leave the decision too late. Killcaid's muscles tightened in anticipation. Still he refrained from giving the order.

Finally, Killcaid considered the time to be right and nodded to the huntsman. The huntsman took the lead hound to where Matthew had spent the night to introduce him to his scent. Ever eager the remaining hounds milled about, their excitement now erupting in shrill falsetto barks and whimpers. Then the lead hound began to circle, nose riveted to the ground. The pack suddenly fell silent, serious with intent.

The lead hound picked up the scent beyond where the crowd had been and began tentatively to follow the trail. Only when he was certain did he pause and lift his head. A low, bass booming cry came from deep within. The rest of the pack homed in and soon the air was filled with the musical cacophony of the chase, a sound beloved of huntsmen the world over. The entire pack surged as one brown and tan stream along the path Matthew had taken.

The horses and men about Killcaid caught the fever of the chase and stirred restlessly. But still Killcaid would not give the signal to follow. Even to his helpers Killcaid's actions were a puzzle, but some caught the sinister notion of his intent and glanced, white eyed and uneasy, at each other.

"Aint we going after dem hounds?" asked one at last.

"There's plenty o' time for that," re-joined Killcaid in a leisurely fashion. "That boy aint no use to no-one. He don't work. He aint nothin' but trouble. This way he's goin' to trouble no-one no more." And he spat on the ground with satisfaction.

One of the slaves laughed, but it came out as a falsetto bark. Even to them Killcaid's plan seemed wrong.

"He ain't no more'n a boy," ventured one of the men and instantly regretted it as Killcaid glowered at him.

"Boy's vermin," growled Killcaid emphatically.

"Sure is Masser. Aint no more'n use than a pesky 'coon," agreed the slave who had spoken out, fearing he had already gone too far.

By now the baying of the hounds was a distant clamour barely audible on the light morning breeze. The huntsman was clearly anxious above all others to be up with his hounds. But still Killcaid restrained them. A grim smile of satisfaction played about his lips for now he had finally made up his mind. He meant to make sure that they would arrive upon the scene of Matthew's capture too late to stop the hounds from doing what nature dictated they should. After this morning's near rebellion it would be a chilling lesson to those who had enjoyed his discomfiture and would bring them back in line as nothing else could.

217

For a few more moments, until he was certain of the outcome, he savoured the heady wine of revenge before nodding to the others to begin the pursuit and even then, he restrained the riders from quickening their pace. Even the huntsman was not allowed to move in front of Killcaid.

35

Dining With The Family

Ruth had feared this moment, her first experience of sitting at table with a white family. She had witnessed enough of how they behaved at table to have no fears on that score, but it was the ability to live the lie that she and her mistress had concocted which was her greatest fear. Meeting casual strangers presented few difficulties, but now she had to sustain the subterfuge among people she would get to know and who now would get to know her. Mary had provided her with the necessary attire, subdued and not too grand, and had given her some of her own jewellery to wear. She had even provided her with fresh underwear, for servants talk. Now it was all up to her. She had to remember the whole story she and Mary had concocted and stick to every detail less they should contradict each other.

She had prepared her toilet with care, assisted by Maggie, who had proved to be a talkative child and plainly not used to her role as lady's maid. She spoke with a thick German accent and was clearly curious to hear what life was really like in the grand houses of the southern states. She compared them in her mind with the heavy stone *Schlosser* from Bavaria, her country of origin. For Ruth, having her hair brushed and prepared and being assisted to dress was a surreal experience, but she reflected with some relief that it was a good thing that both she and Maggie were new to their respective roles.

When she was ready she dismissed Maggie and went along to Mary's room so that they could go down together. There Mary had greeted her with a look of open admiration.

"Well, just look at you!" she cried with obvious pleasure, "truly all eyes will be upon you."

That is the last thing I want, thought Ruth, but she was pleased with the compliment. For the first time, she really did look at herself in the mirror, not as someone trying to evade detection, not as a slave, but simply as a woman in her own right. She saw before her a mature, handsome woman of dark, more Mediterranean than African complexion, whose eyes now sparkled with pleasure and excitement at the transformation she was witnessing. Truly, she realised with growing confidence, no-one looking at her would think she was anything other than what she pretended to be. With a flutter of excitement, she began really to look forward to playing the part of lady's companion to her mistress and acting the part of a white woman. With this thought her heart overflowed with gratitude to her mistress, "O Missus'," she cried, "I is so grateful for all you has done for me."

The answer she received was a mild rebuke.

"Whilst we are here in the North you must never address me so, even in private, or our secret will be out."

Ruth nodded. How quickly she had forgotten the ability of slave or servant to become an invisible yet sentient part of the furniture. Fortunately though, Mary's maid had already been dismissed. The moment of euphoria had passed, and she reminded herself again of her former fears lest the excitement of playing her new character should cause her to betray herself. She remembered then the penetrating stare of Mary's mother and her sudden perceptive accusation.

"Do you think your mother will denounce me again?" she asked with sudden trepidation.

"No, my dear. She will have forgotten all about it. In fact, it will probably have done us a service, for now everyone will be anxious to save your blushes."

"Do you really think so?" asked Ruth not utterly convinced.

"Certain of it."

Together the two ladies descended to meet Mary's family and some friends who had been invited for the occasion.

Ruth had to school herself to proffer a hand when being introduced and to resist the temptation to bob. She watched carefully how Mary's various cousins and aunts, relatives and old friends behaved and was careful not to stand out. Any fears she had of betraying herself by something she said were hardly put to the test for Mary's father insisted on monopolising the conversation at every turn. But he was an entertaining host and soon gales of laughter were sweeping round the room.

It was at the point when she was beginning to relax and almost to savour the occasion that all her old fears were once more aroused. A voice with an unmistakeable southern accent suddenly sounded in her ear, "Ah fancies Ma'am that you and I are the odd ones out here." It was the man she had been introduced to as Colonel Gladstone. He was indeed the odd one out as clearly a man of the South. He was no relation of Mary's but was an old friend of the family before the days of the present conflict. He was a handsome man of military bearing and courtly southern manners. He had been introduced as the personal guest of Henry Bragg and a colonel in the Southern Army. He had been captured outside St Louis and was now on parole waiting the chance to return south in exchange for a Yankee officer of similar standing.

"My good friend Colonel Gladstone," Henry Bragg had announced putting an arm about the Colonel's shoulder. "Though on the wrong side of our present divide, our friendship goes back a long way. We were, so-to-speak, trading partners. When I heard he was awaiting repatriation, it was the least I could do to offer him the comfort of my hospitality until the wait was over, to show that we of the North are no barbarians in this conflict."

Colonel Gladstone had bowed in acknowledgement of this sentiment.

"Someday our great nation will be a union once more," continued Mr Bragg, "and we will offer again the hand of friendship, to be at one and to trust one another again, north and south, a partnership of equals."

"Amen to that," said the Colonel.

It was a pretty speech and one or two of the ladies present had softly clapped their gloved hands in agreement with the sentiment. Colonel Gladstone with his easy manner and charm had quickly integrated with the company. Quite what his connection was with Henry Bragg had been left rather vague, but the two seemed much at ease together almost as if engaged in some joint enterprise. His presence though, coming from the South, made Ruth feel uneasy and she wondered whether there was more to his remark about them being the odd ones out.

"How so Sir?" she had challenged at the time, perhaps too quickly. He had eyed her quizzically.

"Why surely that we two are the only ones here Southern born and bred. Mary, God bless her, is a Northerner by birth, though she has lived long enough amongst us." She wondered whether the sharpness of her response might not have aroused some suspicion in Colonel Gladstone's mind. Despite his easy manner and charm, she sensed that he was a dangerous man and one to be treated with a respectful caution.

At that point dinner was announced and Ruth found herself being escorted in by a distant cousin of Mary's. During the meal, she relaxed once more, but every now and then she would look up to find the Colonel's eyes fixed upon her. She felt sure somehow, he had seen through her deception and was just waiting for her to betray herself.

Despite the ominous presence of Colonel Gladstone, she found herself otherwise enjoying the evening and the feeling of emancipation it gave. The company treated her with friendliness and respect. Her views on the present conflict were sought and listened to with serious consideration. For the first time in her life she tasted the heady wine of being treated by white people as an equal, as a person in her own right whose opinions were important and counted for something. Part of her still hankered after the old life where she was not living a lie, but this was infinitely more exciting and had given her a taste of the fruits of true freedom. She realised suddenly that this was the way her life could be, should be and she meant to ring from it every drop of enjoyment before the shackles of slavery fell over her once again. But could she, she wondered, now return to that old life. Surely Mrs Styles would take care of Matthew and make sure he was not sold. But she knew it was but a fancy. Had she known at that moment the perils facing her son, her present musings would have instantly been thrown aside weighed against the instinct of a mother to protect her young.

36

The Chase

Matthew forced down the initial panic he had felt on hearing the distant clamour of the hounds. But he had heard many tales, told in the slave cabins at night, of fugitives outwitting the hounds and those that hunted with them. He was not without hope either. He immediately changed direction although it would take him longer to reach the safety of the bayou. He altered course towards a small stream and for a short time ran towards the commotion of the hounds, then crossing the stream he continued for a while in the same direction away from the safety of the creek. Then he carefully retraced his steps hoping thereby to set the hounds on a new course away from the line he was taking.

Once back at the stream he continued splashing through the muddy waters hoping that they would flush away his scent trail. But it was hard work. At times he found himself forcing his way through knee deep mud which rapidly sapped his store of energy. His legs began to tire, and he found himself breathing hard. After about half a mile he clambered out of the water, judging that he had left a big enough gap in his trail to delay the hounds. But the diversion had cost him dear, for the strength seemed to have left him. Briefly he scanned the horizon for any other signs of pursuit, but to his relief he could see no riders above the line of the tobacco plants. In the far distance though, he thought he could see a disturbance in the sun's reflection from the sea of tobacco plants, like an invisible snake gliding unseen through the long grass. It marked the progress of the Nethergate pack.

He continued his course, but now his route lay across the tobacco fields. Due to the fall in demand for tobacco, the plants in this section had been left untended and had grown high enough to conceal his passing, but he had to force his way through. The going became increasingly difficult. He was getting near to exhaustion. Soon, come what may, he would have to pause to rest. It was at that point that he ran full tilt into the arms of a slave, who seemed to have appeared from nowhere. He was immediately locked in an iron-like embrace. He was a huge man and Matthew realised at once that he was powerless to resist. Too exhausted to struggle, despair suddenly sapped him of the will to fight.

A sobbing cry of anguish half escaped his lips, but the man clapped his hands about his mouth. Matthew struggled for breath. The slave's physical power was immense. He was pulled to the ground. Only then did Matthew realise that the stranger was signalling for him to keep quiet. Slowly the man released his hand and indicated that he had run into a working party and that above all they must escape the notice of their overseer.

He wasn't a slave Matthew recognized from the Nethergate Estate. He realised that he must be from another plantation. Often estates would bring in hands from other farms for specific tasks. There was a calm authority and dignity about this slave that was instantly impressive. He knew instinctively that he could trust him. He seemed to know what he was doing, for when the distant mounted overseer had turned away, he indicated that Matthew should climb onto his back. He carried him with an easy loping gait as if he were no heavier than the shirt upon his back. This way he retraced Matthew's trail through the plantation for a short distance. Then he branched off at right angles. After a time, he set Matthew down. Removing his own shirt, he rubbed it vigorously over Matthew's body and legs so that it became heavy with Matthew's scent. He paused for a moment with his head on one side, to listen to the distant clamour of the hounds. Then he seemed to make up his mind. Not a word had been spoken, but Matthew could feel the man's goodwill as if it were a whole army of silent supporters. He indicated that Matthew should change his course at right angles to his original trail.

"It's an old trick," he whispered, "but it might delay them for a bit. God be with thee my son," was all he said. He laid his hand briefly upon Matthew's head as if in benediction. There was a deep bass timbre to his voice. It was a voice that Matthew felt he could have listened to for ever. He longed to know more of this man. His heart overflowed with gratitude at this totally unexpected help from a stranger. He waved farewell and left the man busily wafting his shirt now heavy with Matthew's scent over the trail he had originally followed.

He set off with renewed purpose and vigour. This simple, spontaneous act of courage and goodwill, by a total stranger, had an almost miraculous significance. Words he had heard from the Bible came to his mind. 'He gives strength to the weary and increases the power of the weak'. He had the strangest feeling that he had been in the presence and held in the arms of a truly saintly man. When he was exhausted and ready to give way to despair, the man had suddenly appeared from nowhere. He had carried him and given him hope. He felt that the man's goodwill and purpose was with him yet. He longed to know more about him. He didn't even know his name.

Just then the note of the pursuing hounds faltered in the

distance and then died away. He paused to listen. They had reached his first false trail. They would now be casting about along the line of the stream trying to pick up his scent once more.

He was making good time now buoyed up by the intervention of the saintly stranger. He felt that perhaps he was meant now to escape from bondage. He had once again turned in the direction of the creek and safety. It would not be long now before he could plunge into the morass where only he knew the secret ways. The dogs would find it impossible to follow his trail. He was aiming for where he had left the dug out. Once in that he would leave no trail and his escape would be complete.

Despite his renewed hope, it wasn't long before fatigue began once again to drag at his heels. Every stride now became a separate act of will, every breath a conscious effort. Exhaustion seemed to be denying his body all sense of co-ordination. He had to rest. He fell to the ground as weak as a kitten. Hope had evaporated almost as soon as it had been born, dashed now with the sense of his own frailty. The temptation to lie here until the hounds overwhelmed him was almost too great to resist. What hope had he for a future anyway? Then suddenly the note of the hounds changed. Once more they had hit upon his trail. Their great booming chorus was enough to drive him again to his feet. But his progress now was desperately slow.

He had cleared the plantation and was moving through the thick scrub that bordered the bayou. He could see tantalisingly close the dark green belt of the trees and vegetation about the swamp where safety lay. He was walking, no longer able to run. Every few yards he had to pause to gain his breath and to muster the energy for a few more steps. The ground was waterlogged and ever more difficult to move over, sucking at his feet and sapping his energy with every stride. He cast about for sign of the horses which surely must be following the hounds. Their dust cloud was nowhere to be seen. The green horizon seemed impossibly far, his progress achingly slow. Then in the distance he heard the note of the hounds change to excited yapping and confused barking. He smiled to himself as he pictured them all milling about among the slave working party. He saw his unknown helper, standing a giant among the Lilliputians. Who was he, he wondered? Why had he risked so much for a total stranger? Then he wondered how long his subterfuge would hold them.

Killcaid too had noted the changed chorus from the hounds. "Have they got him now?" he asked with barely concealed relish.

The huntsman listened. "No. Don't reckon they has Mr Killcaid. They'm more confused by the sound of it. Best I go and see." With that he set off in pursuit of his hounds. Killcaid and the others followed. They soon came across the hounds milling about a huge black slave holding a shirt in his hands. It was the shirt that seemed to interest the dogs. The man himself showed no fear, but simply stood in dignified stillness whilst the volatile pack seethed about him. The huntsman, who was experienced in such matters, immediately summed up the situation.

"That thar shirt'll be the key. Mark my words Mr Killcaid. Seen it done afore to confuse the hounds. The fugitive marks his scent upon jus' such an article as that thar shirt and an accomplice then lays a false trail with it. Ask him? I'll wager he can tell us which ways he went."

The slave drew himself up with dignity and looked scornfully at Killcaid every line of his bearing speaking a noble defiance.

"That so? That the truth?" growled Killcaid with rising fury. All the frustrations and anger of the morning's events seemed to surge up within him like flood waters boiling about the base of a dam.

"Truth?" queried the slave in measured and sonorous tones that boomed out from deep within his great frame. "What do your sort know of de Truth? There is only one Truth and that is the word that cometh out of de mouth of the blessed Lord Jesus, the only son of God. When you spend your time hunting down one of God's own critters, his own creation, like they was no more than the lowest animal that crawled in God's earth, that is not de Truth, that is an offence against the very Word of God and is hateful and abominable in His sight."

For a moment Killcaid was astonished at these words, delivered with such assurance, authority and passion.

"Of course I aided de fugitive as it is my God-ordained duty so to do." There was a rustle among the tobacco plants as some of the other slaves within earshot came unbidden to join them and to listen to their Pastor. Matthew had, by a stroke of good fortune, run in to the arms of no ordinary slave, but a slave preacher. He was a man who by his sheer physical presence commanded respect. He would never let pass an opportunity fearlessly to ply his cause and proclaim the Gospel when he sensed he might have an audience. Other slaves, looking up, noted the movement and came to join the party. Such was the Preacher's authority that the overseer had learnt not to interrupt these proceedings. He simply added on the time lost at the end of the day. "Alleluia! The Lord God be praised!" continued the preacher as if he was addressing a great congregation. Yet more slaves stretched, laid down their tools and made their way to listen to their preacher. He was always entertaining.

Killcaid however had other business afoot. "Damn you and your Alleluias," he roared, "Which way did the varmint go? Or I'll flay you alive!"

The preacher raised his head and fixed Killcaid with a quizzical look as of a schoolmaster staring down an impudent pupil. At this presumption, the dam of Killcaid's self-control burst. Changing the grip on his whip he swung the lead-loaded end like a cudgel at the defiant slave. All the anger and frustration of the day's events lent force to his arm.

The black man did not attempt to save himself. He did not try to ward off the blow. Indeed, he seemed to welcome it. It was his martyrdom. It was a token of his love and trust in his God. With a sickening thud, the heavy whip-end fell on the side of the preacher's head where the skull is at its thinnest. With a barely audible groan the great man swayed. Then he fell to his knees for all the world as if he were offering himself to his Maker, as indeed he was. The dogs scattered in alarm to leave him space. His mouth worked. He tried to speak then pitched forward and lay still. A sudden convulsion shook his great frame and then left him. His body relaxed in death and surely the good man's soul departed to his own special reward in the loving arms of his Maker.

Those present were shocked into stillness by this sudden savage act and its awful consequence. The hounds which had been milling about as though their job was done suddenly fell back, startled at this sudden explosion of violence. One came across and incuriously sniffed at the corpse, not understanding. Then sensing by the silence of the onlookers that something awful had taken place, it slunk off. Another hound gently took the preacher's shirt, impregnated with Matthew's scent, which was still clasped in his hand. Slowly he let it drop. He examined it with his nose and then slunk off guilt-stricken with his tail between its legs, as if he had been the cause of the dreadful deed that had just been played out.

37

The End Of The Chase

Apart from those with Killcaid there had been one other witness to the scene. From a distance, the overseer of the hired slaves had been watching the events, not wishing to stand in the way of the Preacher. Now he rode over and reined in his horse. "Good day to you Silas," he said. The two were clearly no strangers. "Looks to me as you has finally paid our Preacher off. Not that he's any loss to me, but Mr Lock won't be best pleased. He's a good worker for all his mouthing. Nothing personal Silas you understand, but it'll cost you dear. Otherwise Mr Lock's as like to take the sum from me for not taking sufficient care o' my charges. He's a hard man as you well knows."

Silas Killcaid considered the situation. He felt angry. He had not meant to kill the man. He was annoyed with the slave for provoking him. He had not wanted things to turn out this way. He felt some remorse that the incident had taken place. That is to say, he regretted the inconvenience and the delay in the pursuit of Matthew. But no matter these difficulties could always be resolved. He moved his horse close to that of the other overseer so that they could converse in private. They soon came to an agreement as is the custom on such occasions and shook hands upon the deal as gentlemen do.

Then Killcaid turned to address those present.

"A sad business," he acknowledged, looking down at the crumpled form of the dead preacher, "to which you all bin witness. We come across the bloodied corpse of this here Preacher fellow, lyin' as we see him now. Clearly, he had tried to apprehend the fugitive, as is every Christian man's duty so to do," and he paused here sorrowfully to shake his head. "An' you won't come across a much more Christian soul than this poor Nigger boy. It were that black-hearted varmint Matthew who even now we is huntin' who has struck this poor Preacher fellow down. Struck him with a rock to make good his escape. Struck him and killed him stone dead," and he chuckled mirthlessly at his pun. Then with a steely purpose he continued, "Do I make myself clear? Do you all understand?" Picking up a rock from the ground he moved over to where the victim lay. Then lifting high his hand he struck the preacher's head a second time leaving the stone smeared with the Preacher's blood, leaving no doubt as to how the poor man had died.

He looked from face to face and did not move on to the next man until each of the riders had nodded their heads in agreement. He did not bother with the slaves who had now gathered about their preacher's body with loud cries of lamentation and appeals to God.

"Good. We all understand. Now we mus' double our efforts an' capture him, dead or alive, an' bring him to justice, before some other poor Nigger is kil't." Then turning to the other overseer, he added, "You has my word upon it. Mr. Styles will compensate your Mr Lock for the loss of his hand as he's liable in law for the action of one of his slaves. Now we have work to do. To catch the murdering swine as did this terrible thing."

What had at first been a half-formed intention had now become a firm resolve. It was imperative to Killcaid now, that the dogs catch up with the fugitive before he reached the safety of the bayou. The dogs must be allowed to do their work before the hunters arrived on the scene in time to call them off. That way there would be no loose ends. No-one would dare to contradict Killcaid's version of events and summary justice would be seen to have been done. Turning to the huntsman he urged him once more to cast about for Matthew's trail. It wasn't long before the lead hound let out his long baying call. Noses down, the pack all converged and once more took up the cry until soon the entire pack of coonhounds were coursing along Matthew's trail with their noses hard pressed to the ground, filling the air once more with their music.

The huntsman moved off to keep pace with his hounds, but Killcaid called him back. "Let the hounds do their work," he growled. "The boy's a common murderer now." The huntsman hesitated, then at the look in Killcaid's eye fell back and took up station behind him. Such was the force of Killcaid's personality that the huntsman almost believed in the truth of what Killcaid had just said. In the circumstances, it seemed a reasonable thing to do.

Meanwhile Matthew's progress was now ever more laboured. Beyond exhaustion, will power alone drove him on. He could see the birds wheeling effortlessly in the sky above the trees where the bayou began. How he wished he had their wings to soar effortlessly up to safety. He knew what the hounds would do to a fugitive with no huntsman to call them off. Fearfully he glanced behind him again. The hounds had been silent a long time. His unknown benefactor must have succeeded in delaying them for longer than he had dared hope. He offered up a silent prayer of thanks for the action of his giant saviour.

Then he heard the sound he was dreading as a single long

baying note told of a trail re-discovered. Soon the pack was once again in full cry. Matthew could not respond. All his reserves were spent. All he could do was to stagger forward and hope.

He could see the hounds now, moving with incredible swiftness. Ominously there was still no sign of the riders. Matthew now grasped with a dull certainty Killcaid's intentions. How was it possible that Killcaid's rancour would go to these lengths? His mind was filled with the thought of those teeth, savage and bloodied, ripping and tearing into the softness of his body. His breath came now in great wracking sobs. If only he could move faster. But now his legs refused to respond.

The baying of the hounds filled the air. He turned and spotted the first hound breaking through from the tobacco field. Soon they were all through, their heads down the air full of their commotion, a single, undulating brown wave surging relentlessly in his direction.

The welcoming green canopy was now no more than a hundred yards away. A quick sprint and he would be there. But it was impossible. Matthew realised that he would never reach the fringe of green and the cool dappled shelter of the swamp before the leading hounds were upon him. Frantically he searched for a tree or some other refuge to escape the hounds. There was nothing. Desperately he sought for sight of the riders. There was no-one. He would die alone and unseen.

He was certain now. He knew with sickening horror the satisfaction that Killcaid would draw from his demise. He could hear the counterfeit regret with which Killcaid reported his heroic efforts to reach the fugitive before the hounds had done their worst. Would the Master swallow the lie? But he had accepted Killcaid's version of George's rescue from the swamp in the face of his own son's denials. He couldn't believe that hatred would drive even Killcaid to such lengths. No-one could call the hounds off now. They would complete their bloody business.

The brown avalanche was now bounding and leaping across the green scrub to where he stood. Their heads were up. They had spotted their quarry. Their excited clamour filled the air. At that moment, Matthew suddenly spotted the horses breaking cover. Hope lifted within him. If they galloped hard they might yet reach him in time? He recognised Killcaid's distinctive hat. Then the figure raised his hand and the other horsemen reined in.

With cold certainty now, he knew Killcaid's intention. He was going to enjoy a ringside seat at his destruction. He wasn't going to survive. He was filled now with a strange calm. He would not die fleeing the hounds.

The pack was surging across the scrub. Their excited yelping drowned all other sound. He glanced once more at the horsemen in the distance. Only Killcaid's horse faced him. The others were half turned away, not wishing to be part of what would now follow. Matthew could see Killcaid shading his eyes the better to enjoy the spectacle. He could imagine the thin sneer that would be playing about his lips and the cruel glint of triumph that would sparkle in his hard, humourless eyes. In his mind, he could see it all and he pitied the man. He thought of his mother. She would find his letter when she returned, so full of hope for the future, but she would read them knowing of his cruel fate. He wished he had told her how much he loved her.

Then Matthew drew himself erect and turned to face the hounds.

38

At Bay

The horsemen about Killcaid could not quite believe what they were witnessing. They were used to Killcaid's casual cruelty, but this was something different. They were all a party to a deliberate act of murder. But none stirred. Only a few dared look on.

The lone figure had turned now to face the streaming mass of black and brown surging relentlessly to where he stood. There was something almost biblical in his stance which was not lost on the watching slaves. The hysteria of the hounds drifted towards them. The character of the sound had changed now they had sighted their quarry. Even at that distance the solitary figure radiated defiance. In a moment, it would be savagely wrenched down and buried in a mound of ripping and tearing teeth.

At last one of them spoke in tones almost of disbelief. He voiced all their thoughts. "The lad'll be killed." Then he instantly regretted his intervention. Killcaid stared him down.

"That so?" he remarked. Then after a pause, "The lad's a murderer, isn't he? He ain't nothin' but trouble. The likes o' him spread disaffection like a disease. They all needs a lesson. That understood?"

Mutely they nodded. "Furthermore, all of you," and he stared at each one in turn till they looked down from his glare, "all o' you remember that we did all we could to save the lad, but despite all our efforts we was jus' too late. Remember it were the Master as give permission for us to set the hounds on him." Again, all heads nodded in assent.

Killcaid then turned to savour Matthew's meeting with the hounds. His mouth cracked into a thin humourless smile and his eyes sparkled, hard as enamel, with the savagery of his anticipation. He only regretted he could not be closer. His tongue flickered out about his lower lip tasting the triumph of the moment. He was a man on fire, a man empowered.

Matthew, a lone, erect figure, was standing fearlessly with his hands by his side in the moment before the hounds would engulf him. It was an image that burnt like a bright light upon the minds of the watchers. But as they watched, something strange was happening. The hounds were all milling about him. Some it is true were jumping up to him, but none were pulling him down. Instead the pack was silent, but for some excited barking and yapping. The whole concourse now moved slowly together towards the sheltering green of the bayou. The hounds were now meekly following their quarry, a lone figure in their midst. They had ceased their clamour and were moving alongside Matthew much as when the huntsman took them on a normal exercise outing. Some even had lost interest and were investigating the ground about as hounds will do when the chase is over.

Killcaid could not understand the evidence of his eyes. For once the Nethergate Pack seemed to have failed its savage reputation. Matthew was on the very edge of the bayou. He turned to look in the direction of the horsemen. Then he stooped and began ostentatiously to fondle the hounds that still milled about him, a clear signal that he was entirely at ease. Once more he turned to face Killcaid and raised his arm in a final mocking salutation. With that he vanished into the green of the swamp.

Killcaid could not believe what he was seeing. Mouthing obscenities, he roared, "Get after him! Damn you all!" With that, he urged his horse forward into a frantic gallop. The others followed. But when they and the huntsman reached the hounds, they were just in time to catch a glimpse of Matthew moving easily over the morass where none dared to follow. By then the feared Nethergate pack had broken up into casually exploring groups of hounds.

Killcaid turned on the huntsman. "What the devil's the matter with the hounds?" he demanded.

The huntsman scratched his head. "Blessed if I knows. It was almost as if they knew him."

The huntsman cracked his whip and called in his hounds. Heads came up and they all obediently massed at the huntsman's feet with the air of a job well done.

"What are you waiting for? Set them off again!" Killcaid bellowed at the huntsman, beside himself with fury at the thought that Matthew might make good his escape.

The huntsman, the scion of an English family, famed for producing generations of huntsmen, shook his head emphatically. "Impossible," he said looking out over the boggy marshland, "There bain't no trail left to follow in that lot and I'll not risk loosin' the hounds getting bogged down out thar'."

Killcaid was left to rant impotently. Matthew had escaped. How it had happened he could not comprehend. But happen it had.

The group returned to Nethergate with heads down, proclaiming their defeat. Though what they really thought at the day's events, none could tell. Some even believed they had witnessed a miracle.

Killcaid rode on ahead in a black mood nursing his anger and frustration and still wondering how Matthew had escaped from the renowned Nethergate pack. His only consolation was the thought that Matthew would find it hard to survive in such a place as the bayou with nothing but the clothes he wore. Most likely he would be trapped and sucked down to a lonely, lingering death or succumb to the poison of the snakes which abounded in the bayou. Even if he did survive, he would soon be driven by hunger to seek food on the estate. If that happened, he would soon get to hear of it. With that crumb of consolation, he returned to the work of the day. But none dared speak to him unbidden such was the savagery of his mood.

The huntsman, with the help of his whips, gathered in his hounds and set off in Killcaid's wake, back to the kennels, the hounds following at his horse's heels, their tails up thoroughly satisfied with their day's outing. They were perhaps the only ones who had enjoyed the events of that day.

As for Matthew, he had known true fear when the pack was nearly upon him. Then he remembered the times he had watched the ritual of the hounds being fed in the past. When there had been an excess of game and Old Mo had told him to feed it to the hounds, he had always enjoyed following the huntsman's ritual. Now he recognised Jezebel, the lead hound. She was always first to be called.

"Jezebel sit!" he roared, when the hounds were all but upon him. Instantly Jezebel had recognized his voice. In that moment, the nature of the entire pack had changed. Suddenly Matthew was surrounded by friendly dogs, each eager for his touch, milling about him in case he had some extra titbit about his person. In that way, he had made his way, wearily with his canine escorts, to the familiar edge of the swamp, where he and Old Mo had so often trod. There he had contemptuously acknowledged the watching Killcaid before dismissing the hounds and making good his escape.

Matthew made his way to where he had left the boat. In the cool of the swamplands and in the dappled shade of the giant Cypress trees he felt instantly secure, the harrying cries of the chase now just a memory. In a state of near collapse, he found the dug out and began paddling towards the hut that Old Mo had built. There would be no food but plenty of water from the rainwater system Old Mo had devised. At last he reached the refuge of Old Mo's cabin in the swamp. Never had it seemed so welcome, so luxurious or so safe.

After the exertions of the day he was consumed by a raging thirst. He drank his fill, then fell exhausted onto the bed of animal skins and was instantly asleep.

39

Matthew's Miracle

That night whilst Matthew slept the sleep of the exhausted the story of his escape took wings amongst the superstitious ranks of the slaves.

The miraculous way in which the dreaded Nethergate Hounds had been tamed by Matthew spread like wildfire among the slave community. The more the story was whispered, the stranger and more supernatural it became. As always, such mystical happenings were linked in people's minds with the stories from the Bible. Matthew was likened to Daniel taming the lions under King Darius.

The story took wings. When the hounds were almost upon him he had turned to face them. A strange light had suddenly surrounded him and it seemed that somehow, he was raised up. Then he had spread out his arms and the baying of the hounds instantly ceased. As one the whole pack had laid down at his feet and cowered in fear before him. Then he had blessed the hounds and they had risen to their feet, jostling among themselves for the privilege of carrying him on a carpet of their backs into the bayou. Once in the watery waste of the bayou he had stepped off the backs of the hounds and like the Saviour himself had walked across the waters of the bayou to vanish into the green, mysterious arms of the spirit of the swamp. None had dared to follow. He was Elijah spirited away from the eyes of the Israelites. Even the awesome spirit of the swamp, who swallowed up those who dared to venture into her domain, had welcomed him with open arms. Thus, the story spread, an admixture of Biblical tales, spiced with the swirling undercurrents of witchcraft and magic from the African continent. Matthew came to be credited with the mystical powers of the saints themselves.

If few had witnessed Matthew's escape from the hounds, all had witnessed the abortive flogging. That event too now became imbued with mystical and miraculous properties. They had all seen the way in which Matthew had cast aside the hands of his captors who had been leading him to the whipping post; how he had spread himself on the post waiting for the leathers to be tied about his wrists. Then it seemed the overseer who was tasked with administering the flogging had turned aside unable to cast the lash. Killcaid himself had taken the whip, but even he had dared not administer the punishment and had handed it to the son of the Master himself.

When the Master's son had raised the whip, Matthew had broken free of his bonds as St Paul had broken free from his prison cell and then had simply vanished from sight. Morella's instructions had conveniently been forgotten. Instead, it was Matthew who had sent his spirit into the crowd to confuse his pursuers. His witchcraft had delayed the departure of Killcaid and the huntsmen until he had made good his escape. He had frozen the feet of the horses so that they could not start their pursuit.

Many were the cries of, "Glory be," and "The Lord be praised," as the slaves talked of these events among themselves. The more they talked the more they saw the guiding arm of the spirit world. Even the dreaded spirit of the swamp itself had embraced him.

The slaves were not the only ones troubled by that day's events. George could find no rest in sleep. He went over and over in his mind what he might have done. Would he have administered the flogging to his friend? But if he had refused, a flogging administered by Killcaid's hand would have been infinitely worse. What would Matthew have done if the tables had somehow been turned? Why had his father simply not listened to him when he had tried to tell him what had really happened out in the bayou? Could he be that much under the influence of Killcaid that he refused to believe his own son?

All these thoughts churned round in his mind. Then out of them came one single determination. He would do whatever he could to help Matthew either to live in the swamp or to escape entirely. How the latter was to be achieved he was unsure, but he believed that Matthew could survive indefinitely on the bounty of the bayou, augmented by what he would bring him. Together they would build a shelter as they had laboured together to manufacture the dug out. With that resolution like a beacon before him, he was at last able to sleep.

Not so with Killcaid. He was another that night who found the comfort of sleep denied to him. He seethed with a rage that even the whiskey bottle could not still, as he ground his teeth in frustrated fury. Matthew had now become an even greater thorn in his side. From being a smug and pampered slave who had silently mocked and scorned him secure under the protection of the old Mrs Styles, he had now become an even greater menace. At the very moment when he had been about to subdue and humble him he had escaped in circumstances which put at risk the whole obedient cohesion of the plantation workforce. The more he mulled it over in his mind, the greater his anger grew.

He had had no difficulty in convincing Anthony of his new debt to his fellow planter over the death of the preacher-slave. He had not been pleased, but he acknowledged his responsibility for the action of one of his slaves. It added further ammunition for when he justified his actions to his mother against her favourite.

Killcaid however drew comfort from one thought. Matthew had fled into the swamp with only the clothes he stood up in. If he survived without being sucked into the treacherous morass, hunger would soon force him out into the Estate to seek food and shelter. Then he would surely get to hear of it. But with his enhanced reputation among the slaves, would they not give him shelter and hide him away? In the past, he would have had no doubt of the outcome, for he was a very present fear above all else to his workforce. But now Matthew seemed to have acquired an almost holy status as a man who could walk on water, tame the hounds and work miracles. Killcaid well knew what stories would now be whispered about concerning the day's debacle. But then he reflected, Matthew's reputation would not last long in the face of the reality of the slave's daily toil. He would be a nine-day wonder. If he managed to survive even that long in the bayou. He would be a very sorry figure when he returned, far from the mystical being he had now become in their minds, who could shrug aside the bonds of slavery and vanished at will. He who could once quell the fury of the Nethergate Pack and dance upon the waters of the bayou, would cut a sorry figure when driven out in rags from the shelter of the swamp by the ravages of hunger.

Gradually rationality began to filter through Killcaid's rage. If Matthew had perished in the swamp, he would soon become just a memory. If he survived, he would hardly emerge in a state to be hailed as the all-conquering hero. This time he would ensure that he himself administered justice at the whipping frame or better still that he be given over to the justice system who would be only too willing to convict an escaping slave of committing murder to evade capture. There would be no shortage of witnesses and no escape a second time. This time he would be hung and if the old Mrs Styles returned, even she would not be able to stall the wheels of justice. Matthew would receive his just desserts for murdering the preacher.

He had discovered that the preacher was almost an iconic figure among the slaves, who deeply mourned his loss. He felt that Matthew now truly deserved to die to expiate for the crime of killing such a noble nigger. It was a curious side to Killcaid's character that he now truly believed the murder to lie at Matthew's door and felt real indignation for those who now mourned his passing. By now he had repeated the lie so often that he himself believed it to be true. He had repeated the story to Anthony with such anger at Matthew's conduct that the Master had no doubt as to the villainy of Matthew and this added to his rancour at having to pay his neighbour for his loss.

As for the slaves of Nethergate, it was fear that kept them in order and productive, Killcaid reflected. Above all it was the fear of him. Killcaid resolved to enhance that reputation on the morrow. He would make them all work longer in the fields, increase their work quotas and reduce the rations for those that failed to reach them. He would lay on his beloved lash with ever greater fury. Furthermore, he would find some way of blaming Matthew for these extra privations. In their present mood, he believed the slaves would believe whatever claptrap he might choose to feed them.

With that consoling thought, his whiskey mug fell from his hand and he too slept at last sprawled across the table in his cabin.

40

Settling In

Manuel was full of remorse when he woke his master the next day. He knew he had failed him by doing what Killcaid had dictated, but what choice did he have? He feared Killcaid above all creatures on earth. He still felt the stinging blow administered by his young master, not so much for the force of the impact as by what had driven his young master to administer it. He was consumed with guilt.

When he woke George, he could no longer contain his shame. "Oh Masser George, I is so sorry for what I say yesterday. It were Mr Killcaid, he made me say dem things that were not true. He made me lie to you and the Master. I truly deserves a whippen'."

George was still angry at Manuel's betrayal, but too he was angry with himself for having lost control. He also felt guilt personally at having taken the whip. He still did not know whether he would also have laid on the lash. In a way, he had been entrapped in the same sort of dilemma as Manuel. As a means of assuaging his own faults he was ready to forgive Manuel his failings too. However, he now had the measure of the limits to which Manuel could be trusted. But nevertheless,

Manuel would now have to play some part in his resolve to help his friend in any way he could. He realised that his servant must be kept ignorant of anything that would lead to Matthew's betrayal if indeed he had survived his flight into the bayou.

"I forgive you Manuel. For God's sake let's have no more talk of whipping and I regret raising my hand to you in anger. It is not my way." Tears welled up in Manuel's eyes at the generosity of his young master and he swore to himself that he would not give in again to his fear of Killcaid. Thus, master and slave were reconciled. "And now Manuel," George continued, "there is something you can do for me, something that must be conducted in the utmost secrecy."

George then dictated to Manuel a list of the things of which he thought Matthew would have the most immediate need. As far as he knew Matthew had only the clothes he was wearing when he had escaped. He had already made out a list as he had lain in bed that morning. Matthew would need: food, clothing, blankets, plates and mugs, knives, spoons, rope canvas and cord for traps and for constructing a shelter, hammer and nails and so the list went on. Only Manuel could lay his hands on such commodities without giving rise to suspicion, and only a slave could be seen carrying such items.

That morning Manuel did his utmost to acquire most of what his master had ordered and bit by bit concealed it along the track that led to the bayou at a point that George had indicated. If he suspected what his master was up to he said nothing, for above all he wished to restore himself to George's affection and goodwill and to make amends for his betrayal. Time and again he repeated his avowal that he would never betray his master again. But in his heart of hearts he was only too aware of his own abject fear of the man Killcaid.

By early afternoon he declared to George that most of what he had ordered was secreted along the track that led down to the bayou. Master and slave together ventured out.

George, mindful of the stresses which Manuel might face if questioned too closely, instructed him to collect all the items together again and to leave them in a further place he had indicated. Whilst Manuel was thus engaged he went on ahead to the spot where he and Matthew used to meet. There he raised his pistol in the air and without loading ball discharged it three times as quickly as he could tamp down the charge and wadding. This was their agreed signal for an emergency meeting should the need arise. George waited for Matthew to appear, but after nearly an hour had gone by, George gave up. He scribbled a note giving the location of the supplies that Manuel had collected and left, heavy-hearted by the thought that after all his friend might have perished in the manner he so nearly had himself.

No sooner had George left than Matthew appeared from the undergrowth and retrieved George's message. With the heightened wariness of the fugitive, he had watched George for some time, still was not quite sure whether he meant to betray him. His heart warmed to his friend when cautiously he followed the instructions in the note and discovered the treasure trove that George had left for him. His friend had been thoughtful and imaginative. There were some items that Old Mo had not yet had time to secrete away in his hiding place, but most of all he was grateful for items of clothing that George had included.

It took him some while to ferry it all to the cabin and to stow it as neatly as Old Mo had stowed everything else. There remained one mysterious item which had been carefully wrapped. When he had feasted on some of the food that George had given him and was feeling rested after the stiffness from the previous day's ordeal, he opened it. What he found convinced him as no other gift could of the true loyalty and affection of his friend. There was a simple note which read, "Take good care of her brother," and wrapped in some sheets of music lay

George's favourite flute. Matthew knew he had spare flutes, but this one he treasured above all the others. He felt ashamed of his own doubts and caution as he had lain concealed and filled with suspicion, watching his friend earlier that afternoon. He felt a warm glow of more than mere friendship for his white cousin. He felt the stirring of that special bond that cements the hearts and souls of true brothers by blood that no power on earth can ever dissever.

41

Dilemmas And Rewards

George had much on his mind. Since the debacle of Matthew's flogging and his subsequent escape, his father now refused even to speak to him. Now that the war had effectively brought an end to any further prospect of his continuing with his education, his father had made some tentative efforts to share with him some of the matters concerning the running of the estate. He would discuss the marketing of the tobacco crop where clearly, he had some confidence and expertise. But in doing so, his father had to reveal just how much reliance he placed upon the services of Killcaid and how deeply entrenched was the latter's influence. The presence of his son had made it ever more difficult for him to hide from himself his subordination to his own Chief Overseer.

Because of this perhaps, he had become increasingly dismissive and critical of George and all he did and of his views when he cared to air them. After George's open defiance of his father at Matthew's flogging, Anthony had declared that he was to be shut out from any further participation in estate affairs until he had acquired the necessary degree of maturity to cope with such responsibilities. With that brief exchange, his father had maintained a stony silence.

George's relationship with his mother too had grown ever more remote for he could not hide his resentment at the spite and cruelty of her treatment of Ursula. Life at home, he reflected, was becoming increasingly intolerable and the attractions of life away from the family were becoming ever more appealing.

Now however, to add to his burdens, he had even weightier matters to consider. Posters from the Nethergate Estate offering a reward for the capture of an escaped slave had no real permanence. They were rarely renewed once they had been published. They soon faded from public view and were forgotten. Now though, posters had appeared on the estate from the Sheriff's Office, concerning the slave Matthew Styles, wanted for the murder of the slave preacher, Peter Lock from Spielberg, Mr Lock's estate adjoining Nethergate, "to be captured dead or alive". George had no idea how this had come about but guessed that Killcaid was at the root of it. However, it now made his task yet more hazardous. Now he was breaking the law and sheltering a wanted felon. He could not believe what he was seeing and longed to contact Matthew to find out what had been the true course of events.

If this were not enough trouble for his young shoulders, that night there had been a gentle, insistent knocking at his door. Cautiously he had opened it to see the figure of Ursula standing like a wraith in the moonlight before him. The dim lustre of the moon caught her face and lingered in her eyes that were brimming over with tears. She was deeply distressed. Glancing quickly up and down the moonlit corridor he ushered her in. As soon as the door was closed she fell sobbing into his arms. George held her in a tight embrace as her body trembled and shook with the violence of her distress. Her face was buried in his shoulder. He began to caress her hair, doing his best to console and comfort her. His heart was filled with concern, but he could not help but be aware of the firm young shape of the body which lay beneath her nightshift and he felt his own body stirring despite himself.

She had changed so much in the service of his mother. When she had first come to Nethergate Hall, laughter and smiles had followed her wherever she went. But bit by bit her natural gaiety had been subdued under the relentless persecution of his mother. Her shoulders had dropped, the laughter had leached from her eyes and the lightness left her step. Only when she was alone with him at their secret meetings had the buoyancy and merriment returned and she seemed to come alive again. But when they parted she always seemed to cling to him as if she could not bear to let him go.

At last her sobs became more controlled and she broke away from him.

"O George," she murmured for he had told her to drop the 'Master' title when they were alone, "I is so, so unhappy. I cannot do anything to please the Mistress. Whatever I does she finds fault, even if I spend hours in getting her things just exactly as she instructed with ever so much care, she says that I am stupid an' I deliberately go against her wishes. Then she whip me with her riding crop six or seven time so I hop about like I is dancing on hot cinders, till I screams for her to stop. She keep the whip now on the window, so I can always see it there. It were never like this with the old Mrs Styles. She were kind and patient. She never hit me. O George what will be the end o' me. Will this go on fo'ever?" The words fell from her lips in a torrent of misery.

All George could do was hold on to her yet more tightly. For the first time, he had a glimpse of the hopelessness of the slave's lot when welded to a cruel master or mistress. He had a sudden insight into her life of bleak, relentlessness, never-ending servitude. All he could do was to murmur, "Oh Ursula,

Ursula. My poor dear Ursula. My Mother she was never like this before we came to this great place. She always had a temper, but she was never cruel. I don't know what Nethergate has done to her."

In the moonlight, he could see the wide orbs of her eyes, shiny-wet with tears and the pearl lustre of her skin as she tilted her head to look up into his face. His heart filled with tenderness and a desire to protect her from his mother's harshness. But now Ursula was talking again.

"O George. Dearest George you is so good to me, but that ain't the end o' it. She say now she goin' to have me whip' same as she did for Samuel. She often say that to me, but this time I hear her tell Samuel to have the whipping cart call next Saturday to take me in fo' a public whippen. To be strip to de waist in front of all dem people and then to be whip." She shuddered, and her small frame shook with the dread and humiliation of it.

A sudden wave of anger swept over George at the injustice of his mother's behaviour. Once again all he could do was to hold her yet more tightly and to sooth her distress with tender caresses. His hand wandered down to her bare arms and he felt her suddenly stiffen and draw back, but not before he had felt the livid ridges that were still imprinted there.

"Whatever have you done to your arm?" he asked, but then knew the answer before the question left his lips.

"It were the riding crop," she murmured with shame. "It were my own fault. I was preparing the mistress's bath and I heard her calling, Angela! Angela! Come here this instant!" for a second her sense of humour had returned, for she gave such a perfect imitation of his mother's voice that George almost laughed out loud. He felt an overwhelming surge of renewed affection for this simple, lovely creature who even in her distress could find room for laughter.

"O Ursula," he murmured chuckling once more.

But she continued, "I thought, this time I won't answer to

that name. I told myself, my name is Ursula. My mother she give me that name. So I started to hum and sing to myself, louder and louder as I poured the water from the hot jugs into the tub and stirred it about all the time pretending and pretending I could not hear. The next thing I felt was the sting of the crop. She kep' on and on, till I thought she would never stop. All the time she was cursing me. But it were my fault dis time, 'cos I was bein' so ordinary a' purpose. I truly deserve that beating."

George could only wonder at how she could blame herself for such savagery on the part of his mother. But the thought now uppermost in his mind was the image of her being stripped to the waist in public with voyeurs and poor whites lewdly looking on, filling the air with their coarseness. His mind revolted at the thought of the whip across the beautiful, amber creaminess of her naked back, tearing and scarring her flesh. It was more than he could bear.

"Ursula, we must get you away from here, somehow we must get you away." But even as he said these things he could think of no way in which it could be achieved. Instead he steered her to his bed. She did not resist. He covered her with the sheets and blanket. Trustingly she snuggled into his embrace and gave herself utterly to the protection of the man she loved and trusted. Afterwards she slept feeling a happiness and security such as she had never felt before in her short life.

As for George, he could not sleep. He was conscious only of his delight and wonder in this simple creature who lay beside him. He was still awash with the marvel of what he had discovered in her embraces and full of a desire to protect her forever from whatever life had to throw at her. How he might do this he was unsure but do it he surely would.

42

Reflections And Plans

Matthew had that evening assembled the flute that George had given him and tried out the first pure notes and then trilled up and down the scales. The sound seemed strange at first in the wilderness of his surroundings, but soon he embarked on some of his favourite tunes and filled the bayou with his own music, losing himself in the melodies. When he paused for breath he could hear nature's own accompaniment continuing all around him. He looked about his little oasis of comfort in this wild place and felt what so few of his kind had ever felt in this new world; a sense of belonging, a sense of ownership and above all a sense of freedom. He was a slave no longer. He vowed he would never be anyone's slave ever again. He would rather die. He had freed himself. That thought made him think of the extraordinary man who had so selflessly helped him escape. Without his intervention, the hounds would surely have found him before he could reach the safety of the bayou. He could still feel the strength of the man that had radiated from him and it wasn't just a physical strength. He longed to know more of the man and somehow to thank him.

Now though, thanks to that strange and powerful being,

he was the master of his own destiny. He would stay here for as long as was necessary until the hue and cry had died down. Then he would slip away and join the ranks of the Yankee Army and fight for the freedom of his brothers still held in bondage.

His thoughts turned to Killcaid. In a way, he felt a strange feeling of gratitude. Had it not been for his vindictiveness and hatred he would never have taken the steps that now he had. Left alone perhaps, he would not have had the incentive, the courage even, to take his liberty into his own hands. He might have suffered under Killcaid's lash, trusting on his mother's influence with her mistress to rescue him on her return. But in his heart of hearts he knew that would not be so. He would have rebelled and be tempted into some rash act that would have placed him beyond any help that the old Mrs Styles might have been able to render. He might even have ended up as a fugitive from justice.

He felt a sense of contentment steal over him after the tension and trauma of the last few days. He looked about him. When the time came, he would be sad to leave this little place that Old Mo had created. When he left, it would soon revert to how it had always been. The wood of the cabin would slowly rot and crumble and it would be as if Old Mo had never been. But it would live on in his mind for as long as he lived as his first true home and a tribute to the indomitable old man who had built it. It was home now because it was his. A sudden wave of sadness passed over him at the thought of Old Mo, who had dreamt and created this haven, only for it to be snatched from his grasp at the eleventh hour.

He longed to have known how and if the indomitable old character had survived. But now he would never know. He fancied like so many before him that Old Mo would simply have been swallowed up in the army of condemned souls that wound their way down to the mouth of the Mississippi and the rice fields. There they would simply vanish as if they had never been. A man as old as him would not survive for long. In many ways, Old Mo was the father he had never known. He would not let his memory die.

At the thought of Old Mo and the injustice done to him, his resolve hardened. He would fight and, if necessary, die for the freedom of his brothers in slavery. He would join the Yankees. Becoming a Yankee soldier had, in the early days of the war, been a lottery. Sometimes the Yankee Army accepted escaped slaves as 'contraband', or they simply handed them back to their rightful owners through third parties and shared the rewards from their return. Increasingly though, as Yankee casualties mounted, they were accepted into the Union Army to cook, dig latrines and defences and generally help about the army encampments. Although labelled as 'contraband', they were nevertheless paid good money for their services, like any free man. Some he had heard were even allowed to bear arms, to wear the Union uniform and to fight for the cause of freedom. There was rumour of a completely black unit where even the officers were ex-slaves. The more he thought about it the more he longed to take part in the momentous events that were engulfing his country. He wanted to be a soldier in the fight for freedom rather than a passive spectator, to be able to tell his grandchildren how he had fought all those years ago, for their freedom. Much the same longings, he reflected, as George might feel, only with him it was to preserve the only way of life that he had ever known.

He could not conceal from himself a certain tremor of excitement at the prospect of war itself. He acknowledged that the quickening of his blood at the thought of battle against his oppressors was not only for the freedom of his brothers. He was filled with a savage anticipation at the vision of conflict for its own sake. It was the ultimate test of manhood. He wondered how he would rise to the challenge. Would he be able to stare death in the face without flinching? It was what he and George had discussed so many times, with the sure knowledge that they would be on different sides, but both for sincerely held reasons.

He was anxious now for George's next visit to discover what Killcaid was doing to recapture him, or whether Killcaid might have banked on him meeting a watery grave as George so nearly had a few days before. With George's help, he was now certain he could stay in the bayou for as long as might be necessary. He knew that now he could trust George to reveal to him the existence of Old Mo's Cabin. His sense of isolation receded as he imagined the long hours they might spend here at their ease, lounging in the two chairs that Old Mo had constructed. They would enjoy each other's company and their burgeoning sense of brotherhood, talking, playing music, laughing and putting the world to rights until the time was right for them both to become soldiers and fight each for the privilege of killing what the other held most dear. They could not both be winners, but somehow it did not matter, for their kinship he knew would survive whatever the outcome.

As the shadows began to lengthen in his own little paradise he began his preparations for his second night of freedom in his own home. On his first night, he had been too exhausted to appreciate anything other than the absolute necessity of rest. Now he had time to be more reflective.

His thoughts turned to his mother and he wondered how she was taking to life in New York. She had explained a bit of what she and the Mistress had planned. He missed her; her gentle, serene affection and her wisdom. He wondered too when he might see her again. He would be long gone before ever she returned to Nethergate. Somehow, he thought, he must get a message to her.

His mind turned with fondness and respect to the old Mrs Styles too. She would see through whatever excuses Killcaid might fashion for his treatment. No doubt by then he would have a reasoned and logical account of trumped-up lies of him luring George to his death, but he was confident the shrewd old lady would not for a moment allow herself to be duped. He realised suddenly that it mattered to him what she thought of him. She could do little though about his escape. He hoped though that he would be clean away and serving in the Yankee Army before both returned.

He would have to wait a few months at least before attempting to escape from the bayou, until Killcaid would be confident of his demise. But he was in no hurry and would savour this life of freedom he now enjoyed with no-one to tell him what to do and no-one to serve but himself and only a little loneliness to contend with.

There was of course an alternative to fighting, which had long been used by slaves. That was to take the 'Underground Railroad' along tenuous escape routes to freedom in Canada. To be successful that had to be carefully planned so that each station down the entire route was manned chiefly by Quakers and the fugitive passed safely along each successive stage. People ran incredible risks for no gain but the satisfaction of having done their Christian duty. The penalty for being caught could cost them their farm or dwelling. There were those too who made a good living from tracking down escaped slaves and returning the 'contraband' to its rightful owner.

Most slaves however simply ran away when circumstances made life intolerable, much as Matthew himself had done. They trusted to luck to fall into the hands of Quakers, or such like people who, out of religious conviction, might help them. The majority, though, were quickly fielded, for no-one wanted a desperate escaped slave skulking about their outbuildings, hiding in the woodpiles and stealing food or valuables. The punishment for capture was swift and severe.

Matthew knew there could be no return to the easy life he had known in Nethergate House, for even Mrs Styles could not persuade the Master to overlook such a criminal act as escaping.

In any event the malevolent influence of Killcaid would never countenance it. But Matthew didn't care. Instead he thanked God for dealing him such a workable hand. He planned the days ahead. There was almost a month's growth of weed to clear from Old Mo's homestead farm and there were traps to be laid. He had already harvested some of the root crops Old Mo had planted to augment the food George had left. He lay for a time awake listening to all the sounds of the night as they widened about him.

As he imagined the days ahead he felt an extraordinary sense of peace wash over him and a sense of being at one with his world.

43

George's Dilemma

In the early hours of the morning George had escorted Ursula back to the slave quarters before the day's work began. He was tolerably certain that she had not been missed. In the gathering light of the early dawn they had embraced once more, and he had felt again the warmth of her body pressed tight against his, renewing again his wonderful remembrance of the intimacies they had so joyously shared. His heart was full of happiness and quiet resolve. Somehow, he would save Ursula from the ordeal of the public humiliation that his mother had planned in her relentless campaign to destroy Ursula's will to resist and to crush her into utter submission.

He returned to his bed to await the appearance of Manuel with hot water for his shaving. Try as he would he could not understand why his mother should have changed so much from the mother he knew when they had all lived in the ordinary ease of their New Haven home. As for his father, he seemed to be totally overwhelmed by the weight of the responsibilities he bore for the survival of the family estate and utterly under the cruel and sinister influence of Silas Killcaid. His own life, he reflected, had over the few years he had grown up at Nethergate changed utterly too. He had lost the circle of everyday friends and the life of an ordinary schoolboy in exchange for the trappings of grandeur and for private tutors. He had enjoyed the change at first, but now he felt overwhelmed by it. Through it though, he had discovered the extraordinary friendship with a strange enigmatic slave, a slave related to him by blood, a gift born of the savage lust of his uncle for a beautiful slave girl. They shared, he reflected, a brotherly bond so strong that both had been prepared to risk their lives for the other.

The terror and helplessness of being trapped in the bayou suddenly surged up within him once again, turning him suddenly cold with a paralysing fear. He remembered how in extremity it had been to Ursula that his thoughts had flown. Had he perished, he would never have known the unbelievable union with another human being that he had experienced but a few short hours ago.

Now he too, like his uncle, was linked to a slave girl, but in a vastly different way. The irony did not escape him. In her he had discovered the love of a woman for the first time, a love that was pure and above all a love that was returned. She trusted in him somehow to save her from this latest humiliation that his own mother had incomprehensively planned for her. It all seemed such a hopeless muddle, but there must be a way out. For the sake of Ursula, he was determined to find it. Now also there was the anxiety he faced as to whether his slave friend had survived his miraculous escape into the bayou.

With sudden resolution, he decided not to wait for Manuel. He dressed quickly determined to find out if his fears about Matthew's survival were real or imagined. He made his way in the fresh coolness of early dawn down to where Manuel had left the store of survival goods for Matthew's use. As he neared the spot his heart began to beat faster. If the goods were still there it meant that Matthew had perished.

They were all gone. There was no note from Matthew, but then he thought Matthew was much too cautious to leave such a tell-tale clue, but he now felt an overwhelming sense of relief. His friend had survived. The next step was to make contact and to see if there was anything he could do to assist his escape. He needed to warn him too that he was now wanted for murder. The fact that in doing so meant he was committing a criminal offence himself for which the penalty was imprisonment weighed not a jot with him.

With a lighter step, he made his way back to Nethergate Hall. The knowledge that Matthew had survived somehow gave him new courage. He had come to a decision. He would seek the aid of Samuel somehow to circumvent the punishment in store for Ursula, for Samuel he reasoned had the wisdom born of many years of experience at the vagaries of the various rulers of Nethergate. Samuel had endured the same humiliation himself at his mother's behest. He would surely be on his side now that Ursula faced the same terrible punishment. Once back at Nethergate he called for Samuel.

"You wished to see me Masser?" intoned Samuel with his usual urbane dignity.

"Yes Samuel," he replied wondering how he should broach the subject and not at all sure now how Samuel might react. He might regard such intrusion by him as an act of disloyalty and feel obliged to inform his master of such transgressions, for Samuel was always correct in all his dealings. He might even think that George was trying to lay a trap for him to test his loyalty to his parents. Perhaps fear of once more facing a similar punishment for a second disloyalty, would temper his judgement and he would refuse to help. He decided he would skate about the point to try and find out how Samuel regarded such things. "I hear there is to be another flogging," he opened tentatively.

"I believe so Sir," replied Samuel. A long silence followed in which George hoped Samuel might find it necessary to provide a little more information. It worked for Samuel added, "I believe it is the mistress's personal maid, young Ursula, who is to suffer this time."

George's heart leapt at Samuel's use of the word 'Ursula', for there had been, he was sure, a deliberate pause before Samuel had used the name. Samuel was far too correct to have used her Christian name in error. Encouraged by this covert signal as to where Samuel's sympathies lay, George continued his line of questioning. "Are you aware of the offence she has committed?" he inquired.

Samuel paused. "She has displeased the Mistress in some way. I believe it was over the matter of the new name Mistress has seen fit to give her."

George decided to take the bull by the horns. "Is that a just reason for such a punishment?"

Samuel was silent for a long time. "You must know Sir that it is not my place to cast judgement in such matters, though if she had received a given name before the Lord, I believe that in the Almighty's eyes she has that name forever. As to the punishment she is to endure..." he paused as if considering the matter and then seemed to change the subject. "In my own case, I had clearly transgressed in sheltering an escaped fellow slave. The punishment was justly deserved. I was fortunate in not appearing before the courts and I must be grateful to Mistress for that small mercy."

George's spirits fell. Clearly, he was not going to get Samuel to commit himself one way or the other and he would have to try another tack. But Samuel had not finished.

"The lass is clearly in the wrong and she should never seek to defy the Mistress. However..." continued Samuel, with all the solemnity of a judge, "I think Mistress was in the wrong in trying to change Ursula's name given before God." With the second use of the name 'Ursula', George sensed that surely Samuel was on his side.

"What's to be done do you think Samuel?" he asked directly.

"I think first we might delay the calling of the whipping cart. I think that can easily be arranged by the pretence that my message to the carrier had somehow been misunderstood, that will buy us a little time. Then we must see what Ursula's wishes really are. I have seen how hard she tries to please her mistress and how harsh the Mistress is on the girl, but that of course is her right and she is not by nature an easy one to please."

George realised that Samuel was now going far beyond what a slave should say about his owners, particularly to the son of the owners. In so doing Samuel was taking a risk and George's heart went out to this man who somehow lent nobility and dignity to servitude. He also sensed that Samuel knew far more about his own relationship with Ursula than he had revealed. In a sudden surge of gratitude, he seized Samuel's hand and shook it. "Thank you, Samuel. I am deeply grateful, and I will not utter a word of our conversation."

Samuel bowed in acknowledgement of the words and of the gesture. "But I fear Sir, yours will be the more difficult task, for I see no alternative in the long run but to try to dissuade your mother from taking this course. What I shall do will simply buy a little extra time and if the mistress is still determined to take this course we must ensure that we use the time wisely."

George was not entirely sure what Samuel meant by these last remarks, but as Samuel left, he felt buoyed by the feeling that there might after all be a way out of the problem. Samuel was right, he reflected, about his being the more difficult task. He was not looking forward to tackling his mother on the subject and began to wonder how he might approach the matter.

Overall though, it had not been a bad morning's work. He knew that Matthew was alive and functioning. He sensed that in Samuel he had found an ally who gave him at least some hope of averting the plans his mother had regarding the woman he loved. But above all was the memory of those sweet moments of intimacy he had shared with Ursula and the discovery for the first time of the unbelievable joys in the consummation of that love.

44

A Decision In Haste

Conversation at dinner in Nethergate Hall was usually sporadic unless they had guests. That night, George had so much on his mind that his inclination was to remain silent and to continue to mull things over. However, he knew that he must talk to his parents at least to resolve some of his problems. His mother rarely spoke. When she did it was in brief salvos of challenging statements, ended by staring about her as if willing any of the family to disagree. They rarely did. His father now maintained a stony silence to show his resentment at George's defiance at Matthew's abortive flogging. It was hardly a fertile soil in which to plant the seeds of any communication.

George had always maintained a friendly relationship with the slave community from the time when he was still a youngster on the estate. Now that he was grown to near manhood, he still had the confidence if not friendship of many of the slaves. His father knew that they talked to him as they would to few other white men. In the past, he had let his father know when matters were causing concern. He knew his father often found this useful as a way of stealing a march on Killcaid. He raised the subject now, particularly after the death of Zeb following his flogging, hoping at least to start some sort of conversation.

He received a curt response from his father, clearly determined to let his son stew in his displeasure. A long silence ensued. Then George raised the news of a recent Confederate reverse and added, "But I'm told it was only a temporary setback for our cause. They will assuredly live to fight on another day."

"High time those damn Yankees got their just desserts," interposed Mrs Styles with feeling.

Then more by nature of something to say rather than something he had thought through George said, "I was thinking that I might too join in the struggle. I'm old enough now," he added, trying by this means to get some sort of response from his father. Still, his father refused to be drawn, so George pressed the point. "How would you feel were I to volunteer? I've done my training as an officer with the Militia and I reckon I'm as ready to fight as the next man." Suddenly it seemed a very attractive idea to escape the warring between his parents, the claustrophobic atmosphere of the estate and to avenge the defeat of the Confederates which they had so recently witnessed from Bowling Green.

There had been plenty of posters up in New Haven when last he was there and a group of soldiers from the local Militia had been actively recruiting. He had paused to listen and felt a stirring in his blood at the excitement that war breeds in young men's breasts, but until this moment it had never really occurred to him to join the war himself. Now suddenly it seemed as if this is what he had wanted all along. The only thing that really stopped him was the thought of what might happen to Ursula and Matthew too, but he felt that now at least Matthew could survive indefinitely on his own in the bayou.

Both his parents were regarding him with astonishment. Clearly the thought had not occurred to them either. "I hear

Grenville's son has joined Colonel Trevis' 10th Kentucky Cavalry under General Gordon and is now at Nashville. He hasn't seen action yet, but daily they go to dig out Yankee sympathisers, give them a good drubbing and get them to swear allegiance to our cause," continued George, glad that at last he seemed to have grasped his parents' attention.

"You're not old enough yet, surely," said his mother with unusual uncertainty. Then added with her customary conviction, "You'd need your father's consent and he won't give it."

The veiled command from his wife was not lost on Anthony. Of late, the frustration of somehow never being in control had found expression in a general feeling of resentment particularly directed at those closest to him. He felt his anger rising again, finding expression in a determination to disagree with his wife. "He's over eighteen now and in view of what the other plantation owners are doing, I see no reason to withhold my consent." Turning to George and in open defiance of his wife, he said, "Of course you may join the colours George, if that is really your wish. I will make the necessary arrangements."

George suddenly realised that somehow, he had committed himself to a course that had its appeal, but the implications of which he had not yet fully thought through. "No Father," he said. "You shall give me your letter of consent, if you please. In this matter at least let me make the necessary arrangements."

Stung by her husband's show of independence Mrs Styles decided to once again assert her domestic authority.

"He's much too young. I'll hear of no such thing; besides you need him here to help learn to run the estate." She turned to her breakfast with an air of finality. For a moment, her husband was silent. Then sensing that in this matter at least his wife was outnumbered and that the popular opinion of his peers would support his view he decided for once to stand up for himself.

"The lad is old enough to fight," he said, "and he has

expressed a wholly commendable desire to fight for the Confederate cause in these perilous times. I would not have it known that his mother had refused to let her son join in the struggle. I would never be able to look our neighbours in the eye again." This last remark he knew would strike home, for above all, Amelia valued the opinion of the exclusive clique of influential plantation owners to which she now nominally belonged, but by whom she somehow never felt quite fully accepted.

At this, all Amelia could manage was a disapproving snort, but father and son both realised that victory was theirs.

For a moment though, the awful consequences of one small domestic victory flashed before Anthony's eyes and he felt a rush of sudden remorse.

"It is truly your wish, George?" he asked.

There was no going back now. George was angry with himself. Somehow, he had been engineered into doing something which would make life even more difficult for Ursula and himself. George nodded slowly. "Of course, Father." Then sensing that now would be the right moment, he added, "I was telling you the truth Father about Matthew. It was he who came to my rescue in the bayou, not Killcaid and I can't believe the accusation that he is a murderer as well."

His father wrestled for a moment, then the warmth engendered by this new-found amity with his son won. "I believe you son," he said at last, "Killcaid can be a devious fellow at times and I know he has no love for the boy, but without him, truly I don't think this estate would survive, particularly when the Yankee sea blockade begins to bite. After that there'll be no market and God knows what we'll do. As to the other matter, best let the courts decide, that's if the poor lad has survived out there. I know that your grandmamma will take this hard for she was very fond of him."

It was the closest father and son had come to a meaningful

discussion and George knew better than to press his father further.

"Thank you, Father," he said, "And I am sorry I showed such reluctance before the slaves."

Thus, peace was restored between father and son and a new understanding born. Anthony lent across and placed a hand upon his son's shoulder and squeezed. It was the closest he had come to an embrace in years. "You will let me know if there is anything I can do to help and have a care son," he added. It was all he could bring himself to say, but both knew that more had passed between them than just words.

Amelia looked on at this exchange between father and son and felt a pang of jealousy at what she saw but did not know truly what it was or why she should feel so envious. All she knew was that she was not a part of it. Her own heart, though, was too frozen to know how to make a like gesture. She felt cheated, but there was little she could do other than to plot how she might bring her husband once more to heel. Despite the new danger to her only child, she was not immune to the sympathy such a gesture might engender among those other plantation families whom she most desired to impress. As compensation, she let her mind dwell upon that more comforting thought.

45

Shared Secrets

The next afternoon George again ventured down to the bayou to his meeting place with Matthew. To his surprise, he found Matthew there waiting for him. They greeted each other with enthusiasm and then with laughter as each related his own part in Matthew's escape and the foiling of Killcaid's plans. George then told Matthew of the near cult status he had assumed among the slaves at his seemingly miraculous escape from the whipping post and his taming of the feared Nethergate coonhounds.

"How did you do that? How did you break free from the whipping post and then escape the dogs?" asked George with genuine curiosity. Matthew then explained how he had been given the oil to lubricate wrists and ankles, without saying from whence it came, and how he had so often fed the hounds from the excess of the game that he and Old Mo had hunted. George looked puzzled, for he had never known of the help that Matthew had given to Old Mo. Matthew wondered whether now he should let George into the secret of Old Mo's cabin.

But George had a more serious matter that had been playing

on his mind since hearing of the death of the preacher. Their euphoric mood suddenly evaporated as George asked, "How did the preacher-slave who helped you die?" for Matthew had mentioned how he had been helped by the huge slave.

"Is he dead? What happened?" Matthew was stunned. "It can't be him. He was so massive. It must be someone else." He told George again of the contact he had had with a giant of a man who had helped his escape and how he had done it. He told him too of his sense of gratitude for his entirely unsolicited aid in his escape.

"Truly Brother, I could not have gone on without his help. Ah was so dead beat, ah was ready to give up. I pray to God that this is not the man of whom you speak, for truly I believe I owe him my life. We barely exchanged a word, but I could feel his goodness and his goodwill, like the power of the Almighty himself, urging me on."

"But Brother," George interjected, "You have been named as his killer."

"Who says so?" demanded Matthew heatedly. "It cannot be the same man. He was so huge, so… indestructible."

"By the sound of it though, it is the same man. It is the word of Killcaid. He has witnesses, so Manuel says. The story is that they were following your trail with the dogs and it led to the body of this preacher. The side of his head had been stove in with a rock. He too was a big man an' his killer must have been truly desperate and treacherous to have done such a thing. They say that he must have tried to apprehend you and that is what you have done. There are Sheriff notices out for you now, 'Wanted Dead or Alive'."

"It is a lie! A damn lie!" exploded Matthew. "God forbid it be the same man, for he was a truly Christian soul who help me an' ask for nothing in return. He carried me on his back like ah was a child. If it is the man I am thinking of, I owe him everything." He paused, and his brow darkened. He was filled with an overwhelming regret, if he should have been the cause of the death of such a man. He was certain now that he indeed must have been the victim. He continued bitterly, "This is Killcaid's doing. He must have found out the man helped me escape and lost his temper. Now he wants *me* to hang for it."

"I can see Killcaid's hand in all this too," muttered George. "This way the forces of law are involved should you be captured trying to escape. Not even Grandmamma will be able to help you then."

Their euphoria at Matthew's escape had suddenly evaporated. Matthew crossed himself in sober reflection. "God forbid it should be the same man," he muttered again. But the more he thought about it, the more certain he became. "God rest his soul. That he should pay such a price for my escape…" and he was unable to finish the thought, so deep was his regret.

It did indeed put a different complexion on Matthew's half-formed plans for what his next step might be. If he were caught now trying to escape it would be to face a charge of murder and who would believe a slave against the word of Killcaid, doubtless corroborated by others too frightened to tell the truth. His plan to join the Yankee cause was now perhaps a dream. He was aware that strangely, the two warring sides still co-operated in criminal matters. If his identity was now discovered when he tried to join the Yankees and they found that he was a wanted criminal and for murder at that; they would surely hand him back for a taste of Southern justice. It seemed that all loopholes for the future had been suddenly closed and that Killcaid had triumphed after all. Then abruptly he realised the risk that George was taking in helping him. Even now, by simply being here he was breaking the law. With shame, he remembered his doubts of his friend's constancy. Then with a sudden surge of concern he wondered how all this might seem to George.

"You – you don't believe that I did this, do you?" The anxiety in Matthew's voice was not lost on his friend. He could tell it was not just a matter of innocence or guilt, but it really mattered to Matthew that his friend should believe in his integrity.

"I would not be here otherwise, would I Brother?" George replied simply and placed his hand on Matthew's shoulder. The two stared deep into each other's eyes. Each read the bonds of blood and loyalty that were so plainly written there and wondered with a sense of awe how this had all come about.

It was George who spoke first. "But how will you survive for long out here. It may be months before the hue and cry has died down and everybody here knows who you are."

Matthew was certain now that he could trust George and decided to show him Old Mo's cabin and thus to reveal the length of time he would be able to survive out in the swamp.

"George," he said, mysteriously, "I want to show you something." And he refused to answer any further questions despite George's mounting curiosity.

Using Old Mo's dug out the two paddled out along the confusing lines of waterways with the great Cypresses overhead filtering and dappling the sunlight and the falling cadences of the cardinal bird as a triumphal accompaniment. George was soon utterly lost, but Matthew directed their course with unerring accuracy. In truth, he was overwhelmed with pride and respect for what Old Mo had built; the carefully fenced plots of cultivation that the canny old slave had created and of the use now to which he himself had put it. He wanted to show it off to his friend. He reckoned that he could survive here if not indefinitely, at least until his mother returned to Nethergate and he might be able to consider other plans.

As they paddled, George enlarged upon the news from Nethergate and of the seemingly half-hearted hunt that Killcaid had set in motion for his recapture. There had been none of the usual posters and posting of rewards. It seemed that Killcaid was relying on the forces of the State to do his dirty work. Either that or Killcaid did not want to further enhance Matthew's status among the other slaves by making any special efforts to recapture him. The more George thought about it the more he came to the view that Killcaid thought that he had probably perished in the swamplands as George had so nearly done himself or failing that would be forced through starvation to come creeping back into Nethergate, seeking food and shelter. All the same, the fact that he was now not just a fugitive slave, but also a wanted criminal and for murder too, put an entirely different aspect on his friend's situation.

When they reached the site of Old Mo's cabin, Matthew moored the canoe and led the way through the screen of trees that hid the cabin from the stream. He watched the look of amazement spread over George's face as he saw the carefully fenced plots of cultivated land. True to his expectations, George could only wonder at the sight of Old Mo's cabin and the detail and thought that had gone to make it a place fit for the retirement of a king, albeit perhaps a rather modest one.

They both relaxed on the two simple rush chairs that Old Mo had constructed and sat outside the cabin taking their ease in the late afternoon sun for all the world like two old men at the end of a working day.

Matthew had a list of a few additional things he thought he might need and then George told Matthew of the problem that was uppermost in his mind concerning the punishment planned for Ursula and how Samuel had, for the time being, circumvented it. George could not stay long, and Matthew escorted him back to familiar ground and the two friends parted.

On the way back to Nethergate Hall, George pondered how he might raise the matter of his mother's treatment of Ursula with her. He wondered if his father might have any influence, but his new relationship with his father was perhaps too fragile yet to enrol his support against such a Minervan figure as his mother. He wondered too about the survival of Matthew in the long term. There seemed an awful lot of troubles on his young shoulders.

46

A New Amity

George, emboldened by the new amity between father and son, seized the opportunity during dinner that evening to raise the subject closest to his heart. "Father you know you asked me to keep my ear to the ground about the feelings among the slave community. I think you should know how restless the hands really are."

His father nodded. "I don't suppose the debacle of the other day can have helped the situation. I really don't know what Killcaid was playing at." It felt good to criticise his overseer in this way.

"It wasn't only that," agreed his son, "They've been unsettled by the recent troops moving through the plantation and the sounds of battle so close. Some of the more vocal ones have taken heart at the Yankee victory as a hope for their eventual freedom. But more particularly there is an underswell of unrest over the treatment of Samuel. He is deeply respected by the hands and of course now, there is what happened to poor Zeb." He let this thought register, knowing too that mention of Samuel's flogging would register strongly with his mother. He didn't have to wait long for a response.

"Samuel," she declared, immediately bristling, "was lucky to escape with a flogging. By rights he should have gone to jail for helping a runaway. Flogging in the circumstances was a kindness." Her two menfolk considered this statement, both having been witness to the 'kindness' done to Zeb's tortured back. Anthony's thoughts though had turned to the avuncular person of Samuel and his own childhood memories of his dignified and kindly presence; a crucial part of what he had always known as 'home'. He had rebelled at Samuel's treatment at the time but had been powerless to intervene in the face of the evidence of his actions in sheltering a runaway. But it was George who spoke now in softer tones, not wishing to provoke his mother further.

"Nevertheless, his flogging and the dignity he displayed has enormously increased his influence among the slaves and now Matthew's seemingly miraculous escape has raised him in turn to almost the status of a saint in the slaves' eyes. I think the hands have born witness enough to floggings. They only serve to enhance the reputation of the victim and to act as a focus for discontent."

"Wisely said," endorsed his father hastily, before his wife could react.

"I don't know if there are any other floggings in prospect," continued George quickly, "but in the circumstances, it might be wise to postpone them – indefinitely if possible."

George's advice had been sound in the past and this sudden commitment to the adult world made Anthony feel that he had a real ally in his son.

"Thank you," he said, "I'll let Killcaid know my feelings. Truthfully though I know of no other floggings planned and I will certainly advise against it. I do value your advice on such matters George." Father and son solemnly shook hands to seal their new cordiality.

George though was watching his mother. She was unusually

muted, and he knew his advice to his father had not been lost on her. There was an almost savage glimmer in her eye he had not seen before, and he wondered with a frisson of unease at its meaning. Had he been able to glimpse for a moment the riot of emotions that his mother was experiencing at that instant, he would have been filled with more than just unease. Amelia was burning inside, convinced that father and son were engaged in a conspiracy against her. She was used to having things her own way in the past and she had no intention that things should change now. If father and son were to conspire against her so be it, but they would be the losers.

That evening when George was undressing for bed Manuel was present and George gave him the list he had made of the additional things that Matthew needed. Manuel was strangely quiet and pensive, which was lost on George who was delighted at how things had gone to protect Ursula from his mother's vengeance, at least for a time. That and the prospect of war filled him with excitement. He penned a letter to the Colonel of the Militia as he had promised his father he would. These things he knew took a long time and it would be many weeks yet before he expected to hear from them. At least now he felt there was a real purpose to his life, but war would have to wait until the business of Matthew and Ursula was resolved.

That night he had one other thing to do. He had toyed with the idea of riding down to the railroad and sending a telegraph to his grandmother to tell her how things now stood with Matthew, but had rejected the idea, because of the public nature of such communications. Instead he sat down at the desk in his room and penned a letter to his grandmother, telling her what had happened to Matthew and reassuring her that he would be safe for the foreseeable future. He also mentioned his intention to go to the war. He reported all that had taken place in her absence, urging her not to delay too long her return to Nethergate. After much soul-searching, he decided not to mention the charge of murder which hung over Matthew's head, for fear that she might over-react. He wanted to tell her all the circumstances in person. He felt that she alone had the wisdom to bring some sanity to the events that had occurred during her absence. Precisely what she could do, he could not imagine, but he needed an ally and she was the only person he could think of to fill that role. The war initially seemed to have had little influence on the flow of mail between the two sides, possibly because all had friends and relatives north and south of the lines of conflict. Of late though the conflict had grown more bitter in its execution and this had begun to affect the passage of mail, but letters usually got through albeit with some delays.

George's preoccupation with what he would say to his grandmother possibly made him less alert to Manuel's unusual lack of chatter. There was a simple explanation for Manuel's discomfort. Silas Killcaid was nothing if not alert to what was taking place on the estate. He had got wind of Manuel's unusual stream of requests for stores and had sent for him. There had been no reports of Matthew leaving the area and he was suspicious that someone might be sheltering him on the estate.

The interview with Killcaid was playing over and again in Manuel's mind as he busied himself about George's room. When he had gone to see Killcaid, he had been left to stand whilst Killcaid slowly poured himself a bourbon. The silence had lengthened whilst Killcaid sipped at his drink. His eyes though had never left Manuel's face and seemed to Manuel to be boring into his very brain. He felt his bladder suddenly weaken and tightened the muscles of his buttocks. Still Killcaid's stare did not waver.

"You sent for me Massa' Killcaid?" he said at last.

Killcaid said nothing but took a contemplative sip of his

bourbon and let the silence grow on until it seemed to loom like a monolith over the cowering slave. Killcaid's cruel, dark-eyed stare never wavered.

"Well now so I did," he said at last, in a voice soft and gentle. Manuel's knees began to tremble uncontrollably. Killcaid's eyes seemed to be peeling back with delicate precision every layer of subterfuge that Manuel could deploy until it seemed to Manuel the truth lay bare and exposed before them, plain for both to see with him having hardly said a word. Again, the voice soft almost pleading, "Ain't you got something to tell me? BOY!" the last word was shot out like the discharge of a musket. Manuel staggered back his sphincter muscles loosened and a large stain gradually spread from his groin.

Killcaid saw it and a knowing smile spilled across his face. "Now Manuel, you jus' tell Killcaid all you knows and we can remain friends eh?"

Manuel told all he knew. In fact, it mounted to very little other than that the master's son had been getting together stores, he thought to assist Matthew's survival in the bayou, but, 'No he had not seen Matthew and there was no evidence that Matthew had not now perished,' as indeed Killcaid hoped.

Killcaid considered this and then instructed Manuel as to what he should do. Then he let loose the shaken slave, admonishing him as he left, "Now be sure to do as I tell you and remember I shall be right behind you."

Manuel reflected as he returned to Nethergate Hall that he had been forgiven once, but he knew George could never forgive him again. His fear of Killcaid, though, overrode all other considerations. He could think of no way out. As he busied himself about his duties, he longed to tell all to the boyish figure engrossed in writing letters, but he did not dare. Once again, he knew he would betray his master.

47

Treachery

Matthew was filled with content in his own little island of freedom. His only regret was that Old Mo himself had been snatched away before he had been able to reap the rewards of all his labours. All about him were reminders of that indomitable old man with his battered old hat, the terrible scars on his crown and his eyes that wickedly twinkled defiance at the whole world. He only hoped that now he would be worthy of his memory.

If he was lonely at times, he had George's visits to look forward to. Only in very exceptional circumstances would he ever be able to visit the estate again. He wondered if he would even dare to see his mother. He wondered too how long his mother and Mrs Styles would be away from Nethergate. He thought how he might yet escape, perhaps to the north to Canada and true freedom or into the Army of the North. But always over all his dreams there was the spectre of the murder charge that Killcaid had engineered which hung over his head.

Everyone's hand would be turned against him. There would be a bounty on his head. Even if he escaped from Kentucky into the lands over the Ohio River into Indiana or Illinois both of which states had joined in the Northern cause against slavery, he would still be liable to be captured and returned south. Even though the North were fighting against slavery, they were still bound by the laws of property and were legally obliged to return escaped slaves from whence they came. There would be plenty who would be only too happy to reap the financial rewards for so doing, indeed there were some who made a living from it. He knew that the warring sides still shared the same criminal law. If he joined the army there would be inquiries into his background. Even the Yankee Army didn't want killers and murderers in its ranks. He doubted that he would ever escape from the malevolent hatred of Killcaid. Only death itself seemingly would free him from his enmity.

But Matthew felt no haste to venture forth. Game was plentiful, and the vegetable garden was productive. Old Mo had shown him how to gut and prepare every variety of game to be found in the bayou, how to skin and cure the pelt and how to put to good use the rest of the carcass so that nothing useful was ever wasted. He had benefited much from the skills Old Mo had acquired during his wild days as slave to his fur trapper.

He already knew much about the care and tending of the vegetables Old Mo had grown, from the time he had spent in the kitchens and gardens of Nethergate House. Looking after his new domain would occupy much of his time and keep him busy. That and tending his traps would fill his days. He had some books to read in the evenings whilst the light lasted and more promised from George. Then too there was George's beloved flute to play when the light faded. Calmed by the music he created he would retire to his bunk or drag it out to the veranda and listen to the night life in the bayou as he drifted off to sleep. Life was, he reflected, more than tolerable. At least for a time.

Killcaid or someone had been out with the dogs, no doubt searching for him. He had heard their distant clamour. But he knew he was safe here in the bayou for there was simply too much water betwixt the two for any trace of his comings and goings to linger. Most of his food he trapped and had so far not found it necessary to use his favoured Kentucky hunting rifle which had been Old Mo's favourite too and he had found in the cabin. But in truth the sound of a stray shot would long be swallowed by the tall Cypress trees well before it could reach another human ear. These were early days though and he was determined to be cautious and to take no unnecessary risks. Once George had delivered the items he had requested he would be self-sufficient for weeks to come.

He arrived early at their rendezvous as was his habit, to ensure that the site was not compromised and then waited with patience for George to appear. In the early afternoon, he heard sounds of movement announced by the sudden alarm of the birds and cautiously slunk back into the undergrowth. George arrived this time with Manuel in tow carrying the items he had collected for Matthew. Both sat down to wait. Matthew watched them for a while, wondering at the wisdom of revealing himself to Manuel. As he did so he observed something odd about Manuel's behaviour. He was ill at ease. Matthew decided to wait a little longer before coming out of his hiding place. Manuel kept casting fearful looks behind him whenever he thought that George was not looking. Matthew followed the line of Manuel's glance and observed in the distance the tell-tale disturbance of birds rising and circling, but still some way off.

His need of the stores George had brought finally overrode his natural caution and he broke cover, beckoning them in haste to follow him. Sensing his urgency, George immediately responded and together all three carried the stores to where Matthew had left the boat. They quickly loaded up and George went as if to join Matthew in the boat, but Matthew hastily poled out into the bayou.

"What are you doing?" queried George in astonishment at this behaviour.

"Ask Manuel," was the curt reply. "I think he has something to tell you." George turned to Manuel.

"What is it?" he demanded.

Manuel looked suddenly crestfallen. He knew that somehow Matthew had detected the guilt that now was written plainly in his features.

"I wanted to tell you Massa' George, truly I did, but it were Mr Killcaid."

"What was Mr Killcaid?" asked George his brows darkening with suspicion.

"He made me tell him 'bout the stores you was getting. He knew all about it and he suspect it were for Matthew here, but he don't know for sure. He was to follow me at a distance and I was to leave a trail by tearing up de grasses, but I stop doin' that way back, honest to God I did though the Lord knows what will happen to me now." George felt his anger rising. This was the second time he had been betrayed by his servant. But worse still, if his father got to hear of this, as now he surely would, it would destroy their new-found amity, and no doubt leave his mother feeling free to defy her husband too and arrange for Ursula's punishment.

"Well I can tell you one thing an' that's for sure," he exploded, glaring with fury at the stricken slave. "You will go right back to working on the fields and back to Killcaid. You'll never work for me again!"

Manuel's face showed the depths of his despair at the prospect of once more being even more at the mercy of Killcaid and his cohorts, but chiefly he felt disgust with himself for again having failed his young master.

"I is so sorry Massa' George," he muttered his head hanging low, the grown man no more now than a chastened schoolboy, "but I jus' don' know what I could do and Mr

Killcaid he can do anythin' to me. I fears 'dat man worse dan de Devil himself."

"A servant I can't trust is no good to me," retorted George still seething at this latest betrayal and its consequences.

But Matthew had been thinking fast. "Give him another chance Brother," he urged. "Look, let me take from you now only the things for which I have an immediate need. Take the rest back. You Manuel can get word back to Killcaid, that I did not come to the meeting place and that you will be trying again tomorrow. He'll see you bringing all the stuff back and perhaps he'll believe you. This way Killcaid will think I really have perished or that I am heading up north. Either way it'll take the heat off his belief that I am holding out here in the bayou." Then turning to the crestfallen Manuel, he said, "D'you think yo' can do that?"

Manuel's head was nodding almost before Matthew had finished speaking. "Ah sure can do dat." Then turning to George he said, "Ah'll do dat. Ah'll do dat good. And am I still your servant Massa' George?"

George, who could see the wisdom in Matthew's plan, slowly nodded his head, "But if you let me down again, you'll be off to the Louisville sales the very next day. That understood?"

The three unloaded the dug out and Matthew retained only enough for his immediate needs. Then having arranged a different rendezvous for the next day they departed. Killcaid duly observed their return with Manuel still carrying the stores and Manuel got word back to him as promised through one of the other black overseers.

After a few more days of subterfuge, it became clear that Matthew's plan had worked. Killcaid seemed to lose interest in the bayou and turned his attentions to the nearby towns and the routes up north, but in a half-hearted manner. Soon Matthew and George felt that once more they could relax for it seemed clear that Killcaid seemed to have accepted that the bayou had achieved what the Nethergate Coonhounds had so singularly failed to do.

Matthew and George were sitting on Old Mo's veranda where so often now they relaxed. A comfortable silence had fallen between them each wrapped in their own thoughts. George's mind though had turned to the letter he had sent to the Colonel of the Militia. He had received an acknowledgement, but no further communication. In the Militia things tended to move very slowly. He began to hope now that perhaps it might have got to the bottom of some clerk's tray and been overlooked. No news he felt was probably good news. He would have liked to confess to Matthew how things stood but thought there was no point in raising problems which might never materialise.

Matthew too was thinking how long he would be able to endure living in the way he did. He was enjoying his new-found freedom and the independence of his present way of life, but he was wise enough to know that his present euphoria might not last forever. Then, he would have to consider what his future actions might be. He longed to join in the struggle for the freedom of all slaves and to play a part in that great enterprise, but his criminal status would seem to preclude that.

It was Matthew following his line of thought who broke the silence. "How long do you reckon before my 'wanted' status will become forgotten? I can't stay here forever, and I want to join the struggle before it's all over."

"I don't know," answered George. "Reckon if no hair nor hide of you is seen for six months or so, people might consider you perished in the swamp and they might forget it all." George realised that now was an opportunity to confess how far he had already gone down the route to war, but he hung back. Instead he continued, "I suppose you would become a Damned Yankee."

"I certainly would," re-joined Matthew with conviction.

"And I would support the Confederates," stated George with equal passion.

"Brother, you must do whatever your heart tells you to do. But if we met on the field of battle, it would be my duty to kill you."

"And mine to kill you, despite our friendship and what we share here."

"The North needs soldiers, same as the South and I doubt whether they would inquire too deeply into my background, but you never know and if Killcaid had a hand in it, then it would be the worse for me. All the same…" and he let the thought hang in the air.

Thus the two young men who so recently had become such firm friends now had to face what so many families, both North and South of the divide, had also had to face. For a time, the thought hung heavily between them. Then Matthew smiled and caught hold of George's wrist.

"Happen 'twill never take place. At least whilst we is here we can let things be. The war won't never come between us here. Eh Brother?" and he clapped George on the back. The tension that had been building between them faded and things were back to normal once again, but even so both young men knew that a line had been drawn in the sand.

48

Retribution

On the Spielberg plantation adjoining Nethergate there was deep sadness, for they had just laid to rest the body of their beloved preacher. There was not a soul on that estate whose heart was not heavy with sorrow at his passing. There was not a soul who did not have some personal memory of their pastor; a kind word, a shared grieving at the passing of a loved one, some act of generosity or some unsolicited deed of kindness. But it was mostly his sheer presence they missed, his bulk and the resonant timbre of his voice, filling their lives and giving them hope.

They had laid him to rest on a hilltop overlooking the slave lines so that he could watch over them in death as he had watched over them in life. There had been much lamenting and wailing and much beating of chests. The hymns were long and harmonious, as they keened out their grief. Many threw themselves across his coffin weeping and crying out their sorrow.

But in some cabins that night there were whispered, urgent exchanges. There was talk of revenge, for all knew who had laid their preacher low. They knew their preacher would not wish them to entertain such thoughts. But where was the justice from the white men's law? They were only human after all. Such a wanton act of evil cried out for vengeance. They all knew of Killcaid and his cruel and evil ways. Surely, they would be doing no more than God's will to rid the world of the spawn of the Devil. But there was one man there above all others who meant to extract revenge. His name was Paul. He was the preacher's son.

Paul was a hot-head and the despair of his father. He owed his fine physique to his father and his passions too, but he did not share his father's religious fervour. He saw only the wrongs of servitude and could see little advantage in worshipping in meekness the white man's God. It was only the pleadings of his frail and diminutive mother that kept him from seizing his freedom or openly rebelling. Even so, many were the times when the preacher had had to appeal for forgiveness from his owner for his son's misdoings.

Now watching his mother's fragile little body, wracked with grief, sobbing out her supplications to the Lord to forgive her husband's killer, was more than his fiery spirit could endure. Where had his father's God been in his hour of need? "An eye for an eye, a tooth for a tooth." He remembered his father reading that from the Old Testament and he remembered too what had gone before it, "If a man takes a stick and beats his slave and the slave dies on the spot he is to be punished." Then the caveat that followed, which he could never understand, "But if the slave does not die, but continues a day or two, he shall not be punished, for he is his master's loss." He could hear his father's thunderous voice intoning the passage, savouring every syllable. But had his father not died on the spot? The Good Book, his father's book, the book he worshipped and ran his life by, surely that clearly sanctioned retribution. It mirrored exactly the circumstances of his father's death. He had never registered what his father had always said after it; how his Lord had urged his followers meekly to turn the other cheek. The white man's courts would not punish him in this white man's world? Who, then, was going to punish his father's killer now? He knew, with a grim resolve, the answer to that question.

Paul had always quarrelled with his father. Since his very first memories he rebelled against his Christian teaching. He thought that he had hated him for his rigid, God-given beliefs and for his firm administration of discipline. Many were the beating he had had from his father when he had transgressed. Even as a full-grown man, he doubted that he could have mastered his father physically. But his father had never lost his temper or raised his voice. He had always been in control, had always considered the justice in his actions before their execution. Only now when he was gone did he realise how much he loved and respected the man. He longed to have had the chance to tell him that. Now perhaps sitting with his God, he would know from his son's actions how much he cared for him. His spirit would be avenged as the Bible said it should. Justice would be done.

A few days later Paul joined the working party that travelled to Nethergate, filling his father's place, for their work at Nethergate was scheduled to continue for some weeks yet. They were joined as usual by several Nethergate slaves. It was then that he learnt that the slave who his father had helped to escape was being blamed for his murder and now had a price on his head. But all knew who was truly responsible. There had been too many witnesses, for that lie to hold water, at least among the slaves. The news only hardened his resolve that the true murderer should receive his just punishment. Once at Nethergate Paul talked to the Nethergate slaves. Over the next few days a plan took shape and a date was decided.

Killcaid, true to his word, had clamped down with even greater harshness to crush any further thoughts of disobedience after the debacle of Matthew's flogging. Matthew's escape had raised all their spirits. There was too a swell of sympathy for poor Zeb. Morella's balms and potions seemed to have eased the terrible pain from his flayed back, but the wounds were not healing. His mind was gone. He babbled and wept nonsenses to himself in a constant state of fear and anxiety, rocking himself backwards and forwards. He was convinced that Killcaid was in league with Old Nick himself and that between the two of them they had tampered with his food. Ordinary people could eat it without harm, but for him the food would turn to poison as soon as it contacted the juices of his mouth. No-one could persuade him otherwise. He was slowly starving himself to death, convinced that Killcaid's curse was upon him.

Such was the power of Killcaid's personality, that no-one at Nethergate had ever considered taking the law into their own hands and removing their tormentor. The consequences of failure were too terrible to contemplate for them and for their families. In any event Killcaid had built up such an army of informers that he seemed to be aware of their thoughts before even the seed was sown. Suddenly though, Paul seemed to have made it possible in a way in which it would look like an accident and no-one would be to blame. All they needed to do was to create a diversion in the night which would draw Killcaid from his house. Paul would do the rest. Paul would burn down his cabin. His body would be found in the embers and no-one would be any the wiser. It was seductive in its simplicity. Its success depended on Killcaid not catching a whiff of the plot. To this end the true nature of the plan was kept only to a trusted few whose hatred of Killcaid was keenest. All the rest were told was that they were required simply to make as much noise as possible when the signal was given. They were to ignore what Killcaid's black overseers might do to quieten them down. The uproar must continue for that alone would bring out Killcaid himself.

Paul had noticed that their white overseer who accompanied them to and from the Nethergate Estate rarely escorted his charges all the way back to the Spielberg estate. There was a small farmstead half way, where he was always made more than welcome, by the young woman who lived there. Her husband was away fighting and there were always jobs for him to do in exchange for the favours she alone could give. He would leave the slaves to make their own way back to their slave lines at Spielberg, like obedient cattle.

Paul and five other men planned to break away when the overseer left them and return to Nethergate. They would lie up till dark when they would move to Killcaid's house and wait until the noise in the slave lines eventually drew Killcaid from his cabin. He would meet the same death as he had meted out to Paul's father, but perhaps more prolonged. Then they would place his body in his cabin with liquor bottles scattered about and set it all on fire. It would be assumed he had been too drunk to escape the justice of the flames. They would just have time to return to the Spielberg Estate where there would be plenty to swear they had been there all night. Their Overseer would of course confirm that he had safely delivered all his charges back to where they belonged at the slave lines, for fear of his dalliance being discovered.

The plan was perfect. Paul decided that it should be executed on the very next night.

49

Allison

Killcaid's current 'housekeeper', Allison, was a bright young soul now nearly sixteen, as far as anyone knew. She had grown up in fear of Killcaid. When, as she began to mature, he started taking notice her, she had been truly flattered. When she was invited to keep house for him, she became convinced that he was as in love with her as she was with him. She accepted his casual cruelties as just the way he was. At least it meant that he noticed her. When she began to hear whispers that something big was about to take place and noticed how people would stop talking as soon as she neared them, she knew that it must concern Killcaid. By the sense of excitement in their voices, it seemed that whatever it was, was going to occur very soon. She determined to warn Killcaid as soon as the opportunity arose, but as ever she was wary of his temper.

That evening, she prepared his supper in the way she knew he liked and when all was ready, she prepared herself too, for often when he returned from a day out in the fields it was the first thing on his mind. This evening was no exception and she obediently spread herself upon the bed awaiting his pleasure. He lowered himself upon her with a grunt of pleasurable anticipation. She breathed in the sharp tang of his sweat and the smell of horse upon him. His body aroma was so different from that of the black boys she had known. She set herself to please him. Yet it was not to be.

"Damn it all to hell!" he rumbled under his breath, pushing her roughly away. "Go get my supper."

"Have I done sumtin' wrong Masser Silas?" she asked anxiously with a little moue of disappointment as she hastily adjusted her clothes.

"No. Damn you. Get my supper!"

She hastened to do his bidding, for in this mood he was liable to lash out at the slightest provocation. She decided out of fear of his reaction not to let him know yet of what she had been hearing.

But Killcaid was no fool. He had sensed that something was afoot. What concerned him was that none of those who usually kept him informed had come forward. Yet there was something in the air. He could feel it. The slaves in the field would normally look away when he spoke to them, but today their eyes had lingered just a fraction. It was as if they wanted to store and savour his image in their memory. They seemed to hold themselves in a different way. There was a lightness in their step. There was almost a willingness to do his bidding in contrast to the surliness that had followed Zeb's flogging and Matthew's escape. It filled him with unease.

He ate his supper in sullen silence whilst Allison tried to cheer his mood with lively chatter until he told her to shut up. Thereafter she dared not speak. When he had finished eating she offered him some of his favourite Old Kentucky whiskey whilst she cleared away the meal and had her own supper in the kitchen.

She left him alone with his whiskey. When she came back to him the Old Kentucky had worked its magic and his mood had mellowed. Perhaps he had been imagining things. He had a couple of dogs tethered outside his cabin who would give ample warning if anything unusual was afoot. All the same he went to his cabinet and took out his Smith and Wesson revolver to confirm that it was still fully loaded. He swore under his breath. He remembered then that he had been shooting rats in the barn and now there were only three rounds left in the chamber. He made a mental note to replenish his supply of ammunition from the estate office in the morning. Then he settled down with his pipe to contemplate the fire Allison had made up for him. He wasn't getting any younger, he knew. He was now nearly fifty and already there were streaks of grey in the black of his beard. But he was still wiry and fit. He was angry with himself that he had not managed to respond to Allison's body earlier that evening.

On an impulse, he called her over in a softer voice. She came willingly. He invited her onto his lap. She nestled into him. With purposeful deliberation, he unbuttoned her blouse. His large capable hands explored her breasts. There was an exquisite pleasure in the firmness of a young woman's breasts and the hard, brown tenderness of her nipples which he loved to gently roll between his fingers. Young, nubile flesh held a special charm for Killcaid. He began to roam about the rest of her body revelling in the softness and smoothness of her youth until his probing fingers discovered again a warm wetness that made him hard with desire. He had had many 'housekeepers' in the past, but Allison he decided was probably one of the best. Gently, for he could be gentle when he wished, he took her in his arms and carried her to his bed.

Afterwards he allowed her to stay there, thinking he might have need of her once more and enjoying her nakedness next to his. He had not been disappointed. He had performed well and decided that the creeping ague of the years had not touched him yet. At last he slept, all sense of unease dissipated.

50

Paul's Revenge

Paul and his little band had lain concealed in the tobacco plants as darkness gathered. Each man was armed with either a knife or a stout cudgel. When Paul considered it safe, they stole out and made their way towards Killcaid's cabin. They stopped far away enough not to alert the dogs and waited for the clamour to start from the direction of the slave huts. Paul was burning with anticipation for the fulfilment of hunger for revenge and for proving to himself his love for his dead father. The others in his party were simply anxious to avenge the giant Pastor they had all grown to love for his gentleness and his wisdom. In his pocket, he had a lucifer and a rough stone to strike it on, both carefully wrapped in canvas. All that was necessary now was the commotion from the slave lines. They had no means of measuring the passing of time. The night was cloudy and there was no moon. The air was full of the sharper smells of vegetation touched by the first chill of night. Still there was no sound from the slave huts. Paul began to fear that things might have gone wrong. They dare not linger too long for fear of not getting back to Spielberg before their overseers woke them and their absence would be noted.

Then very faintly he heard the distant sound of raised voices carried on the evening breeze. Soon the clamour gained in volume as more and more joined in. Then added to this cacophony came the sound of cooking pots being hammered and clattered until the night air was full of a discordant jangling and rattling.

Paul smiled in satisfaction and his group moved to Killcaid's cabin where the dogs were already barking at the distant disturbance, adding to the general mayhem. They were chained and no threat, but once they became aware of the band of raiders, they became almost hysterical in their frenzy. Paul expected Killcaid to emerge immediately. But there was no sign of him.

Instead a girlish figure briefly appeared. The light in the cabin was abruptly extinguished, leaving only a faint flickering from the embers of a fire. Abruptly the fire flared up as water was thrown upon it and sparks flew from the chimney. Then even that glow was gone, and the cabin was plunged into total darkness. The watchers could see no sign of movement inside. Had Killcaid been warned Paul wondered? Was he playing a waiting game?

Paul suddenly realised that perhaps Killcaid was unaware of the hiatus down in the cabins, for the barking of the dogs now drowned out all other sounds. Perhaps he was assuming that the other overseers would hear his dogs barking and come to investigate. The passing of each minute eroded the time needed to return to Spielberg safely.

"We'll burn the rat in his hole," announced Paul at last.

"What about the girl with him?" one of them asked. "She may have seen us."

"Let the Devil look after his own," was Paul's terse rejoinder, but an unease had filled his conscience. Was he not condemning another to die in the same casual way that Killcaid had killed his father? They could not afford to let the girl go free, for she would know that Killcaid's death was no accident. But he was committed now.

Hastily they gathered kindling and dried wood and piled it against the upwind side of the cabin. All was stillness within.

When he was ready Paul called out, "Come out Masser Killcaid or we'll burn you out."

"We know who it was as killt our Preacher. Now you're goin' to die jus' the same way like he did," yelled another voice.

"But let the girl out first. She won't be harmed, we promise," added Paul.

A harsh unbelieving laugh was all the response they got; that and the whimpering of the girl.

"Let the girl go," repeated Paul. Now he could hear her crying.

Killcaid remained silent.

"You leave me no choice," said Paul striding to where they had stacked the wood against the side of the house. He struck the lucifer. It flared into brilliant light and he applied it to the kindling. A foul sulphurous stench filled his nostrils, but the flames took hold. Soon a fierce blaze was raging along the side of the wooden cabin and was beginning to spread to the roof.

Inside, Killcaid was convinced that his overseers would soon come to his rescue once they saw the blaze at his house and heard his dogs barking. He could not know that they were far too busy quelling what they took to be an open rebellion and were themselves praying that Killcaid himself would come to their aid. When, finally, they did see the fierce red glow in the woods where Killcaid's cabin was located, it could only mean one thing. Killcaid had perished. With that they beat a hasty retreat, leaving the slaves of Nethergate masters of the field. The slaves wandered aimlessly about enjoying the freedom of being out after the curfew. No slave was allowed out after dark, unless on his master's business and only then with a certificate. But there was no-one there to tell them what to do. Now they had their freedom no-one quite knew what to do with it. Some began to sing. Others joined in. The night began to take on a festive air.

Others too had been aware of the unrest in the slave lines. Manuel had come rushing to his master to warn him of the revolt and to suggest he move away from the Hall, before the slaves could reach it. He had seen the glow in the night sky at roughly the point where Killcaid lived and feared that the slaves were running amuck. He totally ignored the presence of Ursula in the bed beside his master. It was as if she did not exist. George hastily dressed whilst Ursula fled back to her room.

Samuel too had been alerted by the noise coming from the slave lines. He had immediately woken his Master and Mistress and urged them too to leave the house. He had sent for horses and the trap for them all to ride to New Haven to seek the aid of the Militia. Anthony had reacted well to the news. He had even toyed with the idea of riding down to the lines and ordering the men back to their huts so used was he to the men doing exactly as they were told. Samuel managed to convince him that such a course would be tantamount to suicide. Only Amelia seemed to truly appreciate the seriousness of the situation. It was her greatest fear. She was truly terrified. Her head was filled with dreadful images of what they might do to her. She could already feel the horror of black hands grasping at her body and violating her person. She was filled with but one desire – to escape.

Down at Killcaid's cabin the house was now fiercely ablaze. To the watchers it seemed impossible that anyone remaining inside would not have perished. Suddenly the door was thrown open and there was Killcaid, framed by the inferno raging behind him. He was holding the young girl in front of him with one arm about her neck and the other firmly clamped about her waist. Both had dampened blankets about them, already beginning to steam from the heat of the flames. Killcaid was peering wide-eyed at the menacing figures outside his cabin, flickering and dancing in the light of the flames. He didn't recognise any of them. Only one seemed vaguely familiar, a giant of a man seemingly their leader. Then his heart missed a beat. For a moment, he thought he saw the figure of the man they called the Preacher whom he had struck down only a few days before. It was as if his ghost was now returning to clamour for vengeance. For a second his determination wavered at the sight of this apparition. Then he realised it was a much younger man than the Preacher. His resolve returned. He was acutely aware of the three rounds in the chamber of his Smith and Wesson and the number of his attackers. The heat all the time was driving him further from the house and nearer to his enemies. They in turn were advancing ever closer, held back only by the fierceness of the flames.

"Leave now!" bellowed Killcaid above the crackle and roar of the inferno. "Leave, or I will throw the girl back into the flames and the fault will be yours."

At this Allison began to struggle as the awfulness of what was about to happen struck her. She had no doubt Killcaid would do just as he said.

"No! No! No!" she screamed. For a moment, the attackers hesitated. Then, Paul raised his club and ignoring the heat charged towards where Killcaid was standing bent only upon clubbing him down as he had clubbed his father down. The others followed.

But Killcaid was quick. With one convulsive gesture, he hurled the screaming Allison into the flames and at the same time wrenched the pistol from his belt. The other assailants had followed Paul's lead and were now charging towards him. Killcaid stood his ground. He knew that he must first kill the leader. The others he hoped would then lose heart. He levelled his pistol at the giant figure of Paul. Until then, none had realised that Killcaid was armed.

With a terrified scream Allison's body hit the flames. The blanket fell from her. For a moment, it stifled the blaze. It was just long enough for her to scramble to her feet. But now her dress and her hair both were alight. She fled from the inferno, trailing fire behind her straight into the path of Paul. He tripped and fell. Killcaid fired. The shot missed. Realising her greater need, Paul instinctively began to smother the flames about the stricken woman with his body. Killcaid turned to the nearest oncoming figure and fired again. The bullet took the man in the throat. The knife flew from his hands. His momentum carried him forward, straight into the flames. With a strangled cry, he attempted to rise. But already the flames had claimed him. He sank forward on his knees as if in supplication. The flames were all about him. His skin was peeling away as the others looked on. The air became rank with the reek of burning flesh. The assailants stopped in their tracks arrested by the suddenness of the horror they were witnessing and too by the realisation that Killcaid was armed.

Killcaid tracked them with his pistol. At the sight of it, the others shrank back. Only Paul remained to complete his task of smothering the flames about the stricken young woman, now moaning in fear and pain. The pistol came to rest upon him. Paul rose to his feet and met the eyes of Killcaid without flinching.

Paul was thinking only of his father. At this moment of truth, he was filled with a sudden overwhelming emotion of love for that indomitable man and for all he had stood for. In this supreme instant, he understood what his father had been striving to do. He only wished he could have been allowed to follow in his footsteps. He thought of his mother. This double blow would devastate her.

Killcaid raised the pistol aiming between the giant's eyes. It was purely a question of survival. Without hesitation, he pulled the trigger.

51

A Miracle

At Nethergate Hall George and Manuel had already left for New Haven to call the Militia. The horses still stabled at Nethergate House had been sent for, but all the able-bodied slaves had left for the slave cabins to join in the night's entertainment. There was no-one to saddle the horses or harness the trap. The distant skyline was still lit up with the flickering blaze from the direction of Killcaid's cabin. The riotous discord from the slave cabins had died down, following the sound of shooting. Those at Nethergate Hall had heard the distant shots and wondered what it meant. Was Killcaid now back in control, or had he been overwhelmed by sheer numbers? There had only been two shots.

Anthony could not imagine a Nethergate without Killcaid and was convinced that all would be well. Amelia, though, imagined hordes of black figures even now stealthily creeping through the shadows towards the Hall armed with clubs, knives and all manner of weapons from the armoury of agricultural implements used on the plantation. She cringed at the thought of those black faces and skins and what might follow. It was almost more than she could bear. Her body began to shudder uncontrollably.

Killcaid stood in shocked stillness outside his blazing cabin facing the giant Negro with his pistol still trained on the slave's forehead. He had pulled the trigger, but the pistol had only clicked. He realised at once what had happened. When he had fired the first time, it was the second round that had been discharged, then the third. He would have to pull the trigger four more times before the only bullet left was back in the firing chamber. By that time the slave would be upon him.

The slave was staring at him. Hardly believing he was still alive. In a moment, he would charge. Behind him was the raging inferno of his cabin. There would be no escape. But Killcaid was not a man to panic.

Paul faced his father's killer. Unbelievably he was still alive. But what Paul could see which Killcaid could not was the body of his comrade being consumed by the flames. It was truly a vision of hell. As the heat seared and shortened the sinews and ligaments the arms and legs moved with the aimless gestures of a small child in a fever. The body twisted. Reason told Paul he must be dead. Then as he looked his belly burst with the heat. Sickened Paul looked away into the eyes of the man who was about to kill him and who had killed his father.

He was filled with loathing and a disgust that almost made him pity the man. "You will rot in hell for what you have done," he said. Then unexpectedly he found himself saying, "May God have mercy on your soul," just as his father would have said. At this extreme moment, his spirit burned with a sudden delight, for with utter certainty, he realised now that his father was somehow with him and knew that his son truly loved him.

Killcaid recognised, echoed in the son, the deep tones of the preacher-slave he had struck down in the fields whilst hunting Matthew. He knew now who faced him and his spirit shrivelled within him. Allison still lying at the slave's feet, gave a low moan of pain and fear. Killcaid felt a rare pang of regret. He had not meant to throw her into the flames. He thought the threat alone would deter his attackers. But he had not hesitated to carry it out when it had failed in its purpose. It was a question of survival.

If he pulled the trigger now, there would be another click. The Preacher's son would instantly attack, thinking he had run out of ammunition. One more click and then the round would be in the chamber. But one round would not stop the momentum of this enraged titan on the move. They would both be driven back into the blazing hellhole behind him. Already the blanket about his back was beginning to scald his flesh.

Killcaid did not pull the trigger a second time. "Go!" he said, "Get out now, before I change my mind," and he waved his pistol indicating where Paul's companions had fled.

To Paul, it seemed like a miracle. He needed no second bidding. He turned, glanced with compassion at the whimpering girl and then ran in the direction of his fleeing companions. When he caught up with them they received him with true elation, for they had assumed when he fell that he was the victim of Killcaid's first shot. Now it was only one of their number whom they mourned. But things had taken longer than they had planned. They would have to move quickly to be back at Spielberg before dawn. Although they had not achieved their aim they all felt that they had at least struck a blow in memory of their beloved Pastor. But it had been at the cost of yet another life.

As they hastened back along the New Haven Road to the Spielberg Estate, Paul had much to think about. Why when he had tripped over the blazing girl, had he not afterwards continued his attack? What made his compassion for her pain overrule his own purpose of vengeance and survival? He had looked into the eyes of the Devil, stared into the jaws of hell, yet his father's God was more powerful than all of these. His hand had made Killcaid's pistol misfire. His hand had stopped Killcaid from firing a second time. It was His will that had made

Killcaid bid him to leave. The more he thought as he hastened back, the more convinced he became that only the spirit of his father's God was powerful enough to bring about such a miracle. He raised his eyes to the early grey of dawn and vowed there and then to change his life and henceforth to 'be about his father's business'.

He was so filled with a sense of elation and purpose that he almost failed to hear the clatter of approaching horsemen. They only just had time to scatter into the vegetation at the roadside before the New Haven Militia rode by with George at its head, hot-foot for the Nethergate Estate.

Spielberg was just beginning to stir when they crept back into the slave lines. Paul's first act though was to go to the mother of their fallen comrade, where he broke to her the news of the death of her son. All who witnessed it were amazed at the compassion he showed and at the comfort he gave to the grieving mother. When he urged them all to join him in prayer, they all knew that somehow the spirit of his father had not left them and that now they had a new champion in his son. There indeed was yet another miracle.

52

Nethergate Restored

It was Samuel himself who had saddled up the horses and prepared the trap for the Mistress. At the last minute Ursula ran to her mistress with a case of Amelia's most treasured things which in her fear she had missed and some food for the journey for them all. Anthony thanked her for her thoughtfulness and even his wife had to admit to herself that it was a considerate gesture. For a moment, she had a qualm of conscience at the thought of the punishment she had in store for her maid. Perhaps she might wait, at least until the present crisis was resolved.

They set off in the greying light of early dawn, to the clatter of horses' hooves on the gravel and the crunch of the trap's wheels. All wondered whether they would see Nethergate Hall again. The glow from Killcaid's burning cabin was still clearly visible as a reminder of what might yet happen to the Hall itself. If he had perished, the ominous silence from the slave cabins could mean only that the slaves were already making their way to wreak their vengeance on Nethergate Hall and its residents. Amelia began to tremble anew at the thought. They took the longer route that avoided going near the slave lines and all breathed a sigh of relief when they were clear of the estate. The road to New Haven lay empty before them.

As they neared New Haven they met up with George and the New Haven Militia and decided to change plans and follow the Militia to Nethergate. The journey back was full of tension. The day by then was well advanced. At every rise in the road the Nethergate party expected to see the horizon smudged with the smoke from the burning Hall, but at each opportunity their hopes began to rise. At last they reached the Estate. All seemed deceptively normal.

The militia halted. Their Captain, a cautious fellow, expected a trap, or at least pretended to do so to enhance the importance of his mission. A scouting party was sent forward whilst Anthony and Amelia waited with growing tension. George, because of his knowledge of the lie of the land, insisted on going with the scouting troops. The men meanwhile ominously eased their swords in their scabbards and checked their weapons.

The scouting party advanced cautiously, using the sides of the track to muffle the sound of the horses' hooves. Even so it seemed to George that the creaking and clatter of their harnesses would more than advertise their presence to any awaiting ambush. He couldn't help feeling that it would have been better for them all to advance confidently into the estate to overawe any would-be rebels. But he could not help but feel a thrill of excitement at being part of an armed group of soldiers. They were climbing an incline, the top of which would give a good view across the plantation. They spread out and breasted the rise together. The sight which met their eyes filled them all with amazement.

The southern fields of the plantation spread out before them. But what surprised them all was the normality; the usual backs of the slaves bent in toil in working groups across the fields with the heads of the occasional mule visible, patiently standing by their carts. Everything was just exactly as it should be. Then George spotted on the road another horseman. Unmistakeably it was Killcaid, but without his accustomed hat. Leaving the soldiers, George urged his horse forward to where Killcaid sat astride his horse.

Despite his dislike of Killcaid, George was delighted to see him looking much as normal. When he got nearer he could see the red soreness about his neck and on his arms and when he drew up close he could smell the smoke on him. But the old Killcaid was still there, the hard glint in his eyes undimmed. The only thing missing was his hat and his beloved Rattler.

"What ever happened to you?" asked George.

"A good deal," was his laconic reply. "Is the Master with you?"

George nodded.

"Best I report to him," replied Killcaid and turned his horse in the direction of the soldiers. George followed anxious to hear Killcaid's story. Now that there was no danger, the scouting party had re-joined the main body where Killcaid gave his version of the night's events.

Anthony was clearly relieved that his head overseer was apparently unhurt, though somewhat toasted, and that order had been restored. He promised that Killcaid should have a new house and that the estate would pay for his lost possessions. Killcaid related how after he had routed the raiders from about his burning cabin he had taken the injured Allison down in his trap to Nethergate House where Morella had taken her under her wing. From there he had gone to the cabins where the commotion they had all heard earlier had by then died down. He had routed out his overseers who, in his opinion, had done little to curb the disturbance earlier on. Once he arrived all signs of unrest had filtered away and threats of retribution in the morning had returned the slaves to their cabins. The whole disturbance he put down to the sad death of poor Zeb. He did not enlighten his listeners that Zeb had in fact died after the riot had started. He had become so confused with the noise about him that he was convinced that this time the Devil himself was coming for him. It had been too much for him in his weakened state and he had gone into a fit and died with terror in his eyes, in time to allow Killcaid to use his death as a convenience.

"But where did the slaves come from who attacked your cabin?" questioned Anthony. "Were they ours?"

"Definitely not ours Master," Killcaid was able to reply truthfully. "They may have come from Spielberg, as revenge for their preacher that Matthew killed or maybe it was just a group of opportune escapees. Whoever they were, they've left one of their number dead and cooked in the flames. I doubt they'll be back."

The Captain of the Militia, anxious not to have had an entirely wasted trip, seized on the suggestion that the perpetrators might be escaped slaves. "I'll do a sweep of the area," he declared. "If any of their number still linger here we'll soon chase them out." With that he roared orders to his men and with the maximum of clatter and display the Captain led his men triumphantly through the plantation and down to the area of the bayou.

"It's no bad thing," observed Killcaid to the Master, seeing the swagger of the militia, "It'll serve to remind any of thems as has silly notions of how quick the military can be upon them to set things right."

Anthony nodded his head in agreement. He now had a second reminder, after the unruliness following Matthew's escape, of how fragile was the white ascendancy over the mass of the slave community.

Killcaid knew however that the uproar in the cabins had been part of a plan to exact revenge on him and that the threat came from the preacher's son from the Spielberg Estate. His own workforce would never have dared to hatch such a plan.

He had that morning had a frank and open conversation with the Overseer from Spielberg, the same man who had witnessed the killing of the preacher. At first, he had denied the possibility that any from Spielberg could have been involved, since they could not possibly have covered the distance and been back in time for their morning check.

"Always assuming they came home in the first place," remarked Killcaid who well knew the ways of his fellow overseers. "I'll wager you have a man missing too," continued Killcaid relentlessly. He then related the happenings of the night before. His description of the preacher's son was too accurate to be denied. His fellow conspirator had then to confess his dalliance on the way back to Spielberg and that the slaves had been entrusted to make their own way home. He had to admit that it was just possible that some of his slaves may have doubled back to Nethergate and been involved. There was indeed, as Killcaid suggested, a missing slave. No-one had been able to explain the absence of one of his hands that morning, though some claimed he had often declared an intention of making a run for the north and freedom in Canada. No-one had believed he meant it.

So yet again the two overseers put their heads together and concocted a tale that would protect both their interests, but this time it was Killcaid who held the whip-hand. To prevent any further colluding between the slaves, it was agreed that further help from Spielberg would not be required. As far as they were both concerned the matter was very satisfactorily resolved.

To cement their agreement the two retired to the smouldering wreck of Killcaid's cabin and dug a hole to bury the slave from Spielberg. A very small hole was required for the fierceness of the blaze had destroyed most of the unfortunate man's body and much of what was left fell into dust when they attempted to move it.

Both men declared themselves satisfied and shook hands again as they had done after the preacher's death in the manner of true gentlemen. The Militia departed back to New Haven having discovered no further signs of marauding escapees. The powers that be were all satisfied.

53

Uneasy Lies The Head

All in all, Killcaid considered that things had turned out very well. He was far from pleased at having lost his possessions, particularly the Rattler, but they could be replaced. The Master had offered him temporary accommodation at Nethergate House, but he had elected to set up temporary home in the estate offices where he would have more freedom. His cabin was to be rebuilt as soon as possible, to his own specifications. He meant to make the most of that. He had put the fear of the Devil into his little band of overseers for their weakness and threatened to sack them all. He knew how they feared being returned to field work when old scores for past wrongs would be settled by the other slaves, once they had lost Killcaid's protection.

His thoughts turned to Allison. He found it strange that she should crop up now so frequently in his mind. At the end of the day he had gone up to Nethergate House to find Morella and ask her how her patient was faring.

"She been very lucky," Morella had assured him, "She 'as a number of burns and is very sore, but there's nothing that's likely to cause any permanent scarring. In a week or so she be as good as new. But she very quiet. She still frightened as a kitten after what she bin through."

Killcaid lived again the moment he had cast her back into the blaze. But it wasn't his fault. That damned preacher's son had been the cause of it all. He alone had forced his hand. He went in to see her. She was looking very pale with patches of vivid red and shiny skin where the flames had scorched her and where Morella had applied her healing ointments. He thought she might blame him, but her face lit up when she saw who it was.

"O Massa Silas. The Lord be praised you is alright," she cried, "and I lookin' so dreadful."

"Came to see how you was," he muttered gruffly, filled with a sudden tenderness for this girl-child whose first concern was for him and seemed able to overlook that it was his hand that had thrown her into the fire. If she wasn't too scarred, he thought he might even have her back to housekeep for him, for a while. She was for her age surprisingly adept at pleasing him and exciting him as few of his housekeepers had done before.

Allison for her part could only see that he had shown concern by coming to see her. She had not expected it. Perhaps he might feel some affection for her after all. She had entirely forgotten whose hand it was that had casually consigned her to the flames.

54

Night-time At Nethergate House And Hall

Anthony had been impressed by the calm and level-headed way in which his son had reacted to the recent crisis. He had watched George when the soldiers had been with them and was struck by the ease he had showed in their company. He felt a sudden flare of pride that his son seemed now so grown up. His contributions too, when he and Killcaid were talking over events, had been sound and reasoned. He felt that at last he had an ally in his son and confirmed in his own mind his new resolution to bring him more into the running of the estate. He might even find in his son a supporter against the dogmatic nature of his overseer. He began to regret his support for his son's wish to take up arms in the Confederate cause. But that had been the start of their new understanding and he dared not challenge his son's desire to fight, for fear of hazarding it all.

When the soldiers had departed, Mr Styles, George and Killcaid had discussed the recent unrest among the work force which had culminated in the events of the previous night. It was decided that as much as possible they would avoid allowing the slaves to gather en masse, when they might feel emboldened by sheer weight of numbers. There would be the natural meetings in the evenings at the cabins, but if the working day was made long and hard enough there would be little appetite for anything else but food and sleep. George had seized the moment to raise the subject nearest to his heart. He had got his father to agree before Killcaid that there would be, for at least the foreseeable future, no more public beatings or floggings for fear of sparking off further unrest. Killcaid, after some sullen resistance, had conceded the point. George kept his composure, but inside he was shouting with joy at having thus saved his Ursula and thwarted his mother's vindictive plans. He could not wait for the opportunity to tell her and for the fruits of her gratitude and confidence in him.

Thus it was that the events of that day allowed many of those who lived at Nethergate to sleep more easily in their beds that night. George had saved his Ursula and received his reward when he had told her so. He slept that night with a heart brimming over with content. He slept with his arms about his Ursula full of the unfolding wonderment of the passions of this, his first experience of love. He was happy too that Matthew was settled in the bayou and would be safe for some months at least.

Ursula too slept secure in the arms of the man she adored, full of gratitude that he had saved her from the awful aspect of a public humiliation. She too was full of wonderment and joy at what she had discovered in the arms of her lover. She lived for the moment, confident that now George would save her from whatever machinations his mother might plan.

Amelia, that mother, full of grim determination slept fitfully, planning how she might thwart her husband's wishes. She pondered how she might yet arrange for the public whipping of the girl who served her with such unselfish loyalty, but for whom she had formed such dark suspicions and whom she suspected of skulduggery at every turn. She had known true fear that day. When she heard the clamour of the slaves running amuck down in the slave lines, the thought of them streaming up the hill to Nethergate Hall had almost paralysed her with fear and suspicion too, as to who might be at the root of it all. She even suspected that Samuel might somehow be in league with them. She didn't agree with the softer approach that her husband now advocated. That way lay disaster. She determined now to rule her household with a yet harsher hand. It was the only thing that slaves understood.

Anthony, her husband, slept the sleep of the contented, comfortable in a new-found amity with his son and rejoicing in the new ally he had found. He had been confident that Killcaid would overcome whatever plots might have been laid against him. His confidence in his Head Overseer remained undiminished, but there would be costs involved in the day's events and that was a worry for the finances of the estate.

Manuel, a minor player in the life of Nethergate Hall, slept perhaps a little less soundly than his betters. His slumbers, though, were tinged with regret for failing his young master through fear of Silas Killcaid. He tried to convince himself that it would never happen again, could never happen again. But he only half succeeded.

Matthew, now seemingly condemned to be forever a stranger to the Nethergate that had been his home for more than eighteen years, slept easily, dreaming of his new-found freedom and of somehow going to war to fight for the cause of freedom for all his coloured brethren. His dreams were full of gunfire, smoke and charging, yelling men and horses rearing and screaming and bands playing somewhere. All would be action and excitement, but no-one really getting hurt. In his waking hours though, these dreams were dampened with the reality of the situation he now faced in having a price on his head. Killcaid who had been such a blight on his life as a slave had even managed to cast his shadow over the new life he craved to lead. He wondered if he would ever be free from his baleful influence.

Now in Spielberg Estate there was another whose life had been changed by Killcaid's influence. Paul had lost his father but had found his father's God. Now his life had taken another direction and that too would never be the same again.

Killcaid slept that night in strange surroundings in make-do premises in the old Estate Office with the shrill squeaking of rats for company. Sleep though obstinately eluded him. His body was still painful in parts from the burns he had received the previous night. He was troubled too as to which of the slaves had been the link with the slaves from Spielberg and had organised the diversion from the Nethergate cabins. He would need to sniff him out. He thought softer thoughts of Allison and wondered how complete her recovery would be.

Finally, his thoughts turned once again to Matthew. Reason told him that Matthew would have perished, not perhaps in the blooded torment he had wished for him, ripped to death by the Nethergate hounds, but perhaps a slower, more lingering demise trapped and alone in the merciless grip of the spirits of the bayou. It seemed that all the hands were still talking of Matthew as if he were some divine creature who could work miracles. Killcaid ground his teeth in fury at the reputation he had unwittingly furnished for him. But it was not knowing his fate, the uncertainty, that kept him from sleeping. He told himself the boy must have perished. George was no longer trying to get stores and equipment on his behalf. Manuel's behaviour was proof of that. But even if he had survived, he would soon be forced to reveal himself for lack of food. He had run near naked into the bayou and had nothing to aid survival in that hostile world. He tried to imagine an abject Matthew, ragged and starving creeping defeated from the bayou, cringing for food like the meanest cur. He would be mocked now by those who had thought him somehow divine, for no-one can worship a fallen idol.

But somehow his imaginings would not play the same game. Instead, he seemed to see Matthew riding triumphant from the bayou, pulled by a team of the Nethergate hounds to triumphant cheering from crowds of slaves led by the giant slave from the Spielberg Estate. He knew that he had but to crack his whip, his beloved Rattler, to dispel this image, but he couldn't find it.

Rationally, he told himself that if ever he did emerge from the bayou it would be to face a trial for murder. He would be there to watch the hanging that would surely follow. But somehow that image would not form in his mind, try as he might. Sleep still evaded him.

In distant New York, Mary slept easily that night, though she would not have found such rest had she been aware of the happenings at Nethergate. She had found new happiness in the companionship of her father and the love they both bore to the stricken lady who was his wife and her mother. She had found, too, that her father had formed a new respect for her judgement and her ability to understand how the Nethergate Estate should be run. This was against a lifetime of conviction that such matters were beyond a mere woman's ken.

Ruth too was content that night, for she revelled in this new-found world that she had been a part of and yet apart from. She had been accepted without question into the white man's world as an equal and had discovered what it meant to be appreciated as an individual with a mind and understanding of her own. But above all she experienced the added delight of being accepted and respected as a woman. The only small cloud in her blue sky was the unfathomable and enigmatic presence of Colonel Thomas Gladstone who clearly had some hidden agenda that she could not yet divine. He watched her when he thought she was unaware of his attention, waiting perhaps for her to make a mistake. Then he would move in to unmask her or perhaps to blackmail her. His presence filled her with unease.

Perhaps though, all those who slept soundly that night might not have done so could they have seen the storm-clouds that were swirling and twisting just over the horizon. So far Nethergate had escaped the ravages of the civil war that was tearing America apart. Soon though the war clouds would gather over Nethergate itself, the storm would break and perhaps sweep that complacency and many of its people away.

Coming Soon…

The Nethergate Trilogy

Book Two – The Storm Breaks

1

Ursula's Escape

Ursula was now no stranger to George's room and frequently crept up the silent corridors of Nethergate Hall when all was still in the early hours to seek the comfort of his arms and the warmth of his embraces. Though she knew it to be an illusion it was the only place in all the world where she felt secure and safe, for she placed herself utterly in his care and protection. There had been no further talk from her mistress of floggings. George had reassured her after his conversation with his father that the Master had declared that for the moment at least, there would be no more beatings. Whenever she thought of him, which was a great deal, she felt that her heart must burst with the strength of her feelings. It sustained her during the endless working hours where, as her personal maid, she endured the spite and bile of his mother. It allowed her to smile and be civil to the woman who so cruelly misused her. It brought back the sunshine into her life and a return of her happy disposition so that all the world smiled with her. And all the world wondered too, how she could be so happy with such a tyrant for a Mistress.

George also was lost in the blissful world of his love

for Ursula but eating at his heart was the thought of his commitment to the Confederate cause and the instruction he might soon receive to serve the flag and join the colours. He now heartily regretted that moment when he had sought to bring his parents to heel. But it was done now and there could be no going back. What would happen to Ursula then he dared not think. He had not yet told her of his volunteering for fear of the anxiety it would cause her. That at least was his excuse to himself.

Some few weeks after George had extracted the promise from his father, the two lovers were lying together in each other's arms after their love making. George was half asleep. Ursula, full of happiness, listened to the pattern of his breathing as his passion subsided. She could feel the warmth of his young hard body close to hers. Not for the first time wondered at the power she had over him, just because she was a woman. She savoured the peace and security of the moment. No harm could come to her now, when she was in his arms. Suddenly she went rigid. She was sure she had heard the floorboards creak outside the room. She listened, hardly daring to breathe. George was immediately alert to the change in her. She placed a finger over his lips in case he should speak out loud.

"There's someone outside," she whispered into his ear. Her immediate thought was that it was his mother, such was the fear that that lady generated within her breast. Both lay still listening. The sounds of the night crept into the room. An owl hooted and received a distant 't'woo' in reply. The wind sighed softly in the old oak outside George's window. The house itself seemed to settle into the stillness of the night. Then it came again; the sound of someone shifting their weight outside the door to George's room.

George eased himself out of his bed and sought frantically for his night shirt. He donned it and crept on bare feet to the door. There was a soft knocking, repeated twice more after a pause. Then the door handle began to turn. The door opened, and a dark shape entered the room. George was about to launch himself on the intruder when he recognised the outline of Samuel.

"Samuel!" he hissed, "What on earth are you doing?"

"Thank the Lord you is awake," replied Samuel. "It's Ursula. I cannot find her."

George for a moment debated whether to try and deceive Samuel but decided against it. "She is here," he said.

"That's good," said Samuel, not seeming in the least bit surprised, "but we must get her away, soon as possible."

"What are you talking about?"

"It's the Mistress. I have had word that she has ordered the whipping cart to call here this mornin' to take Ursula for a public whippin' in New Haven. I knew nothing about it. She must have done it all through Mister Killcaid."

George's heart sank. He looked to his bed where Ursula sat with the sheets pulled up about her. The thought of her creamy smooth back and the gentle curve of her shoulders being scarred and torn with the lash made him feel physically sick. How could his mother be this cruel? She had even, so Ursula told him, recently been surprisingly considerate, so much so that Ursula had thought that things might be getting better between them. But all the time she had been playing with her, like a cat with a mouse. She had been biding her time to defy her husband and to vent her spite on Ursula. She had waited until Anthony was away in Louisville arranging for his tobacco to be routed down the Mississippi and then she had struck.

She would simply present her husband with a fait accompli, knowing he could do nothing after the event. A feeling of burning hatred and resentment swept over him. He felt nothing but loathing for the bitter, vengeful woman that his own mother had now become.

"We must get her away from here immediately," announced Samuel. "Since last we spoke I have tried to prepare a safe place for her to go, but these matters take time and we cannot afford to take unnecessary risks. This has come about before I was prepared."

George realised that Samuel was putting his complete trust in him, for what he was doing was admitting that he had links with the escape chain for fleeing slaves, the so called 'Underground Railroad'. It was a measure of the upright nature of the man that he had not pressed George to secrecy but had simply placed his life and future on the principle and integrity he had assumed that George possessed. He felt humbled before this simple man of such honour and nobility of spirit.

"What can we do?" he asked turning to look at Ursula, who had not moved. She could not hear their whispered conversation and was still looking apprehensive at the obvious discovery of their secret.

"The first thing we must do is to get her away from this house and out of reach of any search for her that must surely follow the discovery of her absence."

George thought frantically, but there was nowhere on the estate that would be safe, but Samuel was ahead of him. "The only safe place is down in the bayou, but someone would have to go with her to report back so that we can find her again when we have found somewhere secure."

Then a thought occurred to George. "Listen Samuel," he said, "Matthew from Nethergate House, is down in the bayou now, he's laying up there until the hue and cry dies down, now he is wanted for murder. There is a safe place there that no-one knows of, where she could stay, secure at least until you could arrange for her to move on. I can take her there."

"If you say so Massa' George," then he paused, "But I don't think you should take her there. If you are not in the house as usual, it will link you with her when she does not wake your mother and her disappearance is discovered. Is there anyone else who could meet up with Matthew?"

Manuel, his personal slave, was the only choice left, but Manuel had already betrayed him twice through his abject fear of Silas Killcaid the head overseer and George doubted that he could be trusted again. "That leaves Manuel only," he said slowly, "But he is weak, and I am not sure he can be relied upon not to talk, particularly if Killcaid gets hold of him." Then yet another thought occurred to him. Manuel would never find the second dug out that lay concealed in the swamp. He would have to reveal to Manuel the signal to summon Matthew, with all the dangers that that might bring. It seemed he had no option. He would just have to trust Manuel. But Samuel was already moving.

"If he is the only one we must trust him Massa' George. I'll wake him when I gets downstairs. In the meantime, we must get Ursula ready for a trip away. I'll prepare things as much as I can." With that he passed through the door and softly closed it behind him, never once glancing over to the bed where Ursula was still sitting up.

George returned to Ursula who was rigid with anxiety. At the news of her mistress's intentions she gave a low moan and began to shake uncontrollably.

"You said the Master was going to stop floggings after what happened with Matthew," she said.

"So he declared," said George, "But you know my mother. She is a law unto herself. I'll bet she has done this just to spite my father. She just waited until he was away and will present him with a fait accompli when he returns. I'll wager Silas Killcaid has a hand in all this too. I cannot believe my own mother could behave like this."

George hastily got dressed and then cautiously escorted Ursula back through the sleeping house to the slave quarters where Samuel was waiting with Manuel shivering with more than the early morning chill. Ursula soon joined them carrying the canvas bag Morella had given her with the brooch and rings from Mary and her mother and the coloured stones that were so special to her. There was little else for her to show for her seventeen years of servitude.

Ursula was shivering too. Her whole life was about to change. Everything she had known, good and bad, was being ripped from under her feet. She was about to become a felon, fleeing from the law where everyone's hand would be justly turned against her. What little protection she had enjoyed from the flimsy arms of the law, would apply to her no longer. She was angry and full of resentment. No-one had asked her. The two men in her life who meant most to her, the one she loved, the other she trusted and respected, had assumed that she would want to make this momentous choice. Strangely her bitterness was directed towards these two who were now risking everything to help her rather than to the woman whose malice was the cause of her misery. But what choice did she have? She knew she would die rather than endure the shame and humiliation of being flogged in public with her nakedness displayed to all.

George hastily scribbled a note for Manuel to give to Matthew explaining the situation and asking for his protection for Ursula saying that he would join them as soon as he was safely able to do so.

Then it was time to go. She cast one last look about all the old familiar things that had become so much a part of her life. Suddenly they seemed the most precious things in all the world, the very walls seemed cry out for her not to leave.

"Oh George! I don't want to go. Isn't there some other way?"

George realised for the first time how desperate a decision it was for Ursula. He had been so preoccupied with the ways and means, that he had neglected to consider how she must be feeling. His heart went out to her in a sudden surge of emotion and he drew her to him caring in the intensity of the moment not a fig for this public declaration of his love for this mulatto slave girl.

George and Ursula embraced once again with a feverish passion, made the more intense now by the uncertainty of what lay ahead.

Acknowledgements

I would like to thank the following people:

Roger Elgood for the onerous task of looking through this manuscript and for his considered comments and much-valued suggestions.

Pam Varey for her eagle eye for errors.

Ted Crellin for the loan of his Civil War research material.

Mike, James and Alexandra Lloyd for IT support.

Anne Brookes, Una Dowding, Jimmy Gilbert (Deceased), Jean Higgs, Elaine Lunt, Sara Mason, Jan Neill, Fred Robson, J.V. Smith, Tony Stowell, Joyce Thomas, Di Whitaker, Charles Hooker, Mike Cooper, Denys Lingard, David Homar; all members of the Cotswold Writers Circle, for listening to much of the story as it unfolded and for their enthusiastic support throughout.

Finally, to my children, Robin, Sue, Emma, and Sally Ann for their encouragement and to my grandchildren Sian, Alex, James, Hamish, Gemma, and Verity for pretending to be interested and occasionally asking how the story was getting along.

About the Author

Derek H Skinner was born in Plymouth Devon and educated at Christ's Hospital. He is married with four children and six grandchildren. He spent thirty years as a soldier serving in U.K., Germany, Aden, Belize, Nepal, Hong Kong, and Cyprus during which time he belatedly completed his education with an OU Degree. He developed a taste for amateur dramatics culminating in performances in the Fringe at the Edinburgh

Festival, when stationed in Scotland. He then honed his acting and storytelling skills by becoming a schoolmaster at Cheltenham College Junior School. For the last five years he branched out from the oral tradition and has been working and researching the Nethergate Trilogy. His interest in slavery was inspired from a spell on Socotra Island in the Indian Ocean, where the charming admixture of inhabitants were descended from those slaves considered too troublesome or weak to make the journey to America and were casually cast overboard by passing 19th Century slavers.